A BLISTERING NOVEL OF AMERICAN HEROES IN THE HELL OF WAR

No matter how many Japs were killed, the jungle was still there—destroying Sergeant Bailey's men with hunger, disease and death.

The squad had to have a rest—or they'd drop in their tracks and rest forever in the filth and mud of a Burma swamp. But GHQ didn't dare trust the Burma Campaign to a bunch of raw, green recruits. They depended on the battle-hardened veterans called Merrill's Marauders. So Sergeant Bailey's men stayed on—slowly being murdered by the Japs, the rotting jungle and, sometimes, in a frenzy of frustration, by each other.

NEVER BEFORE HAS THE HORROR OF WAR BEEN REVEALED WITH SUCH TERRIFYING TRUTH AS IN *THE BRAVE AND THE DAMNED.*

THE
BRAVE
AND THE
DAMNED

David King

PAPERBACK LIBRARY, Inc.

New York

Covers Printed in U.S.A.
Body Text Printed in Canada.

What I expected was
Thunder, fighting,
Long struggles with men
And climbing.

After continued straining
I should grow strong;
Then the rocks would shake
And I should rest long.

What I had not foreseen
Was the gradual day
Weakening the will
Leaking the brightness away,
The lack of good to touch
The fading of body and soul
Like smoke before the wind
Corrupt, unsubstantial.

The wearing of Time,
And the watching of cripples pass
With limbs shaped like questions
In their odd twist,
The pulverous grief
Melting the bones with pity,
The sick falling from earth——
These, I could not foresee.

For I had expected always
Some brightness to hold in trust,
Some final innocence
To save from dust;
Would dangle through all
Like the created poem
Or the dazzling crystal.

WHAT I EXPECTED
—Stephen Spender

This book is a novel. With the exception of references to readily recognizable individuals who were in the public eye at the time this story takes place, no similarity between the fictional characters and actual people is intended.

THIS is the way it was, 100 years ago, 50 years ago, 25 years ago. This is the way war is today.

The 5307th Composite Unit (Provisional), designated by the code word *Galahad* and christened "Merrill's Marauders" by a newsman, was a voluntary infantry guerrilla force of some 2,600 officers and enlisted men recruited in the fall of 1943 for a "secret dangerous mission." After training in jungle warfare at Deogarh, India, their assignment was to harass the Japanese who had overrun Burma. The unit was originally assigned to British Maj. Gen. Orde C. Wingate whose native, long-range penetration groups better known as the "Chindits" provided the one faint spark of hope in an unenthusiastic campaign. Lt. Gen. Joseph W. Stilwell wrested control of the G.I. Marauders from General Wingate in a political maneuver which was as much a part of the war in the China-Burma-India theater as the actual battles.

Merrill's Marauders operated in north and central Burma behind the enemy lines from January 1944, until August of that year when the capture of Myitkina was finally secured after an indecisive, bloody and demoralizing summer-long fight. By this time, the surviving men of the 5307th had been engaged in guerrilla action without relief for seven months. Mentally and physically exhausted, they were in a state of open revolt at the intolerable conditions to which they had been subjected and the complete disregard of their minimum requirements. A congressional committee was appointed to investigate the mess which smelled so foul the findings were never publicly aired.

This book reflects the attitudes of the enlisted men at a time when the group had been fighting behind the enemy lines for almost three months. The magic 90 days General Wingate had specified as the maximum period his Chindits could effectively function in the malaria-infested, Jap-ridden jungles was approaching. The men expected to be relieved.

The entrapment of one of Brig. Gen. Frank D. Merrill's

three battalions by the Japanese at Nhpum Ga is a fact of the campaign. The subsequent rescue of the survivors of that battalion described in this book is reasonably accurate although certain liberties have been taken with the sequence of events. Lancelot Patrol, the men who comprise it and their actions which occupy this book are imaginary. Although the story is fiction, the men and their deeds may be regarded as composites of soldiers and actions which have occurred and do occur when there are battles.

The author gratefully acknowledges the considerable assistance and advice provided during the writing of this book by Jack C. Davis, Sergeant, U. S. Army (Retired) who served with Merrill's Marauders from initial training in jungle warfare at Deogarh, India, until final victory at Myitkina, Burma, when the force was disbanded.

One of the most bitter commentators on the commitments of the 5307th Composite Unit (Provisional) and the disregard of the most elementary requisites of the volunteers who willingly had gone forward to make their best effort has been Charles N. Hunter, Colonel, U. S. Army (Retired). Colonel Hunter was in command of the original Galahad force until its arrival at Deogarh. General Merrill, an old Stilwell favorite, replaced him at that time. Colonel Hunter continued through to Myitkina as second in command and often served as the commanding officer during the frequent periods when General Merrill's heart condition compelled him to withdraw from the field.

After victory at Myitkina and the disbanding of the Marauders, Colonel Hunter was returned to the United States by slow boat. Some three months went by before he arrived. By that time the Marauder affair was obscured by other events. It is an interesting corollary that although Colonel Hunter continued to serve in the United States Army until his retirement in 1959, he was never advanced in rank after the Burma campaign. He had been told at one time in Burma, however, that the stars were waiting to be pinned if he'd keep his mouth shut about what had happened.

—Peter Howe

A SHADOW darted like a chameleon across the gaunt face of Sgt. Henty Holiday. In the misty moonlight, his atabrine yellowed cheeks looked green. He was asleep on a shroud of parachute silk in a damp earth jungle burrow. He had spread his poncho and GI blanket over the blue silk of the drop chute and was fully clothed. Not even his canvas leggings or jungle rotted shoes, still clotted with mud from the trail between Auche and Hsamshingyang, had been removed. His fatigues, soaked in one hundred crossings of the Chengun, Nampana, and dozens of lesser streams, sweat stained in salt patches from the sun that burned into the sharp-bladed elephant grass, were rusty with the red dust of northern Burma. He'd pulled off only his ammunition belt and field pack and the pack was the pillow on which his helmeted head rested.

The fleeting, weightless touch of the shadow brought Holiday to his elbow, swinging his tommy gun from its cradle in his arms. His spine tingled and the hairs rose at the base of his neck. He was snarling and his eyes were icy. He lay taut and motionless, staring into the strangely tangible moonlight, wary and waiting. He had slept in so many foxholes his instincts had become as cunning as an animal's. His nostrils dilated reflexively and he sniffed the thick warm air for Jap smell. The breath of the Tanai valley was fetid but not tainted.

The night was restless. Monkeys made nervous talk and were abruptly silent. The droning cicadas interrupted their night songs with periods of prolonged quiet. The sudden still that followed furtive stirrings in the *kunai* grass was foreboding. It pressed on Henty with a weight that was physical.

His tongue tasted the humid air, his ears listened to the uneasy earth, his eyes roved the vacant edges of his hole. They registered but did not see the inert shape of his ass-hole buddy, Cpl. Domingo Sabado, cocooned with him in the moist dirt trench. Corporal Sabado was in a trauma of exhaustion. He slept in the position he'd fallen when the patrol had dug in.

"Dua," a voice whispered, gentle and nearby, like a breath of wind in the bamboo vines.

Again: "Dua Chicken."

Henty's lungs rasped hot air in his throat and a smile shuddered on his lips. He pushed himself to his knees but did not raise his head above the bunker. In his squad they sometimes called him Hen and more often, Henshit, but only the Jinghpaws, the tough little brown men from the north Burma hills called him Chicken. Jinghpaws: the Burmese called them "Kachins." The words meant savages.

"Meatball?" Henty whispered. He continued, speaking in the language of the tribe: "What brings you here?"

A bare, dark round head rose above the earth mound. The translucent light limned a leering white scar from nostril to ear on the Jinghpaw's right cheek.

"You will please come, Dua. We wait by the river."

Henty's response was unhesitating: "Five minutes."

He hung over the sodden edge of the foxhole on his elbows, peering after the figure that slithered on its belly across the mud of the abandoned rice paddies toward the Tanai River. Without thinking, he covered the Jinghpaw with his tommy gun. His mind fixed on the clump of bamboo into which Meatball disappeared. The ground about the foxhole was steaming after the first, tentative drizzling rains of the monsoon season, not lifting fog but breathing tenuous, moonlighted gray-green vapors. His eyes probed the streamered area of paddies between the river and the air strip south of Hsamshingyang, searching the blobs of dark that marked the patrol's foxholes, glancing toward the edge of the paddies at the three *bashas,* the native bamboo huts that stood on stilts and rose above the mist. Only one was occupied. Most of the officers of the 3rd Battalion were in the bivouac area near the Command Post at Hsamshingyang a mile to the north, but Snotty, the air liaison lieutenant who'd been tagged for this night's duty with the platoon, had installed himself in one of the *bashas.* There'd been room for the noncoms, too, but *bashas* were for officers. Snotty might be high and dry but he'd be the first to get it, Henty thought with grim satisfaction. If the Japs hit us tonight, the *bashas* will burn like haystacks. The foxhole was damp but it was safe and there was no water in it yet.

10

Nothing moved within the perimeter of the platoon. The empty silence was brooding again and nothing seemed to breathe except the vapored earth.

There were guards at the air strip and patrols on the trail to Nhpum Ga six miles south where the 2nd Battalion was dug in, but in the foxholes at Hsamshingyang the men slept in comas, like Domingo, ignoring the buddy alert system. There was a reason for two-man foxholes. While one slept, the other watched. It saved lives. But here, supposedly, it was safe. The men had earned a rest after the abortive attempt to throw a block on the Kamaing Road at Inkangatawng and the retreat under artillery fire all the way from Auche. A momentary respite from crawling through the slashing *kunai* grass, chopping through the bamboo, plodding through the mud. From laying ambushes and beating off the *banzai* attacks. Neither the Japs nor Merrill's Marauders took prisoners. Tonight, at least, Henty thought, my squad can sleep in peace.

He examined Domingo, as well as he could see in the green glowing night. The corporal's head lolled in a broken-necked position against the sticky wall of the hole. The hollows of his cheeks looked like dark holes in his flesh. One leg was straight out, stiff, the other lifted. Between knee and chest Domingo grasped his M-1 tightly, as in death. He was a tough little sonofabitch, he'd almost got it near Inkangatawng, jumped by two *samurais*. But he'd stood his ground, shot one in the throat and bayonetted the other, spilled out the Jap's guts like a string of buttons. And he was starved and exhausted, sick in body and mind. All any of them wanted was to curl up and sleep a week, get up to a decent meal and go back to bed.

Abruptly, Henty smashed his shoe into Domingo's exposed flank and swiftly slapped his hand over his mouth. The corporal spluttered and struggled to sit up but did not shift his legs.

"You shit-assed stupid bastard," Henty whispered fiercely. "Why aren't you standing guard?"

He slammed Domingo's helmeted head against the earth.

"Christ," Domingo lifted his head, "you ain't human. Leave me sleep."

"You got a goddamned watch to stand, you don't sleep. I

11

ought to stick a knife in you for the one I could have got. Where the hell you think you are boy, in India? Back in training at Deogarh?"

"You bastard," Domingo said aloud, quickly lowering his voice to a retching whisper. "I know where the goddamn hell I am, in a rest area, that's where. The last five days and nights I ain't slept for killing Japs, oh God, it seems like that's all I been doing all my life. Killing Japs. But tonight I get to sleep, you understand? We don't need no guards. The lieutenant said so."

"That phony fly boy," Henty whispered scornfully. "Snotty's no platoon leader. He never even saw a Jap."

Domingo pushed his back against the earth and stretched both legs.

"That phony fly boy looks like Jesus Christ to me," he whispered. "Snotty's going to take me back, or someone like him. You know what day it is? The 28th of March, that's getting close to 90 days we been out of Deogarh. They promised us, no more than 90 days. Then out. And the rainy season's coming and you can't move let alone fight. Even Wingate said his Chindits couldn't take no more than 90 days behind the lines. And there's the air strip here at Hsamshingyang and why the hell you think they brought us in? Tonight I get to sleep and tomorrow I'm going home, or at least back to Margherita where there's a real rest camp."

His head flopped against the side of the foxhole and he gasped: "Dear Jesus, no more goddamn Japs. Tomorrow they start to fly us out."

"You get that shit when you wiped your ass?" It was what they'd said all right, 90 days then furloughs to Calcutta: brown tits and black asses. "What Wingate said was we wouldn't get out in 90 days if they transferred us from his command to Stilwell's."

Domingo leaned forward and whispered savagely: "We're going back, we're going back, what's left of us are going back. We've already lost a third, there's only about 1,800 of us left in all three battalions including the 1st stuck up there at Shaduzup. Ain't none of us got the strength to fight no more." His whisper broke into a loud sob. "Leave me sleep. I got to get my rest tonight."

Henty slapped his mouth.

12

"Stop pissing in an empty can. You wake somebody, this outfit is so trigger happy they'll fire at a fart. You've got no bitch. You volunteered for Galahad, everybody volunteered for the good old 5307th. Even the Army mules."

"What stockade did volunteering break you out from, Henshit?" Domingo's whisper was so tight it whistled. "Tonight we rest, see? And tomorrow they start lifting us out. And you know what, old buddy? When we get to Bombay or wherever, I'm going to find you in whatever whorehouse you're shacked up in and I'm going to cut off your balls and shove them down your chickenshit throat."

Henty chuckled softly.

"You're bitter, boy. Maybe you're right about getting lifted out. It's rained the last five days. Maybe the monsoons will be early. But regardless, as long as we're in Burma, we don't relax. Let's stay alive long enough to leave."

"Oh shit, Hen." Domingo's whisper lost some of its intensity but he still grumbled: "Second's on the ridge at Nhpum Ga, there's just the one trail and it's covered. It's tough titty you got bad dreams and can't sleep. Go jack off in the corner."

"You're on guard," Henty whispered harshly. "That's an order. Something woke me up, something moved down by the river. I'm going out. You watch the foxholes and if anyone stirs or shows himself, you pass the word a patrol is out. I don't want to have to come in under fire."

"Oh you goddamn shitass." Domingo paused and whispered accusingly: "You got something lined up. Those Kachin pals of yours got some booze and women."

Henty strapped on his ammunition belt and slid his belly over the side of the foxhole.

"Maybe," he whispered happily.

He dug his way across the gooey paddies with the butt of his tommy gun. The muck was warm, soft and yielding like female flesh. Booze and women——they were the only reasons Meatball would rouse him in this safe area near the Command Post. Several hundred Jinghpaws had joined the 3rd Battalion at Naubaum, north of Hsamshingyang, before the mission to Inkangatawng. They had been in the hills for a thousand years and no one had ever tamed them. Strange, handsome and intelligent people. They spoke a cultured

13

tongue although they didn't have a written language until missionaries contrived one for them of phonetics. They knew the jungle and how to kill. Savages, all right, to their enemies. They'd locate a Jap patrol, drive *pungyis*, fire hardened bamboo stakes with sharpened points into the grass along the trail ahead and draw the patrol into the trap. When the Jinghpaws made a stand with concentrated fire, the Japs would plunge into the grass and impale themselves like ducks on spits. But now and then for a friend, for a sergeant and a squad leader who'd learned a little of their language, there'd be a Burmese girl, never Jinghpaw, and more often some rice wine or the searing liquor they called *shuru-salot* which meant panther piss.

Henty elbowed his body, tommy gun at the ready, from the turbid paddies into the clump of bamboo on the banks of the lazy-winding Tanai. The moon spilled a sheen of silver on the water.

"We wait here, Dua. This way." It was Meatball's voice, still soft but no longer whispering. "It is safe now to arise."

When Henty's eyes had blinked away the luminescent mist, he saw the outlines of four short and sturdy figures in the shadows.

"Who goes with you, Meatball?" He slanted his weapon, wary as he stood.

"Your friends," Meatball said. "Zing Tu La, Ding Ring and Ding Ra."

"*Ka ja-i*, greetings on this peaceful evening," Henty said quietly in their tongue.

Each of the Jinghpaws had guided his squad. Ding Ring and Ding Ra were brothers, men with fine-featured, resolute, dark faces and straight black hair. The Japs had burned their village. Meatball's real name was unpronounceable. He was called "Meatball" because he looked like one but he was solid as a plank of teak. He'd been gashed by the Japs and left for dead. Zing Tu La was a wise old headman from far in the north. He'd been in another village when the Japs had pounced upon his people and massacred all of them. He proudly wore a few wispy strings of hair on his upper lip. They all had dark brown eyes that lusted for revenge.

As Henty's eyes adjusted to the darkness within the trees, he saw that Meatball was carrying a submachine gun and the

14

other three had sheathed *kukri* knives strapped across their bare chests under their left arms. They wore GI shorts and were barefoot.

"You will please remove your outer clothing, Dua," said Zing Tu La.

It was an odd request but Henty shrugged, pulled off his ammunition belt, stuffed his fatigues in his helmet and laid it on the ground.

"Your face." Zing Tu La was giving orders. "Cover it well with mud. We shall concern ourselves with the other portions of your body."

While Henty plastered his face and neck, the Jinghpaws slapped gobs of mud over his legs, chest, back and arms. They had something in mind other than booze and women. It wasn't the arms they carried: no one went anywhere in Burma without a weapon. But they weren't wearing or even carrying their GI shoes. Those shoes were status symbols. They always wore them when they mingled with their people in the villages. They never wore them on the trail. Henty began to feel pleasantly excited.

"There is reason for this," Zing Tu La explained. "We go into the jungle where your clothing would cry out against the grass and vines, and up into the hills where there are no concealing mists. In the light of the moon, your white skin would gleam like a torch. Now you are silent and invisible as the spirit of my grandfather. Conceal your things here, attach the cartridges to yourself, pick up your weapon and we march."

They set off in single file, Zing Tu La in the lead, followed by Meatball, Ding Ra, Henty and Ding Ring. Silent, fleeting shadows in the night, they moved swiftly south along the Tanai, paralleling the trail to Nhpum Ga. Mostly they merged with the bamboo and *kunai* but here and there they crouched to dash, one at a time, over a bare finger of moonlit ground. They continued, unaccustomed silence became oppressive. The hushed night was not calm. It was as if the beasts that lurked in the dark knew men trespassed in their nocturnal kingdom. And watched. And waited. Henty wondered whether the Jinghpaws and he were alone.

Doubt began to gnaw at Henty's gut. Not about this eve-

15

ning. He'd go anywhere with the Jinghpaws, whatever they had in mind.

But about Domingo, he was so damned sure they were going back. Domingo Sabado, that was a crazy name the little American-Mexican lugged around. It meant nothing more than Sunday-Saturday. Out here a name meant no more than did the day of the week. And the days of the week meant nothing except the sum total of them, that magic figure 90. Domingo had to be right. More than two months they'd been crawling up and down mountains, a couple of hundred miles of mountains, and wading through the rivers and hacking through the jungles. Up and down for Christ's sake! Merrill even made them march the Ledo Road where there was transportation.

Get them in condition, he said.

Look at the shape they were in now. A bunch of skeletons with dysentery, malaria and jungle fever, those who had survived the Japs, half the time existing on lizards and weeds. They were exhausted and ready to give up, like drunks who keep on walking as long as you push and half carry them, but who drop in their tracks and pass out cold when you take your arm away. Well, he'd brought through his squad without a casualty, they'd been together from the start and that's the way they were going out.

They had walked rapidly in the shadows beside the shining river without speaking for almost half an hour, almost half of the way to Nhpum Ga, when Zing Tu La halted at a bamboo cluster on a knoll. Ahead, an open area of *kunai* spread up toward the trail. The elephant grass was as tall as a man except for a swath near the middle where the growth seemed short and new.

"Old elephant path," Zing Tu La said, pointing ahead. "Dua Chicken, please come with me."

They crept through the knifing grass pushing it down ahead of them to the edge of the new growth. Zing Tu La squatted, parted the short grass and held it back. Henty stared at the imprint dimly outlined in the moonlighted moist earth. Out of the warm and humid night, an icy finger touched his spine. The mark looked like a cloven hoof. It was the footprint of a Japanese jungle shoe with the big toe separated from the rest of the sole.

16

"Christ!" he breathed hoarsely.

They backed quickly to where the others waited in the silent darkness of the bamboo.

"They have slipped between us," Henty rasped. "How many do they number?"

"A patrol, Dua," Zing Tu La said. "A very large patrol. As many as 70 of them. They are encamped beyond the trail on a small hill clearing within the jungle. It may be there are others of them but we have knowledge only of this group."

Rage surged in Henty's chest.

"Why did you not tell me? You had no need to show me. I believe what you say is true. We have wasted time. They endanger both battalions, at Hsamshingyang and Nhpum Ga. We could have brought a platoon, surrounded and killed them all."

"That is not the way." Zing Tu La was softly reproachful. "I have said there may be others. The sound of combat would alert them. This is a matter we can handle between ourselves."

"Five against 70?" Henty angrily reverted to basic GI language. "For Christ's sake, how the fuck you figure?"

Zing Tu La understood the tone if not the words.

"These beasts of unspeakable ancestry are equipped with the bodies of men. They are weary from fighting. Tonight, even as you, they think they are secure. They have drunk of wine and lie in deep slumber upon the ground. A solitary sentry guards the camp. You and the Meatball will protect us with your automatic weapons." He touched the handle of his *kukri* knife. "Ding Ring, Ding Ra and I will despatch the enemy in silence. You will not fire unless we are discovered and must withdraw. Come now, and when we enter the jungle, grasp the Meatball by the waist. Ding Ring and Ding Ra will move with me."

Beyond the grass at the edge of the Nhpum Ga trail, they plunged through a thick screen of bamboo vines that concealed the elephant path into the blind, confining feeling of utter dark. The jungle enclosed them in a vaulted passage which Henty felt but could not see. It buzzed with mosquitos and hat was the only sound he heard. He reached into the back of Meatball's shorts and they pushed cautiously

17

ahead on the soft, smooth jungle carpet, clinging to the side wall. The air was close, heavy with the throat-catching odor of the festering elephant droppings. It overpowered even the Jap smell that should have lingered. Henty wondered what the smell was the Japs carried with them. They always gave themselves away when they were near.

The ground rose sharply. He felt it in the tugging muscles of his calves. The pace slowed to a crawl but he did not think it was from the incline. Far ahead he could see a hole in the matted roof where light came in from the night. He swung his tommy gun in his arms and flipped off the safety. Soon they stopped, Meatball and he, and although there was no sound, he could feel the others moving ahead. He still clung to Meatball's waistband, scarcely breathing, depending on the Jinghpaw to guide him when the time came.

The Japs were carrying the battle to the Marauders. The thought fidgeted in his mind. They'd have to fight the Japs some more. He tried to shut his mind off. Domingo wouldn't be going back tomorrow. Unless this was an isolated patrol and they got them all tonight. At the thought of combat, a sense of exhilaration began to fill him and now his mind was on the alert.

They waited, perhaps five minutes, perhaps ten and then abruptly he felt Meatball's waistband tighten. He moved ahead with the Jinghpaw. Henty had watched the hole where the night came in but had seen nothing. He had listened to the jungle but had heard no sound. He had felt no one return, yet Meatball had known when the time had come to move.

They crept softly up the hill toward the opening that marked the beginning of the clearing. They were almost there when Meatball stopped, touched his hand reassuringly, and Henty felt the presence of the others. They pressed on together, past a spot where the smell of Jap was strong. The sentry lay there somewhere, stilled and stinking.

Suddenly they were standing at the fringe of the jungle, wraiths that hovered in the dark, but Henty could see now. There was a small cleared hilltop and 50 yards ahead at its edge, a *basha* standing on its stilts in the moonlight. Scattered on the ground were the Japs, sprawled in lumps and mounds. There were no vapors here and he could make out

18

the features of the two near Japs sleeping side by side. The faces looked like rubber masks, molded and unchanging.

Only Zing Tu La unsheathed his *kukri* with its broad, curved blade sharpened on the inside edge. Meatball slipped across the path, standing just inside the jungle, tommy gun pointed at the camp. Henty leaned forward with his finger tightening on the trigger. The three Jinghpaws crept toward the nearest Japs, the two sleeping side by side.

He saw the Jinghpaws bend together, the three as one, over the near Jap. At the head, one throttled any sound, while the other gripped the feet to still the death kick. Henty exulted as the knife slashed swiftly at the throat. He waited tensely for the second strike. But the shadows glided away to the next group of three lumps.

Again they made one thrust and moved on. Henty stiffened and the caked mud crawled on his skin where the perspiration oozed up under it. The Jinghpaws worked into the camp, slitting the throat of one Jap where two or three slept together, by-passing the one who slept alone. Henty moved his gun with the swooping shadows, holding his breath to quiet the rattling in his chest. The Jinghpaws knelt over one of two stretched-out Japs. This man stirred and muttered. The crouching Jinghpaws disappeared, anonymous figures on the ground.

The night grew dim and Henty scanned the sky. Wisps of cloud were dangling over the face of the moon, streamers from a billowing mass moving swiftly with an air current that did not touch the ground. He found the prone figures of the Jinghpaws beside the mumbling Jap, froze his gun on them and stood rigid while the light went out. He listened for motion, for sound. But the Jap stopped his uttering and nothing stirred in the obscured camp.

The scudding cloud unsheathed the moon. His gun was pointing at two still Jap figures in the palish light. He hadn't moved. He swore in his mind until his temples throbbed. His eyes prowled the camp, examining, discarding the forms, some sleeping, some dead. He couldn't find the Jinghpaws. His eyes ached with searching for them. And then Zing Tu La, Ding Ring and Ding Ra were on the trail and Meatball was shoving Henty's band into the waistband.

The throat of the jungle gulped them and Henty made his feet go with Meatball's. Faster, with less caution, as they quit the terror they'd left behind. A growl snarled close at hand. It was where the Jap stench was worst. Meatball stiffened but kept walking. Henty arced his gun. Meatball reached back and pushed it down. Something slunk away on padded feet. A jackal or hyena.

Henty's heart pounded with savage glory at the massacre he'd witnessed. Killing Japs had never done that to him before. But a band about his mind grew tight with the pressing question: Why? Why hadn't the Jinghpaws killed them all? Why had they left half the Japs still sleeping to awaken and kill Marauders in the morning?

They came down the clean floored jungle tunnel to the tramped mud trail to Nhpum Ga. Zing Tu La scouted up and down while the others covered themselves behind the vine wall. Then they were moving through the *kunai* grass to the bamboo clump beside the Tanai River. The Jinghpaws didn't turn north toward Hsamshingyang, but waded into the river.

"Where do you go?" Henty whispered to Meatball. "I must return and report this penetration. I'll have to get a squad, come back and finish the job you started."

Zing Tu La turned at the edge of the gently flowing river, came back and handed a canteen to Henty.

"I take this from an officer. It is not wine but a kind of liquor. Drink. It will quiet your stomach."

Henty snorted but reached for the canteen.

"Nothing is wrong with my stomach," he said and lifted the canteen to his lips. The liquor was fiery. It tasted like brandy, burning in his throat, warming in his gut. "I have to go back. We have to kill the rest of those Japs. Why did you leave half of them alive?"

In the moonlight, Zing Tu La's teeth flashed white.

"Is it not better to strike terror among 1,000 men than to kill 100? When those who still are living awaken and find themselves in the company of the dead, they will flee in panic and their tale will grow in telling until an entire division of the enemy will fear this nameless thing that strikes at night on the hills of Nhpum Ga."

Henty held the canteen halfway to his mouth and looked hard at the Jinghpaw headman.

"I'll be damned," he finally said. He chuckled and swallowed another mouthful of the liquor. "You may have frightened

20

away more than we struck tonight. I respect your wisdom and your methods but I must return and report the incident. There may be other enemy patrols in the area tonight. That one passed within our defenses."

"And what would you do under the blanket of the night?" Zing Tu La took the canteen Henty held to him and passed it to Meatball. "A squad, a platoon, groping blindly in the darkness would only walk into a trap if there are others. Come with us for now and enjoy the reward you have earned. We have some wine and entertainment for a brave friend."

So they did have booze and women; passion warmed Henty's loins.

"I cannot," he groaned, not attempting to conceal his anguish. "The others think they are in a place for resting and are not alerted. A patrol could slip up and take the whole platoon, they way Meatball approached me."

"Your friend La Bu La is at the *basha* guarding the small person of your entertainment." Zing Tu La grasped Henty's arm. "Come. La Bu La will hasten to your encampment and secure the safety of your men. If an alien footstep falls within the jungle, he will signal the alarm."

"Since you put it that way," Henty said quickly and grinned. "I guess another hour won't make any difference now."

They waded the river, warmish and only waist deep at the end of the dry season. On the far shore in the shadows, Henty passed his ammunition belt and gun to Meatball and sloshed his face and body until all the clinging mud was gone. His toes curled in his puddled shoes. He was in an agony of anticipation.

The jungle was not so thick here on the flat ground and the moon came through. Although still wary, the Jinghpaws moved with confidence through the *kunai* and bamboo, following what must have been a trail although no trace of it was visible. In a *lanai* littered overgrowth, Zing Tu La tugged aside the vines and they crept on their hands and knees to a small open place with a *basha* that the jungle had entwined. It was long abandoned and looked deserted. Zing Tu La mounted the steps and motioned Henty to follow. The others squatted on the earth below.

A soft glow of rose briefly illumined the night as Zing Tu

La pulled aside a straw mat that covered the entrance and whisked Henty inside. La Bu La arose from the side of a small fire of bamboo burning without smoke in an earthen pot at the middle of the room. He was an old man, bent a little. Smiling warmly with his mild brown eyes, he padded cross the matted floor to them.

"The task is accomplished with success?" he asked but Henty scarcely heard or saw him.

Henty was breathing deeply, choking back a gasp. The girl seated on the straw pallet beside the firepot couldn't be as beautiful as she seemed to be. It's only that I'm starved, he thought. She was lightly colored, like the Shans, but her body was smaller, lithe and slender. Under a *sari* of blue drop cloth, her breasts were arrogant and challenging. They thrust hard nipples against the silk. He could feel them in his palms. Her lips were full and red and her eyes were gentle, large and dark. Her legs and feet were bare and clean. She smelled clean. Henty had heard somewhere that the women of Burma cleansed themselves with papaya juice and he could taste its faintly musky fragrance in the air. She had glanced quickly at him when he entered but now she was studying her slim long fingers, folded in her lap.

"She is called Gai-ri," Zing Tu La said with a slow spreading smile. "She is not of us and not entirely of Burma but somewhat of a nameless mixture. We captured her in a raid near Shikau Ga. She has not been molested by any one of us although I do not think she is entirely without experience. Take your place beside her and seek your pleasure. I do not believe she will resist since these light colored-ones have a fondness for strong men whose skin is fair. If she struggles, beat her and she will yield."

Henty sat with his knees against his chest to hide the erection that lifted in his shorts.

"Rest yourself," said Zing Tu La. He handed a bamboo cup of *laku* to Henty. "Who can say what the morning has in store? La Bu La departs now for your camp. I shall wait with the others until you are ready to return."

He heard Zing Tu La and La Bu La leave but he was looking at Gai-ri whose eyes he could not see under her downcast, long-lashed lids. The warmth had surged from his loins to his chest and he could feel his cheeks flushing with desire. Christ, he thought: I'll go off in my pants if I just touch her.

Without speaking, he handed the cup of rice wine to her.

She hesitated, looked at him and accepted it. She touched her lips to the cup and returned it. He turned it to the place her lips had been and kissed the rim. Her lips parted and she smiled. It was a warm smile that lighted the depths of her eyes and he could feel his heart plunging into them. He placed the cup of wine on the floor. She placed her hands hesitantly on his thighs. He roughly thrust them away. She worried her forehead into little lines that looked like wounds.

"Gai-ri," Henty said, breathing hard. "I want you. I want to take you. I want to keep taking you all night. But it has been a long time since I had a woman and never such a one as you. I am afraid. If you touch me or I touch you, it all will be over before it starts. I do not know what to do. It is a misery worse than not having you."

Her fingers swept lightly over the back of his hand. She stood, proud and graceful, a taunting trace of a smile on her lips. With slow, deliberate provocation, she unwrapped her *sari* and let it flutter to her feet. For a moment she was unmoving in the small light of the pinkish flame, velvet skin glowing, holding her lovely red-tipped breasts up with her breath for him to admire, casting her eyes invitingly down the dark line from her deep navel well to the soft triangle of curling hair between her legs.

"Take me quickly now," she said, speaking for the first time. She dropped to the mat and lay on her back. "Relieve yourself of this thing that boils within you. Then we shall drink and after you have rested, I shall caress you until you are once more ready and we shall make love all morning."

2

Fᴵᴿˢᵀ Lieutenant Lucius—formerly known as Lucky—
Snodgrass, United States Army Air Corps, detached
service, lay wide-eyed in the dankly dark *basha*, listening to
the silence. He knew what it meant when there were no
sounds in the jungle at night. Things that didn't belong were
moving in its hidden depths. Men. Japs. It was terrifying.

All the old horror came shuddering back, the nightmare that
haunted him even on his clean-sheeted cot in BOQ at
Margherita. Out of the chill black, the agonizing sound—the
spluttering engine, the final cough. The dead propellor.

"Bail out!" he shouted into the intercom, staring wildly
ahead, to the right and left and below into the infinite darkness.
He was blinded by the night.

Beside him, his co-pilot, 2nd Lt. Sam Carothers, was working desperately trying to pump some life back into the engine.
His face was porcelain in the light of his instrument panel.

"Roger, out," Lucky heard twice in his earphones as the
two crewmen stepped into the unknown.

The ship was losing altitude.

"No use, Sam," he yelled, voice shrilling. "Carburetor's
frozen. Jump."

Sam nodded and unbuckled his belt. He stepped out of the
cabin and Lucky, was left alone. He took a hasty final bearing. They were somewhere over the wild and mountainous
neck of northern Burma, in the area of Fort Hertz between
China and India.

The ship was going down in a lazy circle. He set the automatic pilot, left the cabin and leaped out into an inky sea of
nothing.

He felt surprisingly little sensation while he counted 10
and then pulled the cord. There was the frightful moment as
he waited. Then the reassuring solid jerk at his groin and
shoulders as the chute opened. He reached up and gripped the
cords to steady himself, suspended in time, space, life, hanging
in the sky. He could not see anything, not even the chute above

24

him. He still could hear the ship. Its one engine droned fainter and then there was a roaring crash and an awesome explosion that lighted a mountain side far away. Where the plane burned he could see the vague dark outlines of jungle growth below.

They had been over hostile territory, inhabited by beasts and savages, spined with jagged peaks, mazed with impenetrable jungle valleys. But his first reaction was not of terror. It was anger that filled him, consuming rage. And it was directed at Mme. Chiang Kai-shek.

The bitch, the unfeeling, unthinking, stupid, selfish bitch. She'd sent these new, untested C-46's with engines that didn't work, with carburetors that had no defrosters, without fuel transfer systems, to the Air Transport Command. She'd had the unthinkable presumption to go to the United States Congress, to a joint session of the Senate and House of Representatives, and tell them what to do. And they'd listened, believed her when she said China must have more materials of war regardless of the price. For what? The Chinese weren't doing any fighting. And Congress had pushed the Department of the Army, which knew the C-46's were not flight ready by a long shot, into sending them to the CBI.

The Hump hadn't been a bad run, from Chabua, India, to Kunming. Sure, the C-87 was a lumbering old girl, but you could depend on her and she had plenty of firepower. She was a converted B-24 bomber with .50 caliber guns mounted in the nose, turret, waist and tail. She plowed steadily on through the roughest weather and the Zeros kept a respectful distance. But the good lady from China didn't think she carried enough profiteering stuff for the war lords to stockpile. Give the kids the death traps, life was cheap in China and what the hell, Uncle Sam was footing this bill.

So now he was swinging in the murky night, he had his sky hook. For a few minutes. He began to think of what lay below and involuntarily tried to pull up his legs. They were weighted. Pull up your legs, ready to roll, and hope you land in a clear area.

Clear like the green carpeted hills of peaceful southern Indiana where the dogwood daubed the slopes with a million tiny white blooms in the early spring and the air was warm and clean and Ruth taught grade school in a gracious limestone building at Bloomington, taught nice kids like the ones they planned to have themselves when the world paused to catch its breath in its eternal game of war. So long Ruth, it was good being married to you while it lasted, what was it? seven weeks? that was in another life.

A violent jolt stretched him stiff. He hadn't had time, couldn't have brought up his knees. But it wouldn't have done any good if he had. He flailed with his arms and legs, reached above, to the side, kicked his feet. He touched nothing. He was dangling, hung up on something. Be calm, he told himself, you can only wait for morning. But he began to shake. It was a terrible night, what he knew of it. Most of the time his mind was blank.

When he opened his eyes to the first chalky gray outlines of his snare, he saw that he was hanging about 100 feet above the rocky ground from a far up branch of a giant tree where his parachute was entangled. It was a *kanyin*. He'd heard of them. There were no branches below him. The trunk was an arm's length beyond his reach. He tried swinging like a pendulum but the cords were tight on the wrong side. He had a knife. He could cut the lines. But the drop would be like a fall from a 10-story building. He might survive but how far could he crawl with broken limbs? He remembered stories of OSS parties finding bags of bones that festooned such jungle trees as this. Horror seized and shook him. He passed out.

When awareness returned, the sky was blue and the sun had warmed the day. He heard voices. On the ground, half a dozen men were looking up at him and jabbering. He did not think they were Japs. They didn't wear any sort of uniform, they were half-clad. Savages. He knew that headhunters roamed the mountains between India and Burma. He lost consciousness again.

He felt himself being gently tugged. He opened his eyes and looked into the wild face of a brown-skinned man who bared his teeth. The man was secured to the tree by some sort of belt of woven vines which was hitched around the trunk. Another rope of vines encircled Lucky's waist and he was being pulled toward the tree. His body bumped the trunk. He wrapped his arms around it and clung.

The savage attached the vines about the tree and cut the parachute cords. He hitched his own belt down a foot, grasped Lucky's legs and motioned him to start lowering himself.

Lucky's trembling fingers didn't want to work. He froze. The savage pushed himself back up, lowered Lucky's belt and motioned him again to start moving down.

With the savage supporting him and lowering the belt, Lucky was slipped down. When his feet touched the ground and the savage unloosened the vines, Lucky collapsed. The next he knew, he was sitting with his back against the tree and half a dozen of the fierce-looking bare-chested brown men were squatting around him. They gave him a bamboo cup filled with some milky looking liquid. He drank. There was not much taste but it warmed him. The savages watched intently and when he looked up at them, they smiled. One stood, patted his shoulder and indicated that he should get up and walk. He tottered and fell, pushed himself up, tried again. Gradually his legs steadied. The savages nodded approvingly and beckoned him into the jungle.

He started to follow, remembered his crew and called out. When they gathered around him, he pointed to the sky, floated a trembling hand through the air, held up three fingers and drew a circle above his head. Four of the savages left separately in different directions. He went into the enveloping green with the other two.

For four days he stumbled after his savage guides. He did not know where they were taking him but he was afraid not to follow. They ate raw fish scooped from the streams and shoots plucked from the jungle. He shed his flight jacket and the savages buried it. The brush and thorns tore at his flight suit. He burned by day and was chilled to the bones at night. The nights were the worst. He huddled with the savages covered by the jungle growth and trembled at the sounds the prowling beasts made around him.

Then he learned to fear more when he didn't hear the animals. It meant another Jap patrol. There were many of them. Once in the day, the pot-helmeted enemy swaggered along a path so close to their hide-out he could see their evil eyes, hear their rasping breath. Again and again, the only thing that saved him from madness was a numbness that seized his mind.

On the fourth night, the two savages carried him into the little hut encampment and air strip called Fort Hertz which was held by the OSS. Days later, when his lacerated skin was healing and daily nourishment had begun to revive his mind, they told him the savages had been Kachins. They flew him from Fort Hertz back to Chabua. He was the only one of the crew who returned.

He still could not hold a cup in both hands without spilling and requested that he be grounded. When, after 30 days he still refused to fly, they gave him temporary duty as communications officer. He wasn't a radio operator. He was alone in the shack and garbled his response to a request for a bearing. The plane crashed. He still refused to fly and they sent him to Margherita as an operations officer. He was alone at a new auxiliary strip. He laid the signal panels on the left instead of right side of the strip. He'd never put out signal panels on the ground before, only seen them from above. The L-5 cracked up. They volunteered him for temporary duty as liaison officer with the 5307th Composite Unit (Provisional) at Hsamshingyang. Back to the monstrous Burma jungle. Five days he'd been with the Marauders, five nights he hadn't slept.

He sobbed in the *basha* and sat up quaking at the sound of his own voice. It was late, almost two o'clock by the glowing hands of his watch. There was nothing to fear, he told himself. He was surrounded by a platoon of armed men. But these were defeated men, what could they do? The jungle swarmed with thousands of Japs and these men had withdrawn under fire. None of the pitiful handful would survive. And they would never relieve him. He was doomed with them. He sat, holding his knees, rocking and crying softly: Ruth, Ruth, Ruth.

Gradually, he quieted. Once more, he told himself, lying back on his bedroll and closing his eyes. He lay still, breathing deeply. It was then he heard the banshee shriek. He struggled up, limbs chilled and quaking. His hands trembled over the floor until he touched his .45. The screeching grew more piercing. "They've got to us," he gasped aloud and his throat was tight and dry. The Japs were out there slaughtering that ragged platoon of foot soldiers dug in the ground like moles. He had to get out of the *basha,* out of the area, back to the Command Post. But his legs didn't want to move. He began to hear words in the screams, a profane jumble of them, and they ran together in an obscene plea:

"Oh goddamned Lord, let me cross this fucking field in

one piece. Don't let these conniving crappers rise up and shit on me. You Burma bastards, hold your fire and your farts. This is Old Henshit here and I got to puke up to the piss ant."

Lieutenant Snodgrass stepped to the entrance, trembling now with anger. A slumped figure was weaving between the foxholes where some helmeted heads were lifting to watch. The man was dangling a submachine gun. He is drunk, Lucky thought, and he's coming to my hut with a weapon.

He melted back into the shadow against the wall, snapped off the safety and pointed the .45 at the center of the opening.

"Hey there, Snotty," a voice yelled below. "I'm coming up and in. It's just Old Henshit so don't you worry. Let me know you heard me now. Hey Snotty, you awake?"

Lucky couldn't speak but a sound growled in his throat.

"I read you loud and clear," the voice called thickly and a figure followed it up the steps to the entrance.

"Drop your weapon," Lucky tried to say crisply, growing even angrier because his voice cracked in his wrath.

"Sure." The man laid his tommy gun beside the doorway and took a step into the *basha*. "Where you at, Snotty?"

"Halt!" Lucky squeaked in lathering rage. "What did you call me?"

"Snotty." The man stopped and turned his head, peering at the lieutenant. "There you are. I called you Snotty. I don't know your first name."

"First name! You drunken idiot." It was all he could manage. Fury constricted his throat.

"Sorry, Snotty." Lucky was sure the man was chuckling. "Orders. Colonel's orders. First name only and no rank. Don't want some sniper picking off our brass, now do we?"

The man obviously was drunk and that only made the situation worse. You couldn't discipline nor reason with a drunk.

"What do you mean, coming here in the middle of the night, or morning?"

"Got something to tell you."

Lucky didn't hear him: "Breaking security?"

"Only safe way to come through the foxholes at night. Anyone see me crawling up here, he'd fire first and ask questions afterward. When you sing out like I did, they know goddamned well it's a GI with something on his mind. Never has been the Jap who could get that lingo down pat."

"Don't interrupt me!" Lucky shouted. "You are blind drunk. You are insulting. You are assaulting an officer and with a weapon."

"The weapon?" Even in the gloom, Lucky could see the man shrug. "Hell, more orders. You can't even take a crap without a weapon."

"Your behavior has endangered the platoon, the entire battalion and the Command Post," Lucky said icily. His anger had been good for him. It had burned away his fears and now he was in control. "Your name, rank and serial number, soldier. If you do have any stripes, I'm going to see you're busted and spend the next year in the stockade."

"Oh come off it, Snotty," the man said with an irritating, patient weariness. "I've got a report to make."

"At this hour? You've been in your foxhole since sundown. You're drunk and *I'm* going to throw the book at you."

"Sure I had a couple drinks. You can smell it. But I'm not drunk. And I haven't been sleeping in a foxhole. I just came off patrol and you'd better hear what I've got to say, Snotty."

"Don't call me Snotty," Lucky piped, furious again. "If you must call me by name, it's Lucius."

"Okay, Luscious, but I don't think that's much improvement."

"Don't call me anything," Lieutenant Snodgrass shrilled and rage shook his legs. He thought he could hear the men laughing in their foxholes. "Let's have this report that can't wait and then I'll decide what to do with you. First, your name, rank and serial number. That's an order."

"Oh hell. Henty. Henty Holiday. Sergeant. First Squad. You wouldn't remember the serial number. Here's what I came to tell you. A Jap patrol has penetrated the positions of the Second and Third battalions."

"A Jap patrol?" Lucky said quickly. "I knew it, I sensed it. Where? How large? What have we done?"

Henty blew out his breath. He sounded relieved.

"This one was between us and Nhpum Ga, about 70 of them. They infiltrated across the trail at about the halfway point. We took pretty good care of them and I don't think they'll give us any trouble. But it may be part of an encirclement to trap the 2nd. Hell, I don't know what it means but I'm afraid."

"Indeed," Lucky said with grim satisfaction. But he was nervous and bewildered. He hadn't been trained to fight this kind of war and wasn't sure what he should do. "I suppose Command should be advised."

"If I was in your place, I'd be making tracks right now," the sergeant said bitingly.

"You're telling me what to do?" Lucky said angrily and suddenly was suspicious. He wished it weren't so dark so he could see just how drunk this man was. As far as the lieutenant knew, no patrol had gone out from this platoon. It could be Henty's drunken imagination or even a malicious fabrication. He could see himself standing before General Merrill and Colonel Hunter, still groggy with sleep, sounding a false alarm. Yet he did not dare ignore it. "Henty, I will be frank in telling you that I do not like your attitude. You are drunk and you have been insolent and impertinent from the moment I laid eyes on you. There may be some odd regulations in this Command but it seems to me you are taking advantage of them and enjoying it."

"Oh goddamn it, goddamn it, I don't give a fart what you think. But if you don't let Command know what has happened it's going to be your ass. I don't give a shit about that, either, except I've got 11 men in my squad out there who figure their time is in and they're going back. There's the rest of this platoon and the 3rd Battalion and 300 or 400 in the 2nd who may be trapped at Nhpum Ga. If there's going to be some more fighting, let's have at it. But for chrissake, don't fuck up now."

Lucky held his breath and gripped his flaring temper while he tried to consider what Henty had said.

"Well," he said as calmly as he could. "We have radio contact with Command. Bring me the radio operator with the SCR 300."

"You can't send this out in the clear," Henty said harshly. "There may be other Jap patrols. If we do anything, we ought to take them by surprise. *You got to go and tell 'em.*"

"And desert my post?" He would not, under any circumstances, allow this enlisted man to make him lose his temper again. Nor would he permit the man to tell him what to do.

31

And it was a dark and lonely mile through the jungle to Hsamshingyang. He listened to the quiet, felt the security of his *basha*. And thought of the Japs moving in the night. An idea inspired him. "But wait. I am quite sure the General and the Colonel will not mind having their sleep disturbed on a matter of such obvious urgency." If the report was exaggerated, Command would see just how drunk Henty was and they'd discipline him. And Lieutenant Snodgrass would have done his duty. "And I am equally sure they will want this report first-hand. You can spell out the details." He was quite proud of the level tone he maintained. "You may have the privilege of delivering your report in person. That is all. Is everything clear?"

"Very clear." Henty bent and slowly picked up his tommy gun, started out the *basha* and turned on the top step. "I took it on myself to post some guards around the camp."

He clomped down the steps but his voice trailed back and hung inside the hut.

"Good night, Snotty."

Lieutenant Snodgrass was certain the man was laughing.

3

DOMINGO Sabado lay crumpled in the foxhole. Get your ass up, he fuzzily told himself; promised Old Henshit I wouldn't go to sleep.

He rocken himself until he was upright and propped his back against the damp earth. The air was moist and heavy in his lungs. The canteen still was in his hand. He waggled it and heard a slosh. There still was another drink in it. If I didn't hate Old Henshit so much I could almost love him, he thought, bringing me back a canteen full of *laku* for chrissake, Hen didn't even tell me to save a drink for him, the bastard.

That Hen's no bastard, just a plain good old sonofabitch and that didn't make him a bastard. It was Domingo Sabado who was the bastard, the only honest to God bastard in the whole bastard 5307th. An educated bastard. He'd been to high school. Still a bastard. There ought to be another way of saying it. He giggled and hiccupped. Calculated risk, that's what he was, goddamn calculated risk. That's the way Mamma and Papa must have thought of him. Damned old Army had the same idea only they called him expendable. Everyone in the bastard composite provisional 5307th was expendable. Fucked up outfit. Good place for him. He'd been fucked up from the start, back there in San Fernando 21, hell almost 22 years ago. He hoped the old man and old lady had enjoyed it. How about that, Papa? You had your whopping whore who was my mother (was it so good?) and turned the little bastard over to the county. Oh Jesus Christ, Papa, I just wish I'd known who you were; would you have trimmed a Christmas tree for me, made me a scooter, taken me fishing if I'd dug the worms? Shit, I'm still a kid, never was a child. Chrisskae, I'm stupid drunk in a foxhole maybe I'll never get out of but I think I'm going home tomorrow and I wonder where that is.

I told you in my mind when I thought of you, both of you; I've been to high school and I thought you'd be proud of that. It was an orphan school but I learned, I had to. You don't know what it is to be a Mexican and a bastard in a place they don't want you.

Dear Papa, whoever you are, I don't blame you any more. There's times a man has got to crack his nuts. Dear Mamma, whoever you are, I guess you get hot pants, too. Only maybe one of you should have been more careful so I wouldn't be here right now, no good for anything except killing Japs. Oh hell I don't know, I guess maybe I got some little yellow, red, brown, black even white bastards of my own. So I can't say much except I wish I hadn't done it, but only in my mind I wish that. It's a funny thing, it seems I had to think this thing out tonight, not knowing who you are or where you are. And it's even funnier, you'll never know what it is I've thought.

Except maybe you will, maybe I want you to know. I've missed loving you and had to tell you even if I could only think it. And dear God, I'm going back where I belong because now I've thought it out, I'm going home and I'm going to find you. When Henty gets me back, I'm going to find you somehow and everything is going to be all right for all of us. Maybe you're old and need me. By God that Henshit is a good old bastard.

Old Henshit is going to stay in the Army until he has his 30 years and he wants me to do the same but I can't do it now I got this other thing in my mind. Although maybe I should, maybe I should just go home on a long furlough like they promised, find you, Mamma and Papa, but stay on in the Army to help you best. Old Hen knows what he's talking about. Get a little pension money coming in and they can't screw you no matter what you are. That Hen is smart and much man. I'd seen Old Henshit field a grenade like a pop fly and pitch it right back where it came from before his feet touched the ground. Sonofabitch, there were hunks of Japs flying through the air and splattering them with blood.

Domingo rubbed his moist palm over his forehead. It was beginning to ache with thinking or maybe from the *laku*. He tilted the canteen and gulped the last of the wine. It didn't have much taste except like milk but it burned in your throat and kicked you in the ass. For a while you didn't give a shit about the world, not until it started to wear off. Now where the hell was Henty?

It must have taken an hour at the least to empty the canteen, a good deal longer because he'd passed out part of the time, a long time because the sky was beginning to gray with dawn. Jesus, that had been a kick, listening to Hen talk his way through the platoon, sonofabitch, Hen had put it on. He hadn't needed to be so big mouthed, they could have passed the word from hole to hole but Hen had wanted to rile up Snotty. If there was one thing Hen hated worse than Japs, it was officers. What the hell had Snotty done with Hen? And what the hell had Hen wanted to see Snotty for? Hen wasn't taking any *laku* to the flyboy, that was sure. Maybe Hen was drunk and hadn't shown it.

Jeezus.

Domingo staggered to his knees and tottered in a crouch. Wouldn't that be something if Snotty had taken Old Henshit in for being drunk, for chrissake right when they were done fighting and ready to go back. What the hell would happen to the squad? they'd rot in Hsamshingyang without Hen to bull their names onto orders.

He loosened and pushed his helmet back to ease the pressure on his mind and stood, weaving, steadying himself with his hands in the dirt at the edge of the hole. The sky was an opaque gray and he could see the unshadowed area quite well, the foxholes fanning out in dark mounds about the *bashas*. Was that why the officers slept in bashas? Behind a GI screen? No one was stirring in the holes but someone was standing in the entrance to Snotty's *basha*, backing out, and it was Henty, it had to be Henty, the way the submachine gun dangled in his hand.

What the hell was Henty up to?

Henty was dragging his butt. His chest was caved in and his chin rested on it. He didn't look at anything except his feet and he didn't bother to sound off. If he dropped his tommy gun any lower he'd trail it in the mud. He looked as if he'd had his ass chewed out and there was no more fight left in him. It must be something awful, no one had ever beat Old Henshit, not even the Colonel.

Still looking at the oozy ground, Henty plodded to the foxhole and plopped himself on the edge, dangling his feet in it. He glanced at Domingo and tried to smile but it didn't come off. His face was like a grinning skull.

"You'll be a soldier yet, boy," he said in a voice that must have ached the way it sounded. "Didn't think you could stay awake."

Old Henshit never complimented anyone for anything.

"What is it, Hen? What you been doing? What's wrong? Who ate you out?"

Henty's head jerked up and this time he did manage a bleak smile.

"Nobody ate me out, nobody can. I been to Command. I was with the Jinghpaws last night, we tangled with some Japs before we drank the wine. Command says they're going to get me a medal. A Bronze Star or something. Not that it means a thing. Any decoration a GI gets, the brass has got to get his fruit salad first. Not that I give a damn. Anyway, it's all providing. Providing we come through it. Oh shit."

"Come through what?" Domingo asked, slow and fearful.

"The little slant-eyed bastards have taken the trail to Nhpum Ga, about three miles from here. They got two Marauders that were on patrol last night, wounded some others, they got back. The Japs cut off the 2nd, slipped in between. Don't know how many. We've got 200, maybe 300 fit to fight in the entire 3rd and they don't have that many at Nhpum Ga. They'll be on their own up there for a while. Third has to set up a defense for Command and hold the strip and then try to take the trail back. Don't know anything yet except 2nd has radio contact with Command. They're catching hell up there, heavy stuff, 77-mm's."

"Oh Jesus, Hen!" Domingo started to groan but he couldn't piss and moan, not the way Henty looked and talked. He hadn't realized how much Henty was counting on going back, you never knew what he was carrying around inside. "Well hell, it ain't anything we haven't done before. So we got this little shit detail left, we'll mop them up like we always do then they'll have to fly us out."

"Did we mop them up the last five days? At Inkangatawng and Auche, did we? They've got us on defensive and it's going to be rough. Oh, we'll take them. That isn't what's bothering me. Merrill had a heart attack yesterday. They found him flat on his face. They're evacuating him today. Stilwell ordered him flown out."

"Goddamn, Hen." Domingo was puzzled. "That's real

tough and all, but it's no tragedy. Might even be good. He can tell the Boss to his face how things really are. And as far as fighting's concerned, how many times we fought without him? About half the times. The Colonel's okay."

"Yeah, he's issuing orders right now," Henty said gloomily. "This platoon's got a little job to do. We're going up a trail to a Jap camp I was at last night and do some reconnoitering. See whether they pulled out and what they've got beyond."

"That where you tangled with them, you and the Kachins? Sounds like SOP to me, the ordinary patrol. What's got you down? They can't give us anything we ain't had before."

"Oh yes they can," Henty said savagely. "This time we get shit. You know the Marauders, boy. No replacements. You fight with what you've got. On account of we're in such tough shape from casualties, malaria, dysentery, hell! Those goddamned jungle leeches eat holes in your legs and leave your bones rotting. On account of we've got nobody left, the Colonel's throwing everybody into the lines except the medics and the muleskinners."

"Okay, okay, so everybody fights, we got more support than we been having. Makes good sense to me."

Henty slit his eyes and with his yellowed face he looked almost oriental except his emotions showed. They were snarling.

"Listen, boy, what they can give us we haven't had before is this. They're sending Snotty out with this platoon as leader. How the hell am I going to bring the squad back with a handicap like that?"

4

"PATROL, 'ten-*shun!*"

The platoon, Lt. Lucius Snodgrass commanding, shuffled and stood a little less at ease. The men were in a sloppy double-line forming three squads of 12. Their tattered fatigues were bleached and blotched with muck. Snotty, facing them 10 paces out, had been to Command and was wearing new issue. His fatigues were stiff and greener than the jungle. An unbaptized helmet with camouflage netting rode his blond head jauntily. A canteen swung from his web belt at one hip and his .45 was low and loose on the other. He held his well-padded six-feet militarily erect and surveyed his troops with violet colored, rather large and surprisingly clear eyes. The motley command plainly displeased him. But that wasn't all. There was something strange about his eyes. They stared too hard.

"What's the bastard going to have us do?" Domingo muttered. "Close order drill?"

The patrol had formed on a paddy above and beyond the foxholes, near the group of *bashas*. The morning sun had burned away the thin layer of opacity and the sky was deepening in blue. It was very bright and very hot. The moist earth already was caking and sweat splotches were crawling darkly from under the light field-packs the men had strapped to their backs. Beyond the rest area, the crowding jungle was verdant and looked peaceful. In may have been his imagination, but Henty thought he could hear the muffled thudding of artillery in the distance and smell cordite drifting down from Nhpum Ga.

"The Boy Scout just might do that," he growled. He'd had two hours sleep and felt the worse for it. His gut was grumbling and a pain gnawed it. Instant coffee, canned compressed eggs, three soft crackers and one whole fruit bar: he wasn't used to so much food. And a cigarette. They'd had a 10-in-1 drop at Hsamshingyang with their first tobacco in five days and hadn't had to hoard.

"Jeez," said Pfc. Konrad Malinowski standing next to Henty. He was big-framed, like Snotty, but his bones stuck out and his cheeks were hollow, making his blue eyes and chapped lips seem twice their normal size. "I got to shit. If he keeps us here any longer, I got to rip out the seat of my pants and let her go."

The men had been assembled and waiting five minutes before Snotty had come out of his *basha*.

"If he keeps us here any longer," Henty said, "you don't have to worry. Lined up like this, we're sitting ducks. All the Japs have to do is zero in with one mortar shell and we've had it."

"They ain't that close," Malinowski said.

Thud . . . Thud . . . Thud . . . Hollow repercussions from the ridge shook the still air.

"Well they got artillery," Domingo said. "We shouldn't even hear it but we do, and feel it too. Maybe they got it between us and Nhpum Ga. If they have, they can throw one this way."

"Just let me get one decent meal and keep it in me, I don't care," Kon said and grimaced. "My gut's shrunk smaller than my nuts. Wonder if I ever get to eat another Polish sausage."

"Platoon sergeant, report to me," Snotty barked. He squared his shoulders and thrust out his jaw.

The goddamned fool, Henty thought, standing out there in front like that—if there's a sniper in the trees, Snotty's going to get it right between the shoulder blades.

No one stepped front and center.

Snotty's eyes grew fiery and flashed angrily down the front row, came to Henty and sparked with recognition.

"You . . . Henty," he commanded crisply. "Five steps forward, h'arch!"

Henty trudged out of the ranks dangling his submachine gun. Halfway between his squad and Snotty, he halted and slumped.

"Your rank, soldier," Snotty ordered.

"Sergeant," Henty said resentfully. Snotty knew that.

"Are you the platoon sergeant?"

"No." Indifferently.

"Who is the platoon sergeant?" Annoyed.

"Don't have one any more. First sergeant got his head blown half away at Auche."

Snotty's pink-cheeked face writhed, as if a dull knife were sawing at his entrails. I'll bet the sonofabitch can't stand the sight of blood, Henty thought.

"You are 1st Squad leader," Snotty said, subdued, but making the statement an accusation.

"That's right," Henty said, adding maliciously, "Snotty."

" 'Ten-*shun, sergeant!*" Snotty shouted, red-faced now. "We'll have no more of that. You call me Snodgrass. It doesn't have to be the first name. I checked that point."

Henty chewed away a smile and brought his heels together but didn't move his swinging tommy gun. Someone in the ranks guffawed. He thought it was Domingo.

Snotty strode toward Henty. That gut of Snotty's is fat, he thought, real honest to God blubber you get from eating all you want and regular. The lieutenant stood tall enough to glare down. A crimson rim was burning at the edges of his violet iris. The eyes looked spooky.

"I should put you on report but I have to rely on someone," Snotty said in a low malignant voice. Henty sniggered openly. Snotty didn't want the troops to hear him admit that. The lieutenant's face was getting spotty, red and white, but he went on: "Your attitude is insufferable in an enlisted man regardless of circumstances. *I shall not tolerate it!* From now on you will conduct yourself in a military manner.

"Now, you apparently understand the operation of a patrol and I believe you are aware of our mission since you are largely responsible for it. We are to reconnoiter the area between here and Nhpum Ga which you visited without permission last evening. If the enemy is no longer encamped, we are to determine other positions and the extent of the penetration and report back to Command by sundown. You will act as platoon sergeant. Is that clear?"

"You bet!" Henty about-faced smartly. "Domingo, Konrad, get your asses in high gear. Second, Third squad leaders come on along. The rest of you disperse, scatter. Come on Snodgrass, let's get out of the open."

The platoon broke for the bamboo cover by the river. As Henty trotted toward the *bashas,* he could hear Snotty's voice raising in wordless rage. Henty squatted out of the hot sun

40

on the cool, moist earth under the hut Snotty had occupied and waited for the others to join him. Domingo and Kon, grins wide in their shrunken faces, came up first.

"I got to take a crap," Kon said.

"Use the officers' hole," Henty said.

The 2nd squad sergeant, Double Ugly Bailey, hit the dirt and sprawled. His face was a glob with a nose that looked like a shapeless blob of warm putty. He had ridges above his piggy eyes that made his sandy brows stick out like grassy swamp mounds.

"You're bucking for a dirt blanket, Henty, you take this outfit out," he growled. His mouth was almost formless, just a hole that opened and closed. "They'll last about as long as a fart in the wind."

Sgt. Butcher Smiley of the 3rd Squad folded his legs and sat just inside the shelter under the floor.

"I wouldn't fish with a worm like that," he said, jerking his head toward the approaching lieutenant. The Butcher had a deep-lined face like a haggard old man and he was beginning to develop a twitch that grabbed the left corners of his mouth and eye and made you think he was winking at you when he talked.

Snotty stalked up, face livid. He was puffing, with rage or exertion or maybe both. Konrad was stooping over the trench behind the *basha*.

"What's that man doing in the officers' latrine?" Snotty demanded in a thin, high voice. He had to bend down to see under the hut.

"Shitting," Henty said calmly. "You want him to do it in his pants?"

"You are insolent and insubordinate, sergeant!" Snotty shouted furiously but his voice didn't crack. "Why did you dismiss those men? I give the orders."

Henty clamped his jaw and slitted his eyes at Snotty who had unbuckled his knees to get his head under the *basha*.

"Let's get this straight, Snodgrass," he grated, feeling wrathful bile bubbling in his gut. "I told you last night, or this morning, I got 11 men in my squad I brought in here on this stupid-assed mission and I intend to take them out with me. You tell me I'm acting platoon sergeant, sonofabitch I don't want it but that's okay, only now I got 24 more men to worry about. First thing you *don't* know is in a combat area you don't group your men. That's why I dismissed them without wasting time to argue. You want to give the orders, okay, I'll tell you what to say. There aren't any rules to this cowboys-and-Indians game we're playing out here. The only difference between you and me is I've been at it long enough to forget the A-R. If you don't like me and want to put someone else in charge, like Double Ugly or Butcher here, that's okay. You want to take over by yourself, that's okay, too. Only let me handle my own squad the way I learned."

Kon came back grunting.

"My asshole burns," he said, sitting and rubbing his prat forth and back on the ground like a dog. "I can't remember when it didn't burn like it was being reamed out every step I take."

Domingo stretched out, his M-1 across his chest.

"I'm so tired I don't give a shit," he said. "I ache so much all over I can't even feel I *got* a asshole. Jesus, Henshit, wouldn't you say they got to send us back or let us rest at least when we've wiped up this last mess?"

"Relax," Double Ugly said, speaking into the helmet he'd tilted over his face. "After this is over you won't have to fight no more, I promise."

He laughed and the sound was hollow.

Henty looked at Snotty. His cheeks still were flushed and now his eyes looked feverish. He was grimly silent as he studied the five of them.

"Carry on, sergeant," he finally said tightly and sat on the ground away from them, facing out with his back against a corner post.

"Right," Henty said, turning to the others. "They fucked things up for us again, Command or Headquarters or maybe it was the Big Brass in Washington, D. C. We got Japs in here where they shouldn't be and the 2nd Battalion's cut off. So we got to pull some more chestnuts out of the fire. It's going to be a bitch but we got to go in there and find them. First Squad will move out in front again today. We should rotate but I don't know the other squads like I know the First so we got to take the crap. You're scout, Kon, if you think you can make it."

"Sure, Hen," he said indifferently and rubbed some dirt on

his rawboned face. "I got nothing left in me. Anything else until I eat again will be like dry heaves. It may unpucker but it won't poop."

Henty let a quick grin briefly expose his gray teeth.

"It better not because I'll be right behind you. Domingo, you ride their tails and goose them. Anyone starts to drag, you boot his ass. What the hell, they got a good night's sleep. The rest of the patrol as usual. Second Squad to flank when we hit a block. Third to back us up." He shifted his eyes to Snotty whose lips were compressed in a straight line. "You're with the 3rd, Snodgrass."

"And so are you, sergeant," Snotty said. His voice squeaked a little.

"Don't call me sergeant again," Henty said sharply. "Hen, Henty, Holiday, Henshit, Hey You, anything but not sergeant. You call me that out there and I'll yell Lieutenant. And I'm not going with the Third. I'll be up there with Kon. I'm the only one knows where we're going."

"Henshit," Snotty said nastily and ran his tongue over his teeth as if the name tasted dirty. "You're marching with me in the 3rd where I can keep an eye on you. That's an order. Now tell your men where we're going and how to get there."

"Christ!" Henty exploded.

"It's okay, Hen," Domingo said, eyes smoldering and lip curling. "You already told me enough, I know about where the elephant trail goes up the hill. Won't be hard to follow. I'll back up Kon. Once we get to the Jap camp, you don't know what's beyond anyway."

"They ought to let us have a Kachin," Kon said.

"You know they aren't expendable," Henty said.

"What about medics?" the Butcher asked and winked grotesquely. "We ought to have a corpsman on a patrol like this."

"Can't risk them," Henty said. "Anyway, they're carpenters this morning. Doc's got them building him an operating table. All we've got is my first air kit so take care of yourselves."

He crawled from the shelter of the *basha* and the others followed, Snotty trailing.

"What if the enemy is still encamped where you encountered them last evening?" he asked. There was no color left in his face.

"They won't be," Henty said, face impassive but letting his voice slur contemptuously. He turned his back to Snotty. Double Ugly's normally formless mouth quirked. "We take the main trail to Nhpum Ga as far as the elephant path. There aren't supposed to be any Japs that close but that's another thing we've got to learn the hard way. Keep off to the side and close to the trees and take it easy. Kon, if you have to crap, scout ahead 50 or so yards and come back to the squad. Domingo can send someone else ahead. We might as well move now and get this duty done."

"My mother told me there'd be days like this but not so many of them," Kon wailed the old refrain.

Walking away from them, Henty could hear Domingo asking: "What was she like?"

The trail to Nhpum Ga was an old Kachin road, cleared by elephants and wide enough for two men to walk abreast but the patrol moved in a scraggy file, loosely strung out in the three squads. Kon, crouched, wary, rifle at the ready, probed the way ahead. First scout. The most vulnerable position in the patrol. Each squad with the exception of the 1st which was short its leader, Henty, consisted of eight riflemen, a Browning automatic rifleman, BAR ammunition-bearer armed with an M-1, squad leader and assistant squad leader, both of whom carried optional weapons. All of the squad leaders were carrying tommy guns and two of the assistant squad leaders had carbines. Domingo preferred his M-1. The 3rd Squad had a radioman who packed a 30-pound SCR 300 on his back for contact with Command. He also carried an M-1.

The pace, though cautious, was fairly rapid over the well-tramped trail. The bamboo jungle walled it in on either side but it was not roofed over except in splotchy patches at the turnings. The sun and heat came in. The rise was gradual but steady and Henty's fatigues were clammily sticking to his back before they'd gone a mile. The only air stirring in the corridor came from the artillery blasts and you actually couldn't hear them. The thick growth soaked up the sound but you sensed the pounding the ridge was taking from high trajectory mountain guns and heavy howitzers because you'd been through it.

The 2nd can't take it, Henty thought. Christ! They'll all be slaughtered! The Marauders *never* had been on defensive, the

5307th wasn't equipped to stand off artillery. They were guerrillas, ambushing, hitting with close-in striking weapons, BAR's, mortars, machine guns, rifles, grenades, that's all they had to fight with. Just slip in behind the Japs, mow them down in a lightning raid and withdraw. But now the 2nd was dug in on a saddle of high ground on an exposed position. The Japs could just sit back and throw their heavy stuff up on the hill and the 2nd could never touch them. And when the battalion was wiped out, all the Japs had to do was pour it on Hsamshingyang. How in hell had the 2nd and 3rd got into a goddamned stupid position like this?

How had the 5307th Composite Unit (Provisional) got sucked into his campaign at all, fighting for the bloody British Empire? Where the hell were the goddamned limeys? Sitting on their tailored asses in canteens and clubs in India drinking gin and tonics while GI's fought their battles for them. They sucked us in again, Henty thought bitterly. What the hell was Burma? A goddamned English colony. So the Japs take it, General Tanaka runs over it with 70,000 troops, the British hightail for India and who do they send to take it back? Twenty-six-hundred GI infantrymen, or what's left of it. Twenty-six hundred GI's on K rations when they remember to drop them, fig ting howitzers and mountain guns with hand grenades and rifles. Sure, Old Vinegar Puss was supposed to back them up with a couple of Chinese divisions but the Chinese had no guts for fighting, they were only 100 or so miles behind. When the Marauders had the Japs on the run, the chinks came up. And their generals sold the troops the rice we gave them. Christ, the goddamned chinks even sold the arms we gave them to the Japs. Who was that guy? General Ho traded two lend-lease jeeps to a British consul for a Rolls Royce and beat it back to China when the Japs ran the lily-livered limeys out of Burma.

They were fighting for a road to China so we could send a couple billion more dollars worth of stuff to that farty little bastard Chiang Kai-shek who wouldn't even let his troops make a stand against the Japs. The peanut would salt about $100 million for himself in some bank in Switzerland and stash the arms away for a goddamned civil war with Mao Tse-Tung when the Marauders had gutted the last Jap in this part of Asia.

And now this entrapment, with the 1st Battalion at Shaduzup too far away to come in and flank. Vinegar Joe had got too ambitious, stretched his lines too thin, forgotten that his long-range penetration force so-called now totaled less than 1,800 fighting men, all three battalions counted. And where the hell were Stilwell's two Chinese divisions the 5307th was supposed to be spearheading? Had they ever fought a battle? One of them even had a tank outfit. Everyone had heard of it but no one had seen it yet. Maybe it was protecting the Chink's rear from being overrun by the bulldozers the U. S. Army Engineers were pushing through Pick's Pike on the Burma Road from Ledo. What a pile of crap the whole campaign was from the start; a handful of GI's running the Japs out of a British colony, GI engineers building a supply road to China and neither the limey nor the chinks would lift a gun to help. For Christ's sake! the English forestry officials were even trying to collect damages from Uncle Sam for the trees General Pick was cutting down to build the road!

The patrol was nearing the old elephant trail. Henty recognized the clump of bamboo and patch of *kunai*. He started to edge ahead of the 3rd Squad. Snotty reached out to hold him back. Henty jerked away, shook his head in frowning, silent warning, and slowed the men with a hand signal. There had been no Jap sign but now the artillery was less than three miles away and you could hear the relentless steady thumping. Henty slid up the file, slipping from man to man. There was a tenseness, an uncertainty in the squads which he hadn't felt before. The faces of the men were grim and they didn't glance at him. Well, Double Ugly and Butcher could have told them he'd been ordered to the 3rd by Snotty.

He worked his way through his own squad to Domingo and crept ahead toward the scout. Kon was crouched in the *kunai* like a discarded sack of rags. He looked as if he'd been hit. Henty hadn't heard a report, not even the crack of a snapping branch. His aching gut got sick and he tasted its bitterness. He slapped the butt of his weapon to alert the patrol and scrambled to Kon's side, eyes leaping through the trees for snipers. Fifty feet from the bamboo vine entwined entrance to the elephant trail, Kon remained rigid in his bent-over position. Henty grasped his shoulder. Kon looked at him, held his hand to his stomach and winced when he tried to smile. He was crapping

46

again. Henty let out his breath, nodded and motioned him back. As Kon pushed away, Henty went ahead on his hands and knees through the tall, sharp grass.

He poked through the vines on his belly into the green twilight of the jungle tunnel. As once he heard the buzzing of the mosquitos but otherwise it was still and gloomy as death. He could taste the pungent elephant smell but there was no Jap trace. Enough light seeped through to see. He wriggled ahead on his elbows, eyes shifting from the path and tight growth on either side to the strange orderliness of the matted floor, looking for fresh marks. With infinite patience, he covered the entire width of the path for 10 yards, seeing only the single line of new bruises the Jinghpaws and he had made the night before, studying these to make sure they had not been followed. If the Japs who survived had fled the camp, they had not come this way. He backed down, through the vines and elephant grass to the Nhpum Ga trail, sucking air that tasted clean.

The squads had moved up in the grass on either side and were covering him. At his signal, Domingo and Kon trotted up and squatted. Their chests were heaving and sweat was running down their cheeks. Henty started to shake his head at Kon but the big Pole grinned weakly. He and Domingo plunged under the covering of vines and disappeared. A man at a time, the 1st Squad filtered through, followed by the 2nd. Their faces were tight but they glanced at Henty now. A few even bared their teeth a little in what they meant for smiles.

At the head of the 3rd Squad, still beside the trail, Snotty gestured irritably. Henty gritted his teeth and waited. He led the lieutenant and the last squad into the smothering jungle.

It was like crawling up a green, felt-lined funnel. The patrol inched up the edge toward the opening at the top like humping caterpillars. The jungle absorbed all sound from the bombardment at Nhpum Ga but Henty felt the earth shudder under him. Far up, a shadow flitted across the opening as Kon or Domingo darted across the path. Every man of the patrol rooted to the ground like jungle growth. Both Kon and Domingo sprang from the opening and disappeared.

Moments, minutes passed: days, weeks, months probably were being lived in most men's minds but Henty felt his thinking shut off as his reflexes wound up to propel him into action.

He hoisted his haunches, tucked one knee under his chest and dug a toe into the ground. When Kon and Domingo reappeared clearly outlined against the light of day, waving the patrol ahead, he sprinted up the lane and burst into the clearing.

The mound was very green in the bright light. He could see now what he hadn't been able to distinguish the night before. The area was a *tongyaw*, an abandoned rice paddy where some Kachin had burned off a small area, built his *basha* at the side and raised two or three crops of rice in the rich topsoil before moving on. Now, before the jungle could reclaim it, it had become a slaughterhouse. The ground was littered with dead Japs and they were beginning to stink. Henty counted 37 of those little men in brown. Their heads were unhinged from their bodies and their necks were black with flies where their throats had been opened. They were sprawled in the positions that they'd slept but each corpse was missing a part of an arm or hand. The rest of the Jap patrol must have panicked. Rive bags, canteens, even weapons were strewn among the dead.

"A trail circles around northwest on the other side," Domingo said. "They took off that way." He wrinkled his nose. "They smell worse dead than alive."

Kon leered.

"Seeing a sight like this, I even forget my burning butt," he said.

"Take off," Henty told them. "Scout up that trail 50 yards or so and wait. We'll push right on."

The squads entered the camp area and the men fanned out as Domingo and Kon crossed to the *basha* and entered a break in the trees beyond. Snotty elbowed up to Henty. He was breathing hard.

"Henty, I told you to stay with me," he said angrily and then he saw the dead Japs. Horror filled his eyes.

"My God!" he gasped. "Did you have to mutilate them?"

Henty shrugged.

"We didn't do anything except slit their throats. The other Japs did the rest themselves. When one of them is killed, they always try to hack off a hunk, usually an arm or hand. If we're on their tails, sometimes they just peel off some skin. They cremate it and send the ashes to the folks back home. It's part of their religion."

"Even the ears?" Snotty's words seemed to stick in his throat.

Henty swung and examined the nearest bodies. Where the ears had been there were just dark crawling masses of bloated flies. The Jinghpaws had been at it again, he told himself with a sardonic smile in his mind. Well hell, they'd been ordered to stop taking ears but it had been their party and you couldn't blame them. You asked one how many Japs he'd killed and he just emptied his bamboo tube of ears that looked like dried apricots and told you to divide by two. It was neat and you couldn't argue with him.

"Must be some new kind of cult," he told Snotty.

"Heathens," Snotty said, hacking, looking as if he had a throat full of vomit. "You sure the others all have left?"

"Their bandy legs were doing double time," Henty said, watching Snotty with enjoyment. "There's food and weapons they left behind. I just wish they'd burn or bury their own damned corpses. It isn't healthy, the way they pollute the air. Well, we don't have time to do the job. We've got to see where what's left of the patrol has gone. Looks like they're swinging around to hit Nhpum Ga from the rear, unless they figure on slipping down to Hsamshingyang by some old trail we don't know about. I've got to talk with Kon and Domingo."

Before Snotty could protest, he was running across the encampment, zigzagging between and leaping over the bodies. The trail beyond the *basha* looped into the bamboo and began to climb. He examined the ground as he walked. The Japs had made no effort to conceal their passage and the departure had been recent, within the last two or three hours. They had relieved themselves right on the path and when he swept off the flies, the turds were reasonably fresh. And solid. The Nip bastards were eating better than the 5307th!

Domingo was sitting on the trail below a rise where the trees thinned out. Kon was lying in the grass at the top, spraddle legged, head and weapon pointing in the direction the Japs had taken.

"It's clear beyond, at least into the trees," Domingo said and grinned broadly. Even after almost three months in the

49

jungle, his teeth still were white. "You sure scared the shit out of those little yellow bastards."

Henty sat on his haunches to save his sticking-out tailbones from the hard ground. He wanted a cigarette so he fished a dextrose tablet from his pocket and sucked on it. The chalky taste only made him thirsty and he spit it out.

"I don't like it," he said slowly. "The trail's too plain. Looks like they want us to think they tore ass out, leaving all that stuff in camp. Then crapping where we'd find it and know which way to go. I think we're being sucked into a trap. Keep off the side of the trail and use the trees for cover as much as you can. When you come to a turn or overgrown place, have Kon scoot through on his belly and you back him up close. I'll have 1st as near behind you as I can without bunching."

Kon slid down below the crest, rolled over and sat up.

"Call me when lunch is ready, mother," he said, smiling thinly.

Then he was on his belly snaking over the rise.

"Oh Jesus," Domingo said getting on his knees. "All this distance to go back." He started crawling toward the top, stopped and looked around. His eyes were woebegone and when he spoke his voice was forlorn. "Hey, Hen, that shit I gave you last night, about cutting off your balls and shoving them down your chickenshit throat. . . . I didn't mean it."

An unnatural lump stuck in Henty's throat.

"Forget it, boy," he said gruffly.

"Yeah," Domingo said with a twisted smile. "I'm going to cut off your prick instead and ram it up Snotty's ass."

He faded away, through the grass and over the hill.

They're my boys, Henty thought . . . and grinned.

All of them were like that, every walking wreck in the 5307th, the ornery-est, dirty-est, meanest outfit any army had ever spawned, especially the 1st Squad, his squad, the scurvy-est, bloody-est, sneaky-est sonsofbitches there ever were, fighting on their guts alone. Like Ass Drag coming up the trail. A. D. Svensen, that's what they'd named him, just the initials maybe his folks hadn't known a good American name, those initials sure were naturals for the GI handle. The big, dumb Swede, he didn't even know enough to bitch about how bad off he was. Blondish mousey hair, red faced once but getting orange-yellow, washed out blue eyes that looked so weak you wondered how he saw with them but that could spot a Jap in a tree half a mile off, tossing his BAR in his big mitts as easily as a carbine and wearing two bandoliers of clips across a chest that used to be a barrel but now was all ribs, the crazy grinning bastard, he had an ammo bearer, he didn't need to lug around those extra clips for chrissake, he sure could lay down a powerful lot of fire when you needed it real bad.

"You been chasing monkey pussy again, you big baboon, while your buddies are out there swimming in their blood and screaming for you?" Henty ground his teeth at Ass Drag. "You don't have to stop to fart, close in and cover them."

And the big dumb Swede just kept on grinning and dragged his belly over the rise.

Followed by his ammo bearer, Julie Chiruco, a cocky little Italian who hadn't cut his hair since Deogarh and now wore shining black ringlets that curled down his thick neck. And a fierce mustache. He looked like out of a story book except he carried a needle-sharp throwing knife on his back instead of in his teeth. Christ! all he could talk about were the babes he'd raped, he didn't want them to give it to him, he wanted to bust a virgin who'd screech and claw, he liked to fight for what he got. Jesus, if there ever was a sweetheart who'd back you up when the going was rough it was Julie.

"Up yours," Henty told him and prodded him on with a vicious goose.

Julie raised his fingers to his nose and went after Ass Drag.

Henty started back toward his eight riflemen who were strung out on the trail. Here was Injun Joe, as tall as Kon but leaner and harder. If there was another Indian on the reservation who looked the part as much as Joe, Hollywood had missed him. Hawk-nose, beady-eyes, black hair that should be worn in braids, no goddamned nerves or even feelings, he'd rather stick his bayonet into a Jap than shoot him.

Henty sliced across his forehead with his finger.

"Go get 'em, Joe," he said.

Without a flicker of emotion showing in his sculpted face, the Indian moved silently on, treading as stealthily in his GI shoes as if he were wearing mocassins. Good old Joe, no matter what you asked him to do, he just went ahead and did it and never asked you why.

Hari Kari and Old Overshoes, it was Old Overshoes who'd named Harry McCarthy "Hari Kari."

"But the word you mean is *hara-kiri*," Harry had protested mildly. He was a funny Irishman, well educated and quiet until you crossed him and then his red hair stood on end and his whole face got the color of his freckles.

"All I know is you rip their bowels out real good," Old Overshoes had shouted and laughed lustily.

It was funny how they'd got their names. Old Overshoes was Bob Overholt and could just as well have been called Old Overcoat except he wouldn't screw anything without a rubber not even a Red Cross girl and somebody said with him it was like going to bed with his overshoes on. He'd been a head hunter, one of those club swinging, nut cracking guards at some state pen and he still liked hurting people which was all right out here. When he lobbed in a grenade, he'd hold back after he'd pulled the pin and let go at the last minute so the grenade would explode before it hit the ground and catch them in the face.

Henty poked Hari Kari and Old Overshoes in the ribs and jerked a double time hand signal. They grinned right back at him and didn't change their pace.

Katey and Pretty Pussey, now there was a pair. The names they were known by belonged to them, Kenneth Katey and Leonard Pussey, only the Pretty had been added to Len's. Ken and Len. They both were sharpshooters, but there was something fishy about their eyes and while it was all right being buddies and all, there was something strange or maybe downright queer about the way they always kept apart from the squad but never from each other.

Henty's grin for them was a little stiff.

Nick the Greek, what a crazy, conniving bastard. A born pimp. Hell, the Greek even had a 18-year-old girl he'd bought in India for $100 staked out in a mud hut between the training camp and the village of Deogarh, you could get it any time you wanted if you had $10, and if things were slow Nick might even let you on for a fin.

"Peddling much these days?" Henty asked Nick.

"Man, ain't you heard?" Nick Poppas wet his red lips with

his tongue and his black eyes got bright. "Right after this they're sending us back to Deogarh. We draw our back pay and I clean up."

"I heard we're going to Margherita for some free tail," Henty said.

Then Furman, no first name, no nickname, just Furman, always oily and smirking like he was laughing at them all without smiling, he had all the answers. If he was so goddamned smart and a high school literature or some goddamned kind of teacher in Pittsburgh like he said, how come he was a busted buck assed private in the Marauders? There was something sneaky about the way Furman was always watching and studying everybody with his brooding eyes, dark brown and magnified behind thick-lensed steel-rimmed glasses. But he pulled his weight, they all did, and Henty gave Furman a slap in the butt.

He knew these men so goddamned well. It was a crazy damned thing but the squad was like his family. They'd all volunteered for Galahad with him from New Georgia, anything, even a secret mission you knew was dangerous was worth getting off that stinking island. Yeah, and they'd traded a pile of manure for a pile of shit.

The 2nd Squad filed by, weary but jungle-wise and ready for the kill. And then Snotty and the 3rd. Snotty was sweating worse than anyone else. His skin couldn't breathe under his stiff, new fatigues. His eyes looked glassy but smaller. Maybe his face was puffing, it sure was getting red. And he seemed to be having trouble getting enough air in his lungs.

Henty dropped into the lead position with the 3rd, bellied over the hill with Snotty panting at his heels. Still prone across a dip where the elephant grass grew tall and sharp, then back into the jungle. Mostly the trail was tightly fenced with bamboo, too thick for ambush, and they moved erect, silent and stalking. Except for the humming of the insects, it was still. The air didn't move, the sun beat on the canopy of fronds and the heat pushed the breath back in your lungs. The men were tightening, their nerves stretched to the limit. Henty could feel it like a nervous vibration shrilling back from squad to squad.

Over a hump, still wooded, through a ravine. Men ready, waiting, razor-sharp. Up another wooded slope. Henty glanced over his shoulder at Snotty. The tension in him was screwed to the snapping point. Henty saw it in the jerky way Snotty was shifting his eyes, the way the fingers of his right hand twitched on the butt of his .45.

Around a lazy turning where the bamboo thinned out. Ahead, 1st Squad had left the cover of the trees and was crawling through waist-high jungle grass toward a defile where the path squeezed between two dumpy, wooded mounds.

This is it! Henty thought, crouching, quickly moving through the 2nd Squad toward the grass with his tommy gun on the mounds. He could see ripples where 1st Squad edged forward in the grass. Second took cover in the trees and waited.

A burst of machine gun fire, two Nambus firing, slapped the grass. From dug-in, well-concealed emplacements on each mound, the Nambus fired with awful metronomic precision: *spat . . . spat . . . spat . . . spat . . . spat. . . .* A deadly monotony of rhythm.

At the first burst, the lead squad set up a base of fire to hold the Nambus while the 2nd started deploying through the trees to work its way around and flank the Jap positions. The 3rd started moving off the trail into the bamboo to lay down a screen over the 1st. Henty was off and running with the 2nd.

Alone on the trail, Snodgrass shrilled: *"Halt!"*

Unaccountably, all firing ceased. The 2nd and 3rd hesitated. Then the Japs, sensing the uncertainty or understanding the command, opened again with the Nambus backed now with the rackety-clack of .25 caliber rifles and splattering grenades. One mortar shell blasted a crater in the open grassy area showering earth but no arms or limbs, and a second splintered the bamboo at the edge of the trail. The Japs concentrated their fire power above 1st Squad, on the trail and into the trees. The momentary indecision had enabled them to pin it down. Hidden in the grass, 1st Squad held its fire.

Henty crashed back through the trees to Snotty.

"Retreat!" the lieutenant shrieked.

"They can't, you stupid bastard," Henty roared. "The Japs have got them nailed. We got to hit them from the rear."

"Second, Third, withdraw!" Snotty jabbered. "They'll get all of us."

The Japs were covering the trail and adjoining jungle with a steady barrage.

Even in his blinding rage, Henty was fully aware of what he did.

He smashed his weapon to Snotty's jaw. The lieutenant collapsed like a broken paper bag, lay gray-faced and motionless.

"Get those bastards," Henty bellowed, straddle-legged over Snotty. "Flank those sonsofbitches. Everybody out. BAR's up front. Radioman, back here."

Snarling, growling, swearing, the two squads battered through the bamboo. Second circled to the right, Third to the left. First opened drawing fire. The radioman, a punk kid with murder in his bloodshot eyes, trotted back to Henty.

"Drag this hunk of shit off the trail and stay with him," Henty yelled. "Don't let him use your radio. If he comes to, slug him."

Henty crashed after the 2nd.

Enraged and heedless, the two squads bashed through the trees and grass and around the humps while 1st poured a cascade of fire at the emplacement and into the defile. The 2nd rushed down on the Japs immediately behind the mounds and 3rd caught the tail of the Jap patrol. The Japs started pulling out under the automatic fire and the Marauders slashed savagely at them, spilling them on the trail, knifing them as they fell, wading back toward the Nambus. The machine guns were in square-holed, timber-rimmed emplacements, covered with branches, with gun slots fixed forward. Half a dozen men of 2nd Squad reached throwing distance at the same time. Six grenades tumbled through the air and another round followed before the first had burst.

A succession of blasts roared at the mounds and the air was sprayed with dirt and timber, steel and flesh.

Suddenly, the jungle was quiet.

Henty strode down the trail, stepping on and over the dead and dying Japs. He didn't bother to count.

"Third, cover," he shouted, starting through the defile. "First and Second, regroup."

He stamped through the grass without looking to either side, into the trees and back on the trail to the place he'd left Snotty. The radioman, a new man, someone he didn't know but obviously competent, grasped his M-1 for a butt stroke as he stood guard over the lieutenant. Snotty was sitting up, eyes weirdly out of focus and unseeing. An angry red welt on the side of his jaw was getting lumpy. He didn't look at anyone, or speak, or try to speak, or even seem aware of where he was or what had happened.

Henty ground his heel into the dirt and swung to the men who were straggling up. They grouped in little knots up and down the trail and came into the trees, forming a ragged semi-circle at a distance from the lieutenant. Their faces were tight with anger and they were muttering.

"Regroup in your squads," Henty ordered. "Any casualties?"

Kon shambled up. He had his helmet off and was holding a compress against his right cheek. The bandage was brightly stained and blood was oozing to the corner of his mouth. He kept licking at it.

"Just nicked," he said and smiled crookedly. "They'll fix it with a band aid."

"Let me see," Henty said. He pulled away the compress. Blood was running from a raw, seared streak across the cheekbone. He dusted a bandage from his kit with sulpha powder and taped it over the wound. "A scratch, a lousy scratch. Anyway, now you get a decoration. A Purple Heart. It's the only one they give Marauders. Where's Domingo?"

"He's okay," Kon said and spit some blood from his mouth. "He's coming up the trail. Everyone's okay, I guess. I'm the only one got in the way of anything and then I'm not smart enough to get it good and be evacuated."

"Yeah." Henty raised his voice and shouted: "Third, leave a guard, rest regroup." He turned back to Kon. "Check them in. Make sure they're all accounted for. Give the men a break. They can smoke."

He turned to Snotty. The lieutenant's eyes were beginning to roll like loose marbles. The men didn't regroup. They began to close in, shuffling forward a few steps at a time. Their mood was ugly. Henty could feel a slow burning flame spreading.

"He ain't worth taking a court-martial for," Double Ugly said. "The best thing we can do is put a slug in him."

"Wrong caliber," Henty grunted, staring at Snotty. Spit was dribbling from his half-opened mouth.

"We could scrounge a Jap weapon," Butcher said with an uncontrollable wink that was evil. "But I got a better idea.

Let's hang him over one of the emplacements and blow him up with a grenade."

"No," Henty said and hesitated. "Sonofabitch, he's not much of a man but he's still no Jap. I guess we'll have to drag him in and let him charge me."

The sounds the men made were ominous.

Domingo shouldered through the bunched up squads. His jaw was moving but he wasn't saying anything. He slapped his M-1 to his shoulder, aimed at the middle of Snotty's chest and his finger pulled the trigger. He moved so fast no one could have knocked down the rifle if he'd wanted. But the rifle didn't fire. His finger kept on moving but nothing happened.

"What's the matter, what's the goddamn matter?" he sobbed.

Henty smacked the weapon to the ground and stared at the butt. It was sticky with blood. His eyes shot to Domingo's hand. Only a nubbin of a forefinger remained on his right hand. Not enough of it to reach the trigger. Domingo didn't even know the rest of it had been shot away.

He kept yelling, half moaning: "What the goddamn hell's the matter I can't even shoot the piss head?"

"Snap out of it! All of you! Break it up!" Henty shouted, taking Domingo's hand. "Christ now, aren't you the lucky one!" He swiftly laid a powdered bandage over the stump and bound it tight to the wrist with crisscrossed tape. "Hold it on your left shoulder for a minute. I'll put a pressure bandage on your arm to stop the bleeding when I've broken this up. You just made Pfc. Poor fucking civilian. You're out. Now you'll get a pension without your 30 years. Christ, bright lights, blondes, booze. And the only thing you lost is the finger you stick up your ass when you whistle."

The fire went out of Domingo's burning eyes and they got a strange, far-away look.

"It ain't like it was my pecker," he said and giggled. "Jesus Christ, Hen, you mean it? You really mean I'm going home?"

The men had elbowed past, were pressing in on Snotty. Henty shoved them aside. The gawky straw-haired radioman had pulled out his trench knife and was rubbing the blade against his thigh.

"He's mine!" Julie cried.

Henty grabbed his wrist and twisted it as Julie reached back for his throwing knife.

"You damn fool, Henshit," Julie howled. "Don't you know they can shoot you for assaulting an officer in combat? It's mutiny."

"At ease, damnit!" Henty thundered. "You all got shit for brains? With 36 guys, you think one of you won't get drunk some time and fink? Radioman, come with me. Kon, you stay right here on guard. Not so much to guard as to protect. I don't want anything to happen. I'm reporting this to Command right now. Nobody's going to take a murder rap for this fucking creep."

5

KON started to squat on his heels, felt a sharp stab as his
cheeks spread and sat on the ground with his back against
a bamboo no thicker than his spine. He faced Snotty. They both
were sweating and gulping at the thick air. Kon held his M-1
across his knees. The lieutenant seemed to have come out of it
but he wasn't looking at anyone or anything except his hands.
They were on his thighs, palms up, and the big fingers were
clutching convulsively. That's Henty's neck he's working on,
Kon thought, and shifted his gun so the rifle was pointing three
quarters of the way at Snotty.

Henty and the radioman were walking down the trail away
from the patrol. Out of hearing and out of range of any lurking sniper. The squawk box made a prime target when a transmission crackled. You could aim at the sound. Where in hell
had the 3rd Squad picked up the kid, Kon hadn't seen him before anywhere in the battalion, and what had happened to
Jiggs, the regular operator?

The men, still chewing angry words but with some of the
tension eased by the cigarettes they lighted now, sat or flopped
in groups of three and five. Again and again, a raised voice
would lash out and the mumbling would stop abruptly, all
heads twisted to Snotty. Well they couldn't lift a hand now that
Henty was reporting in and that was a dumb assed thing for
him to be doing. He was in a bind.

Domingo was sprawled on his back in the green shadows
next to Kon. He was holding his right hand off his shoulder by
the wrist, close to his droopy lidded eyes and wiggling the
blood soaked bandage on the stump of his forefinger. He
didn't say a word but he had a shit-eating grin on his face.

Kon touched the soggy compress on his cheek: piss on the
luck. A week from Friday was Good Friday. Mom would be
hanging straggly-haired and red-faced over the combination
wood and gas range she wouldn't part with in the lean-to
kitchen at the back of the weatherbeaten farm house on
Kinninnick Avenue that now was in Milwaukee, building

scheiterhaufen for Pop's breakfast. Jesus, he could smell the warm, rich fragrance of those filled German pancakes, the bottom 10-inch cake covered with peas and cauliflower and sour cream, the second with rice and mushrooms and sour cream, the third with browned veal and sour cream and the top one with a sort of gravy made with egg yolk and sour cream, it's Mom's specialty and she made it only twice a year —Christmas morning and Good Friday.

Now how in hell had he known a week from now was Good Friday? All the day meant to him was special food, that must be it. Who'd kept track of the days and dates except the number of days they'd been out of Deogarh? They'd gotten their orders January 7th although they didn't leave India right away but you should be able to count from the seventh and this was the 29th of March, 81 days since the orders came, but still it was funny he'd remembered a week from Friday was Good Friday. If there'd been letters. Mom would have written to remind him. Oh she'd written all right, but there'd been no mail, on mail dropped to the troops since they'd set foot in Burma.

He looked at Snotty, intently furious, half expecting him to be reading an overseas edition of *Time,* the last issue. No mail for the men but the officers got theirs dropped in regular, along with a jug of bourbon every once in a while. Maybe the officers needed a shot in the morale department worse than the GI's, for chrissake. Give a GI a couple of butts and that was supposed to fire him to fighting pitch.

Snotty hadn't changed from his slumped over position but his fingers kept flexing and grasping. Kon's eyes dropped suddenly to the lieutenant's right side. His .45 was in its holster, inches from his hand. Jesus. Henty should have disarmed the lunatic. Kon straightened and his fingers tightened on the M-1. It was a crazy goddamned thing. He'd shoot the sonofabitch if he made a move but he couldn't make himself go over there and lift the pistol. The weapon was part of the lieutenant's uniform and they'd drilled that crap about respecting the uniform into you so hard you didn't dare, you couldn't even think of doing anything disrespectful.

How about Henty? He hadn't hesitated, he'd probably saved my life.

Oh Christ, I don't know, Kon thought. I'm all mixed up. I'm not as tough as Henty, I haven't got his guts. I'd do anything to save my own skin but would I take a chance for someone else?

He fished the butt of his last cigarette from his gritty pocket, considered the two-thirds that was left and tucked it carefully back. Maybe if he saved it, smoked it before the evening rations, it would kill his hunger and he wouldn't have to eat.

Henty and the radioman were returning and the men were staring at them, stopping in the middle of what they were saying, gawking silently and unbelievingly. Something had happened. Henty's head was up and he was grinning. His step was cocky. The radioman was a step or two behind but he was smirking, too. They tramped off the trail into the bamboo and Henty winked at Kon before he faced Snotty.

"Snodgrass," he said sharply. "Report to Command with the casualties."

He insolently turned his back to the lieutenant. His usually cold eyes looked like blue ice with sun in them and his face was exultant.

"Domingo, I'll put that pressure bandage on your arm before you go."

Kon scrambled to his feet with Domingo. Behind Henty, Snotty shook himself and reared. He whipped out his pistol and butt-chopped the top of Henty's spine below his helmet. Henty sagged and fell without uttering a sound. Before Kon or anyone could wrench himself from his shock, Snotty had snapped off the safety and was pointing the .45 at Henty's back.

"Don't move or I shoot," he cried in a thin, high and piercing voice. His face was purple and contorted. "Don't anyone get any idea about shooting me. I'll pull the trigger even if I'm dead."

The patrol stood paralyzed.

A sob wracked Kon's frame. It's my fault, he told himself: I knew he had the pistol and I didn't take it. The M-1 trembled in his hands but he couldn't lift it to fire, didn't dare, for Henty's sake. He remembered Julie's throwing knife.

"Julie, don't!" he yelled. "You can't get him without killing Henty. The reflex will jerk the trigger."

No one moved, no one seemed to breathe. The men froze mute and fearful on the trail.

"Line up in squads," Snotty ordered, a mad note of triumph in his voice, "on the trail to Hsamshingyang."

The stunned patrol grouped dazedly. Domingo and Kon started numbly toward the 1st. Domingo had slung his rifle and clapsed his left shoulder with his right hand.

"You men, halt," Snotty yelped at them. "Drop your weapons. Pick up the prisoner. You will march at the rear with me."

One at a time, he scooped up the M-1's and slung them over his shoulders. When Kon and Domingo had Henty by the arms and his dragging dead weight between them, Snotty picked up Henty's submachine gun, leveled it at their backs and holstered his .45.

"Patrol, 'ten-*shun!*" His command was precise. The squads struggled into some semblance of spiritless order. "All right, men. I'll be at the rear behind these three. Any talking in the ranks, any break in the file, any untoward movement and I'll shoot them first." His voice broke and he laughed shrilly. "At least the three of them."

He's lost his mind, Kon thought wildly, he's a goddamned raving maniac.

And, desperately grasping for some hope, he's forgetting the rear guard from the 3rd, think it quietly, don't show it in your face. Who was the rear guard? he couldn't remember but he was a Marauder, he'd know what to do, take the opportunity when it came, maybe at the Jap camp he'd distract Snotty's attention so they'd have a chance to throw themselves to the ground in that split second before he shot and killed the lieutenant, God! please let him get Snotty with the first one.

"Rear guard, join your squad," Snotty shouted.

I shouldn't have thought it, Kon moaned in his mind. The man dejectedly emerged from the defile and lined up ahead of Domingo and Kon who had Henty between them.

Snotty, leering and glaring at the same time, came out of the trees and strode onto the trail behind them. The unwavering submachine gun extended purposefully.

"Detail, forward *h'arch!*"

The patrol moved off limp-limbed and sunken hearted making no effort at concealment. Henty was out cold. Kon and and Domingo each held an arm over his shoulder by the wrist and now they reached across his back to grasp his waist. His feet bounced over the ground and scuffed the earth.

Maybe the Japs will hit us, Kon thought despairingly, knowing that they wouldn't. Maybe Snotty will get careless, shove that weapon in my back to prod me if I hold back, give me a chance to swing and grab it before he can fire.

It was Domingo who started to drag. He's got the same idea, Kon thought, blood pounding to his tightening mind. He shot a glance at Domingo. His face was harshly etched with graven lines and his eyes were tight as if with pain.

Snotty fell back: "Pick it up."

Muscles bunched at the hinges of Domingo's jaw as he dug in his toes and staggered on. Kon watched him closely. Domingo's chest was heaving. Beaded perspiration, not running sweat, covered his face which was paling. He looked awful.

They stumbled through the ravines, pulled themselves and Henty up the inclines. Kon felt his legs begin to shake and he stopped looking at Domingo and kept his eyes on the trail ahead. Keep going, his mind told him. They had to get back. Get back alive. Suddenly his thoughts were no longer clouded and fuddled. He knew why they had to get back alive with Henty. Command knew what had happened, Henty had reported by radio to them, Command had ordered Snotty in, that's why Henty had been so cocksure. Oh God! don't let anyone try to break, do anything stupid now.

Through the *kunai* and bamboo jungles, into the Jap encampment on the hillock. The stench of the rotting bodies was so thick it filled Kon's throat. He gagged and spit. Domingo gasped. Kon thought it was from the odor and did not look at him, just kept plodding one step at a time toward Hsamshingyang. But he could feel a new uneveness, Domingo was walking unsteadily. He tripped, sank to his knees, rose and tottered on. Kon turned. Domingo was ghastly gray, glassy eyed and giddy legged.

"Snodgrass," Kon pleaded, starting to turn his head.

"Another outburst and I shoot," Snotty shouted in a voice of rage.

They trudged with their burden toward the elephant trail. The sun was directly overhead and burned fiercely. Sweat filmed Kon's eyes, soaked his back and shoulders, ran in streams down his chest. The legs of his fatigues were sopping, he couldn't have so much moisture in him. He blinked his eyes to clear the mist and looked down his left leg, the one that rubbed against Henty. It was dark and sodden with blood. I got it in my hip, he thought but knew at once he could not have walked so far if this were true. It was Henty, the blood was coming from Henty's waist, it was coming from the stub of Domingo's finger where it grasped Henty. The blood streamed with every step they took. Henty's whole leg was soaked. His fatigues were dripping with about a gallon of blood. A moan gasped from Kon's throat. He started to turn his head, to cry out.

"Keep moving, soldier," Snotty growled, low and menacing.

Halfway across the clearing, Henty began to come to, not clear in head, not aware, but beginning to react. Head still hanging, heavy limbed, but trying to pick up his feet and put them down. It was worse than when he trailed them. Domingo was faltering and he moved and weaved like Henty, stupefied and blind.

Come out of it, Old Henshit, pull yourself together, help me get Domingo back. Oh Jesus! I can hardly stand, can hardly see.

They wobbled down the old elephant path, shambling, falling, jerking, gasping, trembling.

They broke through the hole the squads had torn in the vine wall. Domingo went to his knees, dragging Henty with him. Kon tugged and lifted weakly, got them unsteadily to their feet, reeled forward. He pitched on his face beside Henty and Domingo on the Nhpum Ga trail.

Not quite out. He heard vague, disembodied voices, words without meaning floating in the air.

Snotty's: Prisoner, he. . . .

Voice unknown: Corpsman . . .

Voice unknown: Middle guy . . . gut shot . . . morphine . . .

Snotty's: Prisoner . . .

Voice unknown: Hold . . . there . . .

Voice unknown: Litter bearers . . .

Snotty's: Prisoner . . .

Voice unknown: Weapons, we'll take your weapons, sir . . .

Kon lay back and wrapped himself in the soft, warm, still darkness.

6

Henty's head was tied up in a ball of yarn. His fingers groped their way around, seeking the strand that would unravel it. He fumbled, tried to tug but his hands were numb and had no strength. Without emerging, he lay in fuzzy consciousness. There was activity, and then voices, somewhere in the distance. He tried to grasp a piece of the conversation that flowed about him, a word or phrase, but the meaning was submerged. Something was familiar: he knew this woolly feeling. And the smell that bit into his nostrils, the acrid antiseptic odor. It began to come back, hazy pictures drifting across his mind:

The four of them, Shinbone, Bingo, Droopy and he had been sitting on boxes around his bunk in the back corner of the drafty, coalsmoke smelling CCC barracks, playing Hearts. And Slewfoot gumshoed in. They all glanced up, sneered a little at the superintendent and went back to their game.

Shinbone, a shy-eyed Filipino who didn't weigh enough to hold down a newspaper in the wind, led off with the queen of diamonds and next to him, Henty fingered the king and looked at the tenspot. Now what the hell was Shinbone leading from an ace or sloughing a singleton? the little bastard wasn't good for anything but he was sharp at cards. Henty looked around. Bingo wasn't holding anything. His big round face always lit up like a juke box when he held a trick card. You never knew about Droopy. He thought he looked like George Raft and was deadpan all the time.

"Need six volunteers!" Slewfoot's voice sounded hollow in the half empty room.

A dozen heads turned but no one volunteered. Slewfoot's eyes got small and his nose got pinched.

"It's just a little brush fire, maybe an acre," Slewfoot said, voice raising irritably. "I can order all of you out, you know."

Abruptly, Henty slapped his cards to the blanket and jumped up. "We'll go, the four of us."

"What the hell you doing?" Droopy snarled, low.

Slewfoot looked pleased: "Well, that's fine. We'll need two more."

"No," Henty said firmly. "A little brush fire, the four of us can handle." He winked at Shinbone. "The only way we work good is as a team."

"Okay, boys." Slewfoot gave his thin shoulders a twitch that was supposed to be a shrug. "Have it your way. The shovels and axes are in the truck. Pick up the keys at the office and I'll give you the directions."

"On a night like this, pal?" Bingo mouthed to Henty but he pulled on his blue work jacket. "It's damned near freezing."

"You nuts or something?" Droopy said out of the corner of his mouth and jammed a cap over his ears.

Only Shinbone didn't grumble. He was halfway smiling.

"You jerks," Henty said contemptuously when they'd slammed the barracks door and stood shivering on the stoop. "A little brush fire we can put out in an hour, maybe half an hour. We've got the truck, see? We beat it into town when we've got it whipped and drink some beer. Maybe Shinbone can't lift his himself to pee but he's always got a couple bucks he's won."

"I knew you had an angle figured," Shinbone said happily.

The fire was on the Knob, a couple of miles above the town. They could see it coming in, from the rutted gravel road, a good 10 minutes before they reached it. It was an orange flame like a turned-down lamp wick glowing in the black night sky, creeping over the top of the hill away from them.

"Sonofabitch," Bingo muttered. "I hope the wind don't come up. I hope the fire don't get down in that dry stuff in the gulch."

Henty laughed scornfully: "Stupid, that's where we're going to lay our backfire."

They approached the fire from the slope on the opposite side of the gulch. The dry arroya ran into a box at the far end and came out at the foot of the hills on an arid stretch of scoria. There was some smoke in the air but not much. The flames were so low in the cropped grass they didn't light the night.

"This is so easy, I don't know why we bother," Henty said. "Shinbone, on account of it's your party, you can have the fun. We'll start about halfway here and shovel down into the gulch to make a firebreak. Go on over to the other side and up to the box. Start lighting the stuff down towards us from that end. By the time you get back the job is done."

"Boy, we'll be guzzling beer in no time at all," Shinbone said and leaped across the gulch.

Henty worked down the middle with Bingo and Droopy at either side. There wasn't much sod in the sandy soil and the shoveling was scarcely strenuous enough to work up a sweat. At the far end of the little ravine, brush and scrub growth crackled into sparking flame and Henty saw Shinbone silhouetted as he ran away. Then, down a ways, another fire started. The grass fire licked slowly toward the gulch. Opposite Henty, a third flame leaped.

"You're a real firebug, Shinbone," Henty shouted, laughing. "A couple more does it."

A swirling puff of wind, one of those quirky, sudden Rocky Mountain gusts blew his words away. The flames leapt and all the way down the gulch leaned toward the opposite hill, hot and yellow white now. The grass fire flattened and then sprang up and raced down.

"Shinbone!" Henty shouted. "Run into the wind to the top."

He wasn't alarmed. Shinbone might scorch his jeans and shoes but you could almost walk through the grass fire, it was so sparse.

The fire in the gulch flared again and bent some more toward the hill fire. Henty stopped shoveling and watched, warming himself, enjoying the snapping flames and then the red glowing embers in the darkness. The whole job hadn't taken 15 minutes.

"Shinbone!" Henty cupped his hands and shouted. "Meet us at the truck."

Shinbone wasn't there.

They waited, perhaps five minutes.

"Jesus," Henty said uneasily. "You don't suppose something happened to him."

"What could happen?" Droopy sneered.

"Nothing," Henty said but he felt nervous. "He was right across from me. All he had to do was go up the hill." He remembered how the flames from the gulch had slanted to-

68

ward the hill. "Come on!" he said, grabbing a flashlight from under the seat. Let's go have a look."

"If that greasy little bastard is pulling something," Droopy growled. "I'm going to beat the shit out of him, beer or no beer."

They found Shinbone, face down with one foot in the gully, toe entangled in a root.

"Shinbone!" Henty dropped to his knees in the still-hot burnt grass. He lifted the shoulders and turned a blackened face to the glare of the flashlight. "He's still breathing."

He brushed the others aside, tossed Shinbone's skinny frame over his shoulder and started running down the hill. Bingo trotted ahead into the darkness.

"I'll get the truck started," he shouted.

Henty remembered tripping, pitching forward, trying to catch himself, and then his awareness was as black as the night. Next he knew, he was fighting back to consciousness, trying to pull himself out of a sack of fleece. Into a world of white, sharp with the smell of antiseptic.

He was in the hospital.

"Shinbone!" he came to, shouting, sitting up.

"Couldn't do a thing for him," a calm voice said. "Smoke and flame, mostly flame. Seared his lungs. He must have taken a deep breath to yell. Gone when you brought him in. You're okay. Just got the wind knocked out."

He covered his face with his hands, shut out the brightness, sobbing to himself: I did it, I did it, I killed Shinbone for a glass of beer.

"Shinbone!" he shouted now. He was sitting on the ground, head brushing some sort of shelter.

He stared crazily around, breathing hot waves of air that had the solid taste of sunburned canvas. The odor of antiseptic was strong. He was naked, stripped to his dog tags. A blanket that must have covered him was draped across his legs. Half a dozen GI's, some bandaged, some bleeding, some silent, some groaning, were lying under shelter halves on litters. The doc and two corpsmen were working with a saw at a GI on a makeshift table in a three-quarter enclosed bamboo hut not far away.

He was at the aid station at Hsamshingyang.

A corpsman with a round and florid face like Bingo's came over and bunkered down.

"That his name?" he asked.

"Who the hell, what the hell happened?" Henty asked groggily.

The corpsman's face lit up like a juke box when he grinned. He lighted a cigarette, stuck it between Henty's parched lips.

"Goddamn," he said. "You fooled us good. We thought you'd got it in the gut. How you feel?"

"Like I was wrapped in cotton." Henty dragged at the cigarette. The smoke scratched his throat. He coughed and handed it back. "Where's my clothes? What the hell happened? My neck feels like it was busted."

"You'll be okay in a couple minutes. I'll get you some hot Joe. We aren't too busy yet. You're just coming out of morphine."

"Morphine!"

He looked down his chest: ribs okay. Kicked off the blanket: both legs there. Looked at his hands, felt his back, touched the spot that ached between his shoulders. It was tender but it wasn't bandaged. He ran his hands over his head, face. Just that damned place at the back of his neck. He leaned forward and dropped his head between his knees. The stretching hurt but he could twist and lift his head.

The corpsman came back and handed him a hot tin cup of steaming coffee.

"Christ!" Henty said and sipped the coffee. It had some taste to it. He gulped. It burned his tongue and throat but it was good, real coffee, black and strong. He swallowed some more. "What the hell happened? My neck is sore but I'm still in one piece. What's this morphine crap?"

"The way I heard, you were bringing in a couple guys and passed out." The fat-faced corpsman chuckled. "It sure was funny, the way it bugged doc when he couldn't find your wound. Well, you got a free ride and a sponge bath."

"Tell me slow," Henty said and drank some more coffee. His head was clearing and he was relaxing, enjoying sitting on the ground out of combat and doing nothing, even though his neck did ache. "I don't remember one damned thing."

"Well, they said you came busting out of the jungle with

70

a couple other guys and the three of you passed out cold on the Nhpum Ga trail practically at the feet of another patrol coming in. You were dripping blood, soaking wet with blood from your waist down your right leg like your insides were spilling out. First thing without even looking, they gave you morphine. They couldn't find anything and lugged you in on a litter and we couldn't find a damned thing wrong with you either except a bruise on the back of your neck. It wasn't you who was wounded, see, but the guys you were bringing in."

"What guys was I bringing in, for chrissake, sopping wet with blood? I was up there on patrol. Goddamn!" It flashed across his mind: the Jap block, Snotty panicking, calling Command. They'd told him to send Snotty in with Kon and Domingo and to take over the patrol until relieved. "What two guys?"

"One guy with a cheek wound, he was dripping blood but not as much as you and he came to in time to tell them. Another guy with a finger shot off. Too bad about the little guy."

"What little guy?" Henty cried, suddenly agitated. "Not one of our guys. Who you mean?"

"The little guy with the finger shot off." The corpsman lifted his eyebrows in a mental shrug. "There wasn't a pressure bandage but that shouldn't have made any difference if he'd kept his hand up. There wasn't anything could be done for him. He'd already lost most of his blood on you. You wouldn't think you could lose that much blood from your hand, not unless you were dragging something heavy."

"Domingo," Henty gasped. "You mean he's dead?"

"Yeah, little Mex. He your buddy? Too bad."

"Oh God!" Henty groaned. The coffee cup slipped from his fingers and rattled on the ground. He held his hands over his face, trying to blank out the world. All he did was lift Domingo's face up to his eyes: Domingo's far away look, his silly smile: "You really mean I'm going home?" For chrissake, Henty, *you* killed Domingo. You didn't put on the pressure bandage. You murdered your goddamned ass hole buddy.

A great sob heaved from the pit of his stomach.

"Tough, fella." The corpsman roughly knocked Henty's shoulder. "Here's the other one, he's okay."

Henty was numbly aware of someone sitting beside him.

"Pull yourself out of it, Hen." It was Kon, speaking sharply. "We all feel bad and mad. But we can't do shit about it."

"I did it, I killed the little bastard," Henty mumbled. "I knew I should have put on a pressure bandage."

"How the hell could you?" Kon demanded harshly. "You was going to. How the hell was you to know that goddamned lunatic was going to chop you down when you turned your back? And make us drag you in, Domingo and me. I tried to tell him, Jesus I tried to tell him what was happening but he went crazy wild, held your tommy gun on us, said he'd shoot us all, you was his prisoner. Son of a bitch, I should of took the chance regardless, my guts is all water."

"What the hell you talking about?" Henty shouted, jerking to his knees.

"Snotty did it sure as shit, he could see the blood Domingo was losing and the way he wove and stumbled. He knocked you out and Domingo had to help drag you with that hand, blood running like a river from it. He killed Domingo just like he'd shot him in the back."

White fire seared Henty's mind and blinded him.

"I'll kill him!" He bolted naked from the shelter.

Kon grabbed him by the shoulder, shaking him.

"We should of killed him when we had the chance, only you wouldn't let us," he said bitterly. He threw the blanket over Henty's back and stood close to him, gripping his arm. "You can't do nothing now."

"Who says I can't?" Henty raged, trying to pull his arm away. "Even if he's at Command with the Colonel, I'll kill him before they can stop me. I'll kill him slow with my two bare hands, squeeze his throat until his eyes pop out. They can shoot me afterwards but I'll get him first." He glared at Kon. "Where's my clothes?"

"I brought you some new fatigues," Kon said. "You can't do nothing about Snotty because he ain't here."

"What you mean he ain't here?" Henty yelled. "You ain't going to put me off with that shit. You can't stop me. There's no one can."

"There's some clean shorts with the fatigues next to where you was laying, you got to wear your old socks and shoes and leggings, there wasn't any at Supply but yours are dry now." Kon stooped, picked up the shorts and handed them to Henty. He held onto the fatigues. "They already sent Snotty away."

"What you talking about, for chrissake?" Henty stepped into the shorts and sat on the ground fumbling with the socks. They were damp but not bloody, he noticed even in his fury. Someone had washed them.

"They flew him out right away," Kon said grimly, fists tightening on the fatigues. "They knew he'd last about as long as a pigeon in a tiger cage any place in Burma there was a Marauder. You know what? They put it down as a bad case of combat fatigue. Snotty was an officer."

"Oh shit!"

Henty was sick all over again, retching dry at first and then spilling out the coffee he'd just drunk. His intestines writhed. He sat on the ground, motionless, staring blankly at his feet.

"Shake out of it." Kon was sitting beside him. "You think my ass don't burn worse for it? There'll be some of us get out of this, the war can't last forever, there'll be one of us catch up with him even if he's in a booby hatch."

He pulled a two-third length butt from his pocket, looked a moment at it, lighted it and put it between Henty's fingers.

Henty smashed it into the ground with his fist, shredded it.

"All right, Henshit!" Kon said ferociously, staring at the mashed cigarette. "Now you got it out of your system, don't give me no more crap. Get your shoes on. Get into your fatigues. Right now. There's a Captain Gold wants to see you at Command."

"Yeah."

Henty got slowly to his feet. He shook his head and looked at Kon. His vision was clearing. Time and place were swinging back where they belonged.

"Sorry about the butt," he said. "I'll scrounge you another."

"It's okay, Hen." Kon handed the fatigues to Henty.

One second Kons' face looked the way it always did, except for the new bandage on the cheek, and the next it was contorted and he was giggling hysterically.

"They won't fit so good," he finally said shrilly. "They was Snotty's."

7

WITH a tin cup he found by the shelter half in his fist, Kon held his other hand to his bandaged cheek and wheedled coffee and a cigarette from a corpsman. He sat under a *basha* across from the lean-to they'd thrown together for the Command Post and waited for Henty. The rest of the platoon was back in the foxholes they'd dug the night before, beside the river south of the village, taking a break, waiting for new orders after their aborted mission. Maybe they wouldn't have to go out again today.

But it wasn't good, he thought, in fact it was lousy the way the half-fighting-strength 3rd, maybe 300 to 350 men now, was stumbling all over itself setting up defensive perimeters around Hsamshingyang and the airstrip, digging in instead of out there flanking and throwing the Japs off balance, trying to get through the Nhpum Ga where the 2nd was trapped and taking a shellacking.

Well they had to hold: Hsamshingyang was just another Kachin village, half a dozen yellow bamboo *bashas,* some rice paddies and plats of corn, but it was the gateway to the Hukawng Valley where General Pick and his 50,000 engineers were bulldozing the Burma Road down from Ledo.

So far they'd had luck, fighting Indian style, that stupid Wingate and his fancy names, Long Range Penetration Units for chrissake! Wingate thought he'd invented guerrilla warfare when that's the way the West was took. But this was different now. This was it. Their luck had run out. There wasn't a better squad leader in the 5307the than Old Henshit and when casualties started tearing his squad apart, goodbye Marauders. But Henty shouldn't take on the way he did about Domingo, he sure as hell wasn't to blame. Christ, if it had been Old Henshit marching along with Snotty's machine gun covering him, he'd of swung no matter if a burst stitched him across the back and that would of gave somebody a chance to get at Snotty the rotten sonofabitch. Damn it, I know what it is I ought to do but I can't do it, I'm a puking yellow belly.

All of a sudden he was hungry and thinking about Mom's cooking again, about those *Apfel Pfannkuchen* she used to make for him on Sunday mornings. Hell, all that stuff she sweated hours over she made for him, not for Pop. The old man got in on it because there was some left over. That was a funny thing, being an only child with your Mom and Pop both born in the old country. Now that you were old enough to think about it you couldn't help wondering what it was had gone sour with them. Something to do with sex but Jesus, German women didn't dare act like Mom, not with a Pole——and get away with it. Hell, Pop had slept alone in the unheated upstairs bedroom ever since Kon could remember and Mom had her own little room right in front of the kitchen, that was after Kon got older and she'd moved out of the front bedroom that they'd shared.

Pop must have been a big good-looking Pole once when he was young, when he was courting Mom. He still was big, but stooped like he was carrying a load on his back and there was something shifty, almost guilty, about his eyes when Mom spoke to him which she didn't do much and Pop hardly said a word to either of us. It had something to do with that operation but that had been a long time ago. There'd been an awful fight that had gone on about a week, maybe longer only it wasn't a fight but just Mom raving and Pop with his jaws clamped and sort of slinking without talking back and then Mom had gone away for that operation. She'd called Pop a filthy dirty polecat and cried and cried because they had to cut out some of her insides and when she came back from the hospital she'd never slept with Pop again. For chrissake, do you suppose Pop had brought home a dose of clap to Ma?

But no matter how mad she always was at Pop, or maybe because she was, she couldn't do enough for Kon. Pa never did dare to lift a hand or speak harshly to him. Not after that one time Mom caught Pop whaling the daylights out of him with a razor strap in the rickety garage. Hell, Kon had it coming. He'd swiped a dollar from the old man's billfold when he thought Pop was sleeping off a drunk and wouldn't miss it and Pop had raised up growling like something in the zoo and grabbed him by the ear, twisting and pinching all the time he was dragging him out to the garage. And then Mom had busted in red-faced and fiery-eyed and snatched away the razor strop and belted Pa across the face with it.

"Don't you touch a finger to that boy again, he's the only decent thing I'll ever have, if any harm comes to my Konrad I'll shoot you in your sleep, you pig."

I must of taken good advantage of it all through the years, he thought, knowing Mom would always stick up for me no matter what. Christ, it was going to be rough on her with nothing but the old man left if they didn't pull out of this one and he didn't see how they could.

Henty was coming from Command. Goddamn, he looked funny in Snotty's fatigues bagging over his blood-stained leggings and the shoulders hanging down almost as far as he had the arms turned up. He even had Snotty's web belt and canteen and .45. And a Very pistol, Jeezoo! Two-Gun GI Joe. But he was wearing his own helmet and he'd got his tommy gun back. They must have gotten orders because Henty looked perked, he was a crazy-assed bastard, he wasn't happy unless there was some action.

Henty jerked his thumb south and Kon let out a sigh and pinched his cigarette. They shuffled along the dusty trail toward the platoon's foxholes.

The break was over.

"I just figured something," Henty said, grinning with a pleasure that looked evil. "These fatigues stink. They stink like Jap smell. I always wondered what it was the Japs smelled of, you can always tell when you get near them. It's fear. Those little yellow sonsofbitches with their *banzai* attacks and all are afraid. They say a dog or horse can smell you when you're scared. It's the same with the Japs. They're afraid all the time and they sweat and they stink. Snotty was so scared this morning he stunk up these new fatigues as bad as any Jap. I'm surprised he didn't shit in them."

Kon couldn't help grinning even though it tugged at the adhesive they'd used to pull his face together.

"What the hell is coming off?" he asked. "We got sucked into something, okay, but this isn't like the Marauders, digging in and taking it, the way the 2nd is and the 3rd expects to. Are we just going to sit back on our tails and wait for

77

the 1st or maybe the Chinks to come along and bust us out?"

"Well now, I'll tell you," Henty said with a half-assed grin. "General Merrill wanted to talk over the situation with me but I didn't get back in time and the plane couldn't wait, so he went on up to Margherita to get his ticker checked. And the Colonel, well he wanted some advice but he's got the GI Shits and couldn't hold it any longer so he went out to take his crap. But they got this Captain Gold here, he's from the 2nd Battalion and plenty sharp. He let himself get trapped down here instead of at Nhpum Ga. Anyway, they gave the captain the message for me. We get to go right back out and finish that little job we started."

"Yeah," Kon said despondently and kicked himself in the mind: you just were asking for some action, what do you want, some other outfit to tangle? what do you expect, a day off because you got your cheek scratched? "Who they loading on us this time? Not another flyboy."

"Right at this moment, seems as if the 3rd is slightly short on personnel. A clerk sneaked out to lift the butts off a corpse they brought in and got in the way of a Jap .25 slug. There's been a patrol or two sifted through the jungle, stirred things up enough to keep the 3rd pinned down here. Anyway, they had to put a couple of lieutenants on the clerk's job writing the history of the 5307th, so the orders stand as formerly: until relieved, Old Henshit here will wipe your ass for you."

"I don't like it," Kon said, "But I'd rather be out there with you than stay here. I feel safer in the jungle. Got any idea what's happening to the 2nd, they still got contact?"

"They're taking a real shit kicking." Henty turned his head and his eyes seemed to freeze as Kon watched. "Somebody didn't have the right intelligence, or guessed wrong, or figured to make a name for himself or just fucked up in general. We shouldn't have tried to block the Kamaing Road at Inkangatawng. The Japs were in too solid there. Actually, we never did block the road although the reports will say we did. We never got closer than 100 yards from it. When they had the 2nd dig in at Nhpum Ga, they didn't think the Japs could bring up artillery. So there they are, dug in on a perimeter 400 yards long and about 200 yards wide. Pigeons on a roost. There are about 2,500 Japs surrounding the ridge, pouring in all their artillery, blasting them to hell. They're leveling the top and also they've cut off the 2nd from the water hole halfway down. We've got to hold here but we've got to find a way through to relieve the 2nd or the Japs will finish off both of us. Yeah, we've still got contact but only on the radio."

A shiver raised the hairs on Kon's arms.

"It looks bad, don't it?"

"We've had it rough before."

"But not like this."

"No," Henty admitted grimly. "Our first engagement, at Walawbum, was bad. They had artillery there and we fought against them five days, three days without food, and killed 800. But there the front was fluid. All three battalions were in on it and were full strength. Now we're outnumbered four or five to one and not one of us skeletons has the strength to fight his way out of a wet paper bag. It looks bad."

Henty snapped his jaws together. His chin stuck out and his eyes narrowed. For a minute from the side he looked like Jim Jones, a tough little brawling private Kon had known at Hickam Field. They trudged along in silence, scuffing up the dirt in little dust clouds, once in a while hearing a rattle of small arms fire not too far away and feeling the artillery thumps that came so regularly they'd become a normal part of the atmosphere. Kon kept thinking about Mom. Damnit, she'd told him not to enlist.

"If they ever really do need you, they'll conscript you like in Germany," she said, not bothering to wipe away the two fat tears that rolled down her cheeks. "But this country is so terribly big and strong. No one ever would dare to fight another war with it."

"So what's the worry?" he answered lightly. "I can't find a job, there's no work at all. I put in a peacetime hitch, save some money, and meanwhile you got one less big mouth here to feed."

"But if anything should happen," she'd said, "I'd be left all alone."

"Henty?" Kon said and hesitated.

"Yeah."

"There's something I'd like you to do for me."

"Sure. You need $10 till payday?"

They both laughed. If they ever got a payday, it would be a good one, money enough to make any town flap at the hinges.

"No. Serious. I got a funny feeling. I ain't scared, no more than usual, but after what happened to Domingo I ain't sure no more. If anything should happen to me would you write a letter home?" He paused, embarrassed. "Maybe say something nice, it don't have to be the truth."

"Nothing's going to happen," Henty said angrily. "I won't let anything happen. Domingo doesn't count. I was out cold and it wasn't a Jap that got him. Nothing like that is going to happen again, *ever!* Look, all this time, nothing touched us. Now you got a little scratch this morning, one out of 12 men in three month's time. The odds are all with you again. The war will be over and you'll be an old man with grandchildren before your number comes up again. Don't talk foolishness."

"I know you're right." But Kon persisted: "If something should happen, would you?"

"I guess so," Henty growled. "Nothing's going to happen, but I'd write your Mom."

"No." Kon drew a breath and straightened. "I want you to write my Pop. It's going to be hard on him."

8

LIKE slender legged, dusty bodied warrior ants, the men crept from the trees and holes in the ground toward Henty. Field packs humped their backs. He waited in a stand of bamboo where the sun came through the many fingered fronds in bright warm splashes. Behind him the Tanai River, so clear you could see the rippled pale stones on the bottom, gurgled softly. Occasionally you could hear the mutterings of war; distant unsure thunder and the rattling hail of rifle fire, but it was remote and for the moment you could turn your back to it.

The patrol formed an uneven semi-circle in three squads. Some of the men hunched over drawn-up knees munching rubbery cheese from K rations or smoking cigarettes, but most flopped and lay immobile, half asleep with helmets resting on shoved-up packs.

The 1st Squad assembled without direction immediately before Henty. Kon was in the front row, head between his knees. Ass Drag Svensen and Julie were on one side of him, stretched out but propped on their elbows. The big fighting Swede had his eyes on Henty but there was a vague look in them that misted even the washed out blue. Julie's eyes were unnaturally veiled and he was chewing one end of his fierce mustache. On the other side of Kon, Injun Joe sat erect, motionless and expressionless. He didn't even seem to breathe. There was a soldier——he didn't think, he just killed by instinct. The six other riflemen were flat on their backs behind them. Scattered on cither side of the 1st were the 2nd and 3rd Squads.

Henty examined the patrol, the men whose faces he could see. They all looked alike. Their eyes were dull, their cheeks yellow and hollow and their jaws had a slackness to them. The poor goddamned pooped-out bastards, he thought; all any of them give a damn about is getting some place where they can sleep and eat all they want after their stomachs stretch back to normal size for chrissake? They don't even talk about sex any more. Sonofabitch, maybe I've bit off more than I can chew, I'm no goddamned platoon leader, all these guys are on *my* back.

No breeze stirred or freshened the baked air and Snotty's fatigues stifled Henty. They smelled awful. The acrid sweat stench gave him perverse satisfaction and stiffened his spine. He pulled himself up to his full five-feet eight-inches and threw his shoulders back.

"All right, you bunch of balless recruits," he shouted, "at least look alive. We're going back up on the hill. We're going to find where those Jap patrols are coming from and we're going to blast them the hell out of there. Before we always bitched about how we were fighting for the British or the Chinks but we went out and slugged the shit out of the little yellow bastards. Today it's different. They've got us where the hair is short and it's our own damned skin we're fighting for so I figure we ought to do a little better job than we've been doing. We go out in the same order we did this morning only I want the radio operator up near the front of 2nd Squad where I can get at him." He paused and grinned sourly. "Only to let them know what we're doing when we run into something. We won't get any assist. We're on our own. Any questions? Anybody got a TS card he wants punched?"

The men who had been on their backs sat up and the others shuffled their feet and scratched at the ground with their fingers. They didn't like it, they were a sullen, dejected bunch. Henty saw Julie's mustache lift in a sneer as his eyes dropped to the .45 that Snotty had carried.

"No, *sir!*" he cracked and smacked his lips.

Why that little sonofabitch, I'll ream his ass, Henty thought furiously, but he choked back his anger when he noticed Injun Joe studying him with flat-black eyes.

"Tell us one thing straight," Injun Joe said. "What chance have we?"

The Indian never talked, hadn't said a dozen words to any one in all the time they'd been in Burma. No chance at all, you big brave, Henty thought; when Injun Joe starts asking questions we're up shit creek.

"Same as always," he snapped. The men were shifting, talking among themselves, looking resentfully at him. He grinned. "Better than usual, I'd say. We don't have an officer."

There was some laughing at that, not much, there wasn't a belly laugh left in the whole patrol, but it was enough to ease the tension.

"That is good," Injun Joe said calmly. "My wife had a baby boy before we left Deogarh. I made her a promise I would return to my son."

Henty stared at him. An Indian would go to his grave before he showed his heart to any man. Henty hadn't even known that Injun Joe was married.

"It's the Jap's scalp or yours, Joe," he said quietly. "Unless you go after his, he'll come here for yours. We all want to get out of this trap sewer for reasons of our own. But none of us are going anywhere until we break through to Nhpum Ga." Injun Joe's eyes were fixed and Henty had the feeling he wasn't reaching him. He groped for a way to arouse him. "I've got something special for you today, Joe. I want a prisoner to question."

"When we have driven off the Japs this time," Injun Joe went on without acknowledging the challenge, "are we being lifted out of Burma? All the men talk of leaving before the heavy rains. Do you know if this is so?"

The entire platoon seemed to hold its breath and lean as one toward Henty. He didn't know any more than anyone else. They all thought they were going back because that was what they wanted to think. They'd been given some sort of promise and they knew they were in no condition to fight any longer. Their bodies and minds were shot to hell. But who could figure what was turning over in those metal skulls at Headquarters?

"We were told that," he said carefully thinking aloud. "Monsoons or not, we've come as far as we can without rest or replacement. The U.S. Army doesn't assign suicide missions like the Japs. This engagement right now wasn't planned but we're faced with it and the only thing we can do is drive the Japs out. Once this job is done, I don't see how they can do anything except pull us out."

There it was. He'd finally said it and he believed every word was true. The reactions was immediate and overwhelming, more than he anticipated. The ragged, worn-out, shrunken men struggled to their feet, threw their arms around each other, pounded backs and arms. Tears streamed down dirty cheeks between wild bursts of laughter. The babble was incoherent. They'd fight now, he thought gloomily with a new weight on his shoulders. He'd told them what they wanted to hear and they took it as the gospel not because it had come from Old Henshit who lived in the foxholes and fought with them, but because it came from their platoon leader who wore a .45 and had some mysterious communication with Command. Damn those lousy officers who ran this burlesque show, they'd better keep their word and get them out of Burma into hospitals and rest camps or he'd lead everyone who'd follow over the hill and they'd live with the Jinghpaws until the war was over.

He looked at Kon who hadn't responded with the others. He still had his head bowed between his legs. Domingo's death at the hands of a madman infuriated Henty but Kon's premonition of his own impending fate festered. With Kon feeling as he did, Henty couldn't send him out again as scout.

"I can't promise you stripes now or ever," he told him, "but you better take over as assistant squad leader."

Kon lifted his head and smiled bleakly.

"It don't really make much difference, does it? Who you going to use as scout?"

"That's the goddamned problem," Henty said, scanning the faces of his riflemen. Only Injun Joe looked him squarely in the eyes. "It isn't that any of them couldn't do it. It's just that they're all so tired, I don't trust their reflexes."

He settled first on Hari Kari and then on Old Overshoes, but hesitated naming either. He'd taken Kon off the hook and now he didn't want the responsibility of selecting someone else for the most dangerous position in the patrol.

"I will scout," Injun Joe said stoically.

"Well thanks," Henty said and shouted: "On your feet. Let's go."

The patrol quickly formed into marching order. They were peppery. The radioman, shoulders sagging under his extra burden, started toward 1st Squad.

"How about him?" Kon asked, motioning over Henty's shoulders toward the river.

Henty turned and started. Meatball was coming through the

bamboo. He was bare chested and bareheaded, wearing only a web belt of clips and a canteen over his shorts, and his *kukri* knife across his chest. His tommy gun was in his arms. His brown eyes were guileless as he padded toward Henty and then a slow smile spread the crooked scar between his nose and ear.

"Finally the time has arrived for us to depart?" he asked in his tongue.

"You know you cannot come with us," Henty said sharply in Jinghpaw. "It is not that we do not want you. The order from our headman is that you may not be exposed in combat."

"There was no risk last night?" Meatball asked softly and laughed. "But then, we did not ask permission of your Army. So. This is a time of emergency. Soon the rains will drench the hills and the rivers will overpour the valleys. There will be no need for guides because you will not be able to move in the mud. One of your fighting men is missing and he is not the only one who has been killed today. I have discussed this matter with Zing Tu La and he agrees that I should move with you. There are many reasons. For one matter, your other patrols have been withdrawn from the trails for the protection of the village. The Jinghpaws have taken over the road blocks. This is on orders from your Army. I will lead you through the ambushes. For another reason I did not participate as completely as I like in the slaughter of the enemy last evening. My talents become dull when they are not used. And there are other reasons you would enjoy but I do not take your time now to tell them."

Henty shook his head but he was smiling.

"If anything happens to you, it's going to be my ass," he said in English, switching to Jinghpaw: "Your presence is welcome. Lead us in safety. Our scout will follow in your footsteps." He let out his breath and finished in English: "Let's blow before some pea-brained lieutenant comes along and changes my mind."

Meatball trotted to the lead position. At the sight of him, the already brightened faces began to radiate. Sonofabitch! Henty thought, if I sing out with Ca-dence COUNT! they'll all swing into it or maybe do a jig. They'd be hell on wheels today.

He took his position between the 1st and 2nd Squads,

motioning the radioman to his side. He was a kid with adolescent pimples, a thin-shouldered youngster who ought to be at home tinkering with his jalopy instead of in the jungle toting a cranky pack radio.

"Didn't have time this morning for any conversation," he said. "I haven't seen you with the outfit before. How did you get messed up with this? My name's Henty."

"Ha in-sheet," the kid said with a deep-South drawl and chuckled. "Ainy mo' all th' name ah got is Ridge Run-ah, ah'm f'm Miss-iss-ippi. Naivah haid no shoes till ah was took by th' Ah-mee. C'm daown f'm th' Saicund yestid'y with th' cap'n 'n cain't git back up theah. Yoah rad-yo main git one thim j'ngle lee-ches stuck in his peck-ah so ah git shove in heah."

Henty laughed aloud.

"Well bite my ass. How the goddamn hell you make radio-man? It'd take a code clerk to unscramble what you say."

"Thait's wh't they say-ah." The Ridge Runner looked pleased. "Cain't no Jay-up unnahstan' so ah saind in th' cleah anywheah. Ah'll mind n'body gits b'hind y'all again. Ah'm a houn' dawg."

"The brass must have been drunk to figure out anything as smart as that," Henty said. "Okay, Runner, you protect my rear. Stay between the 1st and 2nd Squads. When we hit action pull out and wait for my signal. I'll let you know when I want you."

Again the patrol walked up the familiar sun-baked, mud-caked Nhpum Ga trail. They were keyed up now but tomorrow the artillery would still be smashing at the 2nd if the Japs hadn't already taken the ridge. The men would be more concerned about getting back to Hsamshingyang than getting out of Burma and what the hell was going to raise their spirits then? They were tottering on the edge of defeat. He knew it, just as he knew his men.

Now what the hell was he thinking? He didn't know one goddamned thing about what made any of them tick. Kon going off the deep end and then Injun Joe. Jeez, you'd have sworn you could burn him at the stake and he'd never let out a peep, worried about getting back to his wife and son and admitting it in front of the whole patrol. Damnit, a fighting man didn't have a right to have a family.

Within sight of the torn vines that revealed the jungle entrance to the elephant path, Meatball appeared on the trail. He halted the patrol with one hand and pulled Henty ahead with the other.

"Rest your men off the trail in the trees and grass," Meatball said, smiling slyly. "They are well protected here. Move yourself with me that you may see the nature of the trap we have set to snare any of the enemy who come this way."

"Tell Kon to take 10," Henty told Injun Joe and went ahead with Meatball.

The Jinghpaw chattered a monkey call and was answered from the trees. He laughed delightedly.

Across from the entrance to the elephant path, dug in and concealed in the *kunai*, Meatball displayed two smiling Jinghpaws manning submachine guns. A third Jinghpaw with a Bren gun was hidden almost at the elephant path.

"Within the trees along the way we came are others equipped with rifles," Meatball said. "The machine guns and the other automatic weapons cover both the trail and path. Now come with caution beyond this place."

They crept up the trail in the direction of Nhpum Ga. Meatball stopped once to part the elephant grass and show beds of *pungyis,* some set low to trip a man and others angled high and pointed toward the trail to pierce his body. Grinning, Meatball indicated with his hands that both sides of the trail had been planted with the fire-hardened bamboo spikes. He touched his submachine gun and waved his hand into the trees—Jinghpaws waited there to open fire.

Now he crawled ahead another 50 yards. Near the middle of the trail, he lifted an old footprint of dried mud. In a nest beneath it was a grenade with an attached wire. He replaced the mud cake, moved in five yards and removed a tromped clot that concealed another wired grenade. Wrinkling his eyes and laughing silently, he pointed up the closed-in trail, unclenched the fingers of his left hand six times to indicate 30 grenades, then wiggled a finger at the trees to show where a Jinghpaw was stationed with the charger that would detonate them.

With Meatball clacking more monkey sounds, he and Henty rejoined the patrol.

"It will be difficult for the enemy to approach your camp

but it is to be hoped he tries," he said and now he did laugh.

Henty laughed with him.

"What's the joke?" Kon asked without enthusiasm.

"The Jinghpaws have the trail blocked and beyond it's booby trapped," Henty said. "Anybody comes this way is going to end up mincemeat."

Kon glanced at Meatball and smiled slowly, wincing as the bandage lifted on his cheek.

"They look like such nice little guys. Jeez, I'm glad they're on our side."

"What the Japs have done to us is nothing compared to what they've done to the Jinghpaws, their families and villages," Henty said. "The Japs are stupid, they didn't have to try and wipe out the Kachins. All they want is to be left alone. It's a funny thing about the Jap. Stand up to him, start pushing him around and it scares the piss out of him. But if he thinks you can't defend yourself, he's a goddamned raging monster. The reason the Jinghpaws are our friends is we're fighting their enemy with them."

"You may walk erect like men to the *tongyaw* at the top," Meatball said. "The path is well guarded at both outlets."

The squads swung jauntily up the elephant path and started to cross the cleared area with the bloated, rotting corpses. In the intense heat of the afternoon, the putrid stench was gagging and the men put hands to noses and without being ordered, jogged across the *tongyaw*. Henty saw Kon hesitate, kick a body disdainfully with his heel. Boot him in the ass for me, Henty thought and grinned as Kon stoop to pluck something from the Jap's pocket. If that bastard was taking souvenirs, he'd climbed out of the dumps he'd been in and was planning on being around a while.

Henty was breathing hard and his body was wet inside Snotty's fatigues as they wound on through the jungle. He looked back and the men were beginning to lag. It was bright and the sky was cloudless but the air felt muggy. Meatball kept up a rapid pace over the rise where Henty had talked with Domingo. Jesus, he'd been so close to going home, and through the *kunai* into the bamboo where Snotty had panicked. He halted with Meatball at the edge of the trees, peering across the grass at the mounds where the machine guns had been emplaced. Two blasted craters now.

"Take 10," he told Kon. "Get the men off the trail into the trees and keep them quiet."

He crawled with Meatball through the meadow-like clearing where his squad had been pinned down, beyond the demolished positions and through the defile. There were seven fly-and-maggot-ridden bodies on the trail. The Japs had been back; a hand had been severed from each corpse.

They scouted the trail for snipers and finding no sign of the enemy for 100 yards, returned and climbed to the top of the north mound, lying on their bellies with their eyes fixed up the trail.

"Thirty-seven at the *tongyaw,* nine more here counting the machine gunners, that's forty-six we've killed," Henty said. "Zing Tu La thought there were 70 in this patrol. If we make haste, we can overtake them and kill the rest."

"Dua Chicken has the heart of a tiger," Meatball said and laughed softly. "Always anxious for the quick kill. If you will consider a suggestion, it is possible we may find some better hunting. I know their area of the jungle well. The trail we follow encircles Nhpum Ga to the north. I believe what remains of this group may have joined with others and now make up the force that is irritating your force in the valley by the Tanai-*hka.* I shall lead you away from this trail which is not safe beyond this point to another *tongyaw.* It is on a very high hill that overlooks a small valley from which it is possible to reach Hsamshingyang. This is a safe place of concealment which Zing Tu La and others of us have used from time to time. You may rest your men there. If the enemy is encamped within the valley, their positions will be revealed by their fires when darkness falls."

"I think I know the place of which you speak, the one high hill near a ridge between Hsamshingyang and Nhpum Ga. On our maps it is marked as Hill 307." Henty paused and chided: "But you disappoint me, Meatball. No matter how secure the enemy may feel, he will not light fires in a combat area. You saw there were none last night."

"The enemy had no need for fires last evening," Meatball said, "but tonight many small flames will burn. The enemy will be observing the ceremony of reducing to ashes those portions of his dead he has removed. It is a practice I would not recommend for anyone who does not also seek to join his ancestors but I think tonight we shall attend the rites and benefit from them. The main trail will be guarded but when we see the fires, we shall advance through the jungle under the cover of darkness and fall upon the enemy with sudden fury."

Henty rolled over on his back and looked up at the faded afternoon sky. He yawned.

"You provide these men with a few hours of rest in a safe place and they'll follow you anywhere," he said. "If this was a democratic army, they'd elect you general."

"But I would not wish to take your place," the Jinghpaw said and chuckled.

Henty sat up and stretched his shoulders under his pack. His skin pulled clammily from the fatigues.

"The air feels thick with moisture," he said.

"The monsoons will be early," Meatball said, "but the time has not yet come. Another 16 suns will shine."

"Good!" Henty said in English. "That gives us time to get this raggedy-assed show on the road, mop up these shit-eating bastards and blow this goddamned country."

"What is it that you say?" Meatball asked.

"How do we reach Hill 307, this place you take us to?" Henty answered in Jinghpaw.

"We shall enter the jungle at the place your men broke through the trees to encircle the enemy at this position. If a patrol of the enemy should pass, there will be no sign we have returned and departed the trail."

They started back to the patrol.

"Police it up," Henty ordered. "Don't leave any trace we've been here again."

The progress through the bamboo was slow. Meatball selected his way carefully, keeping just inside the jungle, out of the *kunai* where the trampled grass would mark their passage. He slipped like a shadow between the close growing thin-stemmed trunks and at times the men had to remove their field packs to squeeze through.

About a mile from the trail, Meatball circled a knob on the far side and plunged into shoulder-high elephant grass, beating his way into jungle growth on a rise beyond the knob. Hill 307 towered above the surrounding country deep in the thickness of the jungle. The patrol trudged up the pathless incline, fighting the scrambled growth. At the top an area which had been burned off was knee-high with yellowgreen bamboo shoots. A *basha,* sagging at one corner where a post had collapsed, stood high at the edge of the *tongyaw.* Just beyond, a rock escarpment reached out at the level of the ragged, fringed, green bamboo fronds.

"From the top of the *basha,* you may observe above the trees in each direction," Meatball said as the squads straggled into the clearing and halted. "This valley of which I spoke is clearly visible. If your men will establish themselves in positions around the edges of the *tongyaw,* it will be safe for them to rest." He did not smile but his eyes were laughing. "Have them encircle the area at a far distance from the *basha.* The roof will be an observation post."

Henty called Double Ugly, Butcher and Kon.

"What're you trying to do, surround the Japs with one platoon?" Double Ugly growled and frowned his mounded eyebrows into his eyes.

Butcher twitched off three winks but didn't say anything.

"We're going to hole in here until dark," Henty told them. "Have your men dig in on a perimeter at the edge of the clearing. When you get the foxholes dug, crawl in, get some rest and don't move out of them. Meatball and I will be on guard on the roof of the *basha.* If anything moves, we'll spot it. The Japs are probably encamped in a valley about a mile below and if they are, we're going to make a night attack."

"I feel better when that Kachin's with us," Kon said. "This is one time digging a foxhole is going to be no sweat. I think maybe now we got a chance."

"Like a snowball in hell," Butcher said with a crooked smile and quirked eye.

"They better chew some biscuits," Henty said. "But tell them to save some rations for morning. And no smoking."

The three men started for their squads and Henty walked toward Meatball who was waiting at the *basha.* Halfway there, he turned and trotted back to Kon.

"What was it you lifted off that Jap?" he asked.

Kon sniggered.

"His condoms. It's true what they say. They're pink."

"Well Jesus Christ!" Henty snorted. "A gun or sword I could understand. But rubbers! What the hell you going to do with rubbers, blow them up like balloons?"

91

"We're going back, ain't we? You said we was," Kon said defiantly, and then he smiled slyly. "Going to take them back with me. Bet there ain't a babe in all Milwaukee been screwed with a pink one. Jumping Christ! I'll be sensational."

"Oh shit!" Henty said but he grinned. "By the time you get to use them they'll be so old they'll break."

"They'll still be pink, won't they?" Kon demanded.

The steps to the *basha* had fallen away but the entrance was only shoulder high. Meatball pulled himself up and holled in, reaching down for Henty's tommy gun. His scar was stretched white in a broad smile.

"Why do you make monkey faces?" Henty asked. He raised his elbows to the floor and lifted himself inside.

The old Jinghpaw, La Bu La, in shorts like Meatball and wearing a *kukri* knife, stood just inside the room.

"He has been watching," Meatball said, laughing. "The two of us shall now mount the roof to guard. I spoke of reasons you would enjoy why I should accompany your patrol. The last of them awaits your pleasure here."

Gai-ri, in her blue *sari*, was seated cross-legged on a mat in the far corner, watching him and smiling.

9

Meatball and La Bu La scampered out the hut's one window opening at the back, climbing to the roof while Henty gaped. He was dazed and giddy. When he managed to get his mouth swung shut and his popped eyes back in focus, he let loose with a hoarse shout of raw laughter that brought Meatball scrambling down and peering in. Gai-ri looked confused and frightened.

Henty plopped on the bamboo flooring in the middle of the hut. His tommy gun clattered at his side and he held himself together with his arms. Here, for chrissake, in the middle of the jungle, smack in the center of a bivouac, surrounded by troops in foxholes tensing up for combat, Old Henshit was going to have himself a shack job. Oh good God, he thought, I ought to do it, I ought to strip bare-assed naked and run across the *tongyaw* to Kon's foxhole waving a goddamned hard-on and tell him to give me one of those pink rubbers quick. He laughed silently until his belly ached and his breath was a dull pain in his chest.

"It's all right, it's a piss ripper," he gurgled between sobs, switching to Jinghpaw: "Please try to understand the behavior of this hyena. When I saw the beauty this poor hut contains in the person of Gai-ri, it was like a vision from the pipe and I feared the sun had touched my mind. It was beyond believing that such fortune could be mine."

Meatball grinned with more than understanding and clambered back to his perch. Gai-ri smiled doubtfully, dark eyes more hurt than puzzled. She withdrew a little on the freshly woven mat which she'd probably spent the day preparing and crossed her richly browned arms over the silk cloth that tightly sheathed her breasts. Henty shucked his helmet and pack beside his weapon and crawled to her side.

"Forgive me," he said and smiled, touching her velvet shoulder with a dirty paw. She was even more beautiful than he remembered, here in the muted light of late day, a fragile thing of delicate perfection. "I am coarse and undeserving of you. Gentle hands should cup the molded treasure of your body and hold you aloft for worship."

She tossed her glistening dark hair irritably but there was warmth in her eyes. Sighing, she placed her hands on the mat and lifted her lips to be tasted. They were like sweet, ripe jungle fruit.

"I am of the earth, not to worship but to possess," she said, sitting back and smiling. Her teeth were perfect, white and even. No buck-toothed oriental. "It pleases you that I am here?"

"My heart would tell you but my tongue is thick. I thought last night a fantasy and that such a sweet dream would never come again. But I do not understand. How came you here?"

Her fingers brushed the back of his hand with the lightness of a feather. His skin prickled.

"They told me you were injured," she said gravely. "I wished to go to you at once because when you entered my body you reached my heart. At first they said it was not possible because of the many who would see me. When you returned to the company of your men, Zing Tu La talked long with La Bu La and the one you call Meatball. They considered it would be good for you if I were here to attend you when you came to rest."

"I'm grinning like a Cheshire cat," he said and grinned until he felt like one, continuing in Jinghpaw: "It is a devotion I do not deserve and I am humbly grateful but your safety concerns me greatly. The enemy is treacherous and the jungle abounds with him. La Bu La alone brought you by the trail, armed only with his *kukri* knife?"

"La Bu La is wise and wary. We came by secret ways known only to the Jinghpaws."

She leaned forward to her knees and under the *sari*, the hard nipple of a firm small breast, a breast he knew so well, it fit snugly in his palm, brushed his cheek. His loins grew warm and his fingers reached for the rounding flesh beneath the cloth.

She laughed, a pleased and silvery tinkling, and her hand stroked his cheek.

"My brave one of fathomless passion, would you make love in clothing that smells of the jackal? Remove all you have upon you and lie bare upon the mat. I shall bathe your

94

body while you rest and gather strength. It is well to prepare ourselves for the enjoyment of each other so we may know only sweetness in the fulfillment."

He sat in the middle of the hut, unhooking his bloody leggings, tugging at his shoelaces. Graceful as a leopard, Gai-ri brought an earthen bowl of water from the wall to the mat and knelt waiting. The lingering smile in her eyes provoked him and he fumbled, worked clumsily at his buttons. When he'd pulled off his shorts and stood naked, he looked down his chest at his poor body, suddenly aware of his slat-like ribs, his stomach cavity and spindly shanks.

"Not fit for dog food," he mumbled and walked to the mat.

"Your body needs nourishment," she said as if she'd understood him, "but so does your soul. Lie on your stomach."

She sponged water on the back of his neck with a piece of cotton from a chute used for small drops. The water was fragrant, with flowers or spices, and she massaged him across his shoulders, scrubbed his back, even his ass for chrissake, she wiped his ass for him! Well shit, he thought, it's not as bad as it might have been. I had a sponge bath a couple of hours ago, come on Gai-ri, just get the sweat off and let's go. Oh Jesus, Henty didn't dare laugh again but his sides trembled.

"Something is wrong?" she asked.

"Not a thing, sweetheart. It's just this is the first time I've been fucked by the Army and enjoyed it," he said in English and then in Jinghpaw: "The thrill of your hands upon me makes me tremble with anticipation."

"That is as it should be," she said, smiling faintly. "Now turn yourself."

"Roll me over, in the clover," he sang lightly, and then: *"Violate me in violet time, in the vilest way that you know,"* explaining: "It is a love song in the custom of my people."

"Ah so," she said, clapping her hands and laughing happily. "The words you sing must be very tender."

Her pleasant little laugh continued and he wasn't certain it was for the song. Well, damn it, I'm not ashamed, he thought: maybe I am sticking up in the air like a stud horse but she knows what she's getting into.

She pressed the cool wet cloth over his forehead, his closed eyes, chest and stomach, yes by God, I'm going to be clean all over. He clenched his hands and tried to lie still.

When she had sponged his legs and feet, she took the bowl and stepped away. He leaned on his elbow, watching. The color in her face had deepened and her lips were parted. She dropped her *sari* hastily and came quickly to him. She wanted him as badly as he wanted her. Under her breast, her heart was fluttering.

She lay beside him and he put his hand on her breast. Gently, she rejected his fingers and began herself to caress his body. She was quick and eager, running her hands lightly across his chest, seeking the erotic pressure points of his back, down his ribs, near his hips, under his navel, on the insides of his thighs. Good God, Gai-ri, I don't need this treatment but I love it. Her face was close and moist and she watched him with misty eyes.

"You are sure you are not too tired," she whispered. "You would not rather rest?"

"Baby," he said, "the way things are going you take it when you can get it, this may be the last piece I ever have and I'd take it if it killed me. After what you've done to me, I'd screw you if you were a pig." He let out his breath and grasped her shoulders, turning her on her back. In Jinghpaw, he said: "I have never been more ready. I only hope I can prolong the pleasure so we may enter Paradise together."

She sighed and closed her eyes, waiting for him with parted thighs. He knelt over her body which already was beginning to move, put his lips to hers, seeking with his tongue to enter her body all at once. He felt her hand grasp and guide him into her moist warmth. He tried to move slowly. She would not let him. Their passion heaved mightily and burst from imprisonment.

He lay on her for a moment until his breathing quieted and then sat up. Her eyes were closed and there was a smile on her lips.

"That was quality not quantity," he said. "It didn't last as long as a belch but that was the goddamndest screwing I ever had. Cripes, a guy like Nick the Greek could make a fortune peddling this honey but I'm a sonofabitch if I wouldn't rather be poor and keep it all for myself, I'd kill the bastard that even looked at her."

She sat up quickly, eyes tender and filled with something that looked like love.

"It is correct you should have hunger," she said and hugged him. "I shall bathe us and then I shall feed you."

He held her to him, her skin to his, her breasts against his chest. I wish I was man enough to go again, he thought. This is one thing you never get enough of.

There were mangos in a wicker basket, some kind of coarse bread made with corn, a thick chunk of cold pork and some *laku* to wash it down. There must be a Jinghpaw village somewhere near to get supplies like that. He glanced at Gai-ri who was watching him eat, wolf it down, and he smiled self-consciously. She was eating only mango. The crazy thought flashed across his mind that it wouldn't be hard to fade from sight, just be missing in action, slip away into the hills and live with Gai-ri and the Jinghpaws. Spend the rest of his life living off the land and making love to Gai-ri. Hell, he could take it. Only the Jinghpaws wouldn't let him have it that way until the Japs were driven out.

Well, sonofabitch, he thought, if I can't have it that way, when I do get out of the Army, when I've served my 30 years, I'll marry a girl like Gai-ri who can't speak English and just keep her for the kitchen and the bedroom. When I think something, I'll just let go and say it. Yeah, and when I want to go to bed with her, I'll be too old except maybe once a month.

"Now you must rest until the time comes for you to seek the enemy," she said. "I shall remain here by your side and awaken you when the sun has sunk into the jungle. Perhaps tomorrow you will return to me."

"In a moment," he said. He had an odd, uncertain feeling in his heart. "Tell me something of yourself. You are not a Jinghpaw nor yet of the Kachin state. I know you are not a Shan. You look neither Chinese nor Burmese and you are not from India. You are beautiful and gracious and gentle and kind and together it is a strangeness I have never known before."

"These things are not true of the women of your land?" she asked, not without amusement, adding quietly: "It is a strange thing I do not entirely know myself. It goes back some ways, to the father of my mother. He was from Portugal. And the mother of my mother who was from Burma. So my mother was of that mixture you call Eurasian. Then for my father, it goes to his mother who was of the islands of Polynesia and to his father who was surely Irish."

Henty was bewildered.

"You understand your geography well for a hill girl," he said and thought aloud in English: "Let me sort this out. On one side you're Portugese and Burmese and on the other Irish and Polynesian. I guess that makes you Eurasian, too, like your mother, not that it makes a goddamned bit of difference except to the pukka British." He said in Jinghpaw: "You said the father of your father was from Ireland. Was your own father born here or in the Islands?"

"Oh no," she said and now Henty was certain her dark eyes were laughing. "My own father came to Burma from the country in which he was born, where the father of my father took his wife to live. My father came here to teach his religion to the people of the hills. He was from that country of yours which is called the United States."

"The United States? A missionary from the United States?" Henty burst out in English. "Well for God's sake, that practically makes you an American, I think it does. Oh Christ, I'd like to parade you down Center Street past those gawky-eyed sheepherders at the Wonder Bar and the American in Casper, Wyoming, U.S.A. Their heads would swim. Oh goddamnit, it's too bad you don't talk English."

Gai-ri lifted her eyebrows quizically.

"Oh, but I do," she said in unaccented English and her laughter rippled through the hut. "You see, I was educated in a convent school, before the Japanese came."

Henty sprang to his feet, elated, and then he slumped on the floor and moaned.

"Oh my God."

He held his head with both hands and turned his reddening face away from her.

"Jesus," he muttered. "All the things I said. You understood them."

Gai-ri stiffled her merriment with her fist.

"It isn't right that I should laugh at you. But if only you could see the way you look. As if you had walked into your Sunday school wearing nothing from your waist down. And if you did, why should you be embarrassed? It would be only that your church had taught you to find evil in what is normal.

It is the church that is unnatural. Although I was educated in a convent school because it was convenient, I have never seen my father because his religion would not permit him to take a wife. My mother brought me up among her people. In some things, the hill tribes of northern Burma are like the Rajputs of northern India. They have a saying that the woman is a furrow and the man a plow and it is his duty to plant his seed." She paused and laughed again. "And I did not understand all the words you used. Only what you meant."

10

I<small>NJUN</small> J<small>OE</small> sat facing Kon in a shallow fox hole on the west side of the tongyaw in the long shadows of the jungle. It was very quiet here except for the muffled thumping of artillery at Nhpum Ga which sounded like the slow beginning tom-tom beat for the Sun Dance. There was almost no color left in the burned sky, or perhaps it was not so much the absence of blue as the creeping grayness of gathering moisture. The rains would come although when he could not tell in this strange land. The air had a fertile taste-smell to it and the earth wall of the hole was black and rich with humus.

They were eating the supper package from their K rations and Injun Joe, whose real name was Carlyle Wolf, tongued the dry and tasteless potted meat into a cud and rolled the single spoonful from cheek to cheek. He was indifferent to the look of displeasure in Kon's steel-blue eyes.

"Jesus," Kon said at last. "I can't stand it. I can't hardly eat this crap and you act like you got a slurp of ice cream you don't want to swallow. I guess you get that way from eating jerky on the reservation, huh?"

Carlyle Wolf considered Kon and wondered whether he should answer. Like the others in the squad, Kon had his own preconceived idea of the Indian and didn't want that precious image shattered. The white man always created pictures in his mind that made him feel superior to anyone who was different from him. It was in the name that had clung to Carlyle since basic training—Injun Joe—when he'd been baptized for the college his father had attended. It was in the way they addressed him—Ugh! big brave go scalp 'um—when he'd planned on majoring in English before the Army interrupted such things as education, just as had his mother whose tribal name was Little Faun but who held a Master's Degree in English as Faun Little. It was in the assumption that all Indians lived on the reservations where the white man had first imprisoned them when his family owned 10,000 rolling acres east of Browning, Montana, and ran 30,000 head of sheep.

He shrugged.

"The braves who now are the old men of the Blackfeet could run all day on a few kernels of corn but they chewed each one well. I eat slowly to extract and digest all nutrition possible, not because I enjoy this product."

Kon's head came up with a jerk and Carlyle smiled in the back of his mind.

"Goddamn!" Kon exclaimed. "Maybe you got something there. You're tall and you're skinny like the rest of us but maybe you always was lean. I bet you was. And you ain't been sick like most of us. You think if I ate like you I might get rid of the goddamn shits?"

Carlyle didn't want to talk. I have nothing to say, he told himself, and it is impossible for me to adapt my thoughts or conversation. If I tell this man he has amoebic dysentery, what will it mean to him?

"It would do no harm," he said.

"Yeah, I'm going to try." Kon dug his spoon into his can of meat and chewed purposefully. "Christ, more than before it tastes like sawdust and piss." He swallowed and shook his head unhappily. "I guess it's too late anyhow to do much good. A couple more minutes now, I'll get the shits and Old Henshit said we wasn't to leave the foxhole." An intent look came into his eyes and he leaned toward Carlyle. "You think Old Henshit's trying to make like a officer, sacking in the *basha* now he's platoon leader?"

It is in their heritage to trust no one, Carlyle thought, not even those who lead them. Disgustedly, he glanced across the yellowish green overgrowth toward the *basha* near the edge of the once cleared area. It looked like a crumpled and weathered haystack.

"There are two forms lying in exposed positions on the ridgepole," he said. "The sergeant said he and the Jinghpaw would mount guard while we rested. He is a good soldier."

Kon flushed and looked uncomfortable. Carlyle hoped he would be quiet.

"I shouldn't of said what I did," Kon said. "That's a thing that scares me. We're all of us starting to say and do things we don't mean."

Carlyle silently chewed the statement. It was a more perceptive thought than Kon realized. Bitter, bone-aching and mind-sickening fatigue were breaking down their disciplined ways of thinking and acting into instinctive patterns. Men they'd thought were brave would cringe, men they'd thought were cowards would fight like savages for survival.

Kon went on: "You really think we're getting out of here after we mop up this bunch of Japs?"

Oh shut up! Carlyle thought, I've exposed my feelings enough for one day.

"You heard the answer when I asked the question," he said.

"Uh-huh, you did. You can speak up when you want. I never thought about your not talking much on account of you was an Indian. The answer we got sounded all right." Kon paused doubtfully. "It's getting so I don't understand anything no more. Like you asking about getting to go back and then volunteering for scout. On this kind of dangerous mission. You been in the Army long enough to know you don't volunteer for nothing. The only way I can figure it is maybe you felt you had to do something brave after talking about going back like any of the rest of us. Well, the Jinghpaw saved your ass for you."

Carlyle replaced the top of his meat can, tucked it with the biscuits in his field pack, tilted his helmet over his eyes and leaned back. He did not comment.

"Guess you're right," Kon said. "Save some chow for morning, if there is a morning. Anyway, we got to rest first. G'night, Joe."

Carlyle bit his teeth together.

"Night," he said between them.

Injun Joe. His grandfather, Chief Running Wolf, would disown him, banish him from the tribe if he knew the way Carlyle had acted today. He didn't know why he'd volunteered as scout unless it could be Kon was right. Then everyone must know that fear had seeped into his gut, that he didn't want to fight any more, that he'd felt he had to prove himself and the Jinghpaw had saved him the ordeal. He hated himself but he hated the men of the patrol even more for what they thought of him.

There were times when a blackness filled his soul and he asked himself: Why am I here with these people who in my grandfather's time murdered the men and women and even children of my tribe, stole our land? Why am I fighting with them in their sacred cause of liberty? They peddle freedom like an advertising slogan to the world and it means as little. Whose liberty? Whose freedom? Hell, until they put him in uniform he couldn't buy a legal glass of beer. It was strange, indeed, to find yourself allied with your recent enemy against a people whose ancestors were your ancient cousins.

Kon was scrabbling in his corner, removing his fatigues. Carlyle heard his tight grunts of pain as he relieved himself in his helmet. He emptied it over the side of the foxhole, scattered some dirt over the feces like an animal and then scrubbed the inside of the helmet with earth.

"Sorry," Kon mumbled.

I ought to feel sorry for him, Carlyle told himself, but I can't.

Night pocketed the hilltop when Carlyle opened his eyes. There were no stars, no moon. He felt enshrouded in a palpable pall. There was a feel of rain but it was more a threat than a promise. Insects droned in the jungle. Within the perimeter there was the sound of cautious movement. Weapon tensely ready, he peered over the edge of the hole. Black on black, crouching forms were moving across the *tongyaw*.

"Psst." Whispered from the nearest foxhole. "Assemble at the *basha*. Pass the word."

He'd known that was what the movement was but his relief was immense. He repeated the sibilant order and touched Kon's shoulder. Still shaken, he scrambled over the edge followed by Kon and crawled toward the basha. I have become a weak, old woman, he thought grimly, I must steel my nerves.

Two figures, shadowy outlines, were standing near the tumbled hut. One of them spoke, just above a whisper. It was Henty.

"By squads," he said. "Give your names in your positions. . . . 1st Squad."

"Injun Joe," Carlyle whispered and felt his belly gripe.

"Kon."

"Ass Drag."

They all were there, where else would they be? Julie, Hari Kari, Old Overshoes, Nick the Greek, Pretty Pussey and Katey, Furman. The 2nd sounded off. And the 3rd.

"Ridge Runner!" Henty said tightly. "Where the hell's the Ridge Runner?"

"Heah." From near Henty by the *basha*.

"Damnit, why didn't you sound off like I said?"

"Y'all said b' squads. Ah ain't got none. Ah'm b'tween."

There were a few sniggers but they were nervous and brief.

"Knock it off!" Henty rasped. "We're going to pay a visit to the Japs tonight. They're camped in a valley below us. About a hundred of them, near as Meatball can tell. He's scouted them. The valley is small and clear and it's cramped in by the jungle on two sides and a ridge that angles from here and up around it. There's a rim rock trail along that ridge. It's narrow and exposed but on a night like this no one's going to see us. We'll come down off that ridge through the jungle and hit them from the west. We follow Meatball. Every man hook his hand into the belt or pack of the man ahead and keep in step so there's no stumbling."

"Why not some of that dead phosphorescent wood on our backs so we got something to go by?" someone interrupted.

"If we do hit a patrol, we'd be as easy to spot as fireflies wearing horseshoes," Henty said. "We'll just hang on and move slow and careful. Pick up your feet and don't go kicking down any stones. Just before we start off that ridge through the jungle, you'll see their fires below like the valley was filled with candles. We'll halt inside the jungle when we come out at the bottom. Hug the trees but crawl in the grass when you move to your positions: 2nd, move off about 100 yards to the right . . . 3rd, about 100 to the left . . . 1st, spread out where we are. I'll give you five minutes then I'll fire a Very light over the camp and that's the signal to cut loose. You'll have about 15 seconds to get your bearings. Riflemen, pick your targets. BAR-men cut loose and spray the ones that are bunched. They're squeezed in pretty tight so if you're in your positions and firing straight ahead and not too high, we ought to do a pretty good job of cleaning them out. As soon as you've shot off your first clip, toss in a grenade as far as you can, load up again, shoot off another clip and throw in a couple more grenades and rendezvous at the trail with the 1st. Hook onto any belt you can grab regardless; every man for himself, and we'll beat it to hell back up here. Joe, come up here. I'm starting after Meatball and you follow. Kon, Ass Drag, Julie, Hari Kari, the rest of you."

"Wheah y'all want me?"

104

"Oh shit, Runner! Between the 1st and 2nd, like I said. After Furman."

A few hundred yards through the clinging blackness of the jungle surrounding the *tongyaw* and the patrol reached the rocky outcropping. It was a tight formation, body almost pressed to body, and the men were taut. Carlyle was sure Henty could feel his hand trembling as it grasped his field pack. They snaked along and the unseen emptiness yawned on either side. It might be 10 feet or 100 to the bottom. Ahead, Carlyle could see the form he grasped but that was all. The night was almost blind black and even his practiced eye could not see where the sky left off and the earth began. The sullen sky began to mutter. A hesitation shuddered along the file and he could not say it did not start with him. He scanned the sky for sign of far-off sheet lightning. There was nothing yet but if it came flaring above the jungle, they'd be silhouetted nakedly.

Except for the distant grumbling of thunder, the silence was complete and hollow, enclosing them. Only an occasional shell thudded at Nhpum Ga, just enough artillery to keep the 2nd Battalion dug in and discouraged.

The patrol picked its tedious, painful way along the rocky trail and then Carlyle felt his muscles tighten and knew they were climbing. Only a small incline and then he could suddenly see little orange flickerings dotting a remote and unreal blackness below. Back in the groping column, someone stumbled in the shaggy night. A rock, another and another bounded and clattered. The tight line of men scrunched, face to butt. Carlyle watched the fires and felt perspiration quickly beading his face. The falling stones sounded like hail. The sky mumbled. He cowered before the streaking lightning he knew would come but there was none. The showering rocks piled on some unseen shelf. The fires in the valley did not blink out. There was no outcry, no commotion. Still the patrol waited behind Meatball, a new rocklike ridge formed against the darkened sky.

My nerve is gone, Carlyle admitted to himself, there's no reserve to draw on. I'm worn out and afraid I'll never get out of this alive. They've pushed us beyond endurance and they'll keep driving us until we're dead. But there had to be some hope, some way, there was everything to go home for—soft-eyed, lithe limbed Rosebud who hadn't gone to college as they'd planned they would together, who'd married him instead when he went into the Army and now was the mother of a son he'd never seen; his quiet-speaking mother and warm-hearted father and stern-faced old-browed grandfather, Chief Running Wolf, who'd passed on to him the brave legends of the tribe; the hundred rolling yellow hills of the ranch where he could ride his pinto with the wind, proud and free. And here, nothing but black despair and the Japs, whom he could not despise.

Henty's pack tightened as he arose. Carlyle stood and the silent motion passed down the line. In a moment the patrol was again stealing through the night, picking their way off the ridge and then they were secreted in the jungle. Moving in blackness in an unseen jungle that smothered them. Marching men. Moving feet. Silent GI boots that seemed to rock the matted ground they trod.

They were at the bottom, almost out of the jungle. The fires ahead were bright and there were many of them, but they were small. Some men huddled about them, dark squatting shapes. Others moved between. He could hear them talking quietly among themselves. There was an odor of roasted, or burned, meat. He'd seen Indian encampments or ceremonies that looked like this.

Ahead, Meatball detached himself and crawled on through the grass. Henty reached back and touched Carlyle's hand and followed, flanking the Jinghpaw. Mechanically, Carlyle repeated the signal and started creeping to his position off to the side of Meatball. He could feel the movement of the patrol, the silent setting of the trap as 1st Squad moved up on either side of Meatball's point and then 2nd Squad spread out on one flank and 3rd on the other. The rustling quieted and all was still except for the camp sounds.

Carlyle inched his M-1 against his shoulder in prone position, watching a little fire 50 or 60 yards ahead that outlined the shapes of three Japs. His hand was shaking and his spread legs began to quiver. He swore bitterly in his mind and tried to control the trembling.

A flare exploded like a giant flashbulb and a ball of brilliant white hung in the black night above the camp. In the sudden exposure, the Japs were frozen in stunned positions. The globe of light descended slowly, for an eternity, and searching the camp Carlyle saw ahead a shallow foxhole, hardly more than a trench, between the patrol and first fires. A lone Jap, probably a perimeter sentry, was apparently asleep with his rifle across his chest. Carlyle got the man in his sights.

The fire from the patrol was immediate, concentrated and intense. It streamed into the Jap camp. In each squad, the BAR-men worked their overlapping sectors like machine guns. Then, almost at once, the crackling spewing stopped and several dozen grenades exploded in bright bursts. Across the floor of the valley the Japs were shouting, screaming, moaning. Some of the small fires had blinked out but most of them still flickered. The Japs hadn't fired a single shot. Neither had Carlyle.

When the full firepower of the tight patrol raked the camp again, he began to elbow ahead toward the lone Jap he'd spotted in the first foxhole. Some fire was coming from the camp now but it was sporadic and ineffectual.

Again, the heavy fire from the patrol spattered off to silence and Carlyle flattened himself to the ground against the grenade bursts he knew would come. He lay motionless in the grass near the foxhole. There was no more firing, only crashing noises behind as if a great force were gathering for a charge.

The patrol would regroup now and withdraw to the *tongyaw* where they thought they were secure. Except for the anguished groans of the dying and injured, no sounds came from the camp. Carlyle began to move forward again, toward the Jap he'd had in his sights and hadn't shot. He hoped the man was still alive.

11

T HE last round of grenades exploded brightly in bursts of shattered orange. For a tense moment the squads held their positions. There was no return fire from the Jap camp, no movement, nothing but black silence. The men began to break for the trail.

"Stay where you are!" Henty shouted abruptly, his voice harshly cutting the muggy air, "2nd, 3rd, lob in grenades at will."

Meatball tadpoled back and stood beside him. He was making clucking sounds of pleasure in his throat.

"We caught them flat," Henty said, sharp and exultant. "I'm going to line up the squads, make sure we all get out. Take a position within the jungle on the trail and make monkey noises."

The Jinghpaw trotted off chattering. He was laughing in any language.

"First Squad, withdraw," Henty ordered, admiring the sight and sound of the irregular explosions. "Joe, Kon, anyone make for the monkey and hook onto him. Rest of you pile in and grab onto whoever sounds off in front. Call off by numbers."

Men brushed by, substantial but unseen. They didn't smell, not these men, except of earthy sweat and cordite. And they didn't scurry. They were Marauders. Sonofabitch, they were a mean lot in a crummy command but when it came to fighting they had the guts to win. He'd stake his life on any one of them.

"One-Two." A pause. Someone stumbled, swore. "Three-Four-Five." There was triumph in each voice. "Six-Seven-Eight-Nine." An empty silence. Then: "Ten." No more.

"Where's Eleven?" Henty called tightly, looking around at the thick black wall of night. And laughed grimly: "Shit, I forgot. I make Eleven. Move in sounding off; 3rd keep pitching."

Twelve men sounded off in 2nd.

"Third, party's over. Your turn."

Only 11 responded in the 3rd.

"Someone's missing," Henty shouted tensely, staring helplessly from side to side in the pitch coated night. "Where's Twelve?"

"You took him," a nearby voice answered. "That's the radio operator."

"Oh Christ!" Henty said disgustedly. "Him again, in between. Ridge Runner?"

"Heah." From up the line.

"Shove off," Henty called and repeated in Jinghpaw: "We march."

He pushed his hand into a shrunken waist at the tail of the patrol and they straggled into the stiffling jungle. The sky still was growling like an empty gut and the air felt wet but there'd been no lightning and there'd be no rain. They'd had five days of rain on the Inkangatawng mission but those had been off-and-on showers. This was the beginning of the build-up for the drowning monsoons that Meatball said were two weeks off.

They shuffled up the obscured trail but even in the tired, plodding feet there seemed to be a spring. Someone whispered something and a snicker ran down the column. Henty halted the patrol.

"Hold it down," he ordered. "We still have to cross that ridge and we don't know they didn't have a patrol out. Let's don't push our luck."

They came to the rock and Meatball held them below the crest. They tensed and waited while he moved ahead. Can he really see in this stuff? Henty wondered, or does he smell his way? And complimented himself: Damnit boy, you've done it again, brought them out, not just a squad but a whole platoon this time. But you'd make a lousy officer, you didn't remember to blast off the usual clip from that useless .45.

Meatball chattered and the patrol moved on again, clambered onto the rimrock, automatically crouching against the skyline that wasn't there. They did everything automatically, by numbers; you had to for survival. But they'd be a bunch of wild men, there'd be no battalion of military police that could hold them, they'd unhinge Calcutta when they got back to India.

It was like a grotesque victory snake dance, strung out there on the ridge, like a bunch of high school kids after a hard-fought football game weaving down the streets of Casper, except here they couldn't see where they were going and no one to watch. Where they were going, for chrissake! they sure as hell hadn't seen where they were going back in 1932 when the Natrona County High School had given them diplomas and turned them loose in a starving, jobless land. There'd been one thing they'd been sure of, just one damned thing—there might not be any work and sure as hell no further school for most, but they still were the Lucky Generation, they'd been born between wars, you didn't raise your son to be a soldier, Ma, but after a hitch in the CCC where else are you going to find such a soft spot?

The *tongyaw* on the hilltop had a homey feeling. Meatball guided the file to the *basha* and Henty broke off from the column and stood with his back to the hut, looking at the faceless, almost formless men. He wondered whether Gai-ri waited for him on her mat inside . . . good to be home, dear, had a hard day at the office.

"You gave them hell," he told the men. "There's no telling how many we got but we broke them up. If this was the outfit that was pinning down Hsamshingyang, then we're on the way to Nhpum Ga. BAR-men and ammo bearer from 2nd, dig in on the perimeter where the path we took comes in from the ridge. BAR-men and ammo bearer from 3rd, same position where we came up here from the jungle. Rest of you see if you can find the same holes you were in before. You're all on alert so figure it out for yourselves who sacks in first. Any of you got any butts can smoke but light them in your helmets and cup them. Ridge Runner, tote yo' li'l ol' SCR 300 up heah to ol' Hain-sheet."

"When do we eat?" A soft wail.

"Where do we go from here?" In a hoarse whisper.

"I'm almost out of ammo." Indignantly.

"Me, too." A chorus.

Henty grinned. He was feeling good.

"You lousy chowhounds. You can wait until morning. Divy up your ammo with your buddies. We're halfway to Nhpum Ga and they aren't going to pull us back. I figure we'll just stay dug in here until we get a supply drop. Go grab some sack time."

As the group unscrambled and melded with the night, Meatball touched Henty's arm.

"Dua Chicken, I depart now once more for the valley to observe the numberless dead in the first light of day. I shall return with the rising sun."

"With the ears of the Rising Sun, you mean," Henty said and chuckled. "Inform those who guard the path of your departure and arrival by your monkey chatter."

Meatball clucked softly and his *chit-chit-chit-chit* clicked off toward the ridge. Henty strained his ears for sound of movement within the hut but there was none.

Beside him, the Ridge Runner was swinging his pack radio from his back.

"Y'all want ah git C'mand naow?"

"Yeah," Henty said absently. It was too much to hope that Gai-ri and La Bu La had waited. "They shouldn't have. But it gave him an empty feeling to think she was gone.

The traffic to Command was heavy. Lancelot to Arthur, Lancelot to Arthur, the Ridge Runner droned endlessly. Who in hell had thought up the code names, the same deskbound dimwit who'd dubbed this dismal undertaking Galahad? Well, whatever the meanings of the words, they used ls and rs which the Japs couldn't fit around their tongues. The Runner finally got through, or woke someone up.

"Henshit here," Henty said, grinning, hoping he had the Colonel. "Reporting contact with the enemy."

It was Captain Gold.

"Go on, Henshit." The voice was so tired the words dragged but it was friendly.

"Contacted enemy patrol, estimated strength 100, encamped in valley one mile northwest of Hill 307, attacked at 2200 hours inflicting heavy losses. Determining exact casualties and will report at 0600. Believe this was main base of patrols nipping Arthur's ass. Enemy appears routed. Lancelot suffered no casualties. Now encamped Hill 307. Ammo low, rations gone. Request orders."

The receiver crackled. There was no voice.

"Do you read me?" Henty asked.

"Loud and clear. Just a minute, Henshit."

Getting his orders, Henty thought Captain Gold seemed half-assed decent, he'd given Snotty's .45 to Henty, he hadn't had to do that. The .45 was a useless piece of hardware but it felt good on your hip.

"Henshit, here are your orders. Remain where you are. At 0900 you will receive a three-day supply drop. Proceed immediately seeking penetration west north west to Maggot Ridge. Do you read me?"

Henty wrinkled his mind. The place name was a new one but it could mean only Nhpum Ga.

"Well now, uh, just a second." He paused to let that sink in. "Had some trouble here. I think I've got it."

"Roger. We'll expect your report at 0600." Captain Gold hesitated and added in a tone that was both warm and concerned: "Good luck, Henshit."

Well hell, the poor guy, he was from the 2nd Battalion, his men were at Nhpum Ga.

"Roger, Arthur. Over and out."

The Ridge Runner pushed down the antenna and swung the portable transmitter-receiver by the strap. He sounded a yawn.

"Since y'all be need'n me in the mawnin', m'be ah bettah bunk w'yah. Mind n'body kin s'prize yah."

"Now that's right thoughtful of y'all," Henty said and bared his teeth. It would be the sensible thing to do but suppose, just suppose, Gai-ri hadn't left? "But think of yo' po' l'il ol' ass hole buddy in yo' foxhole. Not getting any sleep because you aren't there to spell him!"

"Yeah," the Ridge Runner said resignedly. "Ah figgered y'd think a' thet."

Henty reached his tommy gun into the *basha* and pulled himself over the stepless, shoulder high entrance. A soft cool hand helped him. Wordlessly but shaking with emotion that overwhelmed him, he put his arms around Gai-ri. He clung to her weakly in the dark and she helped support him. Then her fingers sought the clasps on his belt and helped him remove his weapons, field pack and helmet. Gai-ri took his hand and led him across the room to the mat in the corner.

"I shall remove your clothing," she whispered, "and then while you rest, I shall bathe away your weariness. There is some wine and food for later."

She knelt at his feet, removing his leggings and unlacing his shoes.

He smiled to himself and it was a different feeling smile than he'd ever known. I'm glad I can't see myself, he thought: something strange is happening. He stepped out of his fatigues and pulled off his shorts. When he lay on his stomach, the scented moist cloth in Gai-ri's hand began to massage his back. He was weary but he was content. A soothing drowsiness came upon him and he slept.

Dreamless sleep.

A hand shook his shoulder and he awakened in the dark, tense, rolling to his side and groping for his tommy gun. The hand touched his arm and a finger closed his lips. He remembered.

"Someone is outside the *basha* calling you," she whispered close to his ear.

He started crawling across the floor with the .45 in his hand.

"Henty, damn! Henshit." The voice was low but urgent.

"Who is it?" he asked standing to the side of the entrance, half raising the pistol.

"Kon. Injun Joe ain't in our hole."

"For chrissake, you wake me up to tell me that? He probably dug himself another hole."

"Why'd he do that?"

"He shouldn't have but you probably shit him out of that one."

In the silence that followed, the cicadas sang. Some of the mugginess had lifted and the night was lighter. Henty could make out Kon's stooped shape but could not see his face.

"It could of been," Kon finally admitted. "I been bailing it out pretty regular. You sure he got back in?"

"You heard the count," Henty said irritably. "Eleven counting me in 1st. Twelve in 2nd. Eleven in 3rd, and the Ridge Runner."

"Yeah. I guess so. Well Jesus! What've I got to do, stand guard by myself all night?"

Henty snorted with disgust.

"If you're stupid enough to ask a question like that, you deserve to. Sack in and forget it. There are enough others on alert." He chuckled. "Your gut will be your conscience."

"Whyn't I sack in with you? We could change off."

113

Oh the poor bastard, if he only knew what he was saying.

"I'm not being chickenshit," Henty said, "but we can't leave that gap in the perimeter. You know that, even if you're sleeping. And this isn't exactly a hotel room. It's an observation post. The roof is the highest place around. I'm going to mount guard right now."

"Shit, Henty, I forgot. You was up there before when we was sleeping. Sorry I woke you up."

"Glad you did." He meant that all right and it made him feel a little guilty. Smiling guilt. "Just a second." He patted the floor, found his pack, dug out his K ration package, thrust it down to Kon. "Here. Don't know the food will do you much good but you can use the cigarettes. I owe you that much."

"Aw shit, Henty, you don't have to do that," Kon said awkwardly but he took the package. "I hadn't ought to take it, but I'd go to hell for you, Henshit."

Kon left hurriedly.

Henty stood in the entrance, watching as Kon's outline merged with the night. I'm a first-class bastard, he told himself and padded across the room to Gai-ri.

She had removed her *sari* and drew him to her.

"Well hello, Guard," he said and laughed softly.

Her legs parted and she reached for him. A delicious warmth crept from his thighs and burned through his body. She locked them together with her arms and legs about his back and rocked him in a passionate cradle. He shuddered ecstatically.

The cooling touch of the scented water brushed across his forehead awakened him luxuriantly to gradual awareness and he was smiling when he opened his eyes. Gai-ri in her sari was kneeling at his side, her beauty pastel-like in the soft grayness before dawn. He reached for her face and drew her lips to his. It was not a hungry kiss. It was gentle and shared and very satisfying.

"I must leave you now," she said quietly but he thought her eyes were sad.

"But you can't," he said quickly, sitting up. "At least, not until Meatball returns. You cannot go into the jungle alone. Anyway." He smiled. "You couldn't get out of the camp and I wouldn't want you to try."

Her lips parted. The look in her eyes was tender.

114

"I do not go alone," she said, stroking his cheek. "La Bu La will lead the way."

"But where is La Bu La?"

"On the roof." She laughed. "He has been there all night."

He shook his head.

"I should have known. Where will you go?"

"I do not know. But we shall meet again."

He held her close. There was no passion in his feeling, only contentment.

La Bu La swung through the back wall window opening.

"It is time," he said. He was smiling benignly like a parent pleased with his children.

Gai-ri emptied the water from the bowl out the window, removed a mango and rice wine from the basket and placed the bowl inside.

"Your breakfast," she said. Her kiss was warm and lingering. "Be careful."

Gai-ri and La Bu La slipped out the opening in the back wall and the silent jungle enfolded them as Henty watched.

He dressed slowly, munching the fruit and sipping the wine. He did not understand what it was he felt for Gai-ri. She wasn't just another shack job. When he was with her he had a sense of being complete and that was the strangest part of all. He'd never known a woman that he'd wanted when his passion was spent.

Buckling the web belt with the holstered .45 over his fatigues, he unhooked the canteen and left it in the hut with his helmet and field pack. He started from the window without his tommy gun, felt suddenly insecure, returned for it and clawed his way up the back wall of the *basha*. The bamboo was slick and he had to kick footholds between the cracks and wedge in the butt of his submachine gun for leverage. He lay flat on the pole facing the ridge.

The day was dawning grayblue and cool. All about the *tongyaw* the fringed fronds of the bamboo were green and quiet. Ahead, the rimrock thrust a rheumatic finger pale and boney around the valley. Far below over the cascading tops of the trees he could see the grassy little nook where the Japs had camped. It looked littered, like a municipal park after a Sunday summer afternoon.

It was that hour of silence, of uncertain calm when all

115

the world takes its breath for the new day and even the insects were hushed. I'll bet there isn't a man in camp on guard, he thought without rancor, twisting and squirming as he checked the mounds that marked the patrol's perimeter. He looked into the foxholes, the pitiful burrows where the men curled like animals. They were animals. They stalked their prey at night and killed and crawled back into their holes in the ground.

Knock it off, Old Henshit, he told himself, you're thinking dangerously.

He swiveled his belly back toward the ridge, scanning it for Meatball. It was Kon who came to him first. Henty caught the movement from the corner of his eye, watched Kon come across the *tongyaw*, instinctively hunching over bent knees in a half crouch, rifle slanting across his chest. The rawboned Pole halted at the front of the *basha,* standing erect and waving.

"Old Hen and his chicks!" he called softly and grinned, lifting the dirty bandage on his cheek. It needing changing. "Tell me how to get up there and I'll take over. I saved a butt for you."

"Take the elevator, you dumb bastard." Jesus, Kon was gaunt, the son of a bitch was starving to death. "Pull yourself up into the *basha* and out the back. There are some holds I kicked in the wall."

Kon slung his rifle, pulled himself into the hut and a moment later Henty heard him coming up the bamboo. He scratched up the thatch and straddled the pole facing Henty. His eyes looked more gray than blue and they were luminous, large and staring. Even in the still sunless morning, his hollow unbandaged cheek looked shadowed. He fished a cigarette from his pocket and held it to Henty in fingers that looked like claws.

"Old Henshit, you ought to quit knocking yourself out," he said seriously. "Jeez, you don't get no rest, you push yourself twice as hard as you push anybody else, one of these days you're going to keel right over and then what happens? We get another Snotty."

"Do I look like I'm coming apart at the seams?" Henty grinned, took the cigarette and stuck it in the corner of his mouth. He pointed below. "If you look down there you can see the camp and some of the damage you did last night."

He looked with Kon at the dirty floor of the valley.

"Jesus!" Kon said softly. "We must of got a million of them."

"Yeah." Henty was examining the camp carefully. "Nothing big went up so if they had an ammo dump, we didn't hit it. They must have had rations, rice anyway, maybe wine. There's a drop coming at 0900 but maybe if you took a small detail, say four or five men, you might scrounge up some breakfast, scavenge what you can carry, blow up anything else. You might even find some more rubbers. Feel like it? We move out right after the drop."

"Sure! I'll take Hari Kari and Old Overshoes, Ass Drag and Julie. Maybe some of them bastards ain't quite dead, we'll slit their throats like you and the Jinghpaws done."

"You won't need BAR-men. Take a couple of the others."

"Check."

Kon slid off the pole, still clinging to it, and dug his toes into the thatch. His eyes were gleaming now.

"And thanks," he said and slipped his way off the roof.

Henty sat upright, straddling the top of the hut and lighting the cigarette. The first drag was a pain in the bottom of his throat and made him cough but the second felt good. Kon dropped from the *basha,* trotted across to the perimeter. He knelt beside several holes and in a few minutes was walking toward the trail that led to the ridge with Hari Kari, Old Overshoes, Katey and Pretty Pussey. They all had packs on their backs but they were flat and empty. Just as the canteens bouncing on their hips were empty. The scavengers were out for wine. They filed past the BAR-men and ammo bearer guarding the path to the rock and disappeared in the green. Henty wondered why Kon hadn't taken Injun Joe.

The sun was edging the gray rock with shining gold when Kon and his small party began worming along the narrow trail. Henty stiffened and ground his teeth. The cigarette smoldered forgotten between his fingers. Jesus, they were exposed out there, even crouched they were silhouetted targets. Without thinking and uselessly, he covered them with his tommy gun until the five men dropped off the ridge and were covered by the trees on the slope. Then he slumped and looked at the blister the burning cigarette had raised on his middle finger.

He mashed the cigarette on the butt of his gun and shredded it in the air. You couldn't see the ridge from within the jungle and there probably wasn't a Jap within a mile but he'd done a stupid thing in sending that patrol out. He paused to study that thought. Had he been stupid? The whole patrol was going to move out along the ridge after they'd taken the drop. Kon's advance party was a risk an officer would have taken for the safety of the group, just the way they used a scout, maybe he'd had that idea somewhere in the back of his mind all along. It made him uncomfortable to think he might have. At least he could have waited for Meatball to return.

The sun was coming up fast, making the jungle foliage yellowish with warm light. Henty's eyes prodded between the trees, skipped along the rock looking for the Jinghpaw. He fidgeted. The minutes dragged by and the sun burned into his scalp. Men were stirring in the foxholes. He glanced around the perimeter, saw the Ridge Runner dragging his pack radio and starting for the *basha*. Henty searched the ridge again.

Just coming onto the rimrock from the jungle where Kon and his patrol had entered it were two figures. The one in front was stooped bearing some bulky burden. The one in back was short and walked erect. They were too far away to distinguish who they were or what the one in front was carrying.

"What the hell!" Henty said aloud and left his perch.

He waved the Ridge Runner to the top of the *basha* and trotted bareheaded across the clearing toward the trail to the rock.

"Look alive!" he shouted to the BAR-men. "There'll be three, maybe four of us coming back up this trail in a hurry. Don't get itchy fingers just because something moves."

He ran through the twisting yellowgreen walled jungle alley. The stooped man in front had been carrying a body, someone wounded? a corpse? It had to be. He thrust the thought away but the conviction kept coming back. The holstered .45 slapped his thigh. Goading symbol of authority. Angry anguish pounded in his chest.

Out of the jungle and onto the rimrock, practiced eye automatically noting the treachery of the trail, the precipitous drop, wondering how they'd made it blind.

He met them on a shelf, Meatball prodding a dazed and frightened Jap with Injun Joe slung across his back.

"Put him down," Henty shouted to the Jap whose eyes and face got blank. He stood and shuddered sweat. Henty looked at Meatball, said in Jinghpaw: "Tell him to put Joe down with his back against the rock."

"I do not speak the tongue," Meatball said, stepping beside the Jap, pointing to his burden and indicating with his hand where he should place it.

Henty slipped his arm under Injun Joe's and helped ease him down. Strips of torn brown cloth bound broad green leafs to Joe's right side in a swath from his armpit to his hipbone. The Indian's face was gray, a thousand-year-old graven piece of granite. Henty held his palm to Joe's nostrils and looked at Meatball.

The Jinghpaw shook his head.

"The breath of life grows faint, Dua," Meatball said. "It was almost extinguished when I came upon them and yet he walked. His entire side has been blown away."

Henty looked hatefully at the Jap and back to Meatball.

"You came upon them? I do not understand. Where?"

"Within the jungle, halfway to the rock from the valley, and only this morning shortly before encountering your small patrol. They seemed angry and threatened the prisoner but proceeded on their mission. I did not use the same trail last night but circled to look for sign of withdrawal to the rear. Wounded as your man was, he was working the enemy up the path a footstep at a time at the point of his gun knife."

Henty looked back at Injun Joe. Onyx eyes were open in the sculpted face of stone. The grim lips parted and Henty leaned to hear the words.

"It is the prisoner you wished to question," Injun Joe whispered and closed his eyes . . . and died.

Hard-eyed as Injun Joe had ever been, Henty pulled out the .45 and shot the Jap in the middle of his forehead. He kicked the falling body over the edge of the shelf.

"No one in the patrol speaks Jap," he said.

12

Kon's detail filed downhill grim and silent. The meeting with Meatball and the Jap bent under the shattered body of Injun Joe had enraged them. They followed the trampled growth that marked the trail they'd trod the night before. It was getting hot, beginning to steam, and the bugs were whining. Hari Kari was a yard or two behind Kon with Old Overshoes at his heels. Several lagging paces to the rear, Katey and Pretty Pussey shared their gloomy thoughts.

Hari Kari could feel his Irish boiling. With every pounding step, he felt his blood thrust more brick red to his face. Jesus, Mary and Joseph! the way Injun Joe had looked when he'd opened his pained black eyes to them with not a muscle twisting in his face although what was left of his body was writhing. Why couldn't he have got it clean?

He showed his helmet off his furrowed, sweating forehead and made the first comment.

"We should have gutted the little bastard."

Kon glanced over his shoulder. His tightened neck muscles had pulled his mouth down.

"Yeah. But he was carrying Injun Joe."

"Hell, the Indian was done for. A couple of us could have taken him in, what was left of him. We should have carved out that Jap's insides for what they did to Injun Joe."

"They didn't do it." For once Old Overshoes' voice was quiet and it sounded mean.

Hari Kari angrily turned his head. Old Overshoes was big. He'd been beefy. All he had now was brawn. His face was coarse and his brown eyes had a malignant yellow cast.

"What the hell you talking about, *they* didn't do it?"

"That was a grenade got Injun Joe," Old Overshoes said roughly. "We didn't take any Jap fire to speak of and no grenades. That was one of our own grenades got Injun Joe."

"How do you figure that?" Hari Kari looked ahead at the tangled green growth that bound the trail and frowned. "He came in with us last night, we all did. Henty must have sent him out this morning. He was scout."

Kon stopped and turned. Hari Kari and Old Overshoes halted. Katey and Pretty Pussey came up with their look-alike staring glassy eyes and overlipped mouths. The five of them glanced suspiciously from one to another.

"He didn't come in last night," Kon said, thin lipped.

"You heard the count," Hari Kari snapped.

"He wasn't in his hole," Kon said.

"But the count was right," Hari Kari said stubbornly. "What'd he do? Drop out and go back?"

"We all thought he was with us but he wasn't," Kon said. "The Ridge Runner must of sounded off twice. He must of hooked on with 1st and sounded off and then he answered when Henty called him by name."

"I don't get it," Hari Kari said. "If Injun Joe wasn't with us, where was he? What was he doing? How'd he get in our line of fire?"

"Henshit told him to bring in a prisoner," Old Overshoes said. He made the statement sound ugly.

"Henty didn't tell him to take no stupid chances," Kon said.

"Henshit changed the orders," Old Overshoes said loudly. "We weren't supposed to hang around pitching grenades. We were supposed to shoot off our second clips, lob in a couple and get the hell out. Injun Joe spotted the Jap and went after him when he thought we were through."

"Well Jesus!" Kon said defensively. "Joe heard those orders changed like we all did."

"He was already out there," Old Overshoes shouted.

"Why'd Henshit want a Jap, anyway?" Hari Kari asked uncertainly.

"Why isn't the point." Old Overshoes looked from one man to another, menacing. "The fact is Henshit killed the Indian sure as Snotty killed Domingo."

"Be reasonable," Hari Kari said irritably but his anger was gone and he was troubled.

"Well, it wasn't like he was anybody's buddy or was close to anyone," Kon said. "The Kachin said we got 79 of them and it only cost us one."

Hari Kari looked at Kon in sharp dismay.

Katey and Pretty Pussey didn't say a word but they looked searchingly at each other.

"He was a Marauder!" Old Overshoes raged. "He took his orders from Henshit. It could happen to any of us."

"Let's get on with it," Kon said wearily. He turned and trudged slump shouldered down the trail. "We ain't got all day," he added.

"They all were dismal and dejected, Hari Kari knew it, they all felt something was wrong and it gnawed at them. All except Old Overshoes: he seemed to get some overbearing, brutish satisfaction from the tragic blunder. Whose mistake: Henty's or Injun Joe's?

"Step along and look alive," Old Overshoes called and Hari Kari knew he was sneering without turning. "We got to get back and get our orders, see what Henshit fucks up today."

"He gets his orders from CP," Hari Kari muttered.

"They tell him what to do, not how to do it," Old Overshoes said, gloating and overriding. "The shit head just better not try naming me scout to take the Indian's place. I'll give the stinking little fart some of what he gave Snotty except I'll make it stick."

"Hold it down," Kon said, voice rising. He didn't even glance back.

Kon was in charge of this patrol, he ought to order Old Overshoes to the *tongyaw*. Someone ought to chop the bullying bastard down but they were afraid of him. Hari Kari was afraid of him. That's why he'd made friends with Old Overshoes.

Harry McCarthy, Number 201987, not his Army Serial Number but convict number at Eaststate Pen. Oh, he'd been drilled and was ready for the Army after five years of marching stiffly in rank three times a day to chow except on Sundays when you brought cold soggy buns back from breakfast for your second meal; marching silently every day except Sunday to and from the planing mill; marching tight-faced once a week to the movies, to the showers; marching, shoulders back, eyes straight forward, once a month to the barber shop.

No talking anywhere except in the cells before lights out, in the four-man cages with iron bunks that pulled down from the walls on chains like the ones that bound you. At least they had a four-man private toilet, a goddamned bare bowl without a seat that stuck out in the cubicle between the bunks, you gulped the smell of shit and stink of piss. That's what you were, shit and piss and exterminator. You, exterminated, there was no world. The light of day was always shadowy as if it were not there, filtered through steel-meshed, iron-barred windows in the gray stone walls.

Five damned years of a five-to-ten for breaking and entering, he'd enlisted the day after he was released and hadn't mentioned he was on parole. What the hell, they'd never find him in the Army and revenge could wait, it was sweeter for the savoring. It wasn't that he hadn't been guilty, he'd never denied he'd broken and entered and the charge could have been worse than it was. But he'd been engaged to Eileen, and that sweet little colleen with eyes as green as Ireland was a two timing tramp.

He'd seen them from the cozily lighted bar just off the shadowy dance floor at the Horseshoe Club, the blond pimpy looking punk in the white linen suit, white buckskin shoes, white tie and dark blue shirt, rubbing his belly against Eileen's and pawing up to her breast when they danced to *Stormy Weather*. She didn't mind.

Sure his brain exploded, senses smashed to smithereens in a hot red blast. Once a week he took her out, once a week he spent a buck on himself for beer, nursing the dollars from the $35-a-week he made as a reporter so he could buy the furniture she said she had to have before she'd marry him. So he'd slunk in the dark, tailed them to her one room place, clambered up the fire escape and ripped off the screen when the light went out, beat the shit out of the naked, shaking bastard while Eileen quietly got dressed, went out in the hall and called the law. He'd been slobbering on the edge of the bloodied bed and the punk had dressed and left and Eileen was in the hall, hysterical. She'd gouged her cheeks and scratched her arms and ripped the shoulder off her dress. A casual acquaintance, she told the cops he was, and charged him with breaking and entering. No, she wouldn't say rape ——it was too "embarrassing."

He knew Old Overshoes the day he joined the squad on New Georgia, not who he was, but what he was——a guard, a yard guard at that, at some Midwestern joint, a prowling gorilla with a club who pounced and beat his helpless victims senseless. Old Overshoes made him cringe and crawl inside so Old Overshoes and he were buddies and he tried to outdo the sadistic moron when it came to butchering Japs to keep him off his back.

They were good soldiers, he told himself, bitter and accusing.

At the edge of the valley where they'd halted the night before, Kon lifted a hand and drooped it over his head. Hari Kari closed the distance between them and Katey and Pretty Pussey moved in behind but Old Overshoes stood several paces off by himself, sneering.

"We'll disperse and police the area," Kon said without enthusiasm. "Katey, take the far side by the stream. Pussey, the opposite edge below the ridge. Keep your eyes peeled for snipers. We don't know how many got away or where they went. I'll go straight down the center. Hari Kari, you work between me and Katey." Now Kon looked directly at Old Overshoes and he lifted his voice. "Take my left, Overholt." He turned back to the others. "You come across anything big, ammo or rations, give a hand signal. I'll be watching. We'll blow it up together. Don't bother with anything except beer and wine. To hell with the rice, we got a drop coming and it's as bad as K rations. Don't take no chances, anything that moves, shoot it."

They fixed their bayonets and poked their separate ways into the camp area, prowling the confined valley at intervals of 30 to 40 yards. Kon had taken the good safe middle, Hari Kari thought sardonically and checked himself. It was the place where he could observe them all and he'd done something else. He didn't trust Old Overshoes and he'd separated each man from his buddy. The Pole wasn't altogether stupid.

It must have been a pleasant little place, this valley with its green floor and clean stream winding along one side. A snug place at night sheltered by the tight jungle and buttressed by the rock. But now it was an airless pocket under the blazing sun, a stinking dump filled with refuse. The bodies of the Japs were everywhere, festering with flies. For the first 100 yards, the Japs were entirely dead and mostly bits and pieces. Hari Kari prodded the ones that were intact, turning them over and moving on, stooping to claim a brown bottle of wine. It was funny, the bottles were squatty like the Japs. He didn't bother with beer. He could get that going back if he wasn't loaded.

He looked to his left. Old Overshoes had dropped behind. He was doing a more thorough job than the rest of them. Hari Kari watched with morbid fascination as Old Overshoes stalked five bodies clustered about the charred remains of a small fire and an arm bone. Old Overshoes poised, one knee bent in good form, lunged and lifted a corpse from the ground at the end of his rifle. He shook it off his bayonet, fell back a few paces and thrust at the next body.

Before plunging for the third, he looked up, saw Hari Kari watching and grinned.

"You're doing it by the book," Hari Kari called, hating himself for the acknowledgement, the fawning encouragement. "But you're messing up the follow through. Where's your butt stroke."

Old Overshoes laughed loudly, sounding pleased.

"Don't want to bother wiping the blood and pus off the stock," he shouted.

Old Overshoes might look a little rough but he really was a very tidy person.

Hari Kari pulled his attention back to his lane. When someone had to get it the way Injun Joe had, blown up by his own side, why couldn't it be Old Overshoes? Hell, it probably had been Old Overshoes who'd tossed the one that caught the Indian. If Injun Joe had been on his feet it must have been one of Old Overshoes' delayed pitches.

Ahead, Kon had stopped, was jerking his hand up and down and motioning toward the ridge side where Pretty Pussey was standing and circling the air above his helmet with his fist. Katey already was running the valley and Kon started off. Hari Kari jogged to the left and Old Overshoes waited until he came up. His face was flushed and he was breathing hard.

"Save your strength for the live ones," Hari Kari told him.

Old Overshoes sneered and trotted easily along. He was no more exhausted than if he'd just climbed out of bed with a babe. For him, sticking dead Japs was exhilarating exercise, a kind of lust or passion. Overshoes reached back and patted his pack.

"Picked up something special off an officer," he said. "It isn't beer or wine, some kind of whisky, I think, with a fancy label. I'll hold it out for us. Tonight we'll have a nip from a Nip, how's that?" He chortled noisily. "Just the two of us."

Me and my buddy, Hari Kari thought.

Pussey had stumbled on a little dump of small arms ammo, 15 or 20 wooden cases under a tarred canvas. They were stacked against an exposed face of grayish rock that slanted down from the ridge.

"What'll we do, explode it?" Pussey asked and danced a little jig.

Katey walked over and looked at him with proud eyes.

Kon was examining the pile. He seemed worried.

"We'll have to," he said slowly and pulled some deeper lines into his face. "But Christ! I ain't no demolition expert. There's enough stuff here to blow us all to hell."

"Why you fathead!" Old Overshoes said contemptuously, taking over. "Dump it in foxholes, a case at a time. Toss in a grenade. What doesn't go up is scattered."

Kon glared at him. If the suggestion had come from anyone else, he probably wouldn't have minded.

"Yeah." He was reluctant. "But we better find some foxholes for ourselves first."

"Find your foxholes, the rest of you," Old Overshoes blustered disdainfully. "Lug the stuff over, crawl in your holes and I'll blow it up."

Old Overshoes collected all the grenades. The others including Kon sweated with the cases, dumping them in holes and taking cover while Old Overshoes blew them up. Katey and Pretty Pussey found a cave of their own and Hari Kari shared a shallow trench with Kon. His pupils were small and angry and his lips were pressed together. Old Overshoes handled the demolition smoothly, efficiently, and with a swaggering bravado, falling only to the ground and scorning deeper shelter while the valley echoed with the blasts. The operation took a certain amount of courage, Hari Kari admitted. It was ordered and executed exactly as Kon should have handled it.

The patrol moved back out across the valley after Old

Overshoes blasted the last case of ammunition. Here, at the far end of the camp, there were the blackened remains of many small fires but fewer bodies. The Japs who'd been at a distance from the firing had evidently escaped into the jungle in the cover of the darkness. Hari Kari looked up from his lane. On opposite sides, Katey and Pretty Pussey were advancing cautiously, observing the trees that edged the clearing more intently than the ground. At the center, Kon was a few yards ahead of their ragged line. He paused to roll over the occasional body he encountered. To the left, Old Overshoes made a leap and a savage thrust with his bayonet at an obvious corpse. He rammed the knife into the body repeatedly. Hari Kari tasted acid in his throat.

He remembered the Indian at Deogarh. The man had been an almost naked skeleton, no flesh on his knotted bones. Old Overshoes and he had followed the ferret-eyed native down black and twisting alleys to his filthy, mud-walled hovel to buy a bottle of lousy whisky. They hadn't needed it. It was time to return to camp and Old Overshoes already was drunk enough to keep him mean for a week.

"Five rupees more, sahib," the Indian had wheedled, dull eyes gleaming in the yellow light of the lantern.

"You thieving bastard!" Old Overshoes had shouted in sodden fury, seizing a long handled, short bladed axe that leaned against the wall.

He cleaved the Indian's skull down to his spine, bent and grasped the 10 rupees he'd already paid from the dying man's clenched fist.

They ran blindly through the night until they reached the road.

"God," Hari Kari gasped, shaking uncontrollably. "You didn't need to kill him over five rupees."

"Fifteen rupees," Old Overshoes corrected and laughed harshly. "Best whisky we've ever had. It's free. And who's to know? You wouldn't say anything, now woul dyou, Harry?"

Of course he hadn't said anything, he thought bitterly; he'd been there with Old Overshoes and they'd have had his neck, too.

Off to his right, a shot cracked and Hari Kari dropped, bringing his M-1 to his shoulder. Katey was standing, waving his rifle in one hand and pointing to the ground.

"A *coup de grace! A coup de grace!*" he sang.

Hari Kari pushed himself back to his feet. Kon and Pussey had gone down at the report but Old Overshoes had prodded unconcernedly on. The bastard's lust for blood was insatiable.

Cautiously, Hari Kari probed ahead, approached a huddle. When he turned the body on its back, the almond eyes opened. They were stark with pain and fear. The Jap started drawing his hand toward his right side where the khaki was black with blood. Hari Kari aimed his rifle down at him and shot him in the head. The others turned briefly at the shot but continued on this time. Kon had moved ahead 10 or more yards. Thirty yards to Hari Kari's left, Old Overshoes was only a few yards in front.

As Hari Kari's rifle came up from the Jap on the ground, it was pointing at Old Overshoe's back. He held his weapon in a trance. Slowly, it snugged to his shoulder and Old Overshoes was in his sights. His finger tightened on the trigger. He began to shake and the end of the M-1 wobbled. He shook his head and blinked his misting eyes, glancing up.

Kon had stopped and was looking back at him, watching with a steady, expressionless stare. He made no move nor sound. Then the corners of his wide mouth lifted, the dirty bandage moved on his cheek and he closed his right eye in an unmistakable wink. He deliberately turned his back.

13

A D. SVENSEN, just the initials that meant only Ass Drag,
loomed beside Julie Chiruco, the bearded little Italian
in the sparse shade at the edge of the *tongyaw*. With them
were Nick the Greek and Furman. Their heads were tilted,
helmets biting into the backs of their necks and they were
squinting at the sky, watching the supply drops being kicked
from the circling C-47. The blue and green chutes were
puffing out at 400 or 500 feet and gently floating towards the
ground.

"Let's grab the first, wrap up the corpse and get on with
the war," Julie snarled between his teeth.

They all looked at the long trench just within the perimeter
of the foxholes where Injun Joe's rifle with his helmet and
dog tags already marked the head of the grave. Beside the
dark hole on Hill 307 in Burma, the body was stretched and
stiffening under a pile of soft green, lace-edged fronds.

"It was a shame," Ass Drag lilted, feeling a small frown
pull between his eyes. "And so needless, just like the other, the
Mexican."

"Man, I want *out*," Nick the Greek intoned, shivering and
licking his lips with his tongue. "What's the future?"

"He lost nothing but his chains," Furman said softly. Behind the thick glasses, his eyes were untroubled.

"What the hell kind of crap is that?" Julie yelled and his
dark eyes sparked. "He's dead, ain't he? I want to know why'd
Henshit shoot the Jap when Injun Joe was bringing him in for
questioning? Of all the stupid assed goddamned things to do!"

"He lost his temper when he saw the Indian's condition,"
Ass Drag suggested. He always seemed to be excusing people
to Julie. "He feels bad when he loses someone. We are a heavy
load to carry."

"Yeah?" Julie barked. "He'd better start thinking twice
about what he orders, then. What's been going on down in
that Jap camp this morning? Those ain't firecrackers we been
hearing. What I want to know is who's got it now?"

Furman smirked and shrugged.

"Henty said they were blowing up stores. He has been observing on the roof from time to time."

"I'll bet!" Julie cried shrilly. "I'll bet the cigarettes from my rations that don't all come in."

"Julie!" Ass Drag reprimanded sharply. "You must not talk like that. It is the same thing as willing it to happen."

"Not me, A.D., not me." Julie shook his head and his eyes flashed. "I ain't the one dealing the cards."

The baled supplies were bumping in the clearing, chutes crumpling, and with wary eyes on the ones still in the sky, 2nd and 3rd Squads were pouncing on them.

"Might as well take that one," Julie mumbled as a parachute collapsed nearby. He reached to his back for his knife and ran toward it.

"I'd watch him if I were you," Furman warned Ass Drag. "He's getting wound up too tightly. He'll snap."

Ass Drag lumbered after the short, intense Italian. He hadn't needed Furman's caution. He was worried about Julie. He was worried about all of them, except Furman and himself.

Julie was sawing at the shrouds and Ass Drag knelt to bunch the silk. Furman and Nick the Greek picked up the supply bundle and started with it for the *basha*.

"Why ain't the detail back if nothing's happened?" Julie demanded. "They know we're moving out right after the drop."

"They will be here soon," Ass Drag said with a confidence he didn't feel. "There has been no sound from the valley now for more than half an hour."

He gathered the cumbersome chute easily in his big arms and carried it to the body of the Indian. Carefully, he spread the silk in the clearing in front of the grave and folded it. Nick the Greek and Furman returned and stood to one side as Ass Drag wrapped the cloth about the body of Injun Joe and Julie tucked in the edges.

"Henty's coming down." Furman said.

"He'll have some excuse," Julie said grimly without looking up. "He'll never admit he was wrong."

Henty walked up to the head of the grave as Ass Drag and Julie dropped the body into it. They all turned to him, waiting for what he had to say. His eyes were icy and his sunken cheeks looked gray, as if all the atabrine had drained away.

"I don't know what kind of religion Injun Joe had or if he had any," he said. His voice was firm, even a little angry. "If I did, I still couldn't say the right words. But I can say this. There's a lot going on out here that doesn't seem to make much sense. Maybe some day a few of us will understand what it was all about and I don't know if that will be good or bad. Whatever Joe died for, he was doing what he thought was right. All I'm interested in is getting what's left of this outfit back and out without any more casualties. None of you have to prove how brave you are by being reckless. When you're finished the burial, pick up rations and ammo at the *basha* and we'll hit the trail."

"What about Kon's detail?" Julie asked sharply. "Ain't we waiting for them?"

"If they aren't back, we'll carry their supplies. We'll meet them on the path."

Henty swung on his heel and walked rapidly to the *basha* where the second and third squads already were lining up. Furman and Nick the Greek began to methodically spade the black earth over the enshrouded body of Injun Joe.

"He didn't try to make excuses now," Ass Drag said argumentatively to Julie.

"Maybe," Julie said, darting a fierce look at Henty's back. "He'll never get a chance to make excuses if he gives another bird-brained order like he did to Injun Joe."

Kon's detail did not return and the patrol filed the short distance through the jungle to the rimrock. The sky was beginning to haze, getting moist and hot again. Damn it all now, Ass Drag grumbled to himself, how long did it take to rain? The pounding at Nhpum Ga still was muffled but it sounded heavier, as if the Japs had moved in more artillery. What was the mission of the patrol now, mop up any Japs left over from last night? They surely wouldn't try to break through all the way with this little band.

The 2nd Squad was in the lead this morning, behind Meatball and Henty, and 1st was bringing up the rear. The radioman was by himself between 2nd and 3rd, trudging along and looking at nothing but his feet. He'd admitted answering twice to the count and Henty had chewed all the skin right off his ass.

They were advancing at a cautious pace along the exposed, narrow outcropping when the high-pitched sound of aircraft motors pierced the air.

"Hit the dirt!" Henty shouted and the patrol fell flat faced on the burning rock.

Three P-40's swooped in from the north and whistled overhead. They were sleek and silvery. They darted in a low circle just above the tree tops not far to the south and west with their cannons blazing. The Jap shelling stopped abruptly at the first pass and the P-40's blasted a 50-mm circle around the ridge where the 2nd Batallion was entrapped. As the fighters silenced the heavy guns of the enemy momentarily, first one and then two more Dakotas came in and hovered over Nhpum Ga. Drop chutes bloomed in the sky. It wasn't much, three P-40's and three C-47's with a supply drop but a hoarse cheer broke out from the patrol. Headquarters hadn't abandoned the 5307th yet.

When the drop was completed, the fighters made another circle of the ridge and screamed off after the Dakotas. The Jap artillery opened up again and the patrol got back on its feet. Still no sign of Kon and his detail. The patrol pushed on.

Ass Drag could see Henty every now and then as the crooked trail bent back in the sky. Henty was getting nervous, jumpy. He kept slowing the patrol to scan the way ahead, peer into the treetops on the slope. They were halfway to the path that led through the jungle to the valley.

Jesus, it would be a tragic thing if anything happened to that Pole now. Headquarters was giving them air support and they'd get out of this. They'd have to send them back because there wouldn't be enough Marauders left to fight the Japs. And once they got Kon into a hospital, he'd get a medical discharge.

All the men could talk about was going home. It was a sickness. When they thought about it too much they acted foolishly. Ass Drag hadn't cared much one way or other whether he ever got out of the Army until they paired him with Julie. The fiery little Italian made Ass Drag think of his youngest brother, Lars. He hadn't seen the boy since he'd left the farm 10 years ago now and he could tell from Julie that a boy needed an older man at his side. The farm had been terrible then with yellow clouds of dust burying the crops, choking the livestock, getting into people, eroding their insides while it etched their outsides stark.

There'd been Pa, his empty sack of life filling up with dust. The water wasn't fit to drink and he got to lugging home gallon jugs of moonshine from some farmer who'd found a way to beat the dust storms. And Ma with her brood, there were five of them, A.D. the oldest, 17 the day before it happened and Lars just five. They were snotty nosed and hungry, howling underfoot while Ma shoveled out the dirt and tried to cook up something to fill their aching empty bellies.

Pa came in, slamming the door behind him in a hurry to keep out a gritty gust of wind. He was staggering and his eyes red rimmed. He lurched for a cup on the big square kitchen table where they all sat hunched over their hunks of salt pork and potatoes boiled in their jackets. There was a jug in Pa's fist and he slopped out a drink in the cup.

Ma was a quiet one, never said much of anything, but this night she got a deadly light in her sky blue eyes and her tired voice rang out sharp.

"Emil, this has got to stop. You're spending money you haven't got on that terrible drink while your family starves."

Pa hung his head but not until he'd drunk what was in the cup and half filled it again.

"What am I to do?"

"You're going into town and find some kind of job, I don't care what, and you're going to stop your drinking."

"There's no use looking," Pa said thickly. "There is no kind of work at all."

"How would you know that?" Ma asked shrilly. "You've never tried. I won't put up with this another day. You leave that moonshine here now, go on to bed and sober up."

Pa shook his head hopelessly.

"It's no use, Ma. I don't know what will become of us."

"You've got no choice now," Ma cried. "We can't just sit here and starve to death. You've sold everything you have, your watch, the farm machinery, even my Sessions clock that was a wedding present. There's nothing left to sell for gasoline and moonshine except your shotgun and you can't sell that for the pheasants you might shoot and give us one decent meal."

Pa poured some more whisky in his cup and looked up. There was a little gleam in his pale eyes.

"That's right. I forgot the shotgun, I still have that. There won't be any pheasants here ever any more."

He stumbled to the closet off the kitchen where the milk separator had stood before the skinny cows were butchered.

"Oh Emil," Ma sobbed. "I should have kept my mouth shut. Now you'll sell that, too. At least this time buy some food before you drink it all up."

The kids straggled out, Lars round-eyed, crawled into the beds between cotton sheets that felt filled with sand. In the kitchen Ma nagged on, for how long A.D. didn't know. He was awakened by a blast and a scream and stumbled down the stairs. Ma was standing over Pa's body that was doubled sideways on the floor and tears were streaming down her gray cheeks. The shotgun was on the floor beside Pa and half his belly was torn away.

"I didn't mean to do it, Pa," Ma was moaning.

Pa died but before he did, A.D. dragged the doctor out to the farm and Pa told him he'd shot himself by accident, didn't know the gun was loaded. A.D. never mentioned to anyone what he'd heard his Ma cry out. When she'd collected the insurance, what hadn't been borrowed on, he'd had to leave, he couldn't stand living under the same roof with her. He'd worked in the cold room at the packing house in Omaha. Fifty cents an hour. He'd never seen Ma since, nor any of the kids, they were down on him, the way he'd taken off and never sent a dime. Kids needed their Pa or an older brother. He'd take care of Lars.

The patrol was coming up the ridge to the high place that overlooked the valley, where they'd seen the fires the night before. Meatball held up his hand and they crouched, waiting, getting tight. Old Overshoes came over the mound, saw them and tossed off a jaunty salute. His pack was full and looked heavy.

Ass Drag blew his breath in relief.

Pretty Pussey and Katey tagged after Old Overshoes, hump backed, so loaded they had to keep their thumbs in the pack straps and their eyes on the path. And then Kon shambling along with his burden.

Every man in the patrol was licking his chops and grinning.

Henty had walked up to Meatball, waiting for the scavengers.

Behind Ass Drag, Julie chattered:

"Booze, booze, you see that, A. D.? They're loaded down with beer and wine. They wouldn't bring back nothing stupid."

"You don't deserve any," Ass Drag tossed over his shoulder, "for the crazy things you said. You wanted to bet they wouldn't come back."

"Aw now, Ass Drag," Julie said and sniggered. "We all make mistakes."

The four men were bunched on the trail facing Henty and Meatball. Old Overshoes was waving his arms and it looked as if he and Henty were arguing. Ass Drag couldn't hear what they were saying and watched for Hari Kari. That crazy Irishman would have the biggest bundle of them all, he'd probably have Jap knapsacks hanging at his sides, he'd be pulling up the incline like a pack mule.

Hazed though it was, the sun was frying them on the hot rocks while Henty chewed away at Old Overshoes and the other three. Ass Drag swiped his sticky forehead under his helmet with the back of his hand and shifted his eyes between Henty and the knot of men and the top of the trail. Hari Kari still hadn't appeared.

Whatever they'd been talking about up there seemed to be settled. Meatball pushed beyond the four men of the detail and kept moving. Old Overshoes fell in behind with Katey and Pretty Pussey trailing along and then Kon. It was very strange. They should have exchanged their loads, distributed the beer and wine among the whole patrol, relieved the rest of 1st Squad of the double supplies they were carrying.

The patrol started off again and with the movement an angry report buzzed back through the ranks: *Hari Kari wasn't coming back!* Old Overshoes had killed him and they'd buried him down there in the valley with the Japs.

14

A HEAD of Henty on the narrow backbone of the rimrock, Kon tottered under his bulging pack. He was loaded beyond his strength. All of the men who'd been on the detail were gasping and clucking, lungs hungry for air, and their fatigues were black with sweat. Let the bastards suffer. They could lug a couple hundred bottles up from the valley but they'd left Hari Kari's body down there, lying with his enemy in death.

Henty's eyes were icy but inside his fury flamed. Losing men to the enemy was disheartening but when Marauders killed each other, it was tragic. Three men sacrificed from his squad, the best fighting men there were, and not one could be marked up against the Japs.

"Fall back a little," Henty said sharply to Kon. "Give it to me straight. I don't want any crap."

Kon didn't turn, stumbled on, and when he spoke his voice was labored.

"It's like they said. Hari Kari tried to shoot Overholt. In the back. He missed. Katey saw it. All of us heard the shot. Overholt swung and shot him in the chest. He was back there sticking that goddamned bayonet into him before the rest of us could move."

"But they were buddies," Henty said louder, voice raw with protest. "They boozed and brawled together. It must have been some kind of accident Hari Kari shot at Old Overshoes."

Kon paused a moment, caught his breath, shambled on before he answered, still without looking at Henty.

"I tried to make out like it was. I tried to stop Overholt. Maybe we could of saved Hari Kari. But Overholt was wild."

"There's something goddamned cockeyed about this," Henty said, angrier because he felt helpless. "I just can't believe Hari Kari would try to shoot his buddy. If he did, he wouldn't have missed."

"I told you, Katey saw him."

"How far off was Katey? He could have been mistaken."

"He wasn't," Kon mumbled. "I saw it, too."

"What!" Henty grabbed Kon's stuffed pack. Kon turned unsteadily. They stared silently at each other. Kon's face looked dead but his eyes were burning. "You saw it and didn't try to stop it? What the goddamned hell. You were in command."

"I couldn't of stopped it if I'd wanted," Kon said, snarling. "Hari Kari already had Overholt in his sights. His rifle was shaking but I thought he'd get him. I didn't much give a damn, in fact I hoped he would. Overholt is a bastard."

Behind, Henty heard Double Ugly's feet kick stones.

"Shove off," Henty snapped. "Keep your voice down. Why didn't you pull Overshoes off Hari Kari when he struck him?"

"I told you," Kon muttered, swaying into motion. "I tried but he pushed me off like I was a bag of popcorn. Anyway, Katey and Pussey were as crazy as Overholt. They said anybody who'd try to kill his buddy was worse than a Jap. They wouldn't even lug Hari Kari's body out of that stinking Jap graveyard. Just shoved him in a foxhole where he fell."

"That was just an excuse," Henty growled. "All those two bitches wanted was their beer and wine. They were afraid they might have to leave it if you brought the body out. What made Hari Kari turn on Old Overshoes? They hit it off right from the day Old Overshoes joined the outfit."

Kon walked silently beyond the high place that overlooked the valley. He did not glance down.

"Hari Kari looked like he was in shock," he finally said. He was panting and the words were coming harder. "There'd been a argument. About Injun Joe getting blowed up. Overholt blamed you for it. You watch that prick. He's got it in for you. He was riding all of us. Even Hari Kari. Overholt kept crowing and rubbing it in. Hari Kari just got his craw full and come apart. The way things are, it don't take much. Not much of a push to shove these guys off the deep end."

"Christ!" Henty said furiously. "It's not enough I got to worry about the Japs. Now I got to baby-sit a bunch of psychos. Keep your trap shut about that. About Hari Kari going off his rocker. I'll have to cover up somehow. I can't have this outfit wondering who's going nuts next and taking pot shots at them."

"Yeah," Kon grunted. "You won't forget that letter to my Pa, will you?"

"Shut up about that too, you shithead. I'll watch out for you."

Henty trudged on in vapored, gloomy silence. What in hell was the matter with Headquarters, and that meant only The Boss Stilwell, no one else not even his staff had a word to say about this show—keeping men in combat until they lost their minds. Could there have been some truth in that rumor, that the Marauders had been written off with an expectancy of 85 percent casualties? The idea was too savage and brutal to think about but he did. They'd sat there in Washington worse than any butchers in the Japanese High Command and decided 2,600 slaughtered GI's was the price they'd pay to make Stilwell's Chinese divisions look good.

Take the mission with this patrol, what sense did it make? What chance did they have? He could understand the original orders: Determine enemy positions, contact enemy patrols, relieve the pressure on Hsamshingyang. But penetrate to Nhpum Ga? A patrol? Through enemy artillery?

Well; shit.

Half a mile beyond the path to the valley, the spiney ridge began to reach around to the east. Meatball led the patrol off the rock that burned through the thin soles of their shoes, down twisting setbacks on the western side into a small green pocket between the ridge and a thinly wooded slope. A clear stream rippled between clumped bamboo and there was some shelter from the sun although no breeze stirred the hot dead air.

Henty called a halt. The men staggered into shade and dropped.

"We'll take a break, fill our canteens," he said. "Katey, Pussey, drop your packs and get on top of that next hill with Meatball. Signal if it's clear ahead. I'll relieve you after 10. Overholt, leave your pack and stand guard back on top of that ridge we just came down."

Katey and Pretty Pussey blinked their glassy eyes but shrugged unprotesting from their loads and trailed after Meatball. Old Overshoes didn't remove his pack. He took three paces and hung his big shoulders above Henty. His yellow cast eyes were glaring. He tossed his M-1 to his left hand and clenched his right fist tight.

"Up yours, Henshit," he said.

The next moment, Henty had rammed his .45 in Old Overshoes' gut and he was doubled over and coughing.

Old Overshoes stepped back, straightening, and Henty held the .45 with the safety off steady just above Overholt's web belt. He didn't say a word but his teeth were clenched and bared and he felt murder in his heart.

For a tight second their eyes were locked and then Old Overshoes snarled like a treed bobcat, pulled off his pack and slunk away.

"Jesus," Kon gasped. "He'll kill you."

"Take off your pack and put it with the others," Henty ordered and looked around at the grim, tired faces of the watching men. Some were friendly, some were hostile. Slowly, coldly he spoke: "Hari Kari, one of my riflemen, found a bottle of liquor down there in the Jap camp. He drank it and got drunk. He thought his buddy, Overholt, was a Jap coming for him and shot at him. Overholt killed him in self defense. There won't be any more of that. We're going to pile all these bottles in the stream and leave them after I've checked to see there isn't any more booze."

"Hey!"

"Chickenshit!"

"No!"

Some of the angry men were getting to their feet.

"At ease!" Henty shouted, swinging. His .45 still was in his hand. "Double Ugly. Butcher. Take a couple of men and stash the beer and wine. When the sun is washed off the beer, we'll have a ration. One bottle to a man. When we come back we'll split the rest of the stuff." He glanced up the slope. Meatball, Katey and Pretty Pussey were prone at the top and Meatball signaled. "All right, it's clear. Smoke if you've got them."

He carried one pack downstream beyond the patrol and Double Ugly and the Butcher followed with their two men. Henty sorted through the bottles while the others built two rock adged basins and stored them. When all of the bottles— almost 200 shining, gleaming, tempting bottles of beer and wine—were stacked in the stream, he sent the two men back with the packs and sat with Double Ugly and the Butcher in a sandy circle of mottled shade. They lit cigarettes and stared at the beer and wine.

"Better not," Henty said. "They'll be expecting us to have one and watching for it. What's it like in your squads, the morale, I mean."

Double Ugly loosened his helmet strap and massaged his face with both hands.

"Up and down like a yo yo," he said. "The smallest damn thing sets them off either way. They're high now because you promised some beer. Not this ration. The cold one coming back. That's all they want to hear, that they're coming back." He looked suspiciously at Henty. "That right, what you said about your rifleman, getting drunk and thinking his buddy was a Jap?"

"It's what they tell me, I wasn't there," he said irritably. "I suppose I'll have to report the Japs got both him and Injun Joe. It'll save explaining."

Under mounded brows, Double Ugly's pig eyes studied him.

"You've changed since the rest of us wanted to do in Snotty," he said.

"Well goddamnit, what do you want me to do, throw Overholt to the wolves?" Henty dragged hard at his cigarette and added glumly: "We need every man we've got and Overholt's a killer." He turned. "Butcher, what shape your squad in?"

"Nothing wrong a year at home wouldn't fix," the Butcher said. His old face was jerking. "Or even 30 days in India and a pat on the back from vinegar puss. If he's such sharp Army why didn't he perk them up with a couple tin badges? They don't cost him nothing." He spit and his nervous eye winked. "Your boys getting out of hand?"

"They're edgy." Henty admitted. "Three killed in a row the last couple days and all of them stupid mistakes. They're beginning to think the squad is jinxed."

"Keep losing them like that and they'll make you an officer," Double Ugly said and laughed nastily.

Henty's eyes jerked angrily but the dirty laugh hadn't been for him.

Double Ugly went on: "The only thing that counts is the overall, the Big Plan. You don't win a battle saving lives. The

140

more you can forget they're men, just think of them as so many weapons to take a position, the better officer you are. Take your objective regardless of the cost, in fact the more casualties the better, and you're a hero. They say, now that's the kind of officer we need. He can see the overall. He doesn't get involved with his men, doesn't let little things like people, their lives and kids and folks warp his military judgment. That's the kind of a mechanical mind it takes to win this game we're playing." He took a breath, shook his head. "Shit, it's getting to me, too. I'm a noncom. I'm not supposed to think. They give you any idea what's going on at Nhpum Ga when you called in this morning?"

They all listened. It was still there, the constant far-off muttering threat. They'd have missed it if it had stopped. It was their goal, the end of the road.

"They call it Maggot Ridge now. The slopes on all sides are covered with horses and mules, dead and dying, their bellies bloated and crawling. They couldn't take them into the perimeter and the Japs killed them or they died of thirst. They stink so foul you can't breath the air. They've had about 100 casualties and the Aid Station is right there on top in the perimeter. They were out of water, nothing but what was in the mudholes. Half that drop we saw this morning was water in plastic bags. The Japs are pounding them steady from all sides and all they can do is lie there in foxholes and take it."

"Christ, what a fuckup," the Butcher said. His voice jerked, like his face.

"So what gives now?" Double Ugly asked.

"I don't know," Henty said. He felt a thousand years old. "Maybe if we worm our way through, they'll try to reinforce us by the same route. Maybe they just want to see how much attention the Japs give us. Let's hand out the beer."

Even for the beer, the patrol lined up listlessly, filling canteens at the same time—why make two trips when one would do? Ass Drag and Julie came by. The big Swede's forehead was worried and lines were plowed from his nose to the corners of his mouth. The Italian's eyes blazed. Julie acted like he had a chip on his shoulder. Henty wondered what was eating him.

"A.D., you and Julie take your bottles and go up and

141

relieve Katey and Pussey," he told Ass Drag. "Take along a bottle for Meatball."

Ass Drag nodded, started off with the bottle of beer. Julie stopped in front of Henty.

"Just like a goddam picnic, ain't it, Boss?" he said and lifted his mustache enough to show his fangs. "Only we don't know who's going to get screwed."

"Julie!" Ass Drag called sharply.

The Italian snarled and walked in Ass Drag's direction, slouching defiantly.

Henty gripped his flaring temper so tightly it seared his fists.

Nick the Greek moved up with Furman. Nick managed a twisted smile. Furman looked untroubled, as satisfied as usual with himself, Jesus, that lips-pressed, quirk-mouthed smile was irritating, like Furman knew something the rest of them didn't. Henty sent Nick up to take over from Old Overshoes, lifted a bottle from the stream for himself and sat with Furman on the hard dirt in some sparse shade.

"Where's Kon?" he asked.

"In the bushes relieving himself," Furman said, turning his magnified eyes benignly on Henty. He held up his bottle and nodded at it. "The beer will probably kill him, you know."

"He'll be more comfortable with the drizzlies than tearing himself raw for nothing," Henty said grumpily. "What's with you, Furman? No matter what happens, you moon around with a half-assed grin like you were pleased."

"Generally speaking, I am," Furman said. "This is a satisfying experience."

"Now what the goddamned hell you mean by that?" Henty exploded. "You some kind of a fanatic nut or something?"

"Oh I don't think so," Furman said, smooth and oily. "There are a number of us who are pleased to see four colossal imperialist nations, the United Staes, England, Germany and Japan exhausting their resources and manpower in a gigantic struggle that will defeat them all. This is a war that dooms capitalism. The people of the world will emerge victorious."

"Jesus!" Henty said disgustedly. "So you're one of them, a goddamned Commie."

"My sympathies are with our respected allies," Furman said complacently.

"I don't trust your goddamned Russki friends," Henty said angrily, "but they aren't exactly coming out of this without losing a few men and cities."

"The war is a blessing to Russia," Furman said. "The Soviet Union's resources including manpower are vast. As a result of this war, industrialization will be advanced 100 years and Russia will take its proper place among the nations. In the years to follow, its sphere of influence will be global. And do not forget our other allies and neighbors to the north. Why do you think Chiang Kai-shek and his war lords refuse to commit their armies to the battle? Chiang fears not the Japanese but the hundreds of millions of oppressed who are gathering strength under the leadership of Mao Tse-tung. The people of China will arise and free themselves of the chains that have bound them through the centuries. And in each of the countries where the fighting rages now, in Burma, India, throughout Asia, the Middle East and, yes, Europe, the final victory will go to the people. It is a magnificent moment in history and one I had not dared hope would come in my time."

"Furman, regardless of what you think, how can you see men suffer and die and say it's good?"

"The individual is minuscule," Furman said calmly. "Some must be sacrificed for the collective good. The people will destroy the wealthy and powerful who have exploited them and kept them in poverty and ignorance. The riches will be distributed, the land returned to the people from whom it was stolen. The State will provide and all will share."

"Furman, some people substitute education for thinking and they're the most dangerous people in the world. What you're doing is repeating a lot of theories that you've read without letting them go through your mind. No two men ever were created equal. There always will be the weak and the strong. One will follow where the other leads. The state can provide some things like education but it cannot legislate the law of nature which gives one man more ability than another. In whatever kind of society you have, some men will rise to the top and some will stay at the bottom. The more people have the more they want and that's something else you can't change. Even in Russia, you'll find that a few will end up with much and that the people, as you like to call them, will have little. I don't give a goddamn what name you call it by—Capitalism,

Imperialism, Democracy, Socialism, Communism—the result is always the same!"

He stood and Furman watched him with eyes that were feeling sorry for him.

"You can knock off that superior crap," he snapped. "All you are is a goddamned patsy."

He strode away and Kon came out of the brush.

"Pick up your pack and supplies," he told him irritably. "The rest of the squad's been carrying double."

He saw Old Overshoes scrambling down the setbacks from the ridge, turned his back to him and crossed the shallow but clear and fast running stream, climbing through the trees to the forward guard. He sent Ass Drag and Julie back and lay on the ground beside Meatball. The Jinghpaw rolled on his side and started to smile but his eyes got worried when he looked at Henty.

"You are troubled, Dua," he said.

Henty did not answer right away. He closed his eyes to the warm grayed sky, let the hard earth bake through his hot fatigues, filled his lungs with the heavy air, tasted the fertile promise of Burma.

"When the fighting is finished, what will you do, Meatball?" he finally asked.

"I shall find a woman, build a *basha*, clear my *tongyaw*, raise some rice and a family and hunt and fish," he said promptly.

"But would it not be better if many of you labored together in the paddies, all of you hunted and fished together and shared among you what you produced?"

Meatball looked puzzled.

"It would not work, Dua," he said simply. "It would be then that on certain days I must labor with the others in the paddies and on certain other days go out to hunt or fish with them. It is not every day I wish to labor or to hunt. There are times I wish to be alone with the spirits that surround me. There is also another thing I would not like. Some men work harder and hunt better than others. Such an arrangement as you suggest would take the sweetest fruits of my efforts from me. We will share a portion of our food and shelter with those who hunger and need but this must be because we wish to do it, not because it is ordered so. We also must be free to come and go as we wish. Would you have us share our women and our children?"

Henty sat up, laughing.

"I would not have you change from what you are. In war and peace, my brother, I march at your side. Let us advance once more against our enemy."

He signaled and the patrol, strung out and lethargic, straggled up the hillside. The men were dulled by the beer, fuzzy with the heat, limp with exhaustion and weak with near starvation.

"I'll send someone to back you up," he told Meatball and sent him ahead on the trail.

Double Ugly led his haggard 2nd Squad over the hill and then the Ridge Runner walked by, alone. He didn't look at Henty. The Butcher had 3rd in tow. Henty didn't like his squad leaders out in front but he needed them ahead of the men to set the pace and bolster the sagging spirits. Kon, leading 1st, was weaving, as if he were plowing through loose sand.

"Fall out," he told him.

Kon stood beside Henty, drooping. Ass Drag and Julie filed by. Again, the challenging gleam in the Italian's eye.

"Overholt!" Henty said coldly. "Double time to the lead and back up Meatball."

Old Overshoes let the hate show raw in his eyes but he clenched his teeth and jogged up the line.

Nick the Greek winked.

"Furman," Henty ordered. "Take the lead of what's left in the 1st and don't drag your ass."

Kon looked questioningly at Henty.

"Go on back to Hsamshingyang," Henty told him. "Report to the Aid Station."

Kon's lips trembled. He made an effort and pulled them together.

"I can make it," he faltered. "Jesus, Henty, don't send me back."

Maybe it was courage, maybe Kon really didn't want to leave the patrol. Maybe it was fear of the long trail back alone.

"All right," Henty said and reached back into his pack. He pulled out a bottle and handed it to Kon. "Take a couple swallows. It may help."

"What is it?" Kon asked, looking at the ornate label.

"Some kind of Jap brandy. Overholt had it in his pack. It's been opened."

Kon giggled, pulled out the cork, sipped several times.

"Christ, Henty," he said, wiping his mouth .with the back of his hand and returning the bottle. "If you hadn't done nothing else but this, lift his booze, Overholt would murder you. I ain't bird turding. Keep your eyes peeled. He's going to get you first chance he has."

"Sure," Henty agreed. "Now let's join our army. Think you can step it up a little?"

"That stuff put springs in my heels. Lead off."

"You go ahead."

"Okay." Kon walked more steadily, rapidly than he had all morning. "Where?"

"Up in front, behind Overholt. I'm going to keep my eyes on both of you."

Henty looked searchingly at the men as Kon and he overtook them. Their jaws were set against the pain that stabbed their backs, burned their muscles, gnawed their bones. Their eyes were staring but vacant, aware only of the next few feet of the trail ahead.

Kon fell in behind Overholt. He didn't turn his head. Henty trailed Kon by a few paces. The path was narrow and twisting. It dipped and curled into a bamboo jungle where the insects droned and the air was as thick and wet as a hot water soaked sponge. The sweat crawled over Henty's spine and ribs like bugs and his lungs pumped. Kon tripped. Overholt stopped. Meatball was crouched at an elbow in the trail and his arm was raised with his palm out. Henty motioned the patrol down. They crouched or sank or fell. He started toward Meatball, glancing back. Kon had Overholt covered with his M-1.

"Soon we should make contact with the enemy," Meatball said quietly.

Henty felt the familiar fingers clutching at his diaphragm, the curious elation, the coiling spring of his reflexes tightening.

Together they crept down an aisle off the elbow in the path. One hundred yards ahead, the jungle ended and he could see the day seeping into the dense green and yellow foliage. Beyond a clear space, the earth appeared to loom in a dark rise.

They lay on their bellies and wriggled through the trees

until they looked across the clearing. After 20 or 30 yards of tangled spiney brush, a red dome of clay thrust its barren hump some 40 or 50 yards above the tops of the tallest trees. It looked like a bowl turned upside down. It was knobbed with dirt mounds but halfway to the rounded top, a regular ring of lumps circled the strange bare hill. The dirt that formed these warts was dark, as if it had recently been displaced and the sun had not yet dried it out. There were eight of these positions. At the top, Henty could see no indication of embankments. If there was a perimeter up there, it was beyond his line of sight.

"Foxholes or machine gun emplacements," he murmured, returning to the eight positions. "Christ, I wish we had a couple mortars. They've got a damned fortress here and we don't know what's on top or the other side. A frontal attack would be suicide."

Henty signaled Meatball into the jungle. They backtracked prone beyond the elbow. Henty walked to Overholt.

"Crawl up there to the edge of the trees and watch. The Japs are dug in on a hill. Don't fire no matter what you do. If you see anything, come back on your belly."

"You sonofabitch," Overholt hissed. He started to fix his bayonet and Henty knocked it from his hand.

"Stupid bastard," he said. "It isn't blackened. Let them get a gleam of that in the sun and we've had it."

Overholt scooped the knife from the ground and gripped it, glaring at Henty. Then he replaced it in its scabbard and dragged his body forward with his elbows. Henty left Kon at the bend in the trail where he could watch both Old Overshoes and the patrol. He squatted with Meatball just off the trail with his back in the bamboo and called up Double Ugly and Butcher.

He grinned bleakly.

"They learned their lesson last night in the valley," he said. "They've got us blocked now unless we can pull one out of the hat. And I think we can. It's goddamned funny they never catch on to our tactics. We're going to pull a double reverse end run."

He picked up a branch and scratched a diagram of the dome with its emplacements in the baked earth.

"Double Ugly, you and Butcher cut off from the trail here at the elbow and work your way through the jungle south and north. Double Ugly, take 2nd Squad plus Katey and Pretty Pussey from the 1st, flank to the south and around until you're in position to cover the two far emplacements. Got it?"

He drew lines from the jungle reaching up to the positions he'd indicated.

Double Ugly nodded silently.

"Butcher, take the two far north emplacements, through the jungle like Double Ugly. I'm keeping the Ridge Runner so that leaves you an 11-man squad. Take three riflemen from 1st, Old Overshoes, Nick the Greek and Furman. Okay?"

Butcher bobbed his head, mouth working.

"Now then, both of you work those emplacements over with your BAR's and tommy guns. Give your riflemen cover to get in with grenades. I'll take my BAR-man and ammo bearer from 1st. Ass Drag can lay down enough fire to cover the two frontal positions. Meatball can cover the one to the south of them and I'll take the one to the north. I'll use Kon and the Ridge Runner each between two emplacements. Meatball and I will try to get in and give them an assist. Check so far?"

"Check," Double Ugly said.

"Yeah," Butcher said.

"We don't know what we're going to run into on the top or how many there are of them and we don't have time to scout." Henty glanced from Double Ugly to Butcher. They were good men. They knew what to do. "Flank around and to the rear when you've taken your positions. If you've got any ideas or questions, hold them until I explain to Meatball. He might have some suggestions."

Double Ugly and Butcher bent over the sketch Henty had made while he repeated the plan and instructions in Jinghpaw. Meatball glanced at the diagram in the dirt from time to time.

"The plan is well conceived, Dua," he said and his eyes sparkled. "But warn your men to blow up the emplacements and not to occupy them however much they may need shelter. They are sometimes set as traps even after the men in them are dead."

Henty translated, adding: "Anything else? Questions? Ideas?"

"We start up the hill together?" Double Ugly asked.

"Yeah." Henty glanced at his watch. "We'll co-ordinate at

11:36. I'll say when." He paused, eyes on his sweep second hand. "Now."

They snapped their stems together.

"Thirty minutes to reach your positions," Henty said. "It will be tight but don't hack, slip through somehow. At 12:06 start moving up. Hold your fire until you're fired on. Even if they open up on some of the rest of us, wait until you're discovered, get up as close as you can. Take this one, we'll dig in for the rest of the day and I'll send back for the wine and beer."

"Yeah," Butcher said sarcastically and Double Ugly snorted.

Henty showed his teeth and shrugged.

"I'll do what I can. Butcher, send the Ridge Runner, Ass Drag and Julie up to me and tell Katey and Pretty Pussey to report to Double Ugly. I'll send Old Overshoes to you to go with Nick and Furman. Now beat it."

Henty left Kon at the turn and crawled with Meatball to Overholt. He was prone, studying the claybank with something like awe. Henty motioned him back and Meatball remained to observe. Beyond Kon, Henty stood and faced Overholt.

"Report to Butcher in 3rd," he ordered.

"What's the matter, Henshit, I make you nervous?" he asked, sneering, and saw the neck of the bottle pushed out of the flap in Henty's pack. His hand snaked toward the bottle and he snarled: "You thieving bastard."

Henty whipped the .45 to the side of Overholt's face, raking the jaw and drawing blood. Overholt's face drained pale and he trembled with rage. Henty swiveled on his heel and disdainfully walked away. He grinned. Kon had his M-1 to his shoulder and again it was aimed at Overholt.

There was the sound of motion on the path and Kon let the rifle drop slowly. His hands began to shake. Henty handed him the bottle. Kon gulped this time. Henty secured the brandy out of sight far down in his pack.

"Jesus, oh Jesus, Henty," Kon moaned. "You ain't got no sense at all."

Henty cleared his throat and spit dry cotton on the ground.

"The bastard's as yellow as a Jap."

"It don't mean a shit," Kon said. "You push even a rat into a corner, he'll fight when he's got no other place to go."

The Ridge Runner, then Ass Drag and Julie edged up the

149

trail and squatted with Kon and Henty. The Ridge Runner was red-necked sullen. The big Swede's faded eyes were washed with trouble and Julie's were sizzling.

"For chrissake, all of you, stop acting like you puked in your beer," Henty said hotly. Then he laughed at them and explained the attack in detail. When he had finished, he looked at his watch. "You've got 20 minutes. Get some rest. I'll wake you at 12 and we'll move up with the Meatball."

At 12:06, Henty flung his hand over his head and started scraping through the thorny undergrowth toward the bare earth of the hills. The dome seared its livid scar upon his mind. The edges of the sky were chalky but the sun burned through a ragged hole. Felt hammers at Nhpum Ga thumped on cottony quiet in another world. He wanted to shout and break the silence that plugged his ears.

He started up the hill. The hard red clay was hot and his slithering elbows raised an unseen film of dust that prickled in his nose. He could see his own men moving with him. North and south he searched for the slivered movement his mind suspected but eye could not detect as red earth stained fatigues merged with lumped red earth. The camouflage was perfect. The cloying smell of fear crept down the hill. He rooted where he was. The smell came from him, reeked from Snotty's sweat soaked fatigues and they were new and green.

He lay motionless, fertile growth on the bare red desert, and waited to be shot.

But when the firing started, it was to his right where 3rd Squad was deployed. The Nambus clacked like castanets. Then sharp angry counterpoint, a paradiddle from a tommy gun and deep overtones from a drumming BAR. The cacophony of M-1 fire broke the rhythm.

To his left, the 2nd echoed the clatter.

He ripped his furrowed body from the earth and plowed ahead.

Now the four Nambus in the frontal positions spat down the slope. A row of tenuous dust plants grew in the arid dirt a few feet in front of his eyes where the machine guns planted their seed. He hurled back a handful of slugs. Another. And all around the hill the cackling was the same.

The Nambus kept up their steady, ineffectual sounding

chatter. The men were throwing grenades now but from cramped positions on the ground and they were falling short.

Henty slammed another clip into his tommy gun glancing north and south. They hadn't advanced on the flanks, hadn't knocked out one emplacement.

He got off another burst at the position straight uphill and was slammed into the ground. Dirt pelted his body and hailed on his helmet. Roaring craters were erupting on the hill below the Nambus. The Japs had mortars on the top!

Through the drifting cloudbanks of powdered earth, he saw Julie's twisted face and motioned him back. They had to withdraw to the fragile thatched roof shelter of the jungle.

Julie and Ass Drag skidded down a foot at a time maintaining steady fire. The mortar shells kept showering them with a gritty pall but the eruptions curtained their retreat. Julie and Ass Drag, the Ridge Runner and Kon and then Meatball met him inside the jungle. They were grimed and gasping but each in one piece. The mortar shells kept reaching for them, burrowing into the earth and shattering the trees. They broke and ran down the trail, back beyond the bend, they'd have that marked.

The fireworks except for an occasional hollow blast were fizzling out. Dig up the bottle, these men needed it, there wasn't enough for everyone. Each took a mouthful, didn't talk, huddled into the bamboo and hoped he would be safe. Henty pitched the empty off into the trees.

They had come to the end of the trail. This was no Jap patrol, it was company strength at least.

The other two squads hauled their dragging asses in. They all were safe. Jesus, it was a miracle.

Henty clapped Meatball's shoulder, motioned Kon, the Ridge Runner, Ass Drag and Julie, pointed the trail back to Double Ugly and the Butcher.

"Cold beer." He tried to grin.

The men didn't talk and they didn't walk. They bit their caked lips and moved their feet without lifting them from the ground.

Ahead, not far, perhaps a thousand yards, a jarring explosion uprooted trees and sent them crashing. Each man stopped dead in his tracks. That was not a mortar shell.

Another blast. Closer this time. Henty could hear the splintered bamboo and shrapnel raining on the fronds all about him. It was not coming from the hill behind. No shell had whined overhead.

Julie broke, screamed first, but he was not alone.

"Howitzers!" he shrilled. "We're trapped. They got us in a pocket."

15

THE harried patrol scurried for cover leaving Henty and Meatball alone on the trail. Henty watched the men plunging into the bamboo; the poor, frantic bastards, they thought they'd be safe if they could hide from the shells that were marching through the jungle.

Meatball sat beside the path and looked at Henty. The Jinghpaw's smooth brown face was placid and he waited calmly. Henty's legs were spread and he listened intently, calculating as another explosion rocked the ground and tossed a chunk of Burma skyward. Dirt and bamboo fragments splattered on the thin green ceiling that roofed the men and there were cries of outraged helplessness. This shell had struck within 500 yards and near the trail.

"Ridge Runner!" Henty bellowed, stepping just off the path beside a bamboo clump near Meatball. "Runner! Damn your hide. Get your ass out here."

Bamboo stems rattled and the Runner's face poked out at Henty's knees. It was white and twitching.

"Get Command," he said harshly. "There's something cockeyed. The Japs don't have anything back there. They'd have used it on Hsamshingyang."

The antenna quivered as the Runner shook it up and began working for his contact.

Henty repeated what he'd said in Jinghpaw and Meatball nodded.

Then Captain Gold's voice scratched in the receiver. It was excited.

"Henshit here. What the hell is going on? Lancelot's getting heavy stuff and it looks like Arthur's throwing it. Over."

"Pack howitzers." Captain Gold's voice was exultant. "Merrill sent them down. They were dropped this morning. We're zeroing in. Over."

"Hold your fire, Arthur. Repeat. Urgent you hold fire. Waiting. Over."

"Roger. Hold."

Another shell smashed but this one was some distance to the south. Henty felt a small jolt in his legs but no debris reached the path.

"Double Ugly! Butcher!" Henty shouted. "Get the patrol back on the trail. We got support."

He looked at Meatball and grinned. The Jinghpaw smiled back.

The receiver squawked.

"You there, Henshit?"

"Roger, Arthur. You damn near tore into Lancelot. Look, we can do business. We ran into company and I think about that strength. They're solid on a hill with a perimeter of Nambus and they've got mortars up on top. They just pinned our ears back but if you can shake them up a little, we'll go back and have another try. The azimuth on your third shell was about right but your range was about 1,500 yards short. Hold it until I call you back and I'll walk you in. Over."

"Hang on a minute, Henshit."

The men were untangling themselves from the jungle but they were leaving it reluctantly and clinging to the trees at the edges of the path. They shaped up in ragged squads facing in the direction of Hsamshingyang.

"About face!" Henty yelled.

The men looked puzzled at first and then rebellious. Double Ugly and the Butcher snapped at their heels and herded them about.

The radio cackled.

"We can let you have six, Henshit. Over."

"Jesus, Arthur. Don't hold us down. Maybe you're off target, we might need a dozen. Back me up. Over."

"Sorry, Henshit. What we've got are spoken for. Six is it. Over."

"Goddamnit, Arthur," Henty seethed. "We're on the ground. We can direct your fire. We can take a company off Maggot. Over."

"Is it artillery? Over."

"How the hell should I know? Christ! No, I guess it isn't artillery but it's strength. Over."

"All right, Henshit," Captain Gold said briskly. "Take what you're offered. You're not in the overall. Are you ready for six? Over."

"Oh shit!" Henty fumed. "Throw in six, same azimuth as the third but raise your range another 1,500 yards. We'll see if they do anything. Over."

"Are you in contact now to direct us? Over."

"No, we just pulled off. Over."

"We'll hold until you're back on target. Call in when you're ready and we'll give you one. Call back corrections. You get five more. That's it. Do what you can and report results. Over and out."

Henty looked helplessly at the Ridge Runner. He'd already broken contact and was pushing down the antenna.

They had it all worked out on paper, by the book, back there at CP where they couldn't see one damned thing that they were doing. They'd scatter their shells like birdshot, rip aimless holes in the jungle prodding for dug-in, hidden artillery when a patrol had a chance to overrun a company. But they weren't in the overall. Christ, the way CP talked, the patrol already was written off.

The Ridge Runner stood resignedly at Henty's side and adjusted the straps for his radio pack.

"Reckon y'all want me at yo tail."

"That's right." Henty smiled tightly. "What's the matter, don't you want to be a hero?" He called: "Double Ugly, Butcher."

"Shee-yut. Ah'd druther be a houn' dawg."

The Butcher's left eye was winking as regularly as a clock tick. Double Ugly's mouth was open and he was breathing through the hole. Meatball stood, rolling his shoulders and grinning.

"We got pack howitzers at CP," Henty told them. "They're going to give us six on that hill. If they lay them in, we'll go up. Move just like before, same men, same positions. After the sixth shell, you're on your own depending on what they knock out. Take the top if you can. If you see they're still too strong, pull out and rendezvous where we did before."

He repeated the instructions in Jinghpaw for Meatball.

"The men are pretty beat," Butcher muttered doubtfully.

"Christ, I know it!" Henty shouted angrily. "They'll get the lead out when the Japs open on them. Now tear ass into position. You got 10 minutes this time. I'll call for the first shell at 13:17. When the sixth hits, attack if you can. That's all."

155

He was being curt and irrational and he knew it. The patrol split and walked back toward the elbow in three parties. They were sulky and grumbling. Butcher and Double Ugly were pissed off and made no effort to hold the men down. Good. Let them all bitch. They'd take it out on the Japs.

Henty waited in the hot, still, dust-laden air at the elbow in the trail with Meatball, the Ridge Runner, Kon, Ass Drag and Julie. The Italian's eyes were getitng wild-looking with a lot of white showing around the dark iris and he was mutinously silent. One by one, each of the men was reaching his breaking or boiling point.

When three minutes remained, the six of them crept to the edge of the jungle. The ominous, blood-red hill was pocked by craters and the ring of machine gun emplacements looked like malignant growths.

"If they knock out the mortars, we can take the Nambus," Henty said softly and sent Meatball, Kon, Ass Drag and Julie through the brush.

He pulled the Ridge Runner back into the jungle.

"Get it ready," he said and his eyes followed the split second hand on his watch. At 13:16:30, the Runner called Command.

"Henshit ready, Arthur. We're on target. Lay in the first and I'll correct. Do not acknowledge. Hold."

"Roger," the receiver blurted cheerfully amidst a blare of static. It was not Captain Gold's voice.

The Runner's face turned a sickly, pasty color and he dived into the jungle and scrambled away. Henty sat by the squawk box and waited for the Nambus to open fire on the sound. The response from CP had probably been automatic but he wondered who the stupid assed bastard was. The jungle must have muffled the noise of the transmission because there was no fire. The Runner came back on his belly.

A shell sang far overhead and burst into the trees somewhere beyond the hill. Henty swore and waited for a cloud of dust, something to indicate the impact area. This was going to be a rough target; they'd have to smack it on the bullseye. No marker lifted toward the sky. They should have made the first one smoke. Well he couldn't ask for that now, there were only five to go.

"Trajectory okay, I guess," he reported. "But you put that one in the Bay of Bengal. Try reducing yardage by 100 and give us one more single. Do not acknowledge, repeat, do not acknowledge. Hold."

A minute squeezed by in silence. The second shell whistled over the hilltop almost clipping it and dropped far beyond. Henty was calculating rapidly—drop the elevation only slightly and they could shear off everything on the dome.

"How we doing, Henshit?" the radio voice chattered.

"Keep off the air, goddamnit." Henty blazed. He crouched against the spat of machine guns and when there was none, glanced gratefully at the thick foliage. "You stupid-assed bastard, we're in contact. Do not acknowledge, understand? Keep your goddamn flapping trap shut and just do what I tell you. That last one was close. Reduce your range by 50 yards and throw the other four. Over and out."

Henty dragged his wet palms down his grizzled cheeks and looked at the Ridge Runner. He had shut off the set.

"They must have a replacement from the Pentagon," Henty said and waited for the shells. The yardage he'd given was long but the elevation of the dome should shop the missiles in their trajectory.

One. Two. Three. Four. Explosions rocked the big clay mound and leveled its rounded top. A blast of red roared up and draped the hill and surrounding jungle with a gritty mist of dust. Musty smelling and abrasive, it seeped into nose, eyes and mouth. A weird silence descended with the cloud of dirt. Not a Jap screamed, not a gun fired.

The nightmarish nimbus began to dissipate and the frontal positions grew fuzzily from the ground.

"Come on," Henty said to the Ridge Runner and ran crouching through the brush. He came up with Ass Drag and Julie, shouted: "Give them a burst."

Standing, Henty sprayed the two emplacements on the frontal north with his tommy gun. Ass Drag opened with the BAR and Meatball's submachine gun chattered. There was no answering fire.

"What the hell is this?" he hollered at the Ridge Runner. "Some kind of trap?"

Firing broke out north and south but it was from his squads and still the Nambus didn't answer.

The Runner wound up and got off a long pitch but the grenade fell short and threw up a blast of dirt.

157

"Go in prone," Henty called. "I'll cover you."

Hugging his knees, he shoved up the hillside firing. Ass Drag, Julie and Meatball went in crouched and the Ridge Runner and Kon wiggled up on their bellies. When they were within 15 yards of the emplacements, Henty signaled them to stop. There had been no return fire from any of the positions.

"Give them a couple," he shouted.

The grenades arced in. The first two were wide. Kon's second sent one emplacement into the air in a deafening explosion that rocked them. The Ridge Runner threw two more before he blew his target. It, too, exploded violently.

"The sons of bitches pulled out and booby trapped the holes," Henty yelled angrily. "Let's get the other two and see what they've left on top."

They all stood and hurled grenades. On the north and south flanks, the squads were blasting their targets. The detonations shook the hill. There was nothing from the top, no mortars, no fire of any kind. Henty signed and from north, south and east, the patrol advanced.

The red hilltop was a ravaged pit, a crater of the moon and hot as hell. Even its atmosphere was unworldly, misted with pulverized grit that screened the blazing sun and surrounding jungle. There was no sound nor sign of life, past or present. The men of the patrol walked in aimless circles, foolish grins on their vapid faces, as if they'd collapse if they didn't keep moving.

"What the hell goes?" Double Ugly growled.

"If it wasn't for those booby trapped emplacements, I'd of said we dreamed the whole engagement," the Butcher rasped.

Henty pulled off his helmet, dropped it in the dirt and sat on it. He laughed bitterly and the sound grated in his throat.

"Know why they pulled out? They thought we were spearheading an attack in strength, positioning them for artillery. That must have shook them. They didn't know we had anything heavy any more than we did. I'll bet they shit when those howitzers started in. They could see from up here better than we could where those shells were landing and they thought we were directing them. They pulled out in a hurry and we gave them the time to do it while we were moving back. What a goddamned opportunity we lost."

"It wouldn't have made any difference," Double Ugly said. "You couldn't call in the range until we got on target. Well, where do we go from here? Jesus, I wish I had one of those cold beers now."

"Don't we all," Henty said, glancing around. Some of the men had squatted, some were lying in the dirt. "We can't stay here on hell's half acre. Every canteen will be dry in 10 minutes. And I'm not going after a company with what we've got. I'll call CP and we'll clear off this joint. It could be another Nhpum Ga. If Command will send reinforcements with some mortars and machine guns and back us up with those howitzers, we might be able to break through all the way. But we'll get back and meet them where the beer is cooling."

Double Ugly made his sagging face look pleasant and Butcher got a smile into his next mouth jerk.

Henty examined Meatball. He was neither breathing hard nor sweating. The Jinghpaw was indestructible.

"I do not like to ask this but it would be of benefit if you could track the enemy from concealment for a small distance. The patrol will withdraw along the way we came. I wish to know where the enemy has gone and whether he has despatched any patrols to observe us."

"The task will be a pleasure, Dua," Meatball said and smiled.

"If you see no enemy within half a mile, return to us."

Meatball bobbed his round head, chattered in monkey language and jogged back down the slope to enter the jungle from cover. Double Ugly and Butcher sat on their helmets with Henty. South of the red hill, the droning of a small plane sounded faintly. Henty thought he saw a moving blob but wasn't sure. The next second he heard the distant smash of two shells and felt a break in the regular thudding of the Jap artillery. Command was reaching for Nhpum Ga with the howitzers and they'd put up an LP to spot the ring of Jap guns.

"We're getting somewhere," he muttered and looked for the radioman.

The Ridge Runner had removed his pack radio and was sleeping with his bared head cradled in the crook of his arm. Henty pulled the radio-transmitter between his legs. It wouldn't be the first time he'd operated the SCR 300 and it probably

159

wouldn't be the last. He lighted a cigarette, got through to Command and it was Captain Gold.

"Henshit here. We occupied the hill without engaging the enemy. Your last four shells were on target but they saw what was coming and pulled out. If you can reinforce us the way we came and back us up, we'll get through to Maggot. Over."

"Negative, Henshit. Arthur has his hands full. Can you see anything of our shelling now? Over."

"Can't see but sounds as if you're interrupting them. Look Arthur, we've come this far, give us something to work with and we'll go all the way. Over."

"Negative Henshit. We need you. Can you position the withdrawal from where you sit? Over."

"Later, it's in the works. Look Arthur, what the hell you want us to do? We're on a hot seat. Over."

"Why, bring Lancelot to Arthur. Didn't I tell you? Over."

"No damnit. We're within a couple miles of Maggot. Can't go farther alone. Send us help. Over."

"We're fitting you in the picture, Henshit. Arthur will talk to you in person. That's all. Over and out."

Henty pounded his fist on the ground and choked on the dust. He shut off the pack radio, banged down the antenna and shook the Ridge Runner awake.

"Sling that damned thing and don't break security. We're staying off the air."

Double Ugly and Butcher were watching him, grinning.

He stood and shouted: *"On your feet!"*

The men came to and up like sleepwalkers.

"All right," he called hoarsely and tried to swallow. "We're going back, all the way. The Jinghpaw's scouting our rear. I'll take his place and lead off with 1st. Overholt, back me up, then Kon. Rest as usual. Ridge Runner, between 1st and 2nd. Butcher, give us a rear guard from 3rd but don't shoot at monkey noises. Let's move. That beer we left ought to be cold by now."

Worn out as the men were, no feet lagged in the column that skidded down the shot-up hill. They walked upright and almost militarily through the brush and into the jungle. They were going back, yes sir; cold beer served here. They'd take a long break by the small stream below the ridge, flop in the shade, drink a couple of beers courtesy of the Japs. How long had it been since anything like this had happened? Not since Deogarh, that Christmas week when they'd given passes to half of the 5307th and they'd scattered all over India, didn't get back in time for the other half to get their New Year's passes so the rest of the Marauders had taken off without them. Jesus, they'd been a week picking them out of jails and whorehouses from Bombay to Calcutta. The beer bust this afternoon would almost be worth the long trip out and back, if it hadn't been for Domingo, Injun Joe and Hari Kari, of course.

Henty turned the elbow in the path. Around the corner and under a tree, an ice cold beer is waiting for me. Down the long stretch of still shade it seemed they'd trod so many times before to the place the men had broken when they'd heard the howitzer shells. The patrol was pushing him now. Maybe it was Old Overshoes pushing him, maybe the bastard was trying to get up close enough to knife him. Henty grinned. Not with Kon's M-1 in Overholt's back.

Beyond, there was some evidence of the howitzer shells, no real damage, just a few flung clods and splintered branches but no craters. Hell, the men had been safer on the trail than when they'd dive into hiding.

Trees thinning, up the last hill, haze gone, sky blue and quiet, sun hot. He could feel the pressure growing at his back. It was a real physical force, as much as the current in a stream. He wondered whether he could hold them when they reached the top.

Halfway, he halted, swung about face to face with Overholt's glaring eyes and blood-scabbed jaw, ignored him, shouting down the trail loud enough for all to hear:

"There's plenty, plenty for everyone. We'll take a long break and drink it up, all of it. Stay in rank and you get your share. Break rank and you're cut off. Butcher, leave two guards at the top. We'll send theirs up and relieve them in 15 minutes. Double Ugly, you and Butcher help me pass it out and we'll divide it even. Now let's go get it, in rank."

A faint cheer climbed up the hill. It was a hearty sound for the shape the men were in.

Overholt curled his lip and said softly: "I better get an extra for the booze of mine you swiped."

It was hard to tell whether he was threatening or begging.

"At ease, Overholt, or I'll chop you off completely," Henty said and started for the top.

He hesitated a few feet from the crest, took two more paces and halted. Overholt pushed into him and Kon slammed into Overholt. Then the rest of 1st Squad, and 2nd, and 3rd were crowding up, standing stock still and staring. Down in the gulley between the ridge and the hill, one of the howitzer shells had tossed the trees aside and dug a hole that looked like a city dump. The stream was flowing into it, filling it up, but the banks were strewn with bits and pieces of glass that glittered in the sun. There wasn't a bottle in the world that could have withstood the force of that explosion.

16

Numbed mute, Julie Chiruco stared into the valley of shattered bottles. Many colors glinted in the sun from the brown shards. The spectra danced crazily and began to revolve in brilliant wheels before his eyes. He was blinded by the dazzle, couldn't see anything but the concentric pinwheel turnings of the piercing white nimbused flashes of reds, blues and yellows, each the separate aura of a bottle of beer he'd never drink. The resentment that had smoldered in his chest for two days burst fiercely into flame.

"You son of a bitch, Henshit," he shrieked. "You did this to us."

The big hand was on his wrist pinning his forearm against his shoulder even as his fingers touched the knife on his back.

"Let me go, A.D.," he cried, squirming in the iron grasp, knowing without looking it was the Swede who held him fast.

"It was not his fault. Now calm yourself."

The fingers did not relax but the calm, lilting voice was gentle and it quieted him. His breath shuddered from its cage and his insides fluttered. He began to see again, to feel the tight silence that surrounded him, and he turned slowly. Ass Drag's hand let his wrist slip easily and when Julie faced the Swede he found his arm was free and dropped it to his side. Ass Drag's milk blue eyes were not angry but they were pained and sad. Julie hung his head.

"This temper is a terrible thing," Ass Drag scolded mildly. "It will be your ruin. I cannot always be with you to watch. How can you blame Henty for the shell that landed here from camp?"

Ass Drag and he might as well have been alone on an island, not surrounded by the patrol, the way they were talking. It was a good thing no one said a word. He'd have killed anyone who did.

"He was directing their fire, wasn't he?"

"You are not using reason, Julie. Why would any man in his right mind want to destroy our beer?"

"He didn't want us to have it, that's why," Julie flared. "You saw before, one bottle he gives us. He takes liquor for himself but a bottle of beer is all we get. Now he doesn't want us going into camp smelling like he turned us loose in a brewery. He thinks he's Jesus Christ since they hung that .45 on him."

"He wanted that beer as much as anyone," Ass Drag said patiently. "It was when they fired those first shots, the ones that came up the trail, a shell happened to drop in here. They did not know the beer was here anymore than they knew we were on that trail."

"They should of!" Julie began to burn again. "He should of told them, where the beer was and us. All the bastard knows how to do is make mistakes."

"Julie!" Ass Drag's voice was sharp. "We'll have no more of this nonsense. You understand that now?"

"Yeah." Julie sulked. Ass Drag treated him like a kid, there was no one else could get away with what he took from him. "If you say so, A.D."

He chewed his mustache for a moment and then lifted his chin until his long curly locks of black hair were tumbling over the collar of his fatigues, glaring defiantly around the bunched patrol: at Kon, that gutless fink; at Old Overshoes, the yellow-bellied punk; at Katey and Pretty Pussey, those two fish-mouthed fairies; at Nick the Greek, a puking pimp; at Furman, who tried to hide how his mouth shook by smiling with his lips together; at the bird-brained Ridge Runner; at the goonies Double Ugly and Butcher; and last, at Henshit. Henshit was the only one of them who wasn't staring at Julie. Henshit had hiked off to the side, was talking with the Kachin, the guide must have just come in. No one else was saying anything at all, now they weren't looking at him, just shifting their eyes like they all were watching a ping-pong ball.

"Kon!" Henshit called.

Kon went trotting obediently like a dog to lick the hand that whipped him.

Julie glanced back at Ass Drag and sneered: "Well Jesus."

Henshit expected you to kiss his ass every time he did something wrong.

"Men!" Henshit barked.

He couldn't talk normal, he had to try to sound like an officer. And sure, the whole goddamned patrol practically came to attention. Henshit was sticking out his jaw like he was tough but he wasn't, he was just a little shit, not much taller than Julie, and now he was going to make a speech, tell them what to do. Julie turned his ass to the piss head.

"I'm sorry about the beer," Henshit said. "I wanted one pretty bad."

He wanted one. Not the men, he didn't give a damn about how much they needed one.

"Kon tells me his detail didn't go through the whole area of the Jap camp," Henty went on. "He says there's probably more beer and wine down there. Meatball says there's an old overgrown trail from that valley down through the jungle to Hsamshingyang. I'd planned to go back the way we came, through the *tongyaw* where we were last night. The valley will be stinking with corpses and rummaging for bottles will be messy. The beer and wine will be hot if the sun hasn't exploded the bottles. We don't know what's on that old trail. Some Japs got away last night and there's been patrol action around the air strip. We could run into something. But I'm going to leave it to you. I won't guarantee one damned thing but if you want to take a chance on going through the valley and maybe picking up a warm beer or two, that's the way we'll do it."

Why the monkey-peckered baboon, now he couldn't even make his own mind up, he was going to pass the buck. And the mush heads were taking it; hell, they liked it.

"Not us, A.D.," Julie said quickly. "Don't let him suck you in."

Ass Drag lifted his shoulders that used to be strong and dropped his jaw that used to be square against a chest that used to be big.

"But he is doing it for you, Julie."

The dumb Swede, he used to have a mind.

The rising water in the shell crater was thick with sand. Above it where the stream still ran clear, the man drank and filled their canteens. The break was an impatient one, half a butt. Then they crawled like crayfish up to the ridge and plunged from it to claw their way through the breathless steambath of the jungle.

Julie was nudged in the file between Kon and Ass Drag but he didn't talk to either even when they muttered something. The stupid bastards, they'd never learned how to take care of themselves. He reached his hand back, his left hand so the pudding-brained Swede wouldn't think he was reaching for his knife. You had to think things out ahead. He stroked the curling hair and pulled his hand back to his face, patting the luxuriant brush that filled the space between his thin mouth and nose that was pinched like he always was inhaling.

He was proud of his mustache and hair but it hadn't always been that way. That goddamn mother of his back in Albany, New York, she'd gone nuts when the truck had squashed his father and sister. Christ, she'd never had it so good, it had been a big trucking outfit and they'd paid off plenty. But she was a looney, alright, moping around the flat, never going out. Then she had that bright idea, keeping him out of school, making out like he was sick, putting him to bed and fussing over him. Waiting for his hair to grow. He'd been 10 when his father and sister were killed. She kept him in that stinking flat one whole year, calling him Julie like he was a girl, petting him and brushing his hair. She made him frilly clothes, Lord Fauntleroy stuff, and sent him back to school in one of those outfits when she thought his hair was long enough. Hell, it was damn near hanging down to his shoulders in ringlets. In that Irish and Spanish neighborhood. The first morning at recess, a bunch of toughs jerked down his short velvet pants to see whether he sat down to pee. And when he tried to fight back they just fell over and rolled on the concrete and howled, he even fought like a girl except he didn't bite and scratch.

He tried hacking off his hair and she kept him out of school again until it grew out. He took an awful beating for a couple years, hell he was 13 years old before he decided to do something about it. All that time he'd run to school and run back home but they'd always get him on the playground. Then one day when he was 13 he got some guts. He sheared his hair as close to the scalp as he could, gouging holes in his head with the scissors and he threw handfuls of those damned black curls in that Italian woman's face while she rocked and screamed. That afternoon he went out looking for that gang of six roughs in his block who were his worst tormentors. He had a knife. It was just a short bladed paring knife and he clenched it in his fist inside the waist of his pants which weren't knee pants any more but weren't jeans like the other guys wore, either.

It was like the six of them had been waiting for him, they were right there in the street. Red spotted him first. He ran the gang. Red was about 15, big and mean with flat green eyes and a pushed up nose so you could look up the holes into his head. He was wearing a dirty, torn T shirt and overall pants like they all wore.

"Jeez," Red shouted. "Curly Locks whacked off her hair!"

"Yeah, look," the one called Tiger yelled. He was short and fat and greasy. "Now she's playing with herself."

The gang started for Julie.

"We better help her find it and show her what it's for," Red said.

When Red lunged for his pants, Julie slashed a jagged cut that spurted up his arm into the muscle and then the knife thrust upward from his gut. It was funny, he was a born knife fighter, the first time he used that paring knife he knew just how to hold it, thumb along the blade, and to slash up instead of down.

He hadn't cut Red deep enough to do much damage, they only kept him at the hospital overnight, but it scared Red. He and his gang kept their distance, they didn't want anything more to do with that knife. But they weren't through with him. About a month later they caught him by the garbage dump and beat him senseless with tire chains. They must have thought he was dead when they threw his limp and battered body in with the garbage. The garbage truck found him.

He was in the hospital a long time and then he was back at the flat, still in bed, with the doctor coming every day and that woman crooning over him and watching his hair grow long again. She wouldn't have been so happy if she'd seen the insides of his head but the hair hid that. It had started coming to him while he was only partly conscious at the hospital, the bright picture that even had smells to it, popcorn and peanut and animal smells from the one time she'd taken him to the circus. What he saw were shiny blades flashing through the air as the knife thrower stuck them where he wanted all around the nearly naked girl who stood against a board.

There was a way to beat a chain.

After being in the hospital and in bed at the flat for almost five months, the doctor said fresh air would do more good than anything and the woman was happy when he didn't say anything about the hair and didn't want to go out on the street but was content to sit alone in the little boarded-up place in back of the flat building. He practiced throwing knives against the fence. The butcher knives didn't work the way they were. They were too big and clumsy. He filed the blades on both sides to points. The handles were too heavy. He prized off the wood and bound the hilts with black tape. That was better but the blades were still too long. He filed some more and practiced and filed and balanced until he had two needle-pointed, stiletto-like knives that he could send singing into the wood pretty close to where he wanted every time he threw. He made himself another knife, something like a picture of a Bowie knife, for inside fighting. The Italian woman never even asked where her butcher knives had gone.

It must have been six months from the day they beat him with the chains before he went out on the street again. He was 14. His hair was long again, not like a girl's but too thick and curly for any male who wasn't queer. He wore a short jacket made of red corduroy and without buttons, like something the woman had seen in a magazine. She was beaming all over her puffy puss about his hair and jacket, said he looked like Garibaldi. That made him laugh. He was ready to fight like a Red Shirt, too. A throwing knife rode loose in a slit he'd made on either inside of the jacket and the Bowie knife was in his belt just back of his right hip bone.

He went looking for the gang and let them find him, trap him in a boarded-up, half done building that had started to be some kind of warehouse or garage. The brick went up about 10 feet and there were some steel beams for a roof or second story that had been covered with planks which had been stolen so the whole inside was open and light.

They came in after him, one at a time, Red and Tiger and the other four, twirling their lengths of steel links like they were key chains. They were leering and savagely silent.

He let them back him into a corner where he didn't have to worry about anyone getting behind him. They started closing in. Red was a couple of steps in the lead. When he was about 10 feet away, he pulled his arm back to get a good lash started. Julie's hand darted inside his jacket and a knife flashed through the sunlight. It pierced Red's right hand through the palm and came out the back all the way to the taped hilt. Red screamed and his chain clanked on the concrete floor. The other five started forward shaking their chains. Julie had the second throwing knife in his hand and held it back ready to let go. His eyes darted from one of the gang to another.

They stopped where they were and Julie stepped from his corner, threatening first one and then the next. They fell back, all but Red who stood dumbly staring at the knife in his hand. The other five didn't try to rush Julie when he reached Red's side. He jerked the knife out of Red's palm and kicked the chain back. Red sank to the floor holding his wrist and looking at the blood he cupped in his hand. Julie stood in front of him, slipped the unused throwing knife inside his jacket, held the bloodied knife in his right hand and jerked the Bowie knife from his belt with his left. He held the blade pointed upward at Red's throat.

"One at a time or all at once," he said. Except for Red's scream, it was the first sound any of them had made. "I can stick these knives anywhere I want. I'll slit Red's throat first, throw knives right through two of you before you can take a step and take on the other two with my fighting knife. What's it going to be?"

The Bowie knife crept menacingly toward Red's throat.

"Leave me be," he squealed.

Julie kicked him in the nuts and left him clutching his crotch with his bloody hand, the other still grasping its wrist. Julie stalked the other five. They cringed away.

"Drop your chains!" he shouted abruptly.

The chains obediently fell to the concrete.

"Pick up Red and drag him over to the wall, all of you against the wall. By the boarded-up window."

They did as they were told.

"All right, one at a time the way you're lined up, stand

169

by the window and put your right hand against the board. You first, Tiger."

He shook his knife at Tiger who was sweating oil through his blackheads and shrinking to pint size. Tiger sucked his pimply cheeks and moaned.

"You rather have it in your gut or balls?"

Tiger turned his back and his hand trembled against the boards.

"Anybody moves, he gets it."

The knife sliced the air and nailed Tiger's hand. He grunted when Julie tugged it out.

One by one, he impaled their right hands. One by one, they sank to the floor, each holding his wrist and staring at the wound. Not one cried out but three were groaning because the knife had gone through bone.

Julie glared at the six slumped figures and laughed harshly.

"Now you're my gang," he said contemptuously. "Anyone else I decide to take in gets the same initiation. Anybody doesn't like it gets the big knife in his gut. You won't swing chains for a while but they're for punks. By the time your hands are healed, you'll be used to me telling you what to do and I'll get you blades. Up to now you've been nothing, a bunch of hoodlums beating up a loner, snatching a purse or a case of beer. We're going to load this warehouse with stuff we can peddle for dough. I'll never trust any of you but you'll do what I say. Anyone steps out of line or sings gets a knife in his lung. It won't kill you right away and you'll suffer. Most of all, I don't trust you, Red, you're the only one that begged. Just remember, a knife doesn't make a sound. Even if you're in a crowd or handcuffed to a cop, I can get you with a knife and be gone before they know what's happened. Don't ever get any idea of ganging up on me because from now on I'll carry six of these and I can sling them faster than you can talk."

They'd looked at him while he talked, hurting and resentful, but not one could meet his eyes.

"You'll do," he said. "It's up to each of you to get your hands fixed and I want it done by different doctors. Be back here tomorrow afternoon at five o'clock. Anybody doesn't show, I go looking for and he doesn't get a second chance."

He turned and walked casually toward the doorway to

the alley where the boards were loose. Halfway, he looked back. The six of them, his gang, hadn't moved from the wall. He laughed easily.

"Hell," he called. "After I start to put some money in your pockets you might even begin to like me."

It had worked just the way he'd planned, he thought now as the patrol came out of the jungle into the valley that reeked of death. A few purse snatchings, rolling drunks, muggings for working capital. Then Red, who looked 20 when he wore a shirt with a tie and suit, rented a long frame building, two windows wide, with a shed and garage at the back. SECOND HAND GOODS, their sign read but their merchandise was new. They hijacked anything in unattended trucks, just drove the truck away. Lucky for them they hijacked a load of booze almost at the start. The cops couldn't ever find them even with a periscope but a lardy, bald-headed quiet guy named Frank was at their store that night before they'd half unloaded the liquor. They'd made a mistake, he suggested half smiling, and something told them they'd better agree. He looked around the joint, at the radios, plumbing fixtures, fur coats, some cases of lubricating oil, furniture and commented they'd made a good start but it was only a matter of time until even the Law caught on. Now if they were to take down that sign and replace it with another reading STORAGE WAREHOUSE, block off the windows and the public and call a certain number when they had a van load like now, there'd be cash on the line and the stuff would be dumped in Brooklyn. It wasn't many months before they were operating from a brick building and the goods were in and out the same night, not just from Albany, but from Pittsfield, Utica, Amsterdam, and a dozen other communities within a 100-mile radius.

More than three years without a slip-up. The Law: he should laugh so hard. Just because you gave some loud-mouthed beefy fathead a Smith and Wesson and a badge, you didn't give him brains. Christ, he'd been making and spending as much before he was 18 as the payroll for the entire Albany so-called police force. The only system he couldn't beat was the draft. It was funny, in the Army just like in civilian life, it was the jerks who couldn't think their way out of their income taxes who wore the brass and silver on their shoulders and carried the .45's while someone who could figure all the angles picked up the butts and peeled potatoes.

Jesus, what a dumb-assed stunt to bring the patrol down here to this boneyard. It stunk so bad you almost puked. There wasn't anything but rotten egg smelling air and the sun was fierce.

"All right!"

That was Henshit with another crappy command. The boys ranged themselves around him to hear him tell them what to do.

"Work the north half of the valley by squads. . . . 1st will take the middle, 2nd the west and 3rd the east. You'll probably find their knapsacks on the ground. Probe them with your bayonets and pull the stuff away from the corpses. Let's not waste any time in this hole."

The second and third squads spread out quickly, trotting, tired as they were. Henshit held 1st while he called Kon up for a conference. Old Overshoes didn't like that. Henshit was going to have trouble some dark night with that bully boy and Julie didn't much give a shit who came out second best.

Henshit turned, said: "Rest of you ago ahead with Meatball. Kon and I got something to attend to."

Old Overshoes growled, said loudly:

"Like Kon knows where there's more booze."

Henshit snarled back at him:

"Like Kon and I are going to mark the place you dumped the guy you *murdered!*"

Old Overshoes' face got red before it turned the color of watered ashes.

The seven men of 1st Squad trotted ahead with the Kachin while Henshit and Kon walked somewhere behind. This valley filled with puffed up corpses was the worst place Julie had been yet. They were black with big flies that sucked the pus from the rotting flesh. A guy could catch a disease from those flies but it would have to be a new one, some kind of Oriental sickness. They'd already had everything the jungles could give them. Halfway down the valley, they started prodding the knapsacks. Here and there they found a bottle. The Japs must have issued beer and wine like K rations. He'd heard the water in Japan wasn't fit to drink, like in France. Julie slipped two bottles of rice wine in his pack and looked over his shoulder. Back of him, maybe half a block, Kon was sticking the bayonet of a rifle into the ground and Henshit was climbing out of a hole with a helmet in one hand and something in the other. Probably Hari Kari's dog tags. Jesus, anybody that'd crawl into a grave! It was like he knew, Henshit didn't have a goddamned thing upstairs.

Ass Drag walked over, stumbling on his big feet coming up to Julie. There was a grin on his face like he had a turd in his mouth and he was holding three bottles of beer between the fingers of his left hand.

"We'll save them for tonight, that suit you Julie? And we can talk."

The big dumb bastard, trying to get in good again, for three months the square head had been telling him what to do, ordering him around, and he, Julie Chiruco had let him get away with it. Christ, he'd acted like a little kid doing what his Pa told him to so he wouldn't get a licking.

"Stick it up!" he said hotly.

"Now Julie," Ass Drag began.

But Julie stomped away.

The patrol regrouped at the southeast side of the valley. Each man seemed to have found a bottle or two of beer or wine, at least there was not one bitching. In fact, they were acting like a bunch of school kids with all-day suckers. They wanted to sit right there by the side of the trickle of water that was supposed to be a stream while the bottles cooled but Henshit was having none of that.

"We'll cool it in the Tanai when we're back home tonight," he said, grinning like he was doing them a favor. "We haven't far to go, a couple miles, then you can take off your packs, stretch out on the beach and relax. Have your cold beer or wine and a couple butts without thinking about being sniped at or having to get right up and walk again."

And they bought it!

The Kachin found what was supposed to be a foot path along the side of the stream. For about a foot wide, it was a little less tangled, all right, but hardly a path. And every step farther you went, the skinny fishpole trees and spiney grass and brush pushed in closer so pretty soon you were lifting your knees up to your chin. The mosquitos were having a banquet, they hadn't had so many kinds of meat to choose from in all their lives and they kept telling each other about it. There was a dead stink to the heavy air here, too, not of bloated corpses but mixed up rotting odors like old dead trees and grass and fertilizer. Like a city dump when it was wet. You could even taste it. It was pretty much downhill and the stream ran faster and so did you except the Kachin was acting funny and trying to slow you down and how the hell could you hold back when you were practically tripping on your face as it was?

The stream curved to get away from some thorny stuff and the path gave up. The Kachin somehow squeezed through the bamboo the other way and started them winding back and forth toward a little rise where the growth was thin. Julie was breathing hard and every step he took a different bunch of nerves or muscles would jump in his legs and thighs. He bent his head and shoulders over his feet, lifting himself along. And walked into Kon's pack.

"You shit-eating bastard," he said between his teeth.

Kon swung and slapped his helmet with the flat of his hand.

Julie looked up, ready to slug him. Ahead, Old Overshoes was crouched and Henshit and the Kachin were crawling on their bellies through the trees. Oh Jesus! the meathead has led us into another ambush, Julie thought and went down on his knees.

Then Henshit was crawling back, motioning 1st Squad to crawl up toward Meatball, deploying 2nd and 3rd on flankers. Automatically, Julie sided A.D., hooking one thumb in the belt of BAR ammo, scraping out of the trees through the brittle grass, crawling blindly toward a point the Kachin held like a setter bitch.

Then he and A.D. were right up there in front with the Kachin and there was a perimeter, all right, foxholes rimming their side of the rise which probably meant they went all around. But these holes seemed deserted or abandoned, no one opened up on them and there was no sign of life. Maybe they'd be lucky this time.

Henshit came up. With the Kachin on one side and Henshit on the other with their submachine guns, A. D. and Julie began to dig ahead.

One minute everything was calm and peaceful like a day in the country and the next it was like Fourth of July at Coney Island. The whole damned hill blew up like the main event in the fireworks display. There was fire everywhere from the hill and the patrol was shooting back. A.D. was blazing away with the BAR and Julie was sweating out of the belt of BAR ammo and firing his M-1 offhand sort of.

He didn't know what got into A.D. or how it happened. A.D. was lying next to him and then he wasn't. He was diving into the foxhole straight ahead. Maybe he thought he'd got the Jap or Japs who were there and was going to work over the rest of them from cover. A.D. just belly flopped into that hole and then he came out of it again except there was a Jap with him and he was a lively one. He was hanging onto that BAR, swinging from it like it was a trapeze. Outside the hole, the Jap got his feet on the ground and a better hold on the BAR. On both sides, firing petered out to nothing. Both sides held their fire while A. D. and the Jap fought the Battle of Burma in single-handed combat.

A. D. was a good head taller than the Jap but the little guy was strong and huskily built. They kept twisting and turning and the Jap got a leg behind A.D.'s knee. They both went down, the Jap on top, and Julie sighted his M-1. But the next minute A.D. was on top, trying to hang onto the BAR with one hand while he reached for his trench knife with the other. The Jap almost got the gun then and A. D. forgot his knife. He clutched the BAR with both hands and jerked. The Jap didn't let go and the two of them sort of pushed and pulled each other to their feet. Then they were dancing around some more. But A. D. seemed to be weakening, the Jap was better fed and hadn't been in constant combat for three months. A. D.'s feet were stumbling and his hands kept slipping, he had an awkward grip anyway with one hand stuck in the trigger guard, Jesus! it was funny the BAR hadn't blasted them all to hell.

They went down again, pitching from side to side. When they came up this time, A. D. was about done but they still kept waltzing each other around so fast you couldn't risk a shot.

Everybody on both sides had their eyes on the fighters in the ring, Julie knew they wouldn't notice him. He snaked through the grass, got within fifteen feet, reached back for his knife and when A.D. and the Jap gave him their profiles, he furled the blade. He put everything he had into it. It was the most powerful throw he'd ever got off in all his life, it almost threw his shoulder out of joint. The knife went into A.D.'s left rib cage all the way to the hilt and the hilt even shivered a little.

Ass Drag went down dead at once.

Julie buried his face and cried in the dirt. Not that he'd missed the Jap. But because he never missed his target and hadn't missed this time.

17

THE hazed sun was dropping toward the green thatched hills in a veiled and sultry sky when Henty approached the Command shack at Hsamshingyang. The air that crawled along the path was hot and clinging and smelled dirty. Henty's heart was heavy and his feet were leaden. His helmet and tommy gun dangled from one hand and he ran the fingers of the other across his burning eyes and through his wet and matted hair. The patrol had overrun the Jap position on the back trail and come in without further incident, but the new loss they'd suffered bowed his spirit with full realization of the desperate condition all the men were in.

Captain Gold was sitting on a bench at a rough plank table that was strewn with papers. He was studying an old terrain map. A bench in front of the table had a stack of Tech Orders topped with a helmet at one end. An enlisted man was slumped over the control panel monitoring the Command set at the back of the hut.

Dozens of fine lines etched Captain Gold's brittle skin from his eyes to his jaws. The gray eyes were bleary with fatigue and his mouth was drawn down at the corners. When he glanced up, he closed his eyes briefly and smiled faintly.

"You look exactly the way I feel, Henty," he said and although his voice was tired, it was pleasant. "Sit down and have a cigarette while you collect yourself."

He pushed a freshly opened pack of Camels across the table. A mess cup was half filled with crushed butts.

Henty straddled the bench, dropped his helmet and tommy gun to the dirt floor and lighted a cigarette with fingers that trembled. He inhaled deeply and bent his head. His mind felt numb and blank.

"Take a break," Captain Gold called to the man at the radio transmitter. "I'll catch anything that comes across."

Henty looked at the radioman's hollow eyes as he walked from the hut, wondering whether this was the one who'd acknowledged the transmissions from the red hill.

"At the moment," Captain Gold said, leaning back and rubbing his stubbled jaw, "I'm exec, C.Q., adjutant, communications officer. You name it." He laughed quietly. "The Colonel with his howitzers is like a child with a new toy. He's very proud of them. He has found a couple of men from an artillery unit on New Guinea who are manning them. Most of the 3rd Battalion's officers are with him now, discussing an offensive. With two pack howitzers, the Marauders suddenly have teeth."

"They make a difference," Henty said. Just talking, let alone thinking, was an effort.

"I need a complete report of your activities, Henty," Captain Gold said mildly. "I know the shape you're in. Perhaps if you just begin with the night you and the Kachins jumped the Jap patrol and tell it all in sequence, it will be easier. I need to know positions, casualties and so on."

"Yeah, I know," Henty said dully. "I'll just give it to you the way it happened. On the night of the 28th, the Jinghpaws discovered a Jap patrol that had infiltrated about halfway to Nhpum Ga just off the trail. Estimated strength of this patrol was about 70. The four Jinghpaws, you've got their names, accounted for 37 known dead and the patrol withdrew from its encampment. On the 29th, Lancelot patrol accounted for 9 known dead at a trail block beyond the Jap encampment. The enemy position was destroyed. As a result of this engagement, the patrol's 1st Squad suffered its first casualty, Domingo Sabado, but you've got the report on that. The night of the 29th, the patrol engaged a strong enemy position in a valley about a mile below Hill 307. Enemy strength was estimated at 100. Seventy-nine of the enemy are known dead as a result of this surprise attack. The 1st Squad of Lancelot patrol sustained two more casualties, Carlyle Wolf and Harry McCarthy. The enemy withdrew. Today, on the 30th, the patrol engaged the enemy in approximately company strength on a hill about two miles west of Hill 307."

Captain Gold handed the map he'd been following to Henty.

"It's an old survey," he said, "dating back to 1929, I think. But it seems to have some of the trails you've followed.

178

They don't show on our up-to-date versions. Can you mark these positions?"

"Yeah," Henty said, slowly tracing the route the patrol had taken with the stub of a pencil. "This would be hill 307 and this would be the red hill about two miles west." He made an X. "It's a funny looking bare hump of clay. It should be easy to spot from the air. The enemy was dug in there approximately company strength. The patrol attempted to take the position, was driven off by Nambu and mortar fire. Then, when you opened with the howitzers, the enemy withdrew and the patrol briefly occupied the hill. Meatball, the Jinghpaw, says there is a trail circling Nhpum Ga and that the Japs withdrew about three quarters of a mile along that trail which would put that company on the other side of Nhpum Ga." He looked up quickly. "Your howitzers weren't wasted. Meatball counted 13 dead where a shell caught the tail end of their column. The patrol returned through the valley below Hill 307 and down a back trail to Hsamshing-yang."

Henty examined the map more closely.

"This would be the valley," he said, pointing with the pencil. "About here, a mile and a half or so from Hsamshingyang, the patrol came onto an enemy position which we overran after a stiff skirmish. We counted 12 enemy dead. I do not believe any escaped. The 1st Squad again suffered two casualties, both dead. A. D. Svensen, BAR-man, and his ammo bearer, Julie Chiruco."

Captain Gold had been making notes. Now he added a column of figures and looked up with a pleased smile.

"Do you realize, Henty, that you and the Kachins and you with Lancelot patrol have accounted for 150 known enemy dead, relieving the pressure on the air strip and Command, at a cost of only five men?"

"Yes, sir," Henty said bitterly. "Five. And all from my squad."

"I understand," Captain Gold said softly. "It is difficult to reconcile yourself to casualties, especially when the men have been directly under your command and, in this case, were personally known to you. But five men is not too high a price to pay for the results you have achieved."

"No sir, considering," Henty said. "And the first four I

179

can almost bring myself to understand. Even Ass Drag, that's A. D. Svensen. I've got to tell you about him because the fifth was a direct result of Ass Drag's death. A. D. made a single-handed try for a Jap foxhole. It wasn't a very smart thing to do because the Jap still was in the hole and he was alive. They both came up out of the hole fighting for Ass Drag's weapon. The way they kept twisting around, neither side dared fire a shot for fear of hitting its own man. Then Julie Chiruco, who was Ass Drag's buddy, thought he saw a chance and crept up on them with his throwing knife. Ass Drag must have turned just as Julie let go because the knife caught Ass Drag good. When the knife sunk into old Ass Drag, Julie laid on the ground and cried. We'd all opened fire to cover him when Ass Drag went down and I saw what Julie did. He jerked the pin from a grenade and held it with both hands to his gut. It blew him all over the hill. Maybe the first four casualties could have been avoided if the men had been rested and alert but I can take them under the circumstances. Julie's suicide is something different. Even if he did kill his buddy, we all know he didn't mean to. He shouldn't have killed himself."

Captain Gold frowned.

"It may not have been suicide. In the heat of the action, you may not have seen it as clearly as you think. It may have been a faulty firing pin or he may have accidentally dropped the grenade."

"It was suicide," Henty said stubbornly. "It was deliberate."

"Alright, Henty," Captain Gold said crisply. "That's between the two of us. We accomplish nothing now by listing this a suicide. For the record, you'll have to admit it's better that Julie Chiruco was killed in action. For the sake of his parents or survivors and for the history of the unit."

"I don't know," Henty said angrily. "This might wake Vinegar Joe up to the facts. It might tell him better than words what condition this outfit's in. Julie just went out of his mind when he saw what he'd done, the poor kid never would have killed himself if he'd been in anything like reasonable condition. Every man in the patrol is suffering from combat fatigue to the point they're right on the edge of going crazy. There's not one of them I'd depend on. I'm not even sure about myself."

"Henty," Captain Gold said in a weary but kindly voice. "Much as I agree with you, what are we to do? Perhaps I feel more keenly about the situation than you because it's my batallion that's trapped at Nhpum Ga. But if it were the 3rd or the 1st, nothing would be altered. We cannot abandon those men up there. And we have to fight with what we have."

"Yes sir, I guess we all know that. And I think the men will somehow manage to keep going if they only have some kind of assurance that when the battle of Nhpum Ga is won and their 90 days are up, we'll be taken out of Burma. That's what they promised before we left India."

"It was a vague promise, Henty, and I don't think you'll find it anywhere in the orders. It was Wingate's policy to pull out his Chindits after 90 days. When Stilwell managed to get command of the Marauders away from Wingate, he inherited that 90-day business as a hangover but not necessarily as a policy."

"But Christ, sir, if the Chindits, the natives, can't take it any longer than 90 days, how the hell can a kid from Albany? The men are done. It's murder to push them further. You realize that."

"I do, Henty, but it's an odd situation. I don't know what the plans are for this unit after this engagement and I doubt that even General Stilwell's own staff is aware of what he has in mind. Certainly, the men will have to rest, but as for leaving Burma . . ." he shrugged. "If we fail at Nhpum Ga, I would not be surprised if those who survive are relieved. But we cannot fail. And when we succeed, Headquarters may be encouraged to believe the unit has the drive for still another mission."

"Is that official?" Henty asked despairingly.

"No, Henty. It is my personal opinion. We are being frank and I have been impressed with your conduct in the field. We know nothing. General Stilwell's staff avoids Hshamshingyan as if we had the plague, which indeed, we do. There have been a dozen planes in and out during the last few days but no one from Staff. There was one man down from Headquarters, a lower echelon officer. But you didn't know that, did you?"

"No sir," Henty said indifferently.

"Yes," Captain Gold said and worn out as he looked, his face brightened with amusement. "The 1st Battalion has knocked out the Japs at Shaduzup and is being sent down to reinforce us although it will be several days before they arrive. Meanwhile, Headquarters wanted something of a semi-official nature on our situation so they sent this lieutenant. He will report that we shall succeed." He chuckled. "You were recommended for a bronze star, you know, as a result of your sortie with the Kachins. Despite the report that is going in to Headquarters, I am going to recommend you for a silver star instead of court martial."

"Yes sir," Henty said without emotion. "You mean for slugging Snotty."

Captain Gold shook his head.

"No, that incident never happened. It has been written off, forgotten. This is a far more serious offense. You chewed out an officer from Headquarters."

"I did what?" Henty said, voice rising. "Hell, Captain, I never even saw an officer from Headquarters."

"No, unfortunately, you did not see him. But you talked with him. On the SCR 300 when you were directing the howitzer fire. This officer who came down was anxious to get in some, oh . . ." he paused and his eyes twinkled, "some actual combat experience. He took over briefly handling the transmissions. You blistered him unmercifully for acknowledging."

"The stupid son of a bitch," Henty said disgustedly. "I knew it had to be somebody from the Pentagon."

"Not from Washington." Captain Gold lighted a cigarette and pushed the pack across to Henty. "A fully accredited member of the C.B.I.——The Chair-Borne Infantry."

Henty lighted his cigarette and covered his mouth with his hand to hide his smile.

"First Snodgrass," Captain Gold mused. "Then an officer from Headquarters. I must say, Henty, that although your attitude is scarcely defensible, I do find it refreshing."

Henty snorted.

"If it wasn't for what's left of my men," he said deliberately, "it would be worth a court-martial to sit out the rest of this campaign in some stockade where you knew what was going to happen next."

"We pointed that out to the young man, and also that the remarks were directed at me, not at an officer from Headquarters. And also that Henshit was, of course, a code name which might have been used by any of three or four men. He was mollified. The most he will report is a general lack of discipline in command."

"Thanks." Henty grinned. "But now they'll probably have your ass."

"One way or another they'll have it, even if it's plugged with earth," Captain Gold said grimly. "Now then, you mentioned physical and mental fatigue in your patrol. That is a general condition which prevails in the entire unit. Specifically, are there cases unfit for combat?"

"All of them," Henty said irritably and then lifted his shoulders in resignation. "They still perform under fire but there are two who bug me. One has dysentery so bad he'll starve to death if he doesn't stumble into a Jap slug. The other one I think is going nuts. The rest, I don't know. I didn't suspect the little Italian although now I think of it, there had been signs."

"Well, those two you mention, give them light duty."

Henty felt his face gawk and Captain Gold laughed aloud at the look of amazement.

"We can't relieve them entirely as long as they're on their feet," Captain Gold continued. "There just isn't the manpower. But I believe the light duty will be possible for the next few days. Your patrol has had two hard days coming right after the action at Inkangatawng. You have been assigned to guard the air strip here. There is sporadic patrol action but at least the position is stationary. Occupy your old foxholes and get what rest you can tonight. Move into the defensive perimeter at the air strip at 0600 hours in the morning. Perhaps you'd better consolidate what's left of your 1st Squad in your 2nd and 3rd."

"No, sir," Henty said, shaking his head and setting his jaw. "It's still better than half a squad and as long as I've got the Jinghpaw, it's better than most full squads. I've been with the men since New Georgia. I know them and I want them where I can watch them. I've given Nick the Greek, Nick Poppas, one of the riflemen, the BAR. He won't have an ammo bearer but he doesn't give a damn, he'll carry the clips

183

himself as long as he gets to shoot the BAR. The 1st still has fire power."

"You're the platoon leader," Captain Gold said. "The patrol is your command until relieved and it doesn't look as if you'd be replaced so continue to handle the men as you think best. Is there anything I can do for you? Anything you'd like to ask?"

"No," Henty said and changed his mind. "Yes, you can tell me something. I think the patrol could have taken that Jap company with howitzer support. You pulled us in. What is the plan?"

"I know," Captain Gold said. "The fact was, we didn't have an adequate supply of shells and felt at the moment the important thing to do was to give what temporary relief we could to Nhpum Ga by interrupting the enemy artillery. More shells are being dropped and within the next day or two, we will mount a two pronged attack and effect a breakthrough. Khaki column backed by the howitzers will retake the main trail and Orange column will mount a separate flanking attack in the direction your patrol pioneered. The 1st Batallion will be here to reinforce and we have been promised air support."

Henty nodded, scooped his tommy gun from the floor and shoved the helmet to the back of his head. Captain Gold pushed the half filled package of cigarettes toward him.

"Thanks," Henty said, slipping the package in his pocket. "And thanks for this break. The men can use it." He took a step toward the opening, hesitated, said over his shoulder: "Can you use a cold beer?"

Captain Gold threw back his head and laughed.

"If you weren't a GI, I'd think you were joking. Nothing is impossible to you men. You'll probably even confound the experts and drive the Japs from Burma. Yes, I could use a cold beer. It would probably save my life."

"You'll get it," Henty said.

The late afternoon was gloomy and muggy, threatening rain in the hour before sunset. Henty stared moodily at his scuffed and mud-caked toes and walked slowly toward the narrow beach at the bend in the river by the foxholes where he'd left the patrol. Maybe it would rain sooner than Meatball predicted but the coming monsoon season no longer promised anything. Sonofabitch, he almost wished Captain Gold hadn't been so honest with him. Capain Gold believed Headquarters was going to use the 5307th to the last Marauder. Oh, they'd drive off the Japs that beseiged Nhpum Ga, they'd release the 2nd Battalion to fight and die another day. The question was why? Why, with all the millions the United States had under arms, did this little band of 2,600 men have to be sacrificed? Why did they have to fight with knives and knuckles and shed tears of joy for a couple howitzers when all the non-combatant Chinks had to do to equip an artillery division was to send Mme. Chiang Kai-Shek to Washington? The whole damned mess smelled to the hills of dirty politics.

"Hey, man!"

Nick the Greek's call roused Henty from his gloomy thoughts. Nick was sitting back from the beach in a sprout of bamboo. He'd been wiping the BAR with a shred of cloth and he held the weapon tightly across his knees.

"Something send you?" Nick asked and licked his lips. "You look far out like you're gone."

Henty laughed shortly and his eyes skipped over the stretch of sand beside the darkening river. A few of the men already were gulping from warm bottles of beer and wine but most were either sleeping or curled up close to their private stores of bottles in the water. He saw Katey and Pretty Pussey off to the upstream side, heads together in private conversation. Kon was lying on his belly hanging over the stream from a grassy neck. Old Overshoes was on his back with his face hidden in his helmet but every once in a while his ears would twitch and he'd turn his head toward some mumbled conversation. Furman had his back against a bamboo clump. His knees were against his chest and he was watching everyone with time-dusted eyes, a hundred years removed from all of them.

The grunting sounds of muffled explosions came from downstream.

"What's going on?" Henty asked Nick, jerking his head at the series of thumps.

"Double Ugly and the Butcher," Nick said, watching Henty closely. "They're fishing. Bombing the river with grenades. Hell with the K rations, we're going to have a fish fry. I didn't get your message, man, like who reached you?"

"Like I was that high," Henty said and pulled his lips apart in a tight grin. "I was out of this world. There's good news tonight. No duty. Tomorrow we take over on the air strip. Just sit on our tails and take pot shots at the Japs. Also, the 1st Battalion is on its way to the rescue. Hell boy, a night off, beer and fish. What more could you ask in this man's war?"

"Women," Nick said brightly. "No, not a houseful, just one lousey goddamn woman. Man, I'd peddle her ass 30 times tonight."

"Crap," Henty said, thinking of Gai-ri, searching the beach for Meatball. He did not see the Jinghpaw. "There isn't a guy in the outfit could get in the saddle with a ladder."

"You laying odds? Let them get a good whiff and you'll see their color." Nick began wiping the barrel of the BAR again and shrugged his shoulders. "You had me moaning low, the way you looked when you walked up here. I thought maybe they were sending us back to Margherita or Deogarh."

"Isn't that what your palm is itching for?"

"Not since you gave me this." Nick held the BAR at arm's length, saw a bit of grit he'd missed and rubbed it with the cloth. "I got to find out how straight it spits."

Henty saw Double Ugly and Butcher plodding through the sand. They had a shelter half between them. It was heaped with silvery fish and hung like a butt sprung hammock. Henty walked oward them.

"Got another couple loads," Double Ugly said. His face was red and he was puffing.

"Good idea," Henty said. "Get them roasted and the fires out before dark. Tell the men to crawl into their old foxholes tonight and keep half an eye open. The patrol takes over on the air strip at 0600."

"Jesus!" The Butcher almost dropped his edge of the shelter half. "They're putting us out to pasture."

"For a couple days," Henty said and walked toward the piece of ground where Kon was lying.

The Pole was staring at the brown necks of half a dozen bottles that thrust above the rippling water from a scooped out basin.

"Maybe the beer will rip my ass to pieces," Kon said, rolling on his side and grinning gauntly. "But I'm going to drink it. I probably won't ever have another chance."

"Knock that off," Henty said sharply. "It gripes my pee, the way you're always bitching. Things are rough all over. We're here. We're safe. We're going to stay."

"How long?" Kon asked quickly, sitting up. His clouded eyes got lights in them.

"A while," Henty said. "A couple of those beers are mine, aren't they?"

"Two," Kon said. "But I'll split them even."

"You can have the four of them," Henty said. "Maybe they'll fix you up so bad they'll have to lift you out. Go on in to the Aid Station now before they roast the fish. Have them change the bandage on your cheek. It's rotten. And see if they've got any kind of pills they can give you. Take my two bottles along and slip them to Captain Gold."

"Jesus," Kon said, reaching his hand into the stream. "You kissing ass now, Henshit?"

"He gave me some butts," Henty said, pulling out the pack and shaking three from the end. "Here."

Kon laid two bottles on the grass and wiped his hand on his fatigues. He placed the cigarettes carefully in his pocket and started to get to his feet.

"Henty," he said quietly. "Overholt's giving us the fish eye from under his tin hat."

"So maybe he needs something to occupy his mind," Henty said, smiling thinly. "Maybe some light duty like helping clean the fish. He likes spilling guts."

"Listen," Kon said, sitting back. "You got to take that bastard serious. He's planning something. I felt him watching me all the time you was at CP. He hates you and he hates me. He seen you give me butts. Now he sees me go off with a couple bottles. There's no telling what idea he gets."

"Stick the bottles in your pack. I don't give a shit about Overholt but there's no point in advertising the fact that Captain Gold's got beer. It might make it hard on him. But you sure as hell just made up my mind for me. Overholt's going to clean those fish. I'm going to find out right now just how short his fuse is burned."

18

THE refuse pit at the edge of the beach had been dug fairly deep. It was half filled with the slimy guts of a couple hundred fish and buzzed with a couple thousand flies which rose to attack in angry clouds every time a shovel of dirt disturbed them. The handle of the trenching tool was short. Covering the garbage with it was like filling a bucket with a teaspoon.

Bob Overholt pulled his head from the crawling stench and tried to spit out the taste of it that clung to the end of his tongue. He took a step away and faced upstream, filling his lungs with thick night air that didn't taste much better but had a different smell. It was the odor of Burma, old and decayed, like a damp corner of a barn littered with moldy leafs and straw.

Behind him was the flat area of paddies which the foxholes ringed. Between him and the whispering Tanai, the men were putting out the red embers of their cooking fires. Most were smothering them with sand but the woodsmen in the patrol were drowning theirs with piss and you could hear the spitting steam and taste that acid smell, too. The night had dropped quickly on the Tanai valley, dark and heavy. The men were outlined but had no features. He turned. He could make out the *bashas* at the far edge of the clearing and the jungle beyond but only as black cutouts against a background not quite so dark.

"Well shit," he said aloud and laughed harshly.

He stooped, feeling the ground about his feet, and picked up his bottle of rice wine. He hadn't eaten, couldn't have choked down a rotten mouthful if he'd wanted, but he'd drunk almost one bottle of wine while he'd slit the fish and scooped out their insides. He felt a little giddy, as if his mind were slightly out of register. The wine was like a mild anesthetic and he had another bottle of it to see him through the night.

He bent over his spade again.

Henshit's fatal mistake was that he thought everyone was

on his own low level of intelligence. It was the Army's blunder, really, that divided men onto two planes of mental capacity: officer and enlisted man. And Henshit accepted the fact. Henshit had assumed he could treat all of them the way he had the Mex and the little Italian who'd never finished high school and that was where Henshit had tripped himself. He didn't know that Pfc. Robert Overholt had completed two years at a teachers college.

He'd almost laughed in Henshit's teeth when that imbecile had ordered him to clean the fish, the ploy was that apparent. Sergeant Holiday didn't know one damned thing about psychology. Bob Overholt had caught that unskilled maneuver even as his gorge rose dark and bitter. Henshit had wanted to provoke an incident, to inflame him with unreasoning rage by ordering him to the dirtiest duty he could find, the garbage detail. Henshit had thought he was safe, in front of the whole platoon, right next door to CP where he bought favors by passing out the men's beer to the brass, the thieving bastard. And sure, Bob Overholt had burned with resentment, but he could be cunning when the need arose. He'd snapped his mouth shut like a clam and cleaned the stinking, slimy fish. He'd get Henshit but he'd choose the time and place.

Bob Overholt always had been a leader, as far back as he could remember, he didn't have to be shown more than once what made the wheels go round. Even when he'd been in knee pants, he'd had a way with animals and it worked the same with people. You take a puppy or a kitten or even a pony and whip it from the start, let it know who's boss and you never have a bit of trouble. Conditioned reflex, they called it. He'd been doing things right instinctively before he even heard of psychology. So you do the same with people. Like in high school when he was boxing Golden Gloves, he'd figured that out very cute. He'd trimmed his weight down from light heavy, just a shade under the maximum for middle weight, only a fool would fight on even terms. Then he'd get in there fast with a low hard punch that jarred them and they'd be on defensive pedaling backwards from his mitts and he had them nailed. He'd have had the city middleweight championship, too, if it hadn't been for that damned referee who'd called him twice for punching low and then disqualified him. There always was some busybody who only wanted to show off his authority.

He'd played it smart again when he went on to college, entering State Teachers where he carried some real weight as fullback. Christ, his sophomore year he'd been a first stringer. There wasn't any competition. All the teams on their schedule were made up of little guys who weren't fit to carry water for a University eleven, he'd trampled all over them. Best ground gainer State Teachers ever had and he'd have made All-State, too, if it hadn't been for being thrown out of so many games. What the hell, it was just smart tactics to use your fist or elbow when you had a chance.

But even if the System, the little guys who ran things from the sidelines, always was laying for a big man with brains, he'd plowed ahead. Right out of State Teachers, although he had only two years in, he got a job teaching junior high physical ed and hygiene. Best damn swimming instructor they ever had and they admitted it. He knew how to make the pampered brats learn to swim. The first time he got them in class he'd line them up, the non-swimmers, at the deep end of the pool, tell them to jump in and sink or swim. And they'd swim, most of them. Hell, if they held back and didn't do what he told them, he let them have it across their bare butts with the razor strop he always carried, you could cut with it when you got a real bad actor. There was nothing like that razor strop for results and real respect. He should have known there'd be some weak-spined four-eyed kid who'd run home to Pop, bitch about the water he gulped into his lungs and show the old man the welts on his back that had bled a little. A boy with any starch would have been ashamed to admit that he'd been punished for turning up a weakling. And of course, the kid's old man had to have a friend who was on the school board.

Being dismissed from that junior high crap had been a break as he'd soon realized, why work with kids? His talents had been wasted. He was the youngest rookie cop they'd ever had and it didn't take them long to recognize his abilities. They let him handle the preliminaries at the interrogations. They'd leave him alone for a while with the suspect in the little brickwalled, windowless room with just a table and one chair. By the time the sergeant or lieutenant got around to taking the prisoner's statement, he was ready to sign a full confession. Bob Overholt had done a good job, he'd never once slipped up and left any marks where they could show, and he'd liked working for the Police Department. It was a fine job until that young, new district attorney bastard had started playing politics, trying to make a name for himself by investigating police brutality.

But what the hell, the warden knew a top guard when he saw one. They'd been glad to get him at the pen and there was no one who maintained discipline in the yard the way he did. You made your reputation and then you made it stick. There wasn't a day went by he didn't crack his stick on someone's skull whether or not he had it coming. You had to keep those cons off base. He'd still be there at the state pen instead of in this stupid Army where they didn't know officer material when they saw it if it hadn't been for that riot. Well hell, the flare-up didn't last for beans. Some convicts holed up in the messhall and when the guards went for them with water hoses, the bastards set the place on fire. Jesus, he was mad at those sons of bitches. When the tear gas got the prisoners staggering out of there, he beat two of them to pulp with his stick. The warden thought it would be a good idea if Bob Overholt got lost in the Army and look where he was now, gutting fish in Burma and grubbing garbage.

He spaded a last shovel of dirt into the hole, walked across the beach and stooped beside the river. Wetting his hands in the water the night had turned black, he scrubbed them with sand, rinsed them and sloshed water on his face. His jaw was tender where Henshit had slapped him with the pistol. Rage flared anew and burned fiercely. Henshit was going to die for all the crap he'd pulled.

The squad leaders were lining up the men as he walked back to the hole where he'd left his rifle, trenching tool and pack with the second bottle of wine. His mind was alert and sharp but the wine he'd drunk had made his legs unsteady. He stumbled over something lumpy, swore and bent down to feel a still-warm lump of clay. The Kachin guide had been on the beach briefly, had shown the men how to wrap the fish in leafs and clay for baking, and then he'd left. Just disappeared. The Kachin never stayed with the patrol at night. There was something strange about that. The guide knew the country, probably knew where there was a village with decent food and beer. And women. And the Kachin was Henshit's friend.

"First Squad," Henshit called from the perimeter. The moon was obscured but the darkness had grown thinner and you could see him, tommy gun dangling. "Two men to a hole. Katey and Pretty Pussey. Furman and Nick the Greek. Kon and Overholt. Leave a vacant hole between you. Spell yourselves."

Kon, now there's another I've got to get, Bob Overholt thought with a fine glow of satisfaction. He picked up his rifle and trenching tool and slung his pack on one shoulder. Henshit's putting Kon in the hole to watch me; well, I won't do anything as idiotic as slitting his throat tonight but life is going to be miserable for the Pole. Henshit would be sacked in up in one of the *bashas,* too far away to help Kon if he yelled.

"Wheah y'all fixin' f' me t' bunk?" the radioman asked plaintively. "Wheah y'all want me b'tween naow?'

Some of the men laughed.

"I hadn't forgotten you, Runner," Henshit said. "You get officers' quarters tonight, where it's safe. Go on up to the *basha* where Snotty holed up. If anything pops, we want contact."

"Thank y'all kin'ly, suh," the Runner said, sucking ass. "Ah'll tained th' stoah."

But it was exactly as Bob Overholt had figured out, he told himself with a smirk. Henshit would be up there in the *basha* with the Runner and he'd have Kon strictly to himself.

The men were pairing off, straggling toward the foxholes. They were crawling into the ones they'd occupied before. Bob Overholt had marked the hole he'd shared with Hari Kari to the left of a thick clump of bamboo that grew down by the river. It was next to the one Henshit and the Mexican had been in the first night.

He walked toward it and Kon fell in a step or two behind without speaking. He'd like to get his hands around Kon's neck, the scrawny chicken neck that wouldn't take much to twist. But there were other tricks and Bob Overholt knew them all.

When they reached the darkly yawning hole, Bob Overholt

dropped in his pack, tool and weapon, jumped in beside them and deliberately made a clear area at one end, kicking the equipment over to the other side. Let the Pole bastard make something out of that. Jesus, if there was one thing he couldn't stand it was ass kissers like Kon the Runner.

The foxhole was reasonably dry now and he pulled off his helmet, standing, waiting and watching. Kon slid over the edge, still without speaking, and hunched against the far wall with his M-1 clutched to his chest. In a moment, he shrugged off his pack and let it slip down. He had something under his left arm. It looked like a bottle of beer.

Henshit, swinging his tommy gun, strolled by the hole and lowered himself into the one he'd shared with Domingo. Bob Overholt glared at Kon and pulled the wine bottle from his pack. Henshit wasn't taking chances, he was going to be right there on hand to protect his boy. In fact, Bob Overholt thought, suddenly wary, they'd boxed him in with a vacant hole on either side. He took a long dring and felt it in his legs again. He leaned against the side of the hole to steady himself.

"I'll take the first watch," Kon said abruptly, leaning forward and shifting as if he were uncomfortable. "They gave me some pills for my gut and they said they'd probably make me sleep."

"Balls," Bob Overholt said and laughed shortly. "I'm standing guard first. I'm not sleepy. Don't you worry about any pills knocking you out. When it's your turn, I'll damn well see you're on your feet."

He gulped again from his bottle.

"Suit yourself," Kon said and muttered something under his breath. He leaned forward and shifted again from the wall.

"You got to shit, get out of here," Bob Overholt said.

"I don't got to shit," Kon said. "I done that already, all there was. I just got a goddamn pain in my gut."

"Well pain or no pain, you better get your sleeping done now while you can. I don't care if you're doubled over, you're going to take your turn when my time is up."

"For chrissake, it's what I'm trying to do," Kon cried out. "Leave me be."

Bob Overholt smiled and had another drink of wine. He kneeled with his head above the edge of the hole watching Henshit's foxhole. There wasn't any movement visible or even sound of movement but Henshit must have some plan in mind, maybe he'd come crawling over to talk with Kon on some pretext hoping to find neither of them on guard so he'd have another excuse to ream out Bob Overholt.

The night was quiet, almost peaceful and the sky must be clearing because you could see the mounds that marked the entire perimeter. The jungle was dark and the river was dark but you could see a form if it moved. A little breeze had come up, enough to sway the fronds. Bob Overholt had another drink of wine. It was funny, the way the wine left his head clear but made his legs and arms shaky.

Shaky, if anyone had been shaky it had been Hari Kari. It was too bad about him. What the hell had got into Hari Kari anyway? He'd actually liked the guy, much as he'd liked anyone, they'd been buddies. It had happened the way Henshit had said at first, he'd killed Hari Kari in self defense. He'd happened to turn to call something back to Hari Kari and there the crazy bastard was aiming his M-1 at him. Hari Kari had got a weak and sickly smile on his face and started to shake all over and let his M-1 fall toward the ground. Bob Overholt had let him have it. Two quick shots. Christ, once a guy got started that way you never could trust him at your back again. He'd got Old Hari Kari with the first shot but he'd squeezed the second off wide. Just in case. It had worked, too. They hadn't even looked to see if Hari Kari's piece had been fired and he'd had the sense to jerk out the clip before he'd tossed the rifle in the hole with the body. But Jesus, it hurt when a guy you'd buddied with went sour on your hands like that.

From the other side of the hole, Kon's breathing was deep, labored but regular. On top of the marching he'd done in his condition, and the beer, the pills had knocked him out cold. It was going to be a pleasure to kick him around when the time came to get him on his feet.

Bob Overholt didn't actually hear the sound, but he was aware of the silence that followed it. It came from near Henshit's foxhole. He swung his rifle slowly and carefully, grinning. Someone was moving outside the perimeter and he didn't think it was a Jap. If Henshit had left his hole even to take a leak, he was going to get it. Bob Overholt searched the area

194

of paddies between Henshit's foxhole and the bamboo clump near the river for a moving shape. He could see nothing, hear nothing. Then Henshit's head came out of the foxhole and there was another head beside it at the edge. A figure pushed away and Henshit started to turn his head. Bob Overholt sank back into the hole.

He looked at Kon and listened carefully to his breathing. He was certain Kon was sleeping deeply. He swallowed several times from the wine bottle, waited another moment and cautiously lifted his bare head above the ground. One dark shape was nearing the clump of bamboo and another was crawling after it. It was Henshit. He could see the motion of the tommy gun as its butt bit into the ground.

Bob Overholt shot another glance at Kon, edged out of the foxhole and wriggled toward the bamboo until the first figure disappeared in the shadows. Then he lay motionless and waited. He saw Henshit get to his knees, look back around the perimeter and walk into the trees. Bob Overholt elbowed his way rapidly to the side of the clump. When he stood in the trees, he turned to examine the holes. You could see lumps and ridges between but you could not tell what they were. He pushed cautiously through the bamboo and searched the edge of the river. After a moment, he found Henshit and a shorter figure, it probably was the Kachin guide, walking single file, keeping close to the bamboo and grass, secretive and furtive.

He hesitated. He was wobbly and uncertain of his body. He could return to his foxhole, shoot Henshit when he crawled back toward the perimeter and it would be Henshit's fault for being where he didn't belong. But Bob Overholt's mind was alert and his thoughts were racing. If the Kachin was taking Henshit to his village, and food, and beer, and women, Bob Overholt was going to find out where it was located. He'd go back there when the women were alone and take what he wanted. Food. And beer. And women. He laughed to himself and started after Henshit and the Kachin. He tottered a little but his mind was clear. I keep telling myself that, he thought, but it was true. Every time Henshit or the Kachin started to look back, he was hidden in the grass or shadows.

The breeze had freshened and was chasing the clouds across the sky. He had to be more careful because every now and then the clouds swept off the moon and the river glittered and the ground was light enough to show your shadow. He dropped back until he was about 300 yards behind Henshit and the Kachin. And then shrank into a clump of trees. Someone was following him. He could hear the rustle of the movement through the grass and trees. He waited. The sound died away and started up again. He laughed foolishly to himself. The sound was above him and it was the wind in the fronds.

When another cloud darkened the moon, he crept from shelter and hurried on along the river. No longer could he see Henshit and the Kachin. He pushed on faster on wobbly legs, running and stumbling across an open stretch of grass and into the darkness of bamboo that sprouted on a knoll. Ahead lay a patch of tall *kunai* and he could see no sign of movement in it. His arms and hands began to shake as badly as his legs. He'd lost them. Or they were hiding, here with him. Stand still, don't panic, his mind told him clearly but still he shook.

He heard a splash and his eyes skipped across the river. Henshit was climbing out of the water on the other side. He studied the open river, went back upstream, waded to the other side and back downstream until he found the marks where Henshit and the Kachin had stepped out. The cover was thin but he did not see their shapes ahead. He crawled, trailing the tracks they'd made. His whole body was quivering now. It was not fear. It was just the wine.

Water spattered. He skittered off the trail and crouched in the grass, hiding. He had to hide. He didn't dare shoot and he didn't trust his quaking hand to plunge a knife home. Nothing crept out of the water. It had been a fish, he told himself.

He moved back to the pushed down grass where Henshit and the Kachin had walked. I should return, he thought. He was in an agony of indecision. His limbs were trembling uncontrollably as if he'd been seized with a fever. But the village must be near. He'd go on until he found it and then quickly go back to the foxhole. It would be easy going back. With Henshit and the Kachin eating and drinking in the village, he wouldn't have to be so careful. He'd locate the village and then he'd be waiting in the foxhole for Henshit's shape to come sneaking up from the river on its belly.

He bent over the trail again and forced his quivering flesh to go on.

The jungle began to close in and he needed the moonlight now. Each time a cloud threw its shadows above the trees, he had to wait until the veiled moon showed him the track again.

Then he lost the trail. He had it when the light blinked out. When the moon seeped through the curtained jungle again, it had vanished. He circled on all fours like an animal sniffing for a scent, through the trees and brush and grass, in the palish green light and in the dark. He threaded himself into the growth until he no longer could find the way he'd come. He clamped his teeth together to keep them from chattering.

Exhausted, he pulled himself into the vine-laced growth and cringed like an animal in a hutch. He was panting and his throat was parched. The mosquitoes began to drone. His skin crawled under their hot sting. He closed his eyes and tried to breathe deeply to calm himself. But his senses were aware and they told him he was not alone.

He opened his eyes, hugging his rifle. And gradually a wary elation quickened his heart and calmed his limbs. The fragrance of cigarette smoke was faint and elusive but it was in the air. He slowly leaned forward, swept the ground with his hand and crept a foot ahead. A moment before he'd been trembling but now a tenseness gripped his body and he advanced another foot. He was in a narrow, uncluttered aisle. Breathing shallowly through his mouth, he searched it for its secret.

The moon showed its face again. He lay motionless looking at the overgrown outline of a *basha*. A crack looked warm, as if there were a light inside. And laughter sounded softly. It was female laughter.

When the night was thick again with darkness, he inched back, out the vine entangled entrance to the aisle where he'd lost the track and straight across from it into the growth until he was covered by the jungle and the night. He lay there, pulling his lips apart and biting his teeth to keep from laughing aloud. The rifle was hard against his side but his fingers reached for the knife at his belt. He slipped it out and dug its blade into the ground to hide the gleam if the moonlight should strike it.

The knife wasn't for Henshit. Not tonight. Henshit could return safely to his foxhole. The knife was for any Kachin he might have to kill before he took the woman.

19

THE pinkly yellow flame from the bamboo sticks slanting into the fire pot cast grotesque shadows on the wall of the *basha*.

"Oh look!" Gai-ri cried and her silvery laughter tinkled. "You are not a chicken as the Jinghpaws say but a rooster who fills the room."

Henty, sitting crosslegged in his shorts, glanced over his shoulder and his shadow head bobbled on the slanting roof. He held his dog tags to his face, twisted them until they showed flat in shadow and moved them apart and together again.

"Duck," he said. He looked back at her and smiled.

Gai-ri was sitting with her legs folded under her across the earthen pot of flame. Her black hair was soft and loose about her warm-brown shoulders and she wore a yellow orchid tinged with red over one ear. Her *sari,* barely covering the hard pushing nipples of her breasts, was new, of white silk chute cloth.

"You look like a bride," he said.

"You make me feel like one." She held a hand to her mouth but the laughter bubbled out. "Is it because now that I have fed and bathed you, you wish to lie with me?"

He chuckled.

"I should have said you look like a wife. I wish to talk with you."

"Oh!" She pouted prettily but her eyes were merry. "You are going to scold me."

She rose to her knee, reached for his bamboo cup and refilled it with *laku.* When he'd taken it, she touched his cheek. Her fingers were more caressing than a kiss.

"I am sorry, master," she said, sitting back and dropping her eyes. "I did not notice your cup was empty."

"Gai-ri," he said, abruptly serious. "It is hard to believe that only two nights ago I saw you for the first time in this hut."

"So!" she said, eyes flashing and tossing her head. "The time seems much longer? You have tired of me already?"

He laughed with real pleasure.

"A man can be a stranger wherever he is found, but a woman is a woman all the world around," he said.

She lifted her eyebrows and thought about it.

"It is partly true but some things are different," she said, lifting her right shoulder, running her palm over her breast and smoothing the cloth on the curve of her hip. She dropped the pose and almost giggled. "Who said that?"

"I did," he said and pulled his brows together. "It must be something I read. I don't think or talk that way."

"When you are with your men, you are one of them. When you are with me, you are someone else. I have observed this."

"I feel like someone else," he admitted thoughtfully. "When I am with you nothing is the same as it has ever been."

"What has it been before, Chicken? What was your other life? There is something that calls you back?"

He smiled at the bantering way she used the Jinghpaw's name for him but he thought he detected a note of sadness in her voice.

"I am no longer certain of anything. Once I was sure I knew exactly where I was going. You have changed that." Now he laughed. "There is no other woman, Gai-ri, no wife or family. You are the only home I have ever had."

"You must have known many others to read my mind so clearly," she said, smiling faintly and adding quietly: "You, too, are in my heart."

He stretched his arm to his fatigues and reached a cigarette from the pocket, picked a burning stick and lighted it. When he replaced the bamboo in the pot, he pushed the other pieces down to the center so the ends were below the rim. Gai-ri was smiling when he looked at her.

"Have you finished talking so quickly?" she asked.

"I haven't started with what I have to say."

"You should not boast of your many women until you know the customs," she chided.

"I didn't boast, you said that!" He shook his head, smiling. "What customs?"

"When the fire consumes the bamboo to the ends of the sticks, it signifies you wish to find your pleasure in me. If you wish to talk, I shall place more firesticks within the pot but they will be short ones."

He watched with pleasure as she stood in a single graceful flowing gesture and walked to the shadowy corner of the hut. He smelled again the taste-fragrance of papaya, felt the good warmth of desire burn in his groin at the slender body whose strength he knew so well.

"Kiss me, Gai-ri," he said as she kneeled beside him with the sticks.

He did not seek her mouth with hunger nor touch her. The gentle merging and soft withdrawal of their lips was more soothing than passionate. It is this way, he thought, when there is more than lust.

She returned to the other side of the fire and folded her legs under her *sari*. Her lips were smiling and he thought her eyes were pleased.

"I sometimes think you are more of the East than you know," she said. "You have learned or somehow know the second plane of union. The first is physical and I find much pleasure in it. The second is of the mind and that can be even more meaningful. It may be that someday we shall find the third plane together."

"It is strange, but you have explained something that puzzled me," he said, remembering the emotions she had aroused the last time they had been together. The last time, why it had been that same morning. "I wondered why I should still find pleasure in you when I no longer desired your body. What is the third plane?"

"It is of the spirit," she said simply.

"Are these the teachings of your convent school?" he asked, astonished.

"My mother is of the East and she has explained such things to me. But in most religions such concepts are common although they are expressed in different ways." She looked meditatively into the flames and for a moment he felt she went away. But when she lifted her head, lights danced in her eyes. "You did not intend to talk of religion or philosophy but I have a feeling that inside you know of these matters although you may never have learned them. Have you always been a soldier?"

"Almost always," he said, grateful for the question yet wondering whether it was intuition or perception that prompted it. "I have been in the Army for nine years and before that for two years in an undertaking of my government that was something like the Army but called by a different name."

"But the United States has not been at war for nine years," she exclaimed.

"No," he said. "Most of the time I've served has been in the peacetime Army."

Gai-ri's eyes were puzzled.

"But of what use are soldiers and an Army when a country is not at war?"

"It is for defense. If your country is big and strong enough the enemy will not dare attack you."

"But the Japanese attacked your country."

"We were big but we were not strong enough. And at the colleges there were too many students who said they would not fight. It was something called the Oxford Movement that England gave us before she called on us for help. The enemy did not understand our people and believe that we were weak."

Gai-ri looked disturbed and sighed.

"Why should there be enemies among the nations?"

Henty considered her question carefully and then let her think with him as he went over it aloud:

"There is no simple answer but I am going to try to make one which I believe is at least partly the reason we are at war with the Japanese. Many millions of them are crowded on a very small island. The Japanese want great new areas, all of Asia, the Pacific Islands and perhaps Australia where there is room for their nation to grow big and rich and powerful."

"Burma is not your country," Gai-ri said. "Why have you come here to fight them?"

Henty smoked his cigarette down to his fingers and crushed it in the fire pot before he answered.

"I've often asked myself that," Henty said bitterly. "I think the British should have conscripted every slogan-slinging sophomore who signed the pledge not to fight for his country and shipped the idiotic bastard off to Burma. I can only answer you by repeating what I've been told. We fight here to keep the battle from our shores. We fight here to prevent the Japanese from establishing bases that would be dangerous to our allies and to us. We fight here so we can maintain a supply route to our friends. We fight here to prevent the Japanese from going further. We fight here in the name of liberty to halt aggression." He shrugged. "Some of that, I suppose is true."

"And will you defeat the Japanese?"

"Yes."

"And drive them back to their small island?"

"Yes."

"And then will you once more not have many millions of people crowded into a small space? Since their problem will be the same as it was before, will they not still be your enemy and attack you again?"

"Not if we are big and strong enough."

"But before you said. . . ."

"I know," he interrupted. "I suppose it will happen again. Our people forget quickly and soon grow tired of soldiers. We shall try to make friends with our enemies. The taxpayers will complain of the cost of defense although it is a great deal cheaper than fighting a war. A new generation of students who know nothing of fighting will say they will not fight. And whenever and wherever the enemy thinks we are weak, he will attack."

"And you will always be a soldier because you understand how things really are," Gai-ri said with a certain sad pride.

"Yes. No. That's what I thought. Oh, I don't know," he said helplessly. "It's very confused. I enlisted in the Army because it was hard to find work. I'd been in a thing called the CCC before that. I liked the idea of the government taking care of me if I stayed in the service long enough. When the Japs hit Pearl Harbor, I got mad as hell at them. I don't know how much was patriotism and how much was personal resentment because they'd upset my sweet little plan of security. All I know is I hate them and up to now I've figured if I came through this big one alive I'd have earned by pension and I'd stick it out."

Gai-ri nodded her head and her eyes were understanding.

"But something has happened and now you do not wish to remain in the Army after this war is over?"

"No, damnit Gai-ri," he said heatedly.

"Oh now you're angry," she said quickly.

"Yes, but not with you. I meant no, damnit I don't want to stay in the Army any longer than I have to. I've suddenly discovered I want what Meatball, whatever Jinghpaw wants. A house, a plot of ground. A woman that I——." The word came hard: "Love."

Gai-ri clasped her hands in her lap and looked at them. He could see only her long lashes.

"And you have found this woman?"

"Yes, Gai-ri, I think I have." He drew a deep breath. "You."

"As long as it pleases the Jinghpaws and you," she said softly without raising her eyes, "I shall be your woman."

"Wife," he said gently. He remembered his conversation with Captain Gold and the threat of yet another mission for the marauders. "It may be many months before I can be your husband but when it is possible I want you to marry me."

"I will be your woman as long as it is possible," she said with her head still bowed.

"Gai-ri," he said, throat constricting. "Are you telling me that you will not marry me?"

"It is not for me to say," she said with her eyes still downcast. "I am a property of the Jinghpaws and may be bought and sold."

"Why, then I'll buy you from them!"

"Then I will be your woman as long as you may wish and there will be no need to marry me."

An agitation chafed his heart.

"Damnit! I don't want a woman. I want a wife. Someone who wants to marry me. I'll buy you and set you free and then I'll ask again."

"If that is the way you truly feel. I shall tell you now. I shall be very happy to be your wife."

"And I to be your husband," he said, leaving his side of the fire pot and kneeling beside her. He held her shoulders but she did not lift her head to meet his eyes. His heart was trembling. "And strangely humble."

He felt her body shiver and his breath caught in his throat. His eyes were misted and he waited for a tear to creep from her lashes.

But when she looked at him her eyes were shining, both proud and gay.

"Chicken," she said. "The bamboo has burned too long. Tonight let us forget the other planes and make love on the lowest level."

204

20

THE sky turned salmon pink and lilac blue and morning came.

In his night-moist foxhole, Henty awakened stiffly but with a sense of well-being. He sat upright, stretching, puzzling over this satisfying feeling that was almost smug and yet was in a way disquieting. His squad was being decimated. Almost half of the men who'd been his family so long were gone. He'd been anguished at each death. He still was shocked but this morning he could view the losses calmly, almost objectively as the depletions you'd expect in combat. He did not understand his change in attitude.

It was five o'clock. In the early morning hour, he heard the stirrings in and about the burrows. Grumpy phrases hanging half finished in the still-cool air. GI shoes tramping across the dried paddy to the latrine. Shambling through the sand to the upstream beach. Splashings in the Tanai. The slow dribbling of chlorinated water from the listo bag into tin mess cups and canteens. But they'd be using river water for their coffee although the fires they made from the waxed K ration packages wouldn't boil it. Already he smelled the mingling odors, artificial smell of powdered coffee, burning candle smell of breakfast fires. Smells and sounds of soldiers going about their business on another day of war.

He thought of Gai-ri and the patch of ground they'd have. It wasn't much he wanted. A white clapboard house with a green wood shingle roof. A picket fence with hollyhocks. Starchy ruffled snow white curtains at a many-paned bay window. A big stone fireplace. It must be large to hold a spit and fat cooking kettle. At the back, a vegetable garden and behind that a small-fenced pasture with a cow or two. A fast running stream and a view of the mountains. It would be strange to her at first but it really was her heritage. It warmed him pleasantly to think of what he could do for her. The way he'd dress her, bare-backed in summer to show her lovely shoulders and high heeled shoes to display her trim ankles. He'd have to find a job, of course, but that seemed easy, now that he had a purpose.

He lingered with his thoughts, wondered where they came from. They were all the things his mother never had in their weather-roughened ranch house, before the bank took even that away.

Kon sat on the edge of the hole, swinging his legs. Henty tugged his mind back. Christ, Kon's toes were almost coming through his shoes. But they were clean, he'd washed the mud from them. His canvas leggings were frayed but he'd tried to scrub away the stains. They still were damp. As were his worn fatigues. It pleased Henty that Kon was taking an interest in himself. He didn't have on his pack or helmet but he was wearing his web belt and strapped across his chest, sheathed under his left arm, was a curving *kukri* knife.

"Where'd you get that?" Henty asked curiously.

"Traded."

Kon looked much better this morning. His eyes had lost some of their feverish luster. The bandage on his sunken cheek was stained and gray and the adhesive was curling at the edges but it looked as if he'd washed his face and hands. He still was all skin and bones but he looked cheerful, sort of settled. All any of them needed was rest and decent food.

"Traded what?" Henty demanded. "What you want that for, you crazy bastard? You got enough crap to lug around."

"Traded a bottle of beer and my cigarettes to a guy who'd picked it up. It's Kachin but a Jap had it."

"So now you want to bum a butt." Henty laughed. He pulled one cigarette from his pocket and handed it to Kon. "Christ, what characters I got to put up with. I give you a couple extra butts last night and right away you think you're in business. But why'd you want it?"

Kon lifted his shoulders and looked sheepish.

"It was a good deal. Besides, it don't hurt to have a extra weapon. It ain't much to carry and it makes me feel safe."

"Oh Jesus!" Henty said. "You still worried about Overholt? You make out with him okay?"

"Yeah," Kon said with a crooked smile. "He didn't bother me none. But that's what I come to tell you, not about a cigarette. He ain't in the hole."

"Well why should he be?" Henty asked a little sharply,

thinking of Injun Joe. "So he's at the latrine or down at the river or maybe he didn't like the way you smell."

"His rifle is gone but his pack and helmet's there," Kon reported. "And a wine bottle that's got a couple drinks still in it."

"Then he's not far off. What probably happened is he had a couple bottles of wine and he's sick somewhere. You change off guard with him last night?"

"Naw," Kon admitted. "They give me a couple pills at the Aid Station, said they'd help the pain in my gut and maybe let me sleep. After I took them I was out cold until just now."

Henty nodded his head.

"You look a hell of a lot better this morning. I think they helped. You still got the trots?"

"I ain't been to the latrine once yet," Kon said proudly.

"Shit, that's good. You eat yet?"

"Naw."

Henty braced his shoulders, picked up his helmet and tommy gun and climbed out of the hole. The sky was clear and the sun was beginning to warm the paddy area. It was a gentle morning. There was no sound of firing, at least not in the immediate area.

"Now look," he said, standing beside Kon, narrowing his eyes at the big-boned shoulders that were so thin. "You try to eat your eggs and biscuit, lay off that fruit bar. You got to get some strength to go on. We got a couple days coming here at the strip so we get a chance to get back on our feet. Give me your cup and canteen, I'll get some water for coffee."

"They're in the hole, I'll get them," Kon said, standing. He faced Henty and his eyes got perplexed. "How the hell you do it, Henty? You sleep in the ground like the rest of us but in the mornings you look like you just come out of a shower. Shit, you even smell good."

"Sure, I use Lifebuoy." Henty chuckled and added to himself: with papaya.

Overholt had not returned when Henty called the squads to line up for the take over at the strip.

"What'll we do with his stuff?" Kon asked.

"Leave it in the goddamned hole," Henty growled. "I think I know where that bastard is. He's gone to the Aid Station. The sonofabitch has got a hangover. Because we're at CP he figures we got sick call. He's plain goofing off. When he does show up he can get his crap himself and I'm posting him on walking guard tonight."

The air strip lay between the foxholes and the villages. Ridges that formed the terraces between several rice paddies had been leveled off. The sun had baked the ground hard and the short runway was crude and rough but provided adequate landing and takeoff for the light L-4's and L-5's. To the east the furrowed land flattened to the Tanai, glitetring in the bright sun. To the west lay the yellow and green tangle of the jungle. North was the Aid Station and the CP at the village and south, the perimeter of foxholes. Bunkered positions had been dug in on the jungle side of the strip. Henty left the 3rd Squad in the foxholes.

"Spread them out," he told Butcher. "We'll rotate positions. They're all on alert but let half of them rest, spell each other unless there's action. When Overholt shows up, send him up to me."

He dispersed the second squad along the southwest jungle side of the airfield and the 1st filled in to the north.

"What's left of us," he snapped, sending Nick the Greek into a forward position with his BAR and turning to the Ridge Runner. "I want you back where some sniper can't pick you off. You double as runner. That ought to pleasure you."

"Ah spose y'all want me t' keep this thing bleat'n," the Runner yawned. He was drooping under his pack radio and his lids were heavy over his bloodshot eyes. He hadn't shaved and a soft golden fuzz covered his acned cheeks. He smelled beery.

"No, I don't, damnit." Henty rubbed his eyes. The bare ground was beginning to glare. "I said I wanted you to double as runner. We're going to call Captain Gold now and report in and then we're going to maintain silence unless there's an emergency. There's no sense pinpointing a target. Now drag that thing back to your position and pull it off your back. You hear that now?"

"Suits me," the Runner said in a voice that shuffled like his feet.

"It would," Henty said. "And in between you'll snooze."

The Runner's position was a trench halfway between the jungle and the strip and midway between the positions occupied by the 1st and 2nd squads. There was no shade in it now and by noon it would be a Finnish bath. Henty could feel the sweat coursing down his ribs as he waited for contact with CP.

"Arthur to Lancelot," Captain Gold acknowledged loud and clear.

"Christ!" Henty jerked to his knees and turned down the volume control. "Henshit here. In position. Everything quiet except the squawkie. Look, if it's okay with you I'll use a runner except in emergency. Can you do the same? Over."

Captain Gold was laughing when his voice came back.

"Is that an order, Henshit? It's okay for now. Traffic is heavy and I've got a man I can use if necessary. We should have a field telephone out there. Maybe you better check in at about hourly intervals. We'll just give you a short acknowledgement. Over."

Henty lifted his head and peered into the frilled bamboo at the edge of the clearing. Not even a breeze stirred the fronds.

"Roger, Arthur. Will you check at the Aid Station and see if one of my men came in this morning? Over."

"Roger, Henshit. Anything wrong? Over."

"I don't think so. No activity at the perimeter last night. His helmet and pack are in the hole but he and his weapon are gone. I think he's goofing off. Over."

"Is this one of your problem children? Over."

"Yeah, the batty one. Over."

"I'll check it out. You better call back in 15 minutes if it looks quiet. Anything else? Over."

"That's it, Arthur. Wilco. Over and out."

He looked at the Runner and frowned. If Overholt wasn't at the Aid Station—but he had to be. The Runner was pushing the pack set in the corner of the bunker. He looked questioningly at Henty with his little red eyes. They made Henty's burn.

"Okay, kid," he said roughly. "Stay awake until I come back to make that call. Then get what rest you can. You're communications here, not guard."

He studied the jungle once more. A company of Japs could be hidden within 10 yards of their forward positions and the trees and growth would hide them. The sun made the roof of the jungle flat green. The fronds drooped in the heat. They were lifeless. He was grateful for the dead air. They'd all be limp and gasping by night but no one could move in the jungle without signaling where he was.

Henty bellied out of the trench and hugged his knees as he zigzagged across the baked reddish brown earth to the bunker Kon manned alone. The Pole was leaning on his elbows, intent on the area he commanded. It made Henty feel good, the way Kon had bounced back in one night. Some cold beer, some baked fish instead of potted meat, most of all sleep. Kon always had been a good soldier but the goddamned shits had eaten right into his guts. He was a long way from being well but he was on his feet again.

Kon glanced over his shoulder at Henty. The bandage made his grin lopsided. Maybe the scab itched and he favored the cheek. His right hand was resting on the *kukri* knife. He looked ready to use it.

Henty stood beside him and laughed.

"You got more confidence in that pig sticker than your M-1?"

Kon half turned his head and decided to lean sideways.

"If Ass Drag would of had a *kukri* knife I bet he could of chopped that Jap's head off. Instead, Julie got him with his throwing knife. That was a funny damn thing. I seen Julie toss that knife a dozen times for bets. He could pin it smack in the Ace of Hearts every time."

"He would have dropped the Jap except Ass Dragg swung around just as he let go."

Kon shook his head and scowled.

"That's the screwy part, Henty. I was behind but right in line with Julie and Ass Drag. There was a second when Ass Drag and the Jap was standing still just hanging on to the BAR and that's when Julie threw. They weren't moving at all then."

"Jesus!" A dull pain throbbed in Henty's head. "The one time the little Italian missed, he had to kill his buddy. That's why he blew himself up."

"I guess," Kon said and whistled softly. "What they ought to do is issue all us *kukri* knives."

"What the hell, we got trench knives."

"Ass Drag couldn't get at his. A *kukri* is where you can reach it and it handles real nice. You've seen what the Kachins can do with them."

"Yeah! I sure have. They slit throats neat. I wish to hell Meatball would show up. He isn't exactly under orders but its gotten so I depend on him. This morning I could use him. I'd like to have a scout out there in the jungle."

Kon looked him steadily in the eyes.

"Want me to have a look?" he asked.

"No," Henty said thoughtfully. "Jesus, Kon, you changed overnight. The last couple days you've been ready to cash in your chips. Now you volunteer to scout the jungle that may be filled with Japs."

"I ain't afraid of the jungle any more," Kon said.

"I don't guess you ever were," Henty said. "Sick as you've been, you've been first scout and you've performed. I'll do my damnedest to get those stripes for you and I've got to remember to put you in for your Purple Heart. But you don't know the jungle like the Jinghpaw and besides, the 1st is so goddamned thin now I can't spare a man from guard, let alone risk a casualty. Just hang on here and keep your eyes peeled."

He knocked Kon's shoulder and started to climb out of the position.

"Where you going now?" Kon asked.

"I'm calling CP back to find out if they've located Overholt."

"That piss ant," Kon said disgustedly.

Overholt hadn't been to the Aid Station, no one from Lancelot had been anywhere near CP.

"I'm concerned, Henshit," Captain Gold said. "If the man was unstable, he might have wandered off. Over."

"It's possible," Henty admitted. "I don't like it either. I'm going back myself and have another look. I'll leave Double Ugly from the 2nd in charge here. Over."

"Don't take chances, Henshit. Send someone else. Over."

"That crazy bastard has the rest of them scared. I'm the only one can handle him. If there's action these men know what to do. Over."

"You're boss out there. We've got stuff coming in so pass the word. Call me back and let me know what you find out. Over."

"Roger. Over and out."

As Henty trotted across the strip and started toward the foxholes, he kept looking at the cloudless sky, listening for the tinny chatter of the light plane engines. They sounded so unsubstantial you always wondered how they made it. When you came down to it, they were about as substantial as a straw-

211

berry crate. There wasn't anything on the ground right now, but if the Japs were going to hit, they'd probably do it when a ship was coming in, while everybody was looking the other way. There wasn't anything they'd like better than to get a plane or two. Maybe Double Ugly would handle it right but goddamn Overholt, his absence was pulling two men out.

He wondered where the howitzers were this morning. He could feel more than hear the jungle muffled thumps from Nhpum Ga but the area around Hsamshingyang was uncomfortably quiet. There probably were patrols out but this was the third day of punishment for the 2nd Batallion.

The Butcher was in the hole Henty had briefly occupied the night before. He was chewing the inside of his cheek and sweat dribbled down both sides of his tired face. The Butcher was as tough as they came but he was no youngster, hell he was 40 at least.

"What about we move these holes into the shade?" he asked.

"Sure, take a swim if you want, but don't go near the water," Henty said and grinned, squatting beside the hole. "Any sign of Overholt?"

The Butcher shook his head.

"I asked the men. Nobody's seen him since last night. He was pissed off about cleaning them fish."

"That's no excuse for playing games, for chrissake. He's probably holed up somewhere with a jug of wine laughing at us. I've got to find him. Tell your men I may be out. I'll sing when I come back."

"Something could of happened to him," the Butcher said and winked. It irritated him and he tried to brush it away, as you would a fly. "Why risk *your* neck?"

"Yeah, why should I?" Henty hesitated, then said doggedly: "No, I've got to try. He's still one of my men."

"What about the rest of your squad? Hell, you've got the whole patrol to think of. Maybe it's better you stay in one piece."

"The sonofabitch," Henty said between his teeth and stood. "When I find him I'm going to nail his balls to a banyan tree."

"How you going to find him? You're no Kachin."

"Have you seen the Jinghpaw?" Henty asked quickly.

"Not a sign."

"Hell," Henty said. "He's usually around when we need him

212

and I need him bad. I know I'm no bird dog. I'll do what I can. I'm going to circle the perimeter and see if I can pick out a single set of footprints going off by themselves."

"We'll cover you as long as we can," Butcher said.

Inside the perimeter and between the foxholes and the river, the hard earth showed the scuff marks of GI boots. Just kicked up ground that didn't mean a thing. Henty pushed his helmet off his forehead and rubbed away the sweat with his palm. He began to cover the ground immediately in front of Overholt's hole, weaving forth and back and working toward the Tanai. Here, too, the dirt was marked and once he found a clear impression of a heel but no single set of prints.

Halfway to the clump of bamboo where he'd met Meatball, he spotted a slot that looked as if it might have been scooped out by a rifle butt. He got down on his hands and knees and followed a regular series of gouges back to Overholt's foxhole. Grimly now and sweating hard, he wheeled and followed a trail into the bamboo.

The hairs raised on his spine. A red mist filmed his eyes and he thrashed through the growth to the narrow beach. He found wide-spaced prints of uncertain feet, hugging the cover as Meatball and he had done. He broke into a run.

His mind saw what had happened, re-ran the film in detailed sequence: Kon in his corner of the hole, clinging to his rifle but knocked out cold by the beer and pills he'd taken. Overholt swaying defiantly with his wine bottle, glimpsing Henty as he crawled across the paddy after Meatball, watching them disappear into the dark clump of trees. Overholt inspecting Kon carefully to be sure that he was sleeping, scrambling after them across the paddy. Overholt stalking them along the river, drunk but crafty. Fading into the darkness of the night each time they paused, crouching in the grass, waiting with mean cunning until it was safe to move again. Watching them cross the Tanai, creeping after them through the jungle until they reached the pathway to the hidden *basha*. Looking at them from his hiding place, listening to their sounds of laughter.

Seeing Meatball leave with Henty, finding Gai-ri alone with La Bu La who was old and armed only with a knife. Striking at Meatball when he returned with his bayonet. Overholt was a madman with a bayonet.

Overholt had killed the Jinghpaws and had taken Gai-ri!

Henty's mind shut off.

His mouth was open and he was growling in his throat, low and terrible like a wounded animal when he plunged into the Tanai.

21

THE position Katey and Pretty Pussey held at the air strip was between Kon's hole and the first bunker of the Second Squad. It was a forward emplacement within 50 yards of the matted yellow face of the jungle. The clumped bamboo were spindly but tight and *lianas* snaked about the stems. Delicate fronds made a valance on the wall between the red earth floor and the blue sky ceiling. Their trench was large and would have been a good place for a BAR-man with stacks of ammunition. It was so wide that when you kneeled with your head and knees against one side, your feet did not touch the side behind you. It was long enough to lie down in full length.

Kenneth Katey was standing guard, or at least he was looking across the glinting ground into the tangled growth. Under his steel kettle of a helmet, his brown hair was thick and he could feel it curling in his sweat. He had to unbuckle a little at the knee joints to keep the shoulders of his six-foot frame below the ground. He was not so much thin from the campaign as naturally slender. He knew his face was not unpleasant. His eyes were large, greenish gray, and overlidded which he thought gave him a not unbecoming, studious appearance. The eyes did look half-closed and meditative but that was because his eyeballs were so large. He had a thin hooked nose that was almost like a peregrine's but which he felt was patrician. He knew his lips were too full and so he kept them pursed. With his heavy eyelids, he thought it gave his face an overall look of contemplation. Right now he was wondering what was wrong, what actually went on in the mind of Leonard Pussey.

He was annoyed with Len but he kept the irritation from his voice when he turned to him.

"Don't be angry, Leonard," he said, listening to the melodious baritone. Even the months in India and Burma had not impaired his modulation nor slurred his enunciation. His voice retained its stage timbre. "I know I told you after Deogarh that

I wouldn't try it again unless you wanted. But 'these are times that try men's souls.' After all that beer last night, something in me snapped."

Leonard Pussey was sitting on the bottom of the trench with his legs straight out. He didn't think he looked at all like Ken, who was four or five years older, 25 at least. But sometimes when he glanced casually into his polished steel shaving mirror, the reflection startled him. Once he'd turned, thinking Ken was looking over his shoulder. His eyes were velvety brown and try as he would, he couldn't keep the surprised look from them. He was afraid Ken would think it a naive look, not that he cared so much as long as Ken didn't actually say it. He had a turned up nose that Ken said was pert and he realized his mouth looked like a rosebud. Although now he had pouted it into a cupid's bow and he was sulking.

"It's just that you broke your promise, Kenneth." He heard his thin voice rising in exasperation and swallowed to bring it down. He wished he had an Adam's apple to bobble but he didn't think he'd ever have one. "The other boys talk about us as it is. We're always under scrutiny and I will not give them the satisfaction of discovering us in any kind of compromising situation. And I've told you again and again, I really don't know whether I want that sort of thing. I don't deny I'm attracted to you but the implications frighten me. I've just never had relations with anyone, male or female."

"I've told you I'm sorry, Leonard," Ken said with a touch of asperity. "We don't have to discuss the matter in lurid detail."

"But there are times I want to discuss it," Len said. He was being perverse but he couldn't help it. "You know so many things of which I'm not even aware and you've had such a vast experience. Until I met you, I thought it was being brought up by a doting parent and all that that made me think and feel different. Don't you think it helps to be frank? It thrills me, really, to talk erotica with you. But when you try to do things like you wanted to last night, it makes me shudder. I mean, when I think about your thing in my anus I want to squirm." He swallowed again. "What is it like, Kenneth? Tell me again."

"Oh Leonard, honestly, you're such a child," Ken said peevishly. "All you want is sanitized masturbation by remote control."

Ken flushed.

"All right, so I am a hesitant virgin. I don't want to be raped without knowing what is happening to me."

Leonard was contrite at once and angry with himself. Because he was forced to associate with savages, he did not have to assume their brutish ways.

"Forgive me, but damnit, Kenneth, I do not understand you. You have had the same advantages as I. You've been to camps and you went to a private prep school. Hasn't anyone ever tried to touch you before?"

"Once," Ken admitted shamefully. He remembered the way he'd reacted when the tall boy with the sandy hair who was on the tennis team had grabbed him when they were alone in the shower room. "I screamed. I thought he wanted to injure me. Perhaps I could have adjusted if I had lived in a dorm but I wasn't allowed to live-in. My mother was alone, father was dead and she couldn't bear the thought of rattling about that great old house with the servants lurking behind the portieres. I wonder what the old bitch is doing now. She thought sex was filthy. I must have come from a test tube or some kind of immaculate conception. Does everyone do it in boys' schools?"

"In boys' schools and girls' schools." Len sneered. "You even find it among the common people, at the YMCA and the YWCA. But when you do, they are the ones who are abnormal, physically, I mean. It's only among the cultured and privileged where homosexuality reaches its plane of mental refinement."

"You confuse me, Kenneth, truly you do when you make such statements without qualifying them."

"Oh, don't be a dolt. Do you want to spend your life grubbing along the conventional paths, stiffled by propriety, restricted by the mores of a society with which you have nothing in common? If you are ever to experience anything in this dull life, you must dare. How can you say which fruit is sweet and which is bitter if you don't taste them all?"

Len giggled.

"You made a funny."

Ken let me see that he was displeased.

"That's immature, Leonard. It reflects the same coarse attitude that characterizes peasants like our squad leaders."

"I'm sorry, Kenneth, but you see, I do not understand. You

answered with a generality when I asked what you meant about homosexuality reaching a plane of mental refinement."

"Conventions are not for the arts, Leonard. It is only between two members of the same sex that sensitivity and understanding can be expressed without restraint. You cannot be aware and alive and receptive when you must also be aggressive as it is with man and woman. The true artists, the Oscar Wildes, find the compassion they must have in their own sex."

"But Kenneth, I know that not all artists are homosexuals."

"They're either homosexuals or whoremongers," Ken said peevishly. "And if they're whoremongers their art is gross, like that of Diego Rivera and Ernest Hemingway."

"I like Hemingway," Len protested.

"Ah, you are attracted to the masculinity, the virility. The man dominates his art form. That is what I mean."

"Well, what's it like, Kenneth. Tell me again."

Ken's eyes floated away.

"I don't really want to talk about it if we are not going to know fulfillment."

"Please, Kenneth."

"Oh, all right," Ken said petulantly. "Haven't you ever wondered what copulation must feel like to a woman? It isn't quite the same for a man, of course, with another man, but I think it must be better, that penetration of your body and no foolish conflicts. It's unworldly, the thrill of having someone dear become a part of you. Oh Len, don't ask me to go on. You can't blame me for wanting you."

"Tell me how you'd make me ejaculate, Kenneth," Len said softly.

"Sometimes it happens naturally, from what you're feeling and what you're thinking. If it didn't, I'd use my hand."

"But that's just masturbation," Len said, disappointed. "I can do that myself."

"But it would be different," Ken said, beginning to plead. "You shouldn't have asked me to talk about it. Our bodies would be together and I'd be doing it for you, don't you understand? Because I wanted to. I wouldn't be using you only for my own satisfaction, the way the Arabs do with their boys. I'd want you to enjoy it, too. And I told you last night, if you let me I'll take you in my mouth. It's something you'll never

218

experience from a woman, not unless she does it orally for you."

"But I couldn't do it like that for you, Kenneth." Len said with a thrilling kind of terror. "Whatever would I do with the semen?"

"You'd know what to do with it. Oh Leonard, you've got me all worked up. I'll show you. I'll do whatever you want."

"I told you I won't allow it while we're with the boys. I will not be caught."

"They wouldn't care. They'd be jealous. I'll bet there isn't a boy in this whole outfit who would turn me down."

"Oh Kenneth!" Len said, horrified. "You wouldn't."

"I just might. And it would serve you right," Ken said darkly. "The only thing, they wouldn't do it for me. They're just not sophisticated. They masturbate and that's base and despicable because this must be a shared experience. And they'd let me siphon them off and that's all it would be. They wouldn't reciprocate. That's why it has to be us. We'll release each other."

"Not yet," Len said in a gentle voice. "Tell me once more about the first time."

"You're torturing me," Ken said and went on without pausing: "It was the choirmaster at the church. He was an athlete, big and dark and hairy, there's something about hair. I was only 14 and he got my cherry, you know, in a manner of speaking. We'd gone on a church picnic, there were about a dozen of us boys. We went swimming naked and I could swim better than the rest of them and he challenged me to swim across the lake. There was a secluded sandy place in the sun behind a huge rock and we were exhausted and just sprawled willy nilly in the sand. That is, I thought we did. He kept looking at me oddly and running his eyes up and down my body almost as if they were touching me physically, I mean, and then I saw he had an erection. It was massive. He reached a brawny arm around me and before I knew what was happening he was squeezing one of the nipples of my chest, those vestigal things have feeling, and stroking my penis. He didn't say a word but he was breathing hard and had a kind of dull glow in his eyes. I was frightened a little, more because it was strange and, well, forbidden, but I felt warm inside. I had

219

masturbated just like everyone and I thought he was going to do it for me and maybe I should do it for him so I touched that enormous thing of his, I could hardly get my hand around it. There was something almost savage going on inside me, a pounding and swelling like I'd never felt. And then, I don't know how it happened, I was lying on my stomach and he was straddling my back forcing his way into me."

"Didn't it hurt?" Len asked breathlessly.

"Yes, it hurt, but it was such a strange sensation." Ken laughed in falsetto. "Once he started, I didn't want him ever to stop. I was afraid I'd shit."

"And then what happened?" Len prompted. He had a tremulo in his breathing.

"He rolled me over and did it for me, orally I mean. It was the finest sensation of my life."

"Kenneth?"

"Yes, Leonard."

"Have you ever had it with a woman?"

"Just once," Ken said and you could see the recollection was distasteful. "She was like we are, Leonard. And she'd never had a man and we thought we'd find out together what it was like, the way people call normal. It was messy and right in the middle of it, I went limp. It was a nasty experience. She didn't like it, either."

"Are there many like us, Kenneth?"

"That's like asking are there many truly intellectual people. Well, not quite. There are more than you'd think. A lot of people who aren't brave enough to admit prefer their own sex, even people who are married and have families are, well, ambidextrous in sex. You'll always find, the higher the culture, the more prevalent is homosexuality. Why, the old Romans had perfect orgies."

"But wasn't that just before the empire collapsed? They called them decadent and degenerate."

"Oh piffle twaddle," Ken said heatedly. "That's more of the hypocricy of history. If you want to know the truth, it was their athletic competitions that killed them. Instead of maintaining armies, they got in such a lather about chariot races it was all they paid any attention to."

"And it isn't wrong," Len asked quietly although his insides were quivering.

Ken turned his eyes back to the jungle.

"Come up here," he whispered.

Len got up unsteadily.

"Is it Japs?" he asked hoarsely.

"No, silly. I want you to see something."

Ken pointed to the *lianas* that encircled the stems of the bamboo.

"You see, Leonard?"

"What, Kenneth?"

"The trees in the jungle, and the vines that cling to them. They're phallic symbols. See how the trees respond to the embrace of the vines? They writhe and sway and move their fronds in ecstacy and neither asks the other if it be male or female."

"Yes, Kenneth," Len said in a choking gasp.

"Leonard?"

"Yes, Kenneth."

"Do you have an erection right now?"

"Yes, I do, Kenneth."

"I'll let you take me first, the way I wanted you last night."

"But *here,* Kenneth? I told you we couldn't here. And I'm all sweaty."

"You should have sweat," Ken said exultantly. "You've got to have sweat. You've got to have it strong in your nostrils and grunt and feel you're rutting like an animal to enjoy it. Look around you, quickly. Is there anyone who can see into the trench? Is there anyone on the field?"

Len's eyes hastily circled the area. It was going to happen, he told himself joyfully. He'd only wanted to be convinced. He could see nothing but a few helmeted heads poking out of the ground into the bright sun.

"No," he said. "No one will see us if we're in the bottom."

"Then come quickly," Ken said urgently. "Now. I can't stand it."

He squatted, pulling off his pack and belt, tugging his fatigues out of his leggings, jerking out of them and throwing his shorts in the corner.

"I'll lie on my stomach," he said. "Poke it in. I don't care if it hurts. Only hurry, so I can get on you."

Len already was out of his fatigues. He dropped his shorts. They were bare-assed naked when the Japs launched their attack and found the weak spot in the defense.

22

B AMBOO sprouting like blond whiskers from a wart clustered around Bob Overholt's trunk and pinioned his arms. His legs stuck out stiffly from the mound. Muddied hair was matted on his forehead and his head was bowed. Glassy eyes and gaping mouth were open and filled with buzzing flies that could find no place among the hungry horde to feast on the blood that had spilled from the gash in his throat. He was very dead.

Still limp inside and dripping with sweat not entirely from the pallid waves of jungle heat and river water, Henty hunkered with Meatball against the twiney green that had concealed the pathway to the *basha* where Gai-ri had been.

"I don't want to know where you have taken her," he said again, voice struggling unnaturally. "I cannot go to her and reveal her hiding place. I cannot see her again until the last of the enemy has been driven from this valley. I brought evil to the doorway of her shelter and only fortune preserved her from a wound so cruel I do not think she could have lived with it."

Meatball's eyes were filled with grief and his face was agonized. As Henty spoke, he hung his head between his knees and covered it with limp hands.

"This person of tainted ancestry weeps that his lack of ordinary diligence has deprived you of your pleasure," he said in a voice that sounded wretched with pain.

"Put on a cheerful face, my brother," Henty said more calmly. "We mourn when we should rejoice. This has been no fault of yours. It was my clumsy departure from my foxhole that aroused this carrion. Eagerness to be with the woman hastened my clattering feet and enabled him to follow. But the dark purpose he carried with him overcame him like a vengeful spirit."

"It was the benevolent *nats* who dwell in the rippling waters of the Tanai-hka and in the rising vapors of the night who guided the knife that stilled him," Meatball said, still looking at his bare feet. "But for the watchful presence of the nature spirits, I would have brought you worse desolation than you know."

"I am filled with joy that I have been alerted and that she is safe," Henty said, slowly closing and opening his eyes. "In my selfish desire, I did not think of danger. My pleasure now means nothing. I have told you, I wish to live with this woman for the rest of my years.

"It is understood, Dua," Meatball said, lifting his head. His face was still graven but some of the grief had drained away. "Ding Ring and Ding Ra have strengthened La Bu La's hand. One knife leads her, another is at her side and the third follows. I tell you only that she has gone to the north with others of our people. The enemy has become more numerous in the valley and it is best the old ones, the women and the children should be removed. We will secure the person of your woman with our lives. Also, Dua, there will be no more talk of buying her. It gladdens the hearts of all our people you can treasure a gift we make from poverty. When the time has come for her to be at your side, there will be feasting and rejoicing."

"I am well pleased and happy," Henty said. He smiled and laid his hand on Meatball's warm, big-muscled shoulder. "It is done and in good time." He looked over at the corpse in the clump and repeated the question he'd asked before. "Who could have done it? Friend or foe, I owe a debt I never can repay. I know too well what was in that one's mind."

"It was not one of us who came upon him," Meatball said. "I have questioned those who were near. I regret we did not discover him but if we had we would not have killed him. He would have been trussed on a pole like a pig and brought to you for punishment."

"You say the enemy has increased his forces," Henty said. "It must have been a Jap who found him alone and was not aware of why he was hiding or of the *basha*. And yet I cannot understand the enemy not taking his weapon. You did well to remove my woman at the moment in the sunrise when your eyes first beheld this befouled chunk of worthless meat."

"Our lack of wisdom shames us all," Meatball said. He picked up his tommy gun from his side. "It is beyond belief. So careless have we become in our recent victories that we have made a pathway to our place of concealment. I have examined every bent spear of grass, every bush and tree. I have searched even the surface of the water in the river and found only this one's tracks. There are other imprints without number for everyone to see but not a trail to follow."

"This one surely meant great harm," Henty said, standing. "You must count this a sign that the *nats* are pleased and will not forsake you."

"It is as you say, Dua. The *nats* were vigilant when we deafened ourselves with the prideful boasting of our deeds. We shall burn many sticks to them." He looked without emotion at Overholt's body that crawled with ants and insects as well as flies. "Do you desire that we take this husk between us and return it to your camp?"

"No," Henty said, anger tightening the cords of his stomach and making him strong again. "Already he has been the source of death and the well of trouble. He has deprived us of his weapon when we needed it although I am not entirely without blame for tempting him. I now have been absent too long from the camp where my eye is needed to guard against the enemy. Later, when the atmosphere is serene, I shall send some men to bury any of the bones the animals have not carried off. I must leave."

"I shall return no more to my people but take his place in your Army because my lack of caution took him from you."

"You would replace a jackal with a tiger." Henty laughed. "The loss is of little consequence. We shall replace him with a mule. He was fit only to bear a pack. If you will continue to serve us as before, we shall be grateful."

Meatball's brown face shone with pleasure and they walked together through the sun splotched jungle toward the river. It was quiet and calm, perhaps deceptively calm and they were alert but both felt release from their earlier tensions.

"Have you a woman in mind to live with and a place chosen for your *basha* when there is peace?" Henty asked as they approached the Tanai.

"I do not concern myself with the identity of the woman," Meatball said and his teeth gleamed white. "Anyone who is young and not deformed or ugly will suit me. Whatever she is when she comes to me, I shall mold her to a pattern of my liking and she will be as I wish. The land is a consideration. I think perhaps it will be near a stream in a valley between the mountains."

Henty laughed softly: It was what he wanted for Gai-ri and himself.

They searched the opposite shore and finding no revealing movement in the trees or grass, draped their belts about their necks. Holding their tommy guns at shoulder height, they waded into the water.

"Mostly it is peaceful in our hills and valleys," Meatball said as they dragged their legs across the stream. He laughed. "Oh, there is activity enough for sport. From the north and the south, they come repeatedly with weapons and seek to drive us from our land. They say they wish to tame us. In the memories of the most ancient of our headmen, there is no recollection of an invader who has vanquished us or even lived to make his home among us. This present enemy will soon depart our valleys."

"I believe what you say is true," Henty said.

On the beach, Henty shook his shoes. The water sloshed. He ran his fist down the dripping legs of his fatigues and looked enviously at Meatball, clad only in his shorts. They started for the foxholes staying within the shade and shelter of the trees.

"Here in these hills is a very good place to spend all the years," Meatball said. "Life is pleasing and without much effort. The best of meat and especially deer is within a few steps of your shelter which is a simple matter to erect. There are the fishes of the stream for the taking and tender sprouts for the cooking pot grow everywhere. A *tongyaw* is a little work but once the rice is planted, caring for it is a woman's task. When the enemy again retreats as has always happened, I do not think he will come soon again. Those of us who have been warriors will grow fat sitting by our fires, drinking *laku,* telling one another how brave we were and counting ears. What more can any man ask than a substantial shelter, plentiful food and drink, an obedient woman to warm his back and friends to share his happiness? Is that not a good life?"

"A man could ask for little more," Henty agreed.

"You will take your woman to be with you in your distant land?"

"Yes." Henty smiled: Gai-ri would be a wide-eyed child in a supermarket, he wondered whether she'd ever get used to the resplendent novelty.

"It will sadden us for you to leave, Dua, but we shall have a feast to celebrate your contentment. We shall send a *nat* with you for fortune."

"I'll probably need the *nat*," Henty said absently. He thought he heard the buzzing of aircraft.

He stopped. Overhead in the vast, unblemished blue were two dark specks. The faint humming of their engines grew louder and faded off again. They'd be coming in at the air strip soon. The airplanes were alien in the sky above this simple land but they would leave with the Army and all would be as it had been before.

"Where will you build the *basha* for your woman?" Meatball asked as they walked on.

"Not in a village, but away from people where there is space to live."

But even in the country there were super highways, county roads, railroad tracks, telephone lines, REA, fenced-in acres. And he'd need an automobile to get about.

"What is the appearance of the *bashas* in your land?"

"You would not know them." Henty shook his head. "They have solid walls and many rooms."

Building contractor, plumber, electrician, heating, insulation and weatherstripping, storm windows, screens, wallpaper, paint, FHA and mortgage payments, doors with locks, the-drawers-are-sticking.

"Many rooms? And what goes in them?"

"Many things of comfort."

Refrigerator, electric stove, Beauty Rest mattress, silk shaded lamps, Zenith radio, marble topped tables, tapestry chairs and davenport, scenic pictures to brighten your outlook, mirrors to tell the truth, telephone, flush toilet, pink bathtub.

"And you will have a *tongyaw?*"

"We shall have a garden."

Irrigation, a gasoline tractor, seeds in packages, tomato plants, fertilizer and pesticides.

"And there is game and fish?"

Henty nodded his head.

Hunting license, fishing license, game check station, POSTED LAND, out-of-season, outboard motor, you-should-have-seen-the-one-that-got-away.

"I think you will have many different things to eat and drink from what we know."

Kellogg's Corn Flakes, Gold Medal flour, canned creamed corn and frozen spinach, pasteurized milk, oleomargarine, pork chops, hot dogs and catsup, Miracle Whip, dill pickles, Michelob beer and Old Fitzgerald, RISING FOOD PRICES. INCREASED COST OF LIVING.

When Henty didn't answer or comment, Meatball went on:

"I think it must be a different kind of life from what we know with many uncommon things to see and do."

Again Henty made no remark: Yellowstone Park, a World's Fair, White Sox and Golden Gophers, Memorial Day, National Dairy Week, PTA, flashing lights and neon signs, juke boxes, church collection, shave-and-haircut, $1.50, Hollywood and Jack Benny, antidotes for living.

"It will be a new life for your woman."

"Very different," Henty acknowledged.

Fingernail polish, pancake makeup, beauty shop, fur coat, cloth coat, rain coat, housecoat, Nylon stockings, evening slippers, bedroom slippers, overshoes, uplift bra, cocktail dress, evening dress, nightgown, optometrist, orthodontist, neurologist, obstetrician, pediatrician, vitamin pills, don't-you-think-we-ought-to-join-the-country-club?

"This land of yours must be a very happy country, much like ours, where all the people love the freedom which you fight to give back to us."

Income taxes, life insurance, KEEP TO THE RIGHT, No Trespassing, Police Department, RR Crossing, Members Only, MATRON RAPED IN CITY PARK, AFL and CIO, politicians, pedagogues and preachers, city jails, county jails, penitentiaries, insane asylums, WPA and CCC, birth certificate, marriage certificate, death certificate, City Park-Keep Off the Grass, Exit Only, No Dogs, No Cats, No Colored Allowed—my God, that meant Gai-ri!

Henty halted abruptly and looked at Meatball. His happy brown face was innocent as a child's.

"My simple-minded, from-the-mouths-of-babes truth-speaking friend," he said in English. "You have no idea of what you just have done."

Meatball laughed with him. There was no mistaking the delight in his eyes.

"It is settled then," he said in his native tongue which was the only one he knew. "For the rest of your years, you will make your home with us."

Henty dropped his head to his chest to hide his grin.

"You're a crafty bastard and I love you," he said, translating in Jinghpaw: "We shall remain and be one with you."

The sound of the airplane engines swelled in thin crescendo and both he and Meatball looked up. The first of the two L-5's had circled the village and was coming in. Its glide path was steep and it would touch its wheel at the beginning of the short, bumpy strip. The blue star against the white on the fuselage shone like a promise as the plane came above the river. The other ship was halfway around the field, ready to drop as soon as the first had been pulled off the runway. Two frail pigeons.

"All of our people will rejoice at the sacrifice of your decision," Meatball said gravely but there was a twinkle in his eyes. "You will be a headman and contribute your vast wisdom to our councils."

"No, my brother," Henty said, equally solemn, "You will be my headman and I shall seek to learn from you your understanding of the ways of men."

The second L-5 pulled out of a dive and soared over the Tanai a little higher than the first but with its engine stalled for landing. It disappeared and the next moment, the ratcheted clattering of small-arms fire snapped from the direction of the field.

"The Japs have hit the strip!" Henty shouted. He ran in the open on the beach toward the foxholes.

"This way, Dua," Meatball called, plunging into the sharp-edged brush and angling away.

Henty wheeled and followed the Jinghpaw, across the Nhpum Ga trail, pitching into the clinging tangle of the jungle. The intensity of the battle mounted. The firing sounded like a hundred strings of firecrackers set off at once. Now and then, a grenade exploded with a blast like a Fourth of July cherry bomb. Overriding the irregular, staccato spats was the maddening steady beat of a Nambu machine gun. The Japs were attacking in force and the two birds were helpless on the ground.

Twisting, sidling, plunging, Meatball cleaved a passage in growth that seemed impenetrable. Henty could see now what the Jinghpaw was doing. They'd hit the Japs in a tried and tested Marauder tactic from the flank or rear. It might work. There were only two of them but they had submachine guns and they'd take the enemy by surprise. They'd also be with the enemy in direct line of Marauder fire.

Henty knocked off the safety on his weapon and the fighting mechanism in his body took over from his mind. He tripped on a vine, took a header but somersaulted and rolled to his feet with his legs still moving. Meatball glanced over his shoulder and grinned. They were still in the trees but they were near the edge of the paddy area and the air strip.

From their concealment in the jungle, the Japs were pouring their fire into the patrol's defensive positions except at one of the bunkers 1st Squad had held where they'd broken through. Three pot-helmeted little figures in brown already had penetrated the line and were worming over the hot reddish ground toward the Ridge Runner's hole and beyond, the air strip and the L-5's. Others would follow because the Nambu was covering and Kon, the Runner and 2nd Squad's man in the nearest position were pinned down. The rest of the patrol had its hands full with the relentless, savage fire that came from hidden places. The Japs were hurling grenades but they weren't close enough to do much damage except for the three advancing on the communications post, and they had other things in mind.

Meatball got the first Jap, a stubby rifleman lying in the grass, with a short burst, motioned Henty to continue on the flank and disappeared in the bamboo to the rear.

On his knees, Henty caught two Japs from the side and dived as the BAR-man from the 2nd sprayed the earth around him. Christ, he grit his teeth and snaked through the undergrowth that bordered his own patrol's line. His mind tried to tell him this was suicide but his body pushed him on.

A Jap lifted an arm to throw a grenade. Henty's tommy gun traced the arm into the cover. The Jap's head came up with a startled look showing in the flat eyes and the head and arm disappeared. An explosion shook the ground as Henty smashed his face down. Dirt showered his body and something solid crashed onto his helmet. It was a bloody chunk of jaw with three teeth in it, one gold capped.

He scrabbled around the grave the Jap had dug for his shattered corpse and flopped back in it when something moved ahead. Three bursts spit from a tommy gun and the Nambu stopped off beat. Henty ran out his clip in three long bursts and Meatball's weapon answered conversationally and convincingly. Henty rammed in another clip. The only thing now was to make a lot of noise whether or not there was a target. But a Jap conveniently crabbed back and the first burst wasn't wasted.

Meatball's tommy gun quit talking and the Nambu picked up again, except now it wasn't giving cover to the three Japs on the field. It was raking the Jap flank to the north. The Jap firing stuttered away and stammered to a halt. Henty fired away from Meatball into the jungle for the effect the sound would have. Someone screamed and something fell. Sounds faded into the jungle.

"Henshit here!" he shouted with all the power left in his lungs. "Hold your goddamned fire. Henshit coming out with Meatball."

He jerked off his helmet, canted it on the muzzle of his piece and crawled toward the strip with his tommy gun poking above him in the brush.

"Henshit here!" he repeated in a bellow. He heard the chatter of a monkey and grinned. "Answer me you Burma bastards!"

"Come in, Henshit!" It was Double Ugly. "We see you."

"Meatball's in the middle," he called back. "Hold your fire and your positions. They may be back."

Henty waited until he was on the bare earth of the air field before he clapped his helmet on his head. He sat looking up the bamboo fringe for Meatball. From the corner of his eye, he caught motion. Kon's head and shoulder were out of his position and he had his M-1 in his hands. He squeezed off three fast shots toward the Runner's hole and Henty saw the Japs

231

who'd penetrated the defense jerk and lie still. Everyone else had forgotten them except the Pole for Christ's sake.

Meatball walked onto the field, bent under the weight of the Nambu. Henty bared his teeth in a tight smile; the weapon was no good to the Marauders, their ammo didn't fit it, but the enemy wouldn't fire it again. There'd been a time when all of them had been just as sharp as Kon and Meatball.

Henty pushed himself up and ran toward the line, weaving in the direction of 1st Squad's positions. He saw Kon scuttle from his hole toward the trench Katey and Pretty Pussey had occupied, the place where the Japs had broken through the defense. They both must have got it. Henty veered.

Kon was huddled into a corner and the pallor in his cheeks had sludged into his eyes. He looked like he was going to puke. Katey and Pretty Pussey were slumped across each other on the floor. Each had a row of small dark holes across his back.

"Jesus, Henshit!" Kon said gagging. "They're dead but look at them. I never seen nothing like that before. It must of been a goddamn freak grenade that blasted their clothes right off them."

Henty tried to spit the sickening, sulphurous taste of rottenness from his mouth. He'd suspected they were homos and still he'd trusted them. He knew better. The Japs hadn't had to kill them. These boys would have sold out cheap.

"Yeah sure," he said bitterly. "Help me drag their clothes on to their waists and put their belts around them." He looked at Kon fiercely. "And keep your goddamned mouth shut about how we found them and what we did."

Kon grimaced and started to pull one of the pairs of fatigues over Katey's shoes and leggings.

"Okay Henty," he mumbled. He stopped as he was fastening the belt, looking up and brightening. "At least the Japs got them. This time it wasn't Marauders killing off each other. The jinx is broke now, that's for sure."

Squatting, Henty squinted his eyes from Pretty Pussey's sweet little child-like pink mouth to Katey's face with his lips drawn and pursed even in death. His eyes considered the dark clay wall of the trench until he could no longer hold them there. He looked searchingly at Kon's face. It revealed nothing but distaste for what he was doing now, no other knowledge or uneasiness. He looked at the handle of the *kukri* knife under Kon's left arm. A Jap would have taken Overholt's weapon. Henty wasn't sure at all, he wasn't sure of a goddamned thing.

23

THE silence following the Jap's abrupt withdrawal fell over the air strip like a palpable blanket and baked in the sun. It lay uneasily for a few close minutes while the jungle trees wilted back until they stood unmoving and then jerky voices raised shaky bridges between positions.

In his bunker at the north end, Nick Poppas slumped weakly in a corner, running his palm over his wet face and licking his dry lips. He blinked smarting eyes and looked at the BAR he still held with both hands. It trembled in his tight grasp. For the first time, Nick was frightened. His throat was filled with the sickness of fear.

Nick's face twitched as he raised his eyes and looked at the blank wall of the jungle. There was nothing in the trees any more, he told himself. The Japs had all been driven off and the Kachin had even taken their terrible, death spitting Nambu machine gun from them. He looked away quickly, down the line toward the position Katey and Pretty Pussey had held, the hole where Kon and Henty now were. Nick knew what was there. Two corpses. He'd seen the Japs break out of the jungle, seen the grim faces with the hooded eyes under the cover of the helmets. Knew their terrible purpose as they worked under the covering fire of the Nambu straight for Katey's and Pretty Pussey's trench. Even above the clatter of all the other firing, he'd heard the shots sing out from the bunker, knew Katey and Pretty Pussey were dead.

The fire from the jungle had raked the line. It didn't touch him but he'd stood powerless. He'd seen them take Katey and Pretty Pussey and he'd waited for the Japs to break out from their screen, overrun his hole. And he'd shaken so badly he couldn't fire the BAR. It was worse than buck fever. Fear had shot from his gut to his mind and paralyzed him. He'd been under fire from the first of the campaign. He'd laughed at the Japs' little slugs. There had been no warning this terrible thing was going to strike him. To save his life, he couldn't shoot his weapon.

He gasped dryly and ran his tongue over his lips again. His body quivered and the gorge rose in his throat. His chest heaved and he tasted the dry choking but no vomit came. Only scalding tears that blinded him and burned his cheeks. He'd had it. Nick the Greek was done.

Muffled by the cotton in his mind, he vaguely heard someone calling. When he realized it was his name being called, his body jerked in spasm. He felt naked, discovered in his shame. He didn't trust his voice to answer. The call came again.

"Nick! Furman!" It was Henty's voice.

"Coming," Furman answered.

Nick got a sound of some kind from his throat.

"Come down here," Henty shouted back. "We've got to get rid of these bodies while we can."

Nick had poked his head out of the ground. He slid back into the hole at Henty's words. He gagged and shook.

"Goddamn it, Nick! We haven't got all day."

He couldn't puke because there wasn't anything to get rid of and somehow he made his rubber legs propel his body. He squatted beside Furman at the edge of the hole, trying not to look into it. His BAR was jumping on his legs which were trembling and he laid the weapon on the ground. Furman magnified his reproach behind his thick-lensed glasses.

Henty glared up at both of them. He looked angry and beside him, Kon tried to smile weakly and failed. The bodies, both bare to the waist, were propped against the far earth wall. Their chests were a mess of splintered ribs and raw meat. The flies already were working on them.

"They're going to bloat and rot in the sun and we may have some more fighting to do here," Henty growled. He sounded disgusted and annoyed. "Let's get the corpses across the field where they can bury them."

Sick as Nick was, he looked at Henty in surprise: the son-ofabitch was mad at Katey and Pretty Pussey because they'd got killed on him!

Henty was bending over the bodies.

"I'll tie the arms of their fatgues over their chests," he snarled over his shoulder. "We'll hoist them out. You each take one and drag it, by the neck or armpits. Dump them in a clump of trees by the trail. CP can send someone out to dig a pit for them."

Nick felt his stomach churning and turned his head away. Furman was staring at Henty with his mouth gaping.

Kon and Henty got Katey's body between them and hoisted to the edge, heaving from the waist and thighs.

"They got another one last night," Henty grunted. "Old Overshoes. Slit his throat." He motioned to the knife sheathed under Kon's arm. "With a *kukri.*"

The body sprawled on its back in the dirt.

"Let's go!" Henty said sharply.

Furman slung his M-1, got his hands into Katey's arm pits and backed away. He was sweating and gulping.

Pretty Pussey's body pitched from the hole onto the caked hot ground.

"Let me have the BAR," Henty barked. "I'll hold down your position."

"No!" Nick shouted, hugging the weapon across his chest. The only heat in the barrel was from the sun and there was no ejected brass in his position. He took the body with one arm crooked around the neck, clinging to the BAR with his other hand. "I'll manage."

Henty laughed shortly. The way he bared his teeth made him look and sound savage.

"I forgot. I told you the BAR was yours. Well move."

Nick dug in his heels and backed off tugging Pretty Pussey's dragging weight. The sweat broke from his forehead and ran into his eyes. Mistily, he saw Henty with his submachine gun leave the hole and run down the line. My God, Nick thought, he'll know I didn't fire a single shell!

Henty leapt into the hole Furman had occupied. Kon stayed with the two M-1's in Katey and Pretty Pussey's position.

Nick gasped, half turning, stumbling and pushing his legs toward the opposite side of the field. Pretty's body tugged heavily raising a tormenting cloud of red dust. He bent and strained, plodding with death on his arm away from the positions and the jungle and Henshit, that monstrous war machine who fed them to the enemy one and two at a time.

Three more from 1st Squad, his mind kept saying. Henshit drove them until their minds collapsed, until they didn't have minds left to think with, no will left to act. It was what had happened to him when his finger froze on the BAR. It was what had happened to Katey and Pretty Pussey. He knew that, no one could tell him different. He'd seen those three Japs come in and not a shot had either Katey or Pretty Pussey fired in defense. From the looks of their bodies, they hadn't even tried to struggle. It must have been what had happened to Old Overshoes. The way Henshit had beaten and kicked Old Overshoes around, it was no wonder he'd cracked up.

He staggered over the bumpy earth runway. From the corner of his eye, he saw the two light planes, pulled far off at the end. They'd saved the planes. That was the big thing. Get a guy like Henshit who didn't give a damn and let him feed the enemy.

Ahead, Furman had found some thin trees near the path that dropped a little shade. He'd left Katey's body there. Nick let Pretty Pussey's body slip from his arm at Katey's feet and began to shake all over.

"We've earned a break," Furman said, breathing hard. The sweat was a solid film all over his face and his glasses were muddied by the dust. He pulled them off the bridge of his nose and peered over their steel rims. "Let's get away, to some shade, and have a cigarette."

"Sure," Nick said in a weak voice, running his palm over his eyes, staggering as he started for the bamboo on the other side of the trail.

"Wait," Furman said abruptly. "These boys didn't get a free ride."

Nick turned and watched Furman fumble through both their pockets.

"Oh that sonofabitch!" Furman looked up and raged. "Henshit swiped their butts. That's the kind of bastard we've got to put up with. You can't even trust a corpse with him."

"I got butts," Nick said, still faint and trembling. "Let's have one."

They sat in the shade of some bamboo that hung over the trail. The dust stuck to their skin. Furman pulled off his glasses and dropped his head between his knees. Nick closed his eyes and tried to fill his hurting lungs.

"You don't look too well," Furman said huskily and sighed. "Maybe you should see a doctor for a blood count."

237

Nick started and glanced quickly at him. Furman had rubbed some of the dirt from his glasses and had a shaky smile on his face. There was nothing aloof or smug about it. Nick fished two cigarettes from his pocket. They were damp and his hand still shook. Furman lighted the cigarettes and they both had to work to get embers glowing.

"Jesus," Nick said and choked on the smoke. "I don't feel so good. One man last night, two more today and Henshit acts like it was a personal insult."

"I think I know what happened to Old Overshoes," Furman said.

"Henshit said he got his throat slit with a *kukri*."

"I mean, I think I know how he happened to get his throat slit," Furman said. "Henshit sent him on a night patrol alone for spite. Overshoes stumbled onto a patrol. They slit his throat. Henshit will cover up but that's what happened."

"Maybe," Nick agreed dully. "What difference? We're all going to get it. We've reached our limit. Those two today, Katey and Pretty Pussey didn't fire a shot. They'd gone as far as they were able. They just stood there and let the Japs kill them. None of us have a chance."

"Three of us left from the original squad," Furman said. "You, Kon and me. Not counting Henty. He'll take care of himself. And still we totter on."

"A man last night and two today," Nick repeated. His eyes felt hollow. "If there was anywhere to go that wasn't already worse than where we are, I'd make tracks."

"You'd get your throat slit by the first Jap you ran into."

"Maybe that's what happened to Old Overshoes. Maybe he wasn't on a patrol. Maybe he was running. I could understand it."

Furman shook his head thoughtfully.

"You've already said it. There isn't anywhere to go."

"The Hukawng valley is safe, the way we came, at least from Japs."

"No," Furman said slowly, as if he were weighing the possibility. "You've got to eat, you've got to sleep. Even if you did make it as far as the Ledo Road, what good? Are you going to walk up to General Pick, tell him you're a deserter from the Marauders and ask him to furnish transportation to India?"

"So we've got no choice." Nick's arms and legs seemed to be under control again but he ached inside. "We stay here, that's supposed to be a break, a chance to rest. All we get is a chance to roast in the sun until some sniper picks us off. Hell, we aren't even eating different. Then when they're ready, they push us into the Japs around Nhpum Ga. That's funny. Are we supposed to overwhelm them? The Japs must be dug in with pillboxes and fortified emplacements. Do they expect us to blow them up with grenades? I don't even want any more of what we've just had today."

"Oh, they'll back us up with two pack howitzers," Furman said bitingly.

"Yeah, I guess that's the way it is," Nick said, getting heavily to his feet. "I've got over the worst of my jitters but I'll tell you a fact. I don't guarantee how much longer I can hang on. Sometimes there comes a point you aren't responsible for what you do."

Without another glance at the two corpses, they started jogging back separately for the patrol's positions. My will and strength are gone, Nick told himself: I am afraid ever again to be faced with firing a weapon. They'd asked too much too long from the Marauders and now even the pieces were coming apart.

Why were they here fighting on a shoestring? He could have recruited twice as many able-bodied men in his home town of Sioux Falls as they had in all three battalions of the 5307th. He'd gone along without complaining as long as he could take it and there was a fast buck to be had. Now he was used up, that was all. There had to be some way out. And quick. Before the Japs started for him again. Before they pulled the patrol off the strip and sacrificed it at Nhpum Ga.

He was abruptly overwhelmed at that moment in the middle of the baking field by the cool, vanilla-flavored fragrance of the Sweet Palace, his family's joint at Sioux Falls. It was so astonishingly refreshing that the smell and feel of the place was physical. The Sweet Palace with its white-tiled floor and dark wooden booths with little green glass light shades was all at once the embodiment of everything good that had ever happened to him.

He shook his head in bewilderment but the smell lingered. It was a damned strange thing to be happening after the violent reaction to the fighting he'd just had. He remembered clearly his old man, short and fat with a bald head that glistened. And blubbery lips. And the old lady, even the wart on her chin, the way she rolled around the candy counter like a tipsy barrel. Both of them nagging at him all the time. He couldn't do a thing to please them. They thought he should hang around, work the soda fountain. He'd cut out, away from everything. School, the Sweet Palace, the works. And stayed away. Hell, a kid had to have some fun before it all got away from him.

No one could say he hadn't had it before the Army closed in on him. Chicago. The Big Time. Jackpot boards and football pools, a little business in slot machine slugs. He'd made a $150, $200 every week and had a blonde babe he'd set up on North Rush who didn't mind peddling it when he steered in a customer from Iowa or Minnesota who carried some folding money.

You'd think the way he'd lived it up, that's what he'd be panting for, his last days on earth. But he could not and did not want to rid himself of the unforgettable essence of the Sweet Palace. He ought to at least have written the old man and old lady a letter after he got in the Army.

If he knew the lingo like Henty did, he just might be able to make it out of the hills and into India. It had been done before. And he had some money safely tucked away there. For a fleeting moment, he even thought of sounding Henty out, suggesting some kind of deal if he'd make the break. But Henshit would only throw him to the brass or shoot him then and there.

Still, he might be able to do it all alone, work up the Hukawng Valley, move at night. If he were picked up, he could always act as if he'd gone off his nut in shock.

He crouched up to the positions, threw himself flat beside the hole Furman had just entered, Henty glanced up. He even smiled. The bastard didn't have a feeling in him.

"Take your old position, Nick," he said. "We'll switch with the 3rd in the foxholes this afternoon. Meatball and the Ridge Runner are on the line now so the 1st still has got some punch."

Nick scurried to his hole and fell in. The sky was hazing but the sun still made an oven of it. His eyes darted around

240

the earth walls as if there were some way out. His fatigues were drenched and his eyes kept clouding. He peered over the embankment at the jungle from time to time and the BAR shook in his hands each time he did. He was trapped and if the Japs came again, he was dead.

A roaring noise shook him and he felt the leg of his fatigues getting warm before he knew that he'd peed at the sound of aircraft taking off.

He hunched in a corner with his head slumped on his chest. The spattering of firing sounded in the distance. He pricked his ears, listened closely to it. The knowledge washed over him that a patrol was engaged in the Hukawng Valley where he'd thought the way was clear.

A hammer began to beat inside his skull, outward pounding against the heat of his helmet. His face ran with sweat from the throbbing.

There had to be a way.

He began to make small sounds in his throat with each parching gasp of air. He became as inert and lifeless as a corpse and accepted defeat. He might as well be dead.

He might as well be dead; the idea crashed like lightning in his mind. He sat up sobbing and laughing with tears streaming down his cheeks. His body drooped in the great weakness of relief but he stopped trembling. He could escape from everything. It was so simple it made his gasp. And it was safe.

Because he would be dead, officially.

He got to his knees, head whirling now with plans, plotting each crafty detail. He'd be ready when the big chance came. No, he'd make it for himself. He thought of the bodies of Katey and Pretty Pussey. They'd be helpful, a part of one of them at least. But getting it would be difficult and he had to keep his planning simple. It would be better if there were a body but the helmet, weapon, dog tags would be enough. The Army didn't have time to hunt for chunks and pieces of a GI blown to smithereens in a direct blast.

And he knew where he was going to hide, hole up after he'd been killed, officially. Where it was safe and there was food. Right in their very midst. In one of the *bashas* within the perimeter of foxholes. They hadn't been used since Snotty was sent away. And they wouldn't even be looking for him. He'd take along a few K ration packages, slip out from time to time at night or when no one was in the holes, pick up supplies and water.

It was so perfect it made him shudder with delight. At his position, he became wary and alert. Having made his cunning decision, he felt strong and brave. When a sniper's rifle sent a bullet whining near, the BAR leaped to his shoulder and its fire slashed into the trees.

The day continued in flurries of unsustained attacks and harassing thrusts. Nick Poppas returned the fire well and bravely. By late afternoon when the Third Squad moved in to take over, there was plenty of brass on the floor of his position.

"If you had a Jap for every round you fired today," Henty told him, "the battle for Nhpum Ga would be over."

Even then, he was so enmeshed in the cleverness of his design, he did not recognize the need for it had passed.

They trudged into the perimeter of their foxholes in the last hot hours of cloud filtered sunlight. Just the six of them —Henty, Meatball, Kon, Furman, the Runner and himself. The Runner had left his pack radio with the 3rd and that was good. They were spiritless and exhausted. They poked at their tins of potted meat, drank powdered lemon with chlorinated water, gnawed biscuits that stuck in their throats and tried to keep their eyes open.

It was perfect.

"There are six of us to man this perimeter," Henty said, not looking up but staring into his mess cup. "We're all beat to the socks. We've got another couple hours of daylight. Meatball and I each will take one end now and the rest of you sleep until dark. When it's time, I'll crawl around on the inside and wake you. I want three holes between each man. From darkness on, we're all alert. Don't leave your holes for anything. No matter what happens, stay in them. Any sound you hear, shoot at it. Any movement you spot, shoot at it. Don't ask questions. Shoot. Even if it's a fish splashing in the river. I don't care. Shoot. We're a ring of firepower. Now get your canteens filled and get in your holes."

Nick slept soundly and peacefully until Henty roused him in the early darkness.

"Look alive," Henty said. "If anything breaks, we'll need the BAR."

"Okay, boss," he told Henty cheerfully. "So long now."

He spent the next few minutes on the final details. He took his own pack K rations with an extra one he'd scrounged and stuffed them inside his fatigues. He sneered in the dark as he pulled the dog tags from his neck and draped them over the BAR which he stood in the corner of the hole. He piled the clips against its stock. He pulled off his helmet and placed it next to the clips. The field pack he placed in the middle of the foxhole and he laid three grenades on it. His web belt with canteen and trench knife were the only pieces of equipment he kept.

And then he waited, until the worn-out men on guard would be dozing. Waited with his unsheathed knife in hand. Anyone who got in his way was going to get stabbed. When a stringy cloud pulled its dirty lines across the face of a pale and distant moon, he stood, knife in teeth, holding the three grenades. He hurled two away from the perimeter into the bamboo, pulled the pin on the third and tucked it under the field pack. Then he rolled out of the hole. The two grenades near the river exploded a few seconds apart with a merging blinding flash.

Nick the Greek was running toward the *bashas* before the shooting started and the third grenade went off.

24

IT WAS in the chalky gray first light of dawn that Nathan Furman saw the body. It was only 30 feet or so from his foxhole, spread-eagled and bare-headed with the chin half hidden in the crook of an arm but enough profile showing for him to know it was Nick the Greek. It made Furman shiver from his hair roots to his toe nails to think the Japs had penetrated the perimeter three foxholes from him and nailed Nick before the squad's fire had driven off the attack.

Furman shouted for Henty.

Five or ten minutes after the last blast the night before, he'd heard Henty, disregarding his own orders, prowling the positions in the uncertain darkness.

"Henshit on the inside," he'd whisper in a voice too loud for combat. "Sound off if you're okay."

Henty had poked around the foxhole where Nick the Greek had been, calling out his name again and again. After a while, Henty had slid back to his position.

"Just hold tight," he'd muttered.

Hold tight! Knowing Nick had got it, not having any idea where or when the next blast would come. A lot of fire had rattled from the foxholes into the darkness throughout the night but the Japs had not attacked again.

Now Henty came running in a stooped position toward the body. He drew no fire and Furman dragged his belly across the hard dirt toward the corpse. He knew exactly what had happened. After the first two explosions directly in front of his foxhole, Nick had panicked, leaped from his hole in the ground just before they blew it up. He'd been on the shaky edge of bolting the day before. The Japs had moved up and caught Nick running in the light of the third explosion. They might have taken the entire squad.

Henty was squatting beside the body. His face was as gray as the light of dawn. The point of a knife was sticking out the side of Nick's neck, just below his jaw. His shoulder and arm still dripped blood.

Stiffly, Henty got to his feet, coldly kicked the body over. Furman choked back the moan that started and jumped up.

A trench knife was plunged slantwise down Nick's throat as if he'd swallowed it. His eyes were open and had a wild look in them even in their death glaze. His chin was as red as his lips had been in life. The ants had beat the flies this time.

Something lumped inside the sodden fatigues just above the belt. Henty stooped, ripped the fatigues open and two crushed K ration packages spilled out.

"No dog tags," Henty said grimly and strode toward the place where Nick's foxhole had been.

Just like that, the bastard said it—no dog tags. Nick had a trench knife shoved down his throat and the only thing Henshit could think of was he hadn't been wearing his dog tags.

Off to the left, Kon's helmet looking five sizes too large above his wasted face came out of the ground.

"Stay in your holes!" Henty shouted, swinging to Furman. "Not you. Come along. It may do you some good."

With a sickening sudden gripe in his stomach, Furman bent over and trotted toward the perimeter. Henty was in the hole, prodding with his foot in the tumbled earth. The sides of the foxhole had collapsed and in places the loose dirt was piled halfway to the top. Henty's toe probed deeper and he bent, coming up with a helmet and tossing it at Furman's feet. He kicked some more, got down on his knees and burrowed with his hands. It looked almost as if he knew what he was searching for. He plunged his right arm in to the elbow, tugged and pulled out a BAR by the barrel. Dog tags on a chain were slung around it. He threw the BAR up beside the helmet, climbed over the edge and stood with his feet apart looking toward the gashed and splintered sections of bamboo.

"The stupid bastard did everything wrong," Henty said furiously.

Furman lost his temper.

"You're the stupid bastard," he shouted. "You don't give a damn about the men. You're always looking around for what it was that got them dead. What are you afraid of, that you'll get blamed? I don't know who, or how that knife got stuck in his throat but I know what happened. The guy was scared.

He'd lost his nerve. When they started breaking through right here, he lost his head and ran."

Henty turned and walked to Furman's side.

"He ran, all right," he said in a low but savage voice. "Things just didn't turn out the way he'd planned. See those trees? The Japs weren't out in the river throwing grenades. They came from this hole. The bamboo is splintered and torn toward the river. See this foxhole? A grenade was planted in it, probably under his field pack. It was supposed to blow everything up and we were supposed to find pieces of the BAR and maybe a fragment of the dog tags and shreds of the field pack. The force of the blast went out, not up, brought the sides in and buried the stuff. I guess he figured we'd give up searching for a limb or two because we wouldn't have the time. He had two K packages inside his fatigues. He had a place he figured to hide out."

Furman started to sweat in his arm pits: Nick hadn't been able to light his cigarette the day before, he was shaking so hard. He'd talked about being done, mentioned the Hukawng Valley. Maybe he'd had some plan for escaping.

"Well what did he do, ram his own knife down his throat?"

"Maybe he tripped on his cock. How the hell do I know? What do you do when there's a blast behind you or firing around you that may be coming at you? You fall on your face. It's been drilled in you so hard it's instinctive. He'd just thrown three grenades. Maybe he was carrying his knife in his teeth. All I know is he killed himself. That's all."

"He'd had all he could take," Furman said, anger rising again. "He said he wasn't responsible for what he did."

"You . . . dumb . . . shit. If you knew he was going psycho why didn't you report it?"

"What the hell good would that have done?" The sweat was running over Furman's ribs and his eyes were beginning to water. "Would you have given him a three-day pass? If he had planned to try to get away, I don't blame him. He didn't kill himself. The Army did. I've had all I can take of this myself."

"Oh you have!" Henty ground his teeth. "I thought you were the guy who was privileged to see history made. You didn't count the individual where your kind of common good was concerned. What did you think your assignment was, to sit on the sidelines and keep the score? You're just like the rest of the muddle-headed crackpots. You talk a good fight. It's stupid-assed, unthinking, emotional bastards like you who give your blind allegiance to Hitler and Mussolini and Tojo and to Stalin in exchange for empty promises and slogans that make the rest of us fight to preserve what little sanity there's left in the world! I'm sorry about Nick. I'm sorry about anybody who cracks up. He's running away from a situation he can't face. Now drag that corpse over here and throw some dirt on it. Then clean the BAR. You're taking over on Nick's position."

Henty pivoted and walked swiftly toward Kon's foxhole.

Burning with resentment, Furman walked up to the corpse. He averted his eyes, grasping the form by its ankles and dragging it toward the foxhole. At the left, Kon and Henty were watching. Meatball and the Runner probably were watching, too.

Let them. He didn't mind the grave detail as much as the lecture Henshit had presumed to give him. Let Henshit do his flag waving to the troops, like Kon and the Runner and the illiterate Kachin, they'd listen to him because they didn't know better. Henshit had been indoctrinated by the Army. He was just passing on what he'd been ordered to believe, not think. If Henshit had been through what Nathan Furman had endured, he'd sing a different tune.

His own brother, Milton, beaten with rubber hoses by goon squads at the bearings plant because he'd dared to strike. Talk about free speech, the police had knocked out Milton's teeth and called him an agitator when he pleaded with the strikers to hold out for a living wage.

Sweet land of liberty, haven of the oppressed and poor. Milton had it right. What was it he had said? "Economic manipulation to distress the poor and keep them beaten and unprotesting." It always was the poor who suffered in a totally unbalanced society and don't give me that crap, Mac, about opportunity. You were what you were born and they smacked you around like a dead fish when you dared to lift your flipper.

Furman had the body at the side of the partially filled-in foxhole. He rolled it over the edge, went back to his hole for his trenching tool and started to sweat over his entire body as he spaded in the dirt. He hadn't pulled the knife from Nick's throat.

Well, if Nathan Furman had had the opportunity to finish public school and go on to college, he might have been a teacher. He'd told the unquestioning Government Issue morons he was a teacher and he'd certainly have been an officer, which was more than any of the rest of them could say. He'd just never had a break and he didn't doubt the sky was overcast the day that he was born. A gray day in a gray house on a gray concrete street in Jersey City in the gray month of December. Too near Christmas ever to have a birthday. "We'll just celebrate the two together," his Ma would say and he never got more than one gift from anyone. Pa had been a grocer. Aaron's Groceries & Staples. He had one of those dusty-looking, rat-dirt-smelling neighborhood places with windows that got smudged and streaked if you looked through them twice. Broken packages and bent cans on the shelves. Lettuce always a little wilted and vegetables not quite fresh. The kind of stuff a careful operator can buy at a discount and pass off on his customers because they're just as poor and dispirited as he. Twenty-five and fifty cent sales paid for from grubby pocketbooks. People who'd never had any spark to start.

No, Nathan couldn't finish school. There always was plenty around the store to do if you could get it done free. Like his daily morning exercises, sitting in the backroom with a crock of pickle juice wiping the slime off the strings of sausages.

He'd been sick of them all and their shabby lives before he was old enough to know it. Despised because his clothes were shoddy and shunned because he'd never finished school. People had a right to the decent things of life, all of the people, not just the landed gentry and vested business barons. What had they ever done except exploit the poor and helpless? There was plenty of everything in the land. It was just locked in warehouses until it would bring a larger profit. Look at the way things were working out in Russia where all men were equal and shared alike. The time had come to do something drastic about Wall Street wolves and famished families.

He emptied another shovel of dirt on the grave of Nick the Greek and then he stood with both feet on the fresh earth of Nick's final resting place. Somehow, it seemed symbolic.

Henshit pulled all of them away from the perimeter against a string of bamboo clumps near the Tanai as the rising sun began to burn away the haze. The dusty smell of another hot day was lifting from the earth.

"We'll eat here," he said. "But look around now and then."

Furman didn't break out his rations right away. He took up the BAR and examined the big weapon, several inches longer than the M-1. He turned it slowly in his grimed and calloused hands, inspecting its recoil mechanism, and rubbed some dirt from the ejection slot. Nick the Greek hadn't had any right to treat as fine a piece as this the way he had. Furman pulled his other pair of GI shorts from his pack and ripped them. They were rags, anyway. He laid the larger piece of cloth on the ground and began to dismantle the BAR, carefully wiping off each part and placing it on the cloth.

He felt someone watching and glanced up.

"Better eat," Henshit grunted.

Furman nodded and went right on with his job. Henshit wasn't punishing him at all by handing him the BAR assignment. Just as Henshit couldn't touch him with the graves detail or even the lecture which Furman could disregard. The BAR was something. You weren't an ordinary rifleman when you had a Bar. And normally, you even had an ammo bearer. God, it must give you a sense of power to get into a position where you could put the BAR down on its rests and command a field of fire with someone to serve up the clips as fast as you could squeeze them off.

He got a cloth into the bore and it came out black. He was shocked. Nick had fired the piece all afternoon and hadn't even run a rag through it.

Not until Furman was satisfied no speck of dirt remained did he reassemble the BAR, lay it carefully beside his M-1 and get out his breakfast. He mixed his concentrated eggs with a crumbled biscuit and half his fruit bar and heated the mixture in his mess cup over the flame from the waxed container. Henshit was a prick, a mangy martinet when it came to political or economical philosophy, which was to say the same thing. But Henshit would give a man a chance.

He glanced at Henshit enviously. There was only one

weapon he'd rather have than a BAR and it was not a tommy gun. With the BAR you had range. But he would like the .45 that hung from Henshit's belt. Not that it was good for anything. It was just that he'd like the feel of it. Furman supposed it was like Kon with that useless *kukri* knife. What good was a *kukri* knife except for the feeling it gave you?

Covetously, he looked back at the .45. The way things had been going and the way Henshit kept exposing himself, one of these days a Jap bullet was going to have Henshit written on it. And someone was going to pick up the .45.

. Possession of the BAR had removed Furman's sense of helplessness. He felt 10 feet tall, as if nothing could reach him. It was funny, the way a piece of hardware, a certain weapon made a difference in a man's attitude.

Henshit had a few words to say while they finished their cigarettes.

"We're hardly a squad any more. The Runner's from the 2nd Battalion and we borrowed him from the 3rd Squad. Meatball is a guide and he's not assigned. He just personally attached himself to us. I'm acting platoon leader. That leaves just Kon and Furman. Two men don't make a squad. Runner, this morning you go back to the 3rd along with Kon. Furman, report to the 2nd. Consider the unit disbanded."

Furman couldn't understand the sudden agitation that churned his stomach. He reached to his side and touched the satiny feeling barrel of the BAR. Who the hell was 2nd Squad leader? Double Ugly. Christ, you couldn't trust that guy. Much as Furman hated Henshit, he knew him and what he'd do. And damn, even though there were only five of them, the smaller they got the more one man could distinguish himself. There were bound to be stripes in this.

Kon picked at the loose adhesive of the grayed bandage on his empty cheek.

"Don't do that!" Henty said sharply. "You want to get an infection?"

Kon took his hand away from his face and rubbed his butt.

"What you say ain't good, Henty," he said nervously. "That'd be two squads of 13 each. I don't want to be 13th in no squad. There ain't nobody would want to be in a 13-man squad."

To his own surprise, Furman heard himself speaking.

"Look at the firepower we've got with the BAR and," he added quickly, "two tommy guns and two rifles. Look at the way you set it up, with the BAR in the middle flanked by two rifles and the tommy guns at each end. Hell, we can cover a field of fire better than most full squads. We may have had a lot of casualties but as a squad you'll have to admit we've got results. We're down to an experienced hard core. Instead of disbanding why not keep it the way it is and hope we get replacements."

In his enthusiasm he'd said replacements! What in hell was he thinking? He wanted to be relieved, not kept in action.

Henshit's lids closed until his icy eyes were slits. He studied Furman carefully before answering.

"Replacements are out of the question, right now at least. Maybe after Nhpum Ga we might re-form from some other shot-up squad. What do you say, Runner? You want out from this hard-luck squad?"

The Runner pulled at his thin nose and ran his hand over his sore looking eyes.

"Shee-yut, Hain-sheet." He turned his head and spit disgustedly. "Who'd take care y'all 'f ah ain't heah? Ah was think'n m'be y'd git me p'manent."

Henshit said something to the Kachin in his tongue. Meatball shook his round, smooth brown face from side to side, spoke rapidly, patted his tommy gun and laid his hand on Henshit's shoulder.

A glint had come into Henshit's eyes.

"All of you got shit for brains," he said contemptuously but then he pressed his lips together and smiled. "All right, you Burma bastards. Let's go take them."

25

Bᴜᴛ the Burma bastards didn't get to take them that Saturday morning, April First of 1944. At the air strip, there were no Japs to take. The enemy in force had made a determined trust down the Hukawng valley the day before and had been engaged by a Marauder patrol. Jap losses in the savage battle had been severe and the enemy had slunk back to its jungle lair.

It was a beautiful morning, warm but not hot, with a puffy breeze sending billowy cumulus clouds marching across the blue field of sky like armies.

"The monsoons, my brother," Henty chided Meatball. "Will they never come to mire the heavy weapons of the enemy?"

"Another moon phase, Dua, and not even a Jinghpaw will leave his *basha*."

"It is then I would be with my woman."

Meatball smiled at Henty and nodded his head.

"She is secure and will come when you wish."

I wish her now, I wish her here, I wish her always, Henty thought with a gentle smile in his heart and did not ask where she was.

Captain Gold called Henty to CP and questioned him about the firing at the perimeter the night before. His plank desk was even more littered with papers, reports, maps and notations than before. The mess cup with the cigarette butts looked as if it hadn't been emptied for two days and Captain Gold looked as if he hadn't been out of his fatigues for five.

"A small probing action," Henty answered and, remembering the captain's advice when Julie had blown himself up, added: "One of our men was killed."

Captain Gold shook his head and sighed with weariness.

"I wish the 1st Batallion would get here. We lost several dead and a dozen wounded yesterday in the valley. We repulsed them but we suffer losses we can't replace and get no closer to Nhpum Ga. What is your patrol's strength? I've forgotten."

"Two squads intact, but the 1st, that's my squad, is down to two men. We've had nine fatalities."

The captain's tired eyes opened a little and they were admiring.

"You have achieved remarkable results and your disregard for person has been commendable. You and your Kachin with your two-man flanker at the strip yesterday was a daring tactic. With the enemy already penetrating your line, it was military genius."

Henty grunted.

"Necessity. It's hell to sit here and wait with the enemy nibbling away. What is the strength of the 3rd now?"

Captain Gold grimaced.

"At the most, we could muster 300 fit to fight."

"And the 1st?"

"We've lost radio contact." He shrugged. "Probably no more than we have."

"Good God!" Henty exclaimed. The odds would be staggering.

"Yes," Captain Gold said as if he anticipated Henty's thoughts. "We estimate the enemy has 2,500 at Nhpum Ga."

Henty pulled a cigarette from Captain Gold's package and lighted it. He filled his lungs with smoke, seeking some calm before he commented.

"Frankly, sir, it looks pretty bad for the 2nd, doesn't it?"

"We still are in contact with them," Captain Gold said calmly. "Surprisingly, they seem to have settled down and are taking it. Their strength is about the same as ours. With the 1st here, the odds would be the usual ones, about three to one. Water and supplies are being dropped regularly and air support gives the 2nd some intermittent relief from the shelling." He laughed abruptly, a short bitter laugh. "Did you know that one of our howitzers dropped a shell in the middle of the 2nd's perimeter?"

"Oh for chrissake," Henty groaned.

"Miraculously, there were no casualties. They've had to dig in pretty well against the Japs. It's a good defensive position. The Japs can't advance up the hill against them. The howitzers are helping and so is the bombing and strafing.

When we can mount an attack, we may be able to pull this one off. Meanwhile, we're confined to patrol activity, poking through the bamboo, feeling them out for soft spots."

Henty hesitated.

"The 2nd's going to be a pretty pooped out bunch when we do get to them."

"A magnificent understatement," Captain Gold said wryly.

"And the 3rd not much better."

"Agreed."

"And the 1st about like us."

"I think I know what's coming, but please don't let me stop you."

"Well. I know what you said the other day about another mission, but this is dragging on. Our casualties are mounting. Meatball, my Jinghpaw, says the monsoons are practically here. Wouldn't you say now that after we're done with Nhpum Ga, they'll have to evacuate what's left of us?"

"Hope and rumor spring eternal," Captain Gold smiled. It was a wistful smile. "You'd almost think so, wouldn't you? I am in no position to give you encouragement, but I will reconsider my earlier personal opinion." His eyes got hard and the breath he drew thinned his nose. "I do not see how any man can be expected to endure as much as we already have."

That night as the tattered remnant of the 1st Squad, patched by the addition of another disgruntled rifleman from the 3rd and two from Double Ugly's 2nd, heated instant coffee in mess cups over waxed cardboard fires, Henty considered each man carefully before he spoke. There had been no action that day but each man was long since drained dry of spirit. They needed encouragement. Kon was in misery again with his dysentery. His face was white and after one sip from his cup, he bent over and hugged his gut. Furman looked morose. For a while that morning, Henty had thought he'd reached him with his angry words about slogan-followers but now Furman looked as if he'd had a relapse. The Ridge Runner had his knees up to his chin and his forehead was wrinkled. He was far away, dreaming of houn' dawgs. The three men from the other two squads had blank eyes and sagging jaws.

What the hell, Henty told himself: I am speaking for CP this time.

"I think I got the word," he said finally in a quiet voice that made them all sit up. "CP says no more after this one."

There was a stunned silence and then everyone jabbered at once. Meatball glanced around the circle, puzzled but smiling at the sudden excitement. Henty repeated what he had said in Jinghpaw.

"It is well," he said gravely, adding softly: "Then you will leave us, Dua."

"No, Meatball." Henty grinned. "If I am given some time of my own when the enemy is driven from these hills, I shall remain here. You will take me to one of your villages that has been secured and there will be a wedding feast."

Meatball made a great chattering and laughed delightedly. "Your woman will be ready on the moment of this victory."

The others had been trying to break in. Even Kon had straightened and now he shook Henty by the shoulder. His grasp was weak.

"You wouldn't shit us, would you, Henshit?" he asked and smiled wanly.

"Not you," Henty said, smiling. "It came straight from the horse's mouth. We can't take any more. Think you can make it?"

"Well, hell," Kon said, standing erect. "I still got the pink condoms ain't I?"

"Wheah y'all think we git t' go?" the Runner asked.

"If there's any justice in this world," Henty said with a firm conviction that roused even Furman, "they'll rotate us. Back to the states for 30-day furloughs and re-assignment. We've gone further and done more now than they planned when we came in. Ninety days out here is like ninety missions in the Air Corps."

There was no enemy activity at the perimeter or at the air strip that night.

Kon hunkered over to Henty with the rising sun the next morning. He was clinging to his mess cup with both hands and still spilling water. His face was drawn with pain and his eyes were lustrous and feverish.

"I got the shits again," he said. "Bad. I ain't eating nothing and barely drinking but still I got the shits. It's blood."

"Go up to the Aid Station;" Henty said. "Now! They've got their hands full but you're a casualty. Those pills they gave you before helped, didn't they?"

Kon closed his eyes and pulled his brows together. He shook his head.

"Not very damned much. I don't want to go to the Aid Station. I'm afraid they'll hang a hospital tag on me."

"Well Christ," Henty exploded, "isn't that what you've been bellyaching for?"

Kon managed to grin.

"I could of made a joke out of what you said a couple weeks ago. No, it ain't what I'm bellyaching for now. Not if we're getting out of here like you said. All I need is decent food. You think I want to lay in a goddamn GI hospital at Margherita when the rest of you are going home?"

"It'd be a hell of a lot better than being packed home in a wooden box."

"No!" Kon said stubbornly. "You know the goddamn Army. Every chance they get, they'll screw you. I didn't come to ask could I go to the Aid Station. The thing I was wondering was, I think it was the fish that helped me more than the pills. They didn't gripe my gut and I didn't tear my ass to pieces. I was wondering, would it be all right if I tossed a grenade in the river for breakfast?"

Henty laughed.

"Why not? It's no more than a thump in the water. The enemy knows we're here, anyway. Take the Runner with you to pick them up. Get enough for all of us. You'll have to clean them, though."

"Thanks, Henty."

The *kukri* knife hung out from his armpit when he stood.

"Kon?"

"Sure, Henty."

"I know it couldn't be possible with you in the condition you're in, but you were in the hole that night with Overholt. Did you follow him and cut his throat? Now wait a minute. Answer me the truth. Whoever got to him did me a favor and I want to shake his hand, not turn him in."

Kon got an odd, quirky smile on his face but he shook his head.

"I'd like to of. I would of if I had the chance. He was out

256

to get us. But it wasn't me. The beer or the pills made me sleep. I didn't even know he was gone."

"Damnit!" Henty shook his head impatiently. "I've got this doubting hunch it wasn't a Jap. If it had been a Jinghpaw, Meatball would have known. Where'd you say you got that knife?"

"I told you, I traded a beer and some butts."

"I know that. Who'd you get it from?"

Kon looked uncomfortable.

"You didn't say that about not turning the guy in because you thought I might of done it? I mean, that'd go if it was somebody else did it?"

"It goes, Kon. Overholt's already listed killed in action."

"I got the knife from the Runner. He picked it off a Jap in that valley."

"The Runner!" Henty exclaimed in astonishment. "When did you make the trade?"

"The morning after we had the fish and beer. I had one bottle left. I always wanted one of these knives. Anyway, I don't think the Runner could of done it."

"Why?"

"Because he wasn't even on the perimeter that night. You put him up in a *basha*."

Kon boy, Henty thought, that's exactly one of the reasons he could have done it. He could have seen Overholt leaving his hole better than anyone and he could have slipped around the perimeter. The morning after the beer bust the Runner had smelled like a brewery, as if he'd just had a bottle. And he'd looked as if he hadn't slept. And one of the first things the Runner had said when he joined the patrol was that he wouldn't let anyone get behind Henty again.

"I'll be damned," Henty said softly. "Take Furman with you to get the fish."

When Kon and Furman had gone down to the shining Tanai, Henty went over and sat beside the Runner who was stretched out with his head on his pack. He looked up with a friendly grin. Henty pulled two cigarettes from his pocket. He gave one to the Runner.

"Going back to Mississippi on your furlough?"

The Runner sat up rubbing his eyes and lighted his butt.

"Yas, suh! Y'all come t' chat?"

257

Henty nodded.

"Do much hunting?"

"Yas, suh."

"When did they start calling you the Ridge Runner? In the Army?"

"No, suh. Ah haid th't naim f'm fah beck."

"Because you used to trail?"

"Yas, suh."

"And you never had shoes until the Army grabbed you?"

"No, suh."

"You ran the trail barefooted?"

"Yas, suh."

"Pick up a scent like a hound dog?"

"Way-el, ah cain't say ah sniffed 'em ouat but ah sho c'd track 'em."

"Do much skinning?"

"Allus skun 'em ouat."

"Coons and chucks?"

"Yeah. Some deah, some pig."

"Pretty handy with a knife?"

The Runner's eyes shone.

"Yas, suh!"

"You kill, Overholt?"

"Yas, suh."

Henty considered his cigarette and took another drag.

"I'm going to ask for re-assignment here in Burma after we've had our furloughs. You want me to put in for you?"

"P'manent?"

"Permanent."

"Yas, suh!"

Monday morning, April 3rd, was hot and blue. The jungle was peaceful and at Hsamshingyang the lull in the fighting continued. When 1st Squad took over at the air strip, both Butcher and Double Ugly were trying to yawn and grin at the same time when they met Henty. Butcher had practically stopped winking and jerking and Double Ugly had stopped pulling the tufted mounds above his eyes together.

"For once the Army told the truth," Double Ugly said. "They did give us a break here, after the first day. Only thing I wonder, what the hell are they going to do about the 2nd Battalion?"

"I feel sorry for those bastards," Butcher said. "I really do. I like this duty but I'd of gone on. Shit, it ain't right for us to sit here on our butts while they get theirs beat. I'm ready to go any time."

"You know," Henty said. "I've got a funny feeling that time has come."

"Then home," Doubly Ugly said and opened his mouth in a huge grin.

"That's what the man said," Henty said and grinned back.

"Well, what are we waiting for?" the Butcher asked. "You got something to back up your funny feeling?"

"First Battalion's on the way. There's been a lot of activity around CP. We're getting a hell of a lot of traffic on the strip. The Japs are leaving us alone. Probably digging in. It adds up."

"Well, goose them, man, goose them," the Btucher said and laughed.

When Henty had checked the men in their positions, he returned to Kon's bunker. The Pole was leaning against the side of the hole with his head against his arm. He was holding his gut with his other hand and there was blood on the seat of his fatigues. He didn't lift his head when Henty stood beside him.

"Fish didn't help much?"

Kon shook his helmet.

"Look, boy," Henty said and put his hand on Kon's shoulder bone. "You're in no condition to fight. You walk a mile up the trail and I'd have to send two men to carry you back. We've delayed this too long. Now get over to the Doc and tell him your platoon leader sent you with orders to be evacuated before things get busy."

Kon was biting his lip when he turned his head.

"Christ, Henty, don't do it to me. I ain't going to be stuck in no hospital now when the whole shittin' mess is just about wound up. I want to go back to Milwaukee."

"I won't leave you at Margherita. I'll get you out if I have to come for you myself. That's a promise. It's for your own good but even forgetting that, I cant' have you on my hands. Hell, man, you ought to thank me for it. You can sit this one out."

"You're always making jokes." He smiled but his eyes were

watery. "I'll lay this one out on my belly. I ain't sitting again until I get my butt in a bucket seat on a plane that's stateward bound. You won't forget?"

"I won't forget," Henty said and meant it.

It was about noon that Captain Gold ordered Henty to report in person to CP. An L-5, motor stuttering, was dropping in as he started to cross the strip and he waited. It was the sixth plane that had come in that morning. Four of the other five already had taken off again. He hoped Kon was on one of them. Across the strip on the trail to the village, shuffling GI's by ones and twos, squads and patrols were raising a cloud of dust.

As Henty approached the *bashas* that comprised the command compound, the place began to look like a staging area. Supplies were being broken from crates stacked under the *basha* that housed the supply depot and a line of men in netted helmets and jungle stained fatigues straggled toward it. GI's milled between the huts and spilled onto the sun-baked fields and outlying paddies. A group of officers clustered at the entrance to Headquarters, a *basha* that was not built on stilts but rested solidly on the ground. There was a feeling of tense expectancy in the confusion.

The open-faced shack where Captain Gold had his plank desk was across the narrow roadway from Headquarters. Three officers were bent over a map on the table and Captain Gold, unhelmeted and looked harried, was tracing a route. The radio at the back wall was bleating. Henty leaned against a support post and lighted a cigarette. He felt his gut tightening and his heart beat faster. This is it, he thought, but do we attack or withdraw? He had seen no evidence of the 1st Battalion.

"Sit down, Henty," Captain Gold told him and smiled briefly. "That's as near as I can come to saying 'close the door.' "

He puffed out his breath, relaxed and pushed his cigarette package across the paper-strewn desk. Henty held up the one he was smoking. The captain shook his head and blinked his eyes as if to clear them. Each day Henty had seen him, he seemed to have aged a year. When he lighted his cigarette his hands were trembling.

"As you can see, this is a madhouse," he said after a moment.

"Maybe I can collect my senses while I talk with you. What automatic weapon strength do you have in your patrol?"

"Three BAR's, four submachine guns," Henty answered, including Meatball.

Captain Gold considered a moment.

"It should do. I'd like to give you heavy machine guns but that's out of the question. And including yourself, you have 27 men."

Henty nodded, subtracting Kon but adding Meatball.

"Well, the Colonel had a staff meeting this morning. We move against the Japs to liberate Nhpum Ga at 1200 hours tomorrow."

Henty grinned.

"The 1st will be here?"

"We don't know where the 1st Battalion is except it's on the way," Captain Gold said disgustedly. "The point is, we don't have the manpower to absorb further attrition. We attack with the two howitzers and the men we have. All the patrols have been called in, your men will be withdrawn from the strip, we'll use everything but the casualties and mule-skinners.

"When you return to your command. . . ." again the captain smiled briefly, "bring your men in to Supply and draw rations and ammo for three days. No, I misspoke myself. Strip yourselves of equipment, draw rations for three days and ammo for six. I'll tell you why in a moment. Double ammo, got it?"

"Check," said Henty, still grinning. Impossible odds but hell would pop.

"All right. Return to your foxhole perimeter and prepare to move out at noon tomorrow. We will attack in two columns. Orange with the two howitzers will advance up the main trail to a contact with the Jap lines and the howitzers will fire point blank into their artillery positions. Communications will lay wire for a field telephone."

It sounded as if Captain Gold was repeating the orders verbatim.

"Khaki column will follow Orange to within a few hundred yards of its contact with the enemy and then will swing north to flank. Your patrol will be attached to Khaki as far as the elephant path you've been over before. You will then detach yourself and operate as an independent unit utilizing the trail you pioneered. You will attack the enemy from the west and north. You operation will be diversionary and deceptive and you will make as much noise and lay down as much firepower as you command. Your assignment is not to engage the enemy but to deceive him into thinking he is being attacked by three columns in force and compel him to withdraw. You follow?"

"I sure do!" Henty said enthusiastically.

"Good. We are attacking a force of 2,500 men with approximately 300 but the howitzers and air attacks already have softened the enemy. In addition to your operation, the enemy will be further deceived by messages he will be allowed to intercept. They will indicate a sizeable drop of paratroopers is being made. The idea is not so much to defeat the enemy as to compel him to withdraw so the 2nd Battalion can escape its entrapment."

Captain Gold smashed his cigarette into a new mess cup which had replaced the other.

"Your assignment is dangerous and may draw heavy fire unless your deception is successful. Make no effort at concealment. Advance confidently. Tell your men not to hesitate shooting anything that moves. A shadow. Monkeys. Birds. Go in blasting. Use grenades. Use your imagination." He looked questioningly at Henty with red veined eyes. "Well, that's it. Maintain radio contact. I'll be here. You've had your briefing. Anything you want to ask?"

Henty got to his feet. He prickled with anticipation and he was laughing.

"No, sir. Except thank you. This is one assignment I know the men are going to like."

Captain Gold stood and extended his hand.

"Good luck, Henty," he said quietly. "See you in Bombay."

26

H ELMETS rakishly cocked, loaded with ammunition and grenades that dangled from pack straps and belts, Lancelot patrol detached itself from Khaki column at 1347 hours on Tuesday, April 4th. The green tunneled elephant path was sweltering and buzzed with insects that stung and the dead air was foul, but there was a swagger to their gait.

This no longer was a patrol of three squads, or what was left of them: this was a company, a column, and the men were gloriously preposterous. They were 27 against unknown hundreds and they were going into battle with a jaunty swing.

All they'd needed was some glamour, something gaudy, a shoulder patch, a piece of ribbon, a name that wasn't "composite provisional" nor a newspaper catch-phrase. Cripes, you'd think the Pentagon would have realized that when it was "secret dangerous mission" that had lured them to volunteer. Now it was "dangerous diversionary operation" that tickled their imaginations. They accepted the assignment with flamboyant assurance.

The marching order as they sweated uphill toward the *tongyaw* where Henty had watched the Jinghpaws slaughter the enemy one week before was led by Meatball and Henty side by side with slanting tommy guns. Just behind them, BAR-man Furman, puffed with pride, was sided by an ammo bearer borrowed from the 2nd Squad. The Ridge Runner with the SCR 300 was next in line, followed by nine riflemen and Double Ugly with his submachine gun. Behind him, a BAR-man and an ammo bearer, nine more riflemen, another BAR-man with ammo bearer and then Butcher with his tommy gun bringing up the rear.

"We'll use none of our usual tactics," Henty had told them. "At any contact with the enemy, Furman with his ammo bearer will hold the center. Meatball and I will fall in place on either side. The Runner will drop back and get some static on the receiver. To our left, 2nd's nine riflemen, ammo bearer and BAR-man with Double Ugly at the end. Butcher's men, same procedure to our right. The enemy expects one squad to hold and lay down a field of fire while the others flank. We'll form this one line and all let loose with everything we've got. It's a gamble but the strength of the front we show should indicate to them a terrific flanking force. So big they'll pull back fast."

There was talking in the ranks, and laughing. They were a boisterous crew.

"We make no effort at concealment," Henty had said. "Let them know we're coming. A patrol is wary. A column knows its movement cannot be hidden. We're a big force, remember that. Our orders are to advance and go in blasting. They'll already have plenty to think about with the howitzers Orange is using and the mortars and heavy machine guns Khaki has. They'll think we're just as strong. There isn't anything between here and the rimrock trail we used before. Meatball scouted it last night. Once we reach the rock, we turn southeast. From that point on you may fire at will. This is nothing but a deceptive maneuver and we'll try to raise enough hell to make them break and run. Our objective is Nhpum Ga."

The *tongyaw* now was a littered boneyard. Tatters and shreds of clothing, leather, canvas, equipment was strewn over the old rice paddy but the carrion eaters had stripped the flesh from the carcasses. The rotten taste of death lingered in the air and the men jogged across the clearing.

Three P-40's screamed above the leafy jungle and veered in a circle with sharp hot flames licking from 50 mm cannon. They pelted the area around Nhpum Ga with a rattling hail of steel, making four passes before whistling off to the north. A few moments after the fighters had disappeared, two jungle-muffled blasts signaled H-hour. The battle for Nhpum Ga had begun.

Beyond the *tongyaw*, the winding, narrow, up and down trail was peopled with ghosts. Here was the grassy rise where Henty had sprawled and talked with Kon and Domingo that morning when Snotty briefly was in charge. Domingo, that poor little Mexican bastard who never had a chance. When he got a good break and his trigger finger was shot off, Fate got mad, stepped in and booted him in the ass for good. Just as it always had done to all his people. A good little guy who should have hated the world but in whose sorrowful eyes lived the suffering of dead centuries. What the hell had Domingo been fighting for? His way of life?

Henty had left Domingo and Kon that morning, gone back. He remembered the 1st Squad, *his* men as he'd met them on the trail, full of piss and vinegar, snapping along just the way the patrol was going along today. Ass Drag, the slow-moving, slow-thinking squarehead. He had a heart big enough for everyone and he'd never willingly have harmed a person in the world. But you gave him a gun, pointed at a man and said: this is your enemy, kill him. And he did as he was told.

And hot-headed little Julie. Sure the Italian was an untamed punk, but all he really wanted was to be left alone. He might even have found some love somewhere that could have changed his outlook. Any guy who'd blow himself up because he made a mistake and killed his buddy couldn't be all wrong.

Then Injun Joe had soft-stepped by. Of all of them, he had the least quarrel with the enemy. The White Man had unlocked the gate of the Indian's prison long enough for him to go out and die.

Hari Kari and Old Overholt had been next that morning. They both were killers. Maybe Hari Kari had had his fill of killing. Maybe he'd somehow realized that in kiling his closest friend, he'd be killing himself. It had worked the other way.

Old Overholt had gone off his rocker. Henty had seen that, even reported it to Captain Gold. It would upset any man's mental balance to have your buddy try to shoot you. No rational man would follow you into the jungle at night, not when he knew you rendezvoused with Jinghpaws who slit Jap's throats.

Then Katey and Pretty Pussey had come along. It was odd, but with the exception of Old Overshoes, the men had died in their marching order. What in the name of Christ had Katey and Pretty Pussey been doing in the Army? They were unfit for service. You didn't hate a man because he was a leper but at least you put him in an institution and tried to help him.

Nick the Greek was hard to understand, running the way he had. It was like Nick to try to figure out an angle. He'd been dealing for the house all his life and he must have had something big at stake to be worth his last gamble.

Only the first man and the last man of the squad were left. Kon had been scout that day. At least he was safely tucked away. Kon would get back to Milwaukee with his pink condoms whether Furman and Henty made it or not. At least the squad couldn't be wiped out. Henty didn't know why that was important, but it was. Furman had brought up the squad that other morning, now he was out in front. Furman had come along in the Army for the ride to see history made and now he was out in front making it. History wouldn't turn out the way Furman had it analyzed and Henty didn't think Furman himself would continue in the direction he had started. Like every other Commie, Furman wanted to share what the other guy had earned but when Furman got something of his own, he was going to keep it.

Jeez, two men left from his closely-knit, tight little organization. Suddenly Henty felt a little sick in the pit of his stomach and his mouth watered at the back of his jaws. Specks rose and fell on waves before his eyes. It was the goddamned heat.

The hell of the Army was, you were thrown together with a bunch of men. You ate and slept and boozed and whored with them. Some you liked better than the others but you took them for what they were, like in your own family. You might have a bastard for a brother but you'd lie for him and lend him money you knew he'd never pay back and bail him out of jail and fight for him. And if he got drunk and was killed in an auto smash-up you'd feel like hell because he was one of you.

Your own family. Henty sneered at that. If there ever had been a Jukes family, it had been his. He could see the old man now, Happy Holiday. Yellow mustache with waxed points, yellow goatee, yellow Stetson and yellow spats over pointed shoes and they weren't boots. The rancher with his little spread. Who the hell had Happy thought he was fooling? He couldn't have cared less when the bank foreclosed the mortgage on the ranch.

The oil boom was on at Casper. So was prohibition. Standard, Sinclair, they all were there with about ten thousand working stiffs who had bundles of boodle in their mitts and a great dryness in their throats. They put up the dough. Happy obliged with booze. Jesus, how that moonshine flowed. A deputy sheriff was assigned full time at Happy's still to count the drops from the copper coils and collect a buck a gallon.

And Happy had a hunk of the Sand Bar, that worthless piece of flatland on the Platte below the main drag. There were a thousand whores on the Sand Bar and not enough cribs to go around even when you worked them three shifts. Happy had them staked out in tents. One time when Henty was a kid about eight years old, Happy had taken him down to the Sand Bar. An old bag was parked in front of a brown canvas tent on a camp stool with her legs crossed. Her pussy was the only thing she didn't let everyone see for free. She didn't have a stitch of clothes on. Her tits sagged down to her lap. Her eyes were smeared around with black stuff and she had red circles the size of silver dollars on her cheeks. Happy pinched her ass and asked how business was.

"Slow," she said. "Only a dozen so far today."

It was noon.

Happy scooped up Henty and swung him to the sweaty smelling old bitch's lap.

"Give your Ma a kiss," he said. "That witch out at the shack really is your grandma."

Oh, it was a fat old joke, all right, only Henty hadn't been so sure of it for a while.

Like it was a joke about his brother Al. He was the oldest, 10 years older than Henty, a surly straw haired kid but who could blame him? Other boys had paper routes. Al had a liquor run. Happy's little spread was out Poison Spider Road about seven miles from town. He bought Al a bicycle and brought him into Casper every morning. Happy would fill the basket with pints wrapped in newspapers and Al would ride home past the refinery. The men would be waiting for him at noon. One day they got Al in a crap game and he lost half his liquor money. Happy didn't say a damned word about it although Al had been sure he'd get a whaling. Next day, he'd hardly started for the refinery when a deputy picked him up for bootlegging. Happy let him sit in the jug for two nights before he told them to turn him loose. It was to teach Al a lesson, not for gambling but for losing, and the whole town thought it was quite a joke. The only trouble was, Al didn't see it that way. A couple of nights later, he lifted Happy's roll and lit out. They never did catch up with him although Happy swore out a warrant.

It was just for a joke that Happy took Henty's sister Millicent to Tent City on her 18th birthday. She'd always been a shy one, cornflower blue eyes and a fair complexion that burned in the sun and blushed furiously when a stranger spoke to her. Happy left her with an old whore and told her to put the kid to work. It was a put-up job, of course, and Happy was back of the tent with a bunch of steadies, doubled over laughing at the way the girl ran around and around the cot when her first "customer" dropped by. Happy didn't let the man lay a hand on her, naturally, and he drove her right out to the shack when she got hysterical. It wasn't three weeks later that Millicent was picked up for soliciting without a permit. After Happy bailed her out, she took off and they never heard from her again.

Happy's only fault was he liked to gamble. They'd thrown the keys to the joints away and the poker games ran 24 hours. If Happy had any money left when FDR repealed the Eighteenth, it left with him. Ma found some kind of place on a street just above the Sand Bar and took in washing and ironing to keep the four kids going. Henty was the youngest. The other three pulled out as soon as they finished eighth grade but Henty managed to get through high school. It was a bitch of a decade to be a kid in. You were grateful for something in your belly and you didn't expect much happiness.

Henty had been just like the rest of them. He'd gone off to the CCC and let the government take care of him ever since. But now he was done with this Army life. No ma, if you're still alive, I don't want to go home. No little brown home in the West for me. A *basha* in Burma and Gai-ri in a *sari* and let the rest of the world go by. Christ, in a day or two they'd have the honorable Japanese ass in a sling and he'd get married.

The column might have been marching through Georgia, the way they burst out of the *kunai* and started up the wooded slope toward the *tongyaw* with the *basha* where Gai-ri had waited twice for Henty. Back on the main trail the battle was on although they couldn't hear it and maybe Khaki had joined the fight. Hell, maybe Orange and Khaki would break through today and it all would be over before Lancelot fired a shot.

Henty and Meatball reached the top and started across inside the perimeter of foxholes. It would be a place to take a break. Henty turned to yell "Take 10" when a grenade exploded. He whirled and the *basha* erupted in soaring orange flames. A

Nambu began to spit from across the clearing. Someone, he thought it was Furman, squeezed off a burst. There was a scream. Rifle fire rattled from the direction of the rimrock.

"Ambush!" someone shouted.

A few of the men started to break.

"Keep out of the goddamned foxholes!" Henty shouted. "Boobytraps. Set up your front. Open fire. Let them know we're here."

Furman already was on his belly at the edge of the *tongyaw* and he had his BAR on its supports. He was firing across into the trail before the first rifleman was in position. Meatball flopped on one side of him. Heavy fire from the Nambu and rifles splattered but the line, 27 strong, was formed and the firing was interrupted with grenade blasts.

Henty pulled back to the Runner who had turned on the transmitter full volume. You couldn't understand the amplified words and static from CP but the din rose and surged above the sound of battle.

"Get the foxholes!" Henty shouted to each rifleman as he ran down the line to Double Ugly.

The holes had been mined. They began to shower the area with dirt and debris as the grenades fell in them.

Henty grabbed Double Ugly's shoulder.

"Work around the perimeter toward the trail with your tommy gun blazing," he shouted into his ear. "Take a rifleman to throw grenades ahead. I'll send Butcher around the other side."

Double Ugly grinned, rolled to his knees, tapped the nearest rifleman. They took off explosively.

"Keep it hot," Henty yelled at Double Ugly's BAR-man and ran to repeat his instructions to the Butcher.

Back at the point, Furman had a satanic grin on his face as he worked over the Nambu position.

The jungle cracked and rocked in two paths around the *tongyaw*. The flames from the burning *basha* sent licking tongues over the green fronds into the blue. Suddenly there was no more Jap fire.

"Hold it!" Henty yelled.

Gradually the Marauder fire subsided.

The machine guns and grenades continued their encirclement until they neared the path. They halted momentarily and then the tommy guns started walking noisily up the path toward the rock until they faded away in the jungle.

"Reform," Henty shouted, leaping into the clearing and pulling Meatball, Furman and the ammo bearer with him. The column pushed straight across the *tongyaw,* dodged the burning *basha,* entered the jungle on the trail. There was no more firing.

Double Ugly, the Butcher and the two riflemen were sitting on the rimrock, smoking cigarettes, all talking at once and laughing when Henty and Meatball reached them.

"Goddamn, you should have seen the sonsofbitches run!" Double Ugly roared and pounded the Butcher's back. "You ever see anything like it, Butcher?"

From the way the Butcher grinned, he hadn't.

"They're off the ridge and halfway to the red hill by now," he said. "This goddamned operation works. We don't have to kill them. All we have to do is shoot off the fireworks."

"Let's go get them," Furman pleaded. Behind his glasses, his eyes were big and glistening. "We can catch them."

Henty laughed.

"They're going the wrong way. We advance."

"But if we don't go after them," Furman protested, "we'll have them at our rear."

"And I have a hunch they'll stay there," Henty said. "Or try to slip around Nhpum Ga to the west."

"Damnit!" Furman's face twisted with displeasure. "We laid down a hell of a barrage and didn't get one of them."

"We did our job," Henty said, amused.

"I thought I heard a scream," the Butcher put in helpfully.

"That's right," Henty said quickly, nodding solemnly at Furman. "You nicked one with that first burst you squeezed off."

"You think I did?" Furman asked excitedly.

"Sure," Henty said and winked at Double Ugly.

"Goddamned right," Double Ugly agreed. He turned to Henty. "What's the next move?"

"We'll all take 10 for a mouthful of water and a cigarette while I call CP. We're supposed to go south along the ridge and then cut east."

It was too early for much news from the Orange and Khaki columns who were attacking the main Jap positions.

"The howitzers are in place protected by heavy machine guns," Captain Gold reported. "It's a slugging fest but the enemy is not going to find any easy escape route to the east."

"I think maybe a force is withdrawing west of Maggot," Henty said. "A small unit of 30 or 40 with machine guns retreated from mined positions on Hill 307 before the main body of Lancelot company could encircle."

"Insignificant, Henshit," Captain Gold said and chuckled. "Hang on a minute, I want to check something."

Henty grinned at the Runner and waited. Transmissions in the clear with misleading references to the strength of the units operating were part of the deception. He looked at the hot blue sky and as he watched, dark flecks became the sight and sound of another flight of four P-40's, or perhaps it was the first flight returning with full gun belts. The sleek silver ships swooped down, this time shrieking and firing only at the south and west sides of the Nhpum Ga ridge. Air support was being advised of Marauder positions.

The transmitter cackled.

"Arthur here. You still there, Henshit?"

"Roger. In the balcony. Trapeze artists just came on. Good show. Over."

"Henshit, there's a mountain gun somewhere beyond the point of Snotty's snafu. It's troublesome. Take your company back there and remove it. Over."

"Roger, Arthur. Do we continue on the detour? Over."

"From the detour in full strength by the most direct route to Nhpum Ga. Over."

"Roger, Arthur. Over and out."

It was almost 1700 hours when Lancelot reached the old trail that circled through the jungle north of Nhpum Ga. After their easy success at Hill 307, the high-pitched men were grumbling at retracing their steps.

"Let's go!" Furman cried when Henty called a break.

"Okay already," Henty said and knocked Furman's shoulder. "One taste of blood and you're a vampire. Go hang by your toes and sharpen your teeth."

He called Double Ugly and Butcher to the grassy knoll beside the defile. Meatball squatted beside him, rocking and clucking with pleasure. Battle seemed remote in the unsteady

271

thumps that reached them but they were tense and sweating in the humid heat of late afternoon.

"It'll soon be dark," he said. "I'll go for the gamble but I'm not going to be a damned fool. We're not marching up to a protected gun position with drums and bugles playing until we know the lay of the land and who's waiting for us with what. I say now we do a fadeout hidden in the trees while Meatball scouts the situation. Any objections?"

"Why hell no, Henty!" Double Ugly said heartily and Butcher nodded his head in quick agreement.

If the Japs had monitored the transmissions, they must be wondering where Lancelot company is tonight, Henty thought and grinned as he settled in the thick darkness of the bamboo jungle well off the trail. The men were well protected and there was no sign of them anywhere in Burma.

Meatball had returned unheard and unseen sometime during the night. He was resting his chin on his knees and laughing when Henty opened his eyes. Even in the latticed jungle, the sunlight showed it was well past dawning.

"Truly, no beast of the jungle would dare approach you when you sleep, Dua," he said.

"Whew!" Henty aired his lungs and sat up trying to pull some of the stiffness from his shoulders. "And why not, little monkey?"

"A tiger lives in the cavern of your chest and roars he is on guard."

"There is no more truth in you than in the yapping, dog-faced baboon whom you resemble greatly," Henty said and laughed. "If what you say is true, you would have closed my mouth with the sword leafs of the pandanus lest a jackal think me the tiger's prey and nibble at my toes."

"Ah so," said Meatball gravely. "And what has happened to this foot of yours that is gnawed back to the ankle?"

"What you observe is not an ordinary sight," Henty said earnestly. "It is my misfortune to possess a Jinghpaw brother who is fat and lazy. I must urge him along the trail with well placed kicks on his behind. You may judge for yourself how worthless he is by the way my foot has worn away."

Meatball bared his teeth and clicked them in angry monkey protest.

"Shall we feast together?" Henty reached for a ration

package, giving the fruit bar to Meatball and keeping a biscuit. "How shall we entertain the enemy today?"

Meatball bit off a corner of the bar and backed away a few feet, sweeping a small place clean on the jungle floor. He pulled out his *kukri* knife and drew two parallel lines.

"The trail," he explained. "Your men now are at this place."

He drew a line across the trail close to his toes. To the right of the trail he made a half circle with the point of the knife.

"On a small hill that has been cleared to the north of the trail, the enemy has placed a gun with a long barrel. It is well protected."

He made a straight line pointing south from the center of the half circle and plucked several dots on either side of it facing the trail in both directions.

"The enemy also has four machine guns dug into the ground. Two here." He made two boxes, one on either side of the trial nearest him. "And two here." He drew two more boxes flanking the trail on the other side of the hill.

"And what lies here?" Henty asked, indicating the unmarked area facing the gun across the trail.

"It is an empty slope that is tall with *kunai*."

"All of the way up to the path?"

"It becomes less than the height of an ordinary man before it reaches the trail."

"Could our men approach the gun position from this grassy slope without being observed?"

"Yes, Dua, with great caution but they would be advancing directly into the mouth of the weapon."

"Does not the enemy lift the throat of the weapon into the air to reach for Nhpum Ga?"

"That is so, but the weapon can be lowered."

"Do you think the enemy is watchful of the area that faces the weapon?"

"No, Dua. At least not as an ordinary practice. He watches the trail on either side."

"Do you think, little monkey, that you could lead us a few at a time into this grassy valley and conceal us in positions where we could reach the enemy and his long-tongued gun?"

"Yes, Dua, with much care and patience. It would be necessary for your men to move only the length of a hand at a time with many breaths between. It would require most of the day to place the many men you have."

"Then we shall use much care and patience and take most of the day. Now will you guard us from the small hill where we talked while I awaken our men and see whether their hearts are as brave this morning as their words were last night?"

While the men sat on either side of the trail and ate their morning rations, Henty described the gun emplacement.

"Meatball will take us into the *kunai* two or three at a time," he said, eyes leaping from face to face. He saw grimness but no fear. "You'll be looking at the barrel of that Long Tom, some of you most of the day. A shell or two from it will dig a grave for all of us. Once you're in your positions, you can't move. If you've got to piss, do it in your pants. We're going to throw the book away again. The three BAR's will be in the center, no ammo bearers. They'll go with the riflemen. Two tommy guns, Double Ugly and the Butcher on their right, Meatball and I will be on their left. I want the riflemen spread out on either side without weapons. Stack them here. Riflemen are grenade throwers. I'll go in with Furman now. Then the other two BAR-men. Next, Double Ugly and the Butcher. Grenade throwers, two or three at a time, whatever Meatball says. By the time you're all in position, the BAR-men should have the gun crew zeroed in. Meatball will let me know when the last of you is in place and all the automatic weapons will open at once. As soon as we do, get up and start pitching. Hit the machine gun emplacements and the positions around the mountain gun. This time we're not out to make a racket. We're out to take that gun. Any questions?"

"Yeah, wheah y'all w'nt th' rad-yo?"

"You and the squawk box stay here with the weapons, Runner. If we don't make it, let CP know what happened. You'll be able to tell by the firing. If we do make it, get your ass in an uproar. We'll be wanting to make some conversation."

Half an hour later, Henty lay spraddle-legged on his belly, arms pushed ahead and hands grasping his tommy gun. His face was lifted and his chin was on the ground. He was on a downward angling slope, so near the path he could hear the pad of feet when the gun was quiet and the soldiers moved between positions.

Meatball had guided him in first.

"We move only when the weapon fires, Dua," Meatball had said. "It shakes the earth and there is reason if the grass should tremble."

It was a tedious, nerve-racking approach through the slashing *kunai*. Henty had checked the time. It had required more than 15 minutes to crawl from the jungle's edge to his position at the center. Although the positions of the riflemen on the east end of the line would not take so long, those who came in on the west side would have to skirt the valley through the jungle. It would take a minimum of six hours to place all of the men. It was exactly 0900 hours when Henty settled down to wait.

It was going to be hell. The slamming charges of the gun above dropped in throbbing waves and pounded in his head like an ulcerated tooth. Dust from the sun seared earth filtered hotly in his nose and throat.

The mountain gun fired irregularly but there was a pattern. One shell, then a pause, two or three in quick succession and then an interval of silence for 10 or 15 minutes. The pattern repeated itself.

Along toward noon, Henty's thirst became a rawness that felt red. The sun had long since baked him dry and there was no sweat left even in his palms. His throat felt as if it were closing. He chewed at the sharp-edged spear of elephant grass that sprouted near his chin. It did not help. He reached a button on the sleeve of his fatigues and sucked at it. There was no saliva in his mouth. He brought his left arm back by slow degrees from the grip of his tommy gun, reaching back for his canteen.

The gun was suddenly and unnaturally quiet. He stiffened and held his breath. There had been a break in the pattern. One shell had been fired but the two or three that should have followed had not come blasting out. Running feet slapped on the path. He waited for firing to search the *kunai*. Instead, the two machine guns facing east spat away at the trail in the direction of Lancelot patrol. Henty swore. He lifted his head, got his left hand back on the grip of the tommy gun and tightened his right forefinger on the trigger.

The machine gun stopped abruptly, someone shouted, someone jeered. The mountain gun banged off three shells. Henty tried to swallow and only scratched his throat.

The afternoon burned away. Henty slept fitfully. At times he thought he was conscious of movement in the grass but he did not move nor lift his head nor try to reach his canteen again. The only times he opened his eyes were to check the time. It was 1500 hours, minimum time. It was 1530. It was 1600. Now his slitted eyes never left the dial of his watch. At 1617, a hard hand touched his and he jerked rigid and moved his head to look blurily at Meatball. The Jinghpaw inclined his head slightly and Henty responded by the same motion. He waited until the mountain gun had shot once and then three times again. His tommy gun was jerking in his hands before he was on his knees.

27

T HE victory was a piss ripper. The Japs, for chrissake, never knew what hit them.

Henty must have looked like Genghis Khan with his horde to the poor stunned bastards when the Marauders erupted from the *kunai* right into the mouth of the cannon.

The BAR-men caught the gun crew empty handed and flat footed and the tommy guns raked the defensive emplacements flanking the piece. Most of the first grenades were tossed in the four Nambu pits and pieces of machinery and hardware went flying all over the landscape in bright-flashed explosions that trailed black smoke. The best damned part of it was, some big league hurler pitched a fast one right at home plate and blasted hell out of the gun carriage.

The dirty faced, rag-tag wave surged across the trail flipping grenades like firecrackers, shooting for the hell of it.

They mowed them down, opened their bellies and filled them with lead, every sonofabitch who'd been sitting safely back laying those 76 mm high-impact shells on the ridge at Nhpum Ga.

Henty leaped a few feet ahead, whirled and shook his tommy gun in the air with one hand. He had the .45 in the other.

"Hold it!" he yelled. "Goddamn you Burma bastards, don't blow up their wine."

It was over in less than five minutes. It wasn't more than 10 after the first blast from Henty's tommy gun that the Runner came panting up the trail. He had the pack radio on his back but before he ran up the antenna, he handed his canteen to Henty.

"Y'all bettah wet yo' whistle."

Wet it, goddamn, he had to open up the canal first. The water was warm but it trickled soothingly down his throat, a drop at a time. His eyes swept the hillside as he drank. The position looked like an auto junk yard with all the victims still at the scene of accident.

He gave the news to Captain Gold.

"Magnificent maneuver, Henshit. That's going to help a lot and when the enemy learns you're in there with a hell raising company like you've got, they're not going to wait to meet you personally. Over."

"Tell our flyboys to catch them on the west. It's the only way they've got to go. What do you hear from our friends down south? Over."

"In a millpond treading water. Bottling up the flies to kill them. Now, Henshit, march your column straight up to Nhpum Ga from where you are. Mop up everything as you go. Over."

Henty turned, eyes traveling the line the canted gun had sighted, but on the ground not through the sky. The patch of *kunai* on the slope, a tangle of jungle sweeping down to a snarled valley, then a long enmeshed incline, steep and thick with growth until it reached the sheer stark escarpment of the Nhpum Ga ridge. Only a few miles but it looked like a few days.

"Roger, Arthur. Anything new? Over."

"That's it, Henshit. No, wait a minute. Sorry to tell you, but your boy pooped out. Over."

"Oh Jesus, Arthur!" Henty had to pause to find his voice again. "Didn't you get him out of there? Over."

"I know it's tough, Henshit. But the way things are, casualties had priorities. Over."

"Well for chrissake, what was Kon but a casualty?" Henty exploded and then said dully: "Sure, Arthur, I know. Over and out."

He dropped to the ground and sat with his helmeted head hung between his knees. He felt empty. The pillaging troops around him dug in the packs and supply stacks of the enemy. He couldn't argue with the decision to send out amputees or, if it came right down to it, those who had some chance of being mended and fighting again another day. They probably couldn't have done anything for Kon at Margherita except make his last days comfortable. It was just the goddamned Army way of pushing men around, killing a man by slow degrees in his mind or body when the enemy didn't get him. The enemy hadn't been responsible for one of the fatalities in his squad, not even Katey or Pretty Pussey. Those bastards had killed themselves.

He'd write that letter to Kon's Pa, he hadn't known they

were that close, and he wouldn't have to make up a bunch of crap. Kon had been the bravest of them all.

Well, that left Furman.

"Meatball!" Henty jumped to his feet. His eyes were like glare ice and his voice lashed like a whip. "Double Ugly! Butcher!"

They dragged their asses up, gloat fading from their faces in disturbed surprise at the way he looked and sounded.

"Meatball," he said in Jinghpaw. "These men require rest in a place that is peaceful and secure. Do you know of such an area?"

The Jinghpaw's face looked as if his mind were withdrawing and then he slowly bobbed his head.

"There is such a place," he said.

"Let us march there."

Meatball led the patrol with its booty of rice and wine back the trail to where the arms were stacked and then he found a way, not a path or trail but passage through the interlacing vines and trees up to the rimrock which hogbacked east. In the broad valley on the other side was the same stream in which, farther north, they'd stored their beer only to have it blown to bits. The water was clear and cold and they halted long enough to drink and fill canteens. And then Meatball took them away from all sight and sound of battle with the receding rock ridge separating them like a fortress wall from Nhpum Ga.

They came to an oasis in the jungle, a small island of soft green grass, fenced in all around by tightly growing bamboo with the sparkling stream trickling through the middle. It was a haven and they were alone.

The day hushed when the sun dropped below the hills and darkness came. The men drank their wine, smoked cigarettes and slept.

The morning was pinkish when Henty woke up. Meatball was sitting crosslegged at the edge of the stream, head lifted and motionless.

"Have you been guarding us all night?" Henty asked, reproaching himself.

Meatball turned his head. His face was serene.

"There was no need for me to guard, Dua. You are in a sacred place."

"How do you mean that?" Henty asked, sitting beside him.

"You are in my temple of the *nats*," Meatball said quietly. "This place is not known to any other. It is here I come to meditate and talk in nature with the spirits."

Henty looked around the island of grass, at the tattered, blasphemous men who littered the temple.

"I am sorrier than I can say that we have profaned your place of worship," he said.

Meatball smiled warmly and he shook his head.

"You do not know the *nats*. They led me here long ago so that I might have the place to share with you when your need was great. I was telling them that I was grateful."

Henty followed Captain Gold's orders that day against the advice of Meatball. The patrol spent half the day hacking down the slope through the jungle maze and the other half returning to the path at the gun position they had destroyed.

"Henshit here with Lancelot company," he reported in at 1700 hours. "We tried to follow what you mapped out but there's no thoroughfare. Over."

"What do you suggest, Henshit? Over."

"My seeing-eye dog says we take Route 66 nother mile or so and come in over the high bridge. Over."

"Roger, Henshit. You're the driver. Over."

"Did the other vehicles get out of the mudholes? Over."

"They're finding the roads passable but in poor condition. I don't suppose you'll be able to keep your company quiet after all your victories. Over."

"You know it's hard to hide a column, Arthur. I'll do my best but they're bound to make a little racket. Over."

"Boys will be boys," Captain Gold said and chuckled. "Call me again same time tomorrow. I'd miss hearing from you. Over."

"Roger, Arthur. Over and out."

They bivouacked beyond the gun position off the trail, ate half rations and hoarded the rice they'd scavenged with the wine. The next day they ran into a trail block within the first half mile. Here the enemy was stubborn and refused to budge despite their unorthodox tactics and show of force. The front, spread out through the trees on either side of the trail, was static until late afternoon.

"Damnit," Henty told Double Ugly and the Butcher. "We

280

can't get hung up here. Our operation isn't working. They've got these boys chained to their machine guns. We're going to have to pull back, regroup in squads and give them the old one-two."

He was able to report to Captain Gold that night that they'd overrun the block.

"But hell, Arthur, we made only half a mile. Over."

"That was rear guard, Henshit. Don't let it bother you. They're pulling the main body out in your area. They're getting soft down here. Maggot is beginning to relax and enjoy it. Over."

"Roger, Arthur. We're getting hungry. Over."

"They've got dinner waiting for you on the ridge. Can you accept the invitation? Over."

"Will try, Arthur, will try. Anything else? Over."

"Yes, call me early tomorrow. I may have a pleasant surprise for you. Over and out."

A finger of higher ground, still jungle and uphill, pointed toward Nhpum Ga another half mile down the trail. The footwork was not so complicated but even off the path, the Japs were dug in and the patrol was ambushed three times the next day. They'd reverted completely to guerrilla tactics and they flanked and cut through each time after an exchange of preliminary fire. The 3rd Squad suffered two casualties, a shoulder wound and a butt scratch but they were walking wounded. The skirmishes and the jungle held their progress down and they covered less than one mile. It was perhaps another mile or a little less to the ridge but they were enclosed by the trees again and could not see it. The patrol found cover within the jungle late that afternoon and chewed dry kernels of Jap rice.

"On our way, Arthur," Henty reported, "but the county commissioners are doing a lousy job of keeping this roadbed in shape. We can't get traction. We need chains."

"We've got them for you," Captain Gold said. He sounded excited. "First is here. We'll drive a 200-horsepower truck down the turnpike tomorrow. Over."

Henty's stomach churned and collapsed: did the 1st have only 200 men left in condition to fight from the original 800? That meant the total strength of the entire 5307th now was somewhere near 600. He could see why Wingate had said 90 days, no more.

"Roger, Arthur. That's a surprise all right. Over."

"Oh, that's not the one I meant. Maybe I'll have it tomorrow. Over."

He means the Bronze Star, Henty thought disgustedly. Jesus, they could shove that up their collective asses.

"Roger. Look, we're eating pilaf and not because it's Good Friday. Over."

"Well come to dinner, Henshit. They're waiting for you. Over."

"Sure, Arthur. I'll see if I can borrow a tux. Over and out."

The pockets of resistance had softened considerably on Saturday. The pressure of Orange and Khaki columns with the added strength of a third column from the 1st Battalion and the continuing air support seemed to be convincing the Japs that they'd better leave before they found their escape route cut. Lancelot patrol, hungry, thirsty, tired, with a total of five minor casualties, reached the foot of the ridge slope by nightfall.

The ravaged earth stunk of rotted death. Million bits of flesh that had been men were draped from shattered trees. On the ground, the bloated carcasses of the animals, mules and horses were covered with insects so glutted they could no longer fly. Sporadic firing chattered from the perimeter but the artillery that had been smashing it the 2nd Battalion for 10 days was silenced.

"It's almost dark," Henty told Captain Gold. "We'll walk in tomorrow. Jesus, it stinks here. I couldn't eat if we did have food."

"All right, Henshit," Captain Gold said triumphantly. "It's all but over. They're going in from the other side tomorrow morning. I have some reports here that may interest you. We estimate enemy dead at the Nhpum Ga perimeter at 500. You're responsible for your share of them; 2nd seems to have withstood the shelling reasonably well—100 or so casualties and a couple dozen fatals. Over."

Henty couldn't answer right away. Something from his stomach shot up and wedged in his throat.

"Yeah, sure," he said finally. "Anything else? Over."

"That surprise I mentioned isn't here yet. I'm afraid I spoiled it by mentioning it too soon. Over."

"You couldn't spoil it, Arthur. Nothing surprises me any more. I'll talk with you tomorrow morning. Over and out."

Oh for chrissake, Henty thought suddenly as the Runner shut off the set—Captain Gold wasn't talking about any decoration, it was their furloughs and orders he was waiting for.

Meatball approached Henty before he settled back in the trees to get what rest he could.

"In the morning you will enjoy the flower of your victory," he said and laughed.

"It has that appearance," Henty said, thinking of his squad. "But it has not been without its cost."

"The cost is something that lies beyond us, Dua."

"I am not so certain. I think in many things, we set the price ourselves."

"Do not let this victory sadden you, Dua," Meatball said gently. "You have much reason to rejoice."

Henty shook his head and grinned.

"You are right, my little brown brother. I shall be with my woman and my friends again and we shall feast together."

Meatball looked up the bare earth slope through the lacy leafed bamboo.

"Do you believe your feet could find the way from here without your worthless guide?"

"You should share this triumph," Henty said. "More than anyone, you have earned it."

"Perhaps I shall return before the rising sun. I wish now to tell my people the time has come to start the preparations for the gayest of festivities."

Henty laughed aloud.

"Go then, and tell the woman that soon I shall be at her side again."

And then it was Easter Sunday, the Resurrection, and the morning was softly blue and not yet hot. The peaceful air was quiet.

"Let's get up there," Double Ugly growled. "Maybe they got coffee. My gut's growling."

Henty's face twisted into a smile.

"Mine, too. I was waiting for Meatball but maybe he's celebrating. I wouldn't blame him. The little sonofabitch has done twice as much as any of us. Let's line up the men and march up snappy. Tell them to cock their helmets, jangle their grenades. And for Christ's sake, don't let them hold their noses. It isn't military."

He dangled his tommy gun and hitched his belt until the .45 swung low and forward on his hip.

Battle weary, filthy men, patched and bandaged and empty bellied, the column started smartly up the stinking slope.

"Dua, Dua."

Meatball was writhing with agony and tears were washing down his cheeks. He plucked Henty's arm.

"What is it, Meatball?"

Eyes straight, shoulders back. They were watching up above. He couldn't halt the column now.

"Your woman, Dua," Meatball sobbed. "She was in the *basha* at the *tongyaw*. Against the warnings of my people, she had gone there to await you. La Bu La went to guard her. They were in the *basha* when the bomb exploded."

He wept inconsolably.

An iron fist grasped Henty's heart and an iron band wrapped around his head.

"March with me, Meatball," he commanded. "Walk erect like the man you are."

They entered the refuse-littered, shell-pocked perimeter in a military fashion. On the southern edge, the officers of the 2nd Battalion were gathered about their colleagues from the 1st and 3rd.

"Call CP," Henty told the Runner.

The antenna reached its shaky finger into the air.

"Henshit here. As you probably know, we have walked in. I see Khaki and Orange and some officers from the 1st are here and they have a field telephone. Over."

"Yes, sir." Captain Gold's voice was loud and clear for all to hear. "And that surprise I promised you is here, Lieutenant Holiday. You've been given a field commission. Report to Headquarters and sign your orders. You'll want to acquaint yourself with your command before we undertake our next mission to Myitkina. Over."

"Thank you, Captain," Lieutenant Holiday said.

"My pleasure, Lieutenant," Captain Gold said.

Lieutenant Holiday looked around him. The men were tight lipped and resentful. Not about the commission. But they'd heard about the mission. Well, what the hell did they think the Army was, a family picnic? Furman was observing closely, eyes large and thoughtful behind his glasses. Of all the 1st Squad, only Furman the goddamned Commie had survived. Lieutenant Holiday wanted to smash his fist in Furman's smirking face, hurt him, see him cringe.

"Sergeant Furman," he barked. "Report with me to Headquarters."

"Yes, sir!" Furman said with satisfaction.

THE FREEBOOTERS

by Robert Wernick

A wild, hilarious, bitter war novel that's every bit as bold and bizarre as *Catch-22*. "*The Freebooters* makes the reader sit up and take notice."

—*Saturday Review*

54-845, 75¢

HELLBENT FOR GLORY

by *William Chamberlain*

Stark, brutal adventures of GI's fighting their way to glory—from the burning deserts of Rommel's Africa to the sniper-infested jungles of the Pacific; across the frozen rice paddies of the Yalu River; over the bloody battlefields of France and Germany.

53-826, 60¢

WAR CRY

edited by *Noah Sarlat*

In the great tradition of THE GUNS OF NAVARONE—epic adventures in heroism behind enemy lines. American commandos, French and Italian partisans, hot-blooded girl guerrillas fight, love under fire, risk death and torture, to carry out guerrilla missions.

52-815, 50¢

ONLY THE BRAVE

by Robert Granat

"Another FROM HERE TO ETERNITY" (Gary Post Tribune)
"War in Europe with no holds barred. All its brutality of action, language and amorality." (The New Mexican Review)
"Superior war novel . . ." (New York Times)

54-712, 75¢

THE WATCH ON THE BRIDGE

by David Garth

The greatest war adventure since THE BRIDGE ON THE RIVER KWAI
"Impelling force." (Austin American Statesman)

"David Garth knows his soldiers, the ways of making war which the history books will not detail, and the manner of man with a maid. He also has a pithy and moving style." (Sarasota Herald-Tribune)

53-602, 60¢

If you are unable to obtain these books from your local dealer, they may be ordered directly from the publisher.

PAPERBACK LIBRARY EDITION
Department B
260 Park Avenue South
New York, N.Y. 10010
Please send me the following books:
I am enclosing payment plus 10¢ per copy to cover postage and handling.

Book # .... TITLE .... No. of copies: ....

.... TITLE .... No. of copies: ....

Name ....

Address ....

....